A BUTTERFLY

on the

Gowanus Expressway

D.M. FREEDMAN

THIRD EDITION

Copyright © 2023 by D.M. Freedman

Paperback: 978-1-963050-34-9
eBook: 978-1-963050-35-6
Library of Congress Control Number: 2023921974

Ordering Information:

Prime Seven Media
518 Landmann St.
Tomah City, WI 54660

Printed in the United States of America

TABLE OF CONTENTS

PROLOGUE

He drove down the street in a blind rage of hysteria. Daniel Kaplan's whole life had just turned around. All that he had worked for was gone. All that he had hoped for, tried to accomplish, tried to erase and thought that he had was now blown apart. He raced down Ocean Parkway. His heart was beating wildly. Sweat was rising on his forehead. He swerved to avoid a car and drove onto the Prospect Expressway and then onto the ramp of the Gowanus Expressway. There the traffic stopped him dead. He beat furiously on the steering wheel and broke out crying in loud, long sobs.

The traffic inched ahead high on the bridging of the road. He could feel the whole road move from the wind and from the movement of traffic. The smell of the industrial soot and the fumes from the cars made him feel sick. He closed his window and turned on the air conditioning. The traffic stopped again and he sat there frustrated and sad. Daniel had never felt so lost.

As he sat looking out at his windshield, a monarch butterfly alighted on the left wiper blade. It appeared to look at him. He took dim notice of it, bouncing his knee furiously hoping for a break in the traffic. Suddenly, the butterfly flew off. He watched it climb away and out of sight. He looked ahead at the traffic and sighed deeply over the lack of movement.

Then, it hit him. A Butterfly? What was a butterfly doing 100 feet in the air over the dirtiest, most polluted part of Brooklyn? Then a realization came over him. He would be all right. The butterfly was his angel. He breathed deeply. He was not alone. G-d was watching him and his faith, which had been so sorely tested, would be what saved him.

He jumped from the sound of a horn blaring behind him. He stepped on the gas and got the car moving again. He turned his car off the road at the next exit, Hamilton Avenue and headed home.

Book 1

RABBI KAPLAN

CHAPTER ONE

The women all came out to greet their men as they came home from synagogue. They wore long dark dresses, long sleeved and high around their neck. Despite that, their clothing seemed a little too form fitting. Even the older women, clearly wore their finest clothes. They were bedecked with necklaces and rings, showing to all, that they had fine jewelry that they were proud to wear. On their heads were beautifully coiffured wigs. On some of these women, it was almost impossible to tell that they were in fact wearing a wig. On others it was painfully obvious. Children ran around on this hot summer like morning, making noise and playing games. People stopped and greeted each other. They schmoozed about the events of the community and gossiped about their neighbors. Everywhere you looked, Religious Jews were moving about the streets, vibrant in their hustle and bustle. The Sabbath commanded the neighborhood.

Therefore, it was a curious sight to see a tall young man dressed in a black suit and roman collar walk up the street past the women sitting on their porches and the children running around their front yards. It was even more curious that this man stopped at the house of the renowned Rabbi Daniel Kaplan. He looked at the red front door. Then he reached inside his jacket and pulled out a piece of paper. He studied it for a moment then shook his head in the affirmative. He walked up the stairs to the Rabbi's front porch and rang the doorbell. He waited a moment or two. No one answered the door so he rang it again. There was still no answer. He looked at his watch and then back at the door. He walked back down onto the street and over to where several ladies were sitting. He asked them if they knew Rabbi Kaplan and where he might be found.

The Ladies looked suspiciously at him. One of them answered the young cleric,

"I expect that he is in Shul (synagogue) right now. He is usually back around 11:30."

The tall man nodded and looked at his watch again. It was 10:30. He walked up the street, got into his car, and waited. He soon fell asleep.

He awoke with a start. His watch read 11:25. He quickly got out of the car and walked over to Rabbi Kaplan's house. He rang the doorbell, but there was still no answer. He decided to wait in front of the house. He walked a little bit back and forth, looking down the block periodically, hoping to see the Rabbi. People walked passed him with a puzzled look. Nonetheless, the priest waited quietly, continuing to pace in front on the sidewalk.

"He should be here soon"; the lady he had originally spoken to called out to him, "Just wait. You will see him soon. You'll see! He comes back from shul with his family", she said with a heavy eastern European accent.

So he waited. And waited. Although it was only a few minutes, it seemed like hours. Then he saw a crowd of people turn the corner onto the block. There in the distance, he could see a tall man with a long white beard wearing a long black coat and big hat. Next to him was a short woman dressed in a long skirt and wig. In front of this tall man, three boys and three girls walked in animated conversation with the man. It was clear to the young priest that this group was a family. Surrounding them were five young men wearing black suits and fedoras, speaking exuberantly with the tall man, while trailing around the edges of the group. From the distance, the man seemed to be listening intently to what one particular boy was saying as he ran along trying to keep up with the group. The priest could see him shake his head slightly as if he was somewhat deaf. As they came closer it appeared that the tall man was not saying anything at all. As the group became recognizable, the young cleric could see that this man smiled broadly, greeting everyone he passed as if he was campaigning for some political office. Men sitting on their porches ran out to greet him and he shook the hands of many of the men passing by him. As he walked by some of the houses on the block, young men sitting on porches with their families suddenly stood up until he past, as if to show respect. This man was The Rabbi, Daniel Kaplan!

And this was the neighborhood that Daniel Kaplan had grown up in. It was a place he would leave when he was 14 and not return to for almost 20 years. When he did return, he would not recognize this place as the place of his childhood. But then again, he probably would not have recognized himself. For as that neighborhood had changed, so had he.

Although the buildings were the same, they were no longer filled with the people he had grown up with. Rather the neighborhood had become an enclave for very religious Jews. They occupied almost every house as well as most of the stores on Avenue P. The changes in the places seemed subtle, but were distinctive. Armando's Pizzeria was now called Yehuda's Kosher Pizza. The old Pork store on the corner of East 2nd Street was now a Kosher Bakery. Where the old bank used to sit was now a Doctor's office. This bank had once been the scene of a spectacular robbery and hostage taking, one, which had been recreated into a famous movie. The old Claridge Theater was now a Kosher Catering Hall. And so it went. Even the old Italian Men's Club where Daniel's grandfather had occasionally gone into to have a drink was gone. It was now a storefront synagogue. Daniel remembered "the club" fondly. The old men would sit around smoking cigars and playing cards on small collapsible card tables and metal folding chairs. Daniel's grandfather was an insurance salesman and he had written life insurance policies for most of the men who hung out at the club. When Daniel would come with him with his grandfather, there was always a skinny old Italian gentleman named Charley, who tended the uniquely carved and ornate Bar. Charley would look up at Daniel and ask him in heavily accented English,

"Hey buddy boy, you want a milk-a-shek?" Daniel would smile and say, "Sure Charley". Then the old guy would make him a large chocolate milk with lots of whipped cream. He would top it off with flakes of chocolate sprinkled liberally on the cream. He'd make a whole ceremony out of it, pouring the milk, pumping the chocolate syrup from the fountain, shaking it up and so on. When he was done he would put it on a round cocktail tray and serve it to Daniel with a napkin draped over his arm. Daniel always looked forward to the milkshake. The glass was a very tall fluted glass, almost too tall for Daniel to drink from, so he would stand up on a folding chair to do so. Charley would put a plastic straw through the whipped cream. Daniel would suck loudly through the straw. The whipped cream would stick to his nose and cheeks. This always got a laugh from all the men. When Daniel got older, the men used to send him on "errands" to pick up these brown paper shopping bags from the cigar store under the elevated "F" train on McDonald Avenue. They would pay him, sometimes as much as $5.00 for doing the errand. It wasn't until Daniel was much older that, upon reflection, he realized that those shopping bags were the numbers take from the cigar store. When his grandfather died, all of the men from the club came to the funeral. They stood around Daniel as if they were his bodyguards. But all that was gone now. This was a new neighborhood with a new temperament. And it was the place to which he would ultimately return to, because he was now one of those religious Jews.

It was a warm spring day. Late May in Brooklyn blooms with flowers. Memorial Day was just around the corner and the neighborhood was getting ready for the annual escape to the Catskill Mountains that emptied these streets every summer. It was quiet on East 10th Street, the block on which Daniel Kaplan lived.

This Sabbath, as Daniel and his family approached the house they saw the priest standing in front of their house. They all stopped and looked at him. Daniel's wife took one look at the priest and became so startled that she started to look faint. Everyone grew quiet. The Rabbi quickly took his wife's arm and directed her towards the house. He gave the young cleric a quizzical look and helped usher the rest of the family and his guests into his house.

The young priest had not even uttered a word. Now he was standing alone on the street. He could feel the heat of an entire block staring at him and he felt most uncomfortable. He was trying to decide whether to leave, when Rabbi Kaplan came back outside. He stepped down off his stoop and walked out onto the sidewalk to meet the young priest. He reached out his hand to greet him and said,

"Sir, is there something I can help you with?"

The priest swallowed hard and uncomfortably looked around. The whole block had become quiet and seemed to be listening to their conversation.

"Eh, Reverend, Eh"

The older man waited for a moment,

"Reverend!"

The Rabbi called out again, but the young man seemed disoriented. He waited a moment. Then he reached out to shake the priest's hand. The priest did not take his hand, he was still looking around in a kind of a daze. Finally, he took the priest's hand in his own two hands, then he reached up to his shoulder and as he shook the cleric's hand. He smiled and said,

"Reverend?"

"No, . . . it's Father, I am a priest."

"Alright then, Father! Father, are you okay?"

"Yeah, . . . sure!" he said haltingly as he looked around again.

"Is everybody going to watch?" the priest asked.

The tall man laughed.

"I'm afraid so! We don't get too many priests around here during Shabbos and I'm afraid that you are the center of attention for the moment."

The priest look confused

"Shabbos?"

"Shabbos, Sabbath. It's the Hebrew word for Sabbath"

"Oh!"

He looked around again. The older gentlemen, still clasping the young priest's hand, looked at him again and turned him towards his house. They climbed up the stairs and onto the porch. The older man sat down on one of the lawn chairs. He pulled up another one and offered it to the priest. Once they seemed settled, he asked the priest again,

"Can I help you with something, Father?"

The younger man looked around one more time, then seemingly convinced that everything was now okay, gathered himself together and replied,

"Are you Rabbi Daniel Kaplan?"

Daniel looked at him. "Who is asking?

The Priest smiled weakly and put out his hand to shake the Rabbi's.

"I am Father Daniel Fiorentino.

"Fiorentino, hmm. I knew a guy named Fiorentino once." He laughed to himself, "That was a long time ago." Then he looked up at the young cleric and said, "Yes, I am Daniel Kaplan".

The young man was not sure about what he had heard.

"You're not Rabbi Daniel Kaplan?"

"I'm that too!" he laughed gently, "but I don't get many chances to stand on those laurels. To my wife, I'm just Danny and to my kids, I'm Abba, Father in Hebrew. As for me, those are the most important titles in my life. Rabbi? Eh! I am just a man who tries to help people. Maybe I can help you too. So, tell me young man? What brings you to my door?"

"I have a most urgent matter to discuss with you". The priest said earnestly and intensely.

The Rabbi pursed his lips and shook his head knowingly,

"I gather it must be urgent if you came all the way out here to Brooklyn on the Sabbath. You don't look like you are a New Yorker"

The Priest smiled in acknowledgement. Rabbi Kaplan then said, "So, what can I do to help?"

The young man seemed to suddenly come out of his daze. He turned bright red in embarrassment,

"The Sabbath! Oh my! I'm sorry, Sabbath, Saturday, I'm so confused these days. Of course, it is your Sabbath. I should have realized."

He looked away for a second. The Rabbi shrugged his shoulder and smiled.

He started to get up to leave. The Rabbi told him to sit back down.

"You wouldn't have come unless this was very important. So what's the story?"

The younger man agreed, "Your right, it is important." He reflected a moment, "But not so urgent that I should disturb you on your day of rest. Believe me, it's important, but not life threatening."

The Rabbi looked at him closely. This young man seemed so confused. Or maybe he was just shy. Rabbi Daniel shrugged his shoulders.

"You know, it might not be life threatening, but so what? Obviously, you came because someone is in great distress. Am I right about that, Father Daniel? By the way, I like the name."

"The name? . . . Oh!" He laughed, then he looked thoughtfully out onto the street in front of him. "Yes. Someone is troubled, very troubled."

"Well?" the Rabbi asked him.

He nodded at the Rabbi. Then he spoke sort of wistfully. "Troubled, yeah!" shaking his head," However Rabbi, this doesn't have to be resolved just this minute. You have your family and your guests and they must be waiting for you. It can wait until a better time."

Rabbi Daniel looked at him with great concern,

"Listen, if this is a serious matter, it shouldn't wait! Let's discuss it now! I can get the family started and they can eat without me. It will only take a few minutes to make Kiddush (blessing on a cup of wine) and I can be right back. Just wait right here." He got up to go inside, but the priest stopped him.

"No Rabbi, it can wait",

Rabbi Kaplan looked at him with doubt. The priest looked straight at the older man's eyes," Really! It can wait. Tell me. When would it be more convenient? I can meet you in your office or. . . somewhere."

Rabbi Daniel sighed. He wanted to help this young man, but the priest was resolute.

"Alright Father. If you can wait until this evening, after my Sabbath is over, I can discuss it with you then."

"Good. Where should I meet you?"

"Oh", the Rabbi thought for a moment. "Come back here! My family usually sits down for a light meal right after Shabbos. Join us for the meal, and then afterwards we can sit down and talk. Then you can explain the problem to me."

The priest made an unconscious face. The Rabbi continued, "Father, don't be disturbed. This happens all the time, more often than you might think. Many times, I am called to work with clergy from other faiths to resolve an issue. It is all right. If it can wait until tonight, the better, but if this needs my immediate attention, please come in and we will discuss it in my study."

"No! It can wait Rabbi", as he got up to leave, "I thank you for your time in advance. This is a very complicated matter", He shook his head again as if to agree with himself. The Rabbi pursed his lips in concern at how he saw the priest react to everything. Father Daniel continued, "I will join you this evening. Thank you again." Then stepping down the steps, he turned back to the Rabbi and said to him, "Good then, I'll see you at." he looked at his watch for a second.

The Rabbi looked at his own watch and said "9:30. Is that Okay?"

"Yes", the priest answered.

"Oh, another thing", the Rabbi said as he stood up, "Be prepared to eat, my wife is a great cook."

They both smiled. The priest walked back up to the porch and shook the Rabbi's hands. Then, Father Daniel walked down to the street, got into his car and drove away. Rabbi Kaplan watched him as he left, then shaking his head, walked into his house.

CHAPTER TWO

hat was that all about? " asked his wife Rebecca, as Rabbi Kaplan walked into the house. She had been standing just inside the door the whole time and he almost knocked her down when he walked in.

"I don't know." he shrugged. "Eavesdropping?"

She turned red, and then she looked him in the eye and said, "Yes! So what? Tell me, what's it all about?

"Oh, I don't know."

She looked at him skeptically.

"Really, I don't know! I mean he seemed earnest enough, but so nervous. I don't know what it's about. It must be a big problem for him".

He thought for a moment, "You know it's probably something simple like some parishioner he has who is marrying a Jew and he needs help talking him out of it. Or her! Who knows?"

He looked at Rebecca carefully and made a face, "But so nervous! He must be one very new priest."

He stopped for a moment to ponder the situation. Then he started to continue speaking, but then thought better of it. He was silent again for a moment and then started musing as he moved things around a table by the door.

"He said it was a complicated matter. I suppose it must be since he just showed up here. I mean, you know, without calling first. What was strange was that he seemed very sure that he wanted to speak to me and only me." Then he paused, shaking his head and looking down at the table. He was unstacking and restacking books in no particular order, kind of carelessly because finally one of the piles fell to the floor.

"Daniel!", Rebecca scolded him, "What are you doing? Everyone's waiting for you in the dining room, Come on already!"

"I know, you're right. Let's go", and they started walking towards the dining room, "But Becky, I just don't know! This young man seemed so distracted and so nervous. But I don't know. I mean this interfaith stuff, I guess any Rabbi could handle these types of things, but he came out here looking for me." He rolled his eyes for a second in thought. "Interesting, I guess. But I have no idea what it's about."

"Well Danny, doesn't it seem strange? What's a priest doing by our house on Shabbos?"

"I don't know!"

"Well, it's all too weird!"

"Rebecca, why does it have to be weird?"

"It just seems weird"

"Okay, it's weird, you're right, but I'll know what's going on tonight."

"Tonight?"

"Yeah, tonight."

"What going on tonight?"

"I invited him to come by after Shabbos to discuss this problem of his!"

"Tonight? Oh Danny, why tonight?" She looked at him in disgust. Then she shook her head as if this was the norm and said, "Okay, but what time is he coming? And what about dinner?" she asked him.

"He can join us. Maybe it won't be so complicated on a full stomach"

"Oh, Danny, you make me crazy."

She shook her head and walked away back into the kitchen. She was not happy. "To be entertaining a priest in the house, especially right after the Shabbos", she muttered to herself, "What is that man thinking? She had a lot to do on Sunday and Saturday night was the one night of the week she could relax with her husband. And Daniel had to relax. He rarely allowed visitors on Saturday night for that reason. The rest of the week, people came and went with a frequency that was mind-boggling. Everyone had a question for the Rabbi. There were "problems" that only the Rabbi could solve. She stopped and smiled for a moment. In her mind's eye, she saw him wading through all of it with an easy demeanor. She saw his smile. She saw the gentleness and patience that eased people's minds and gave them hope. That was what she had seen in him 20 years earlier and that was why she had married him.

Rabbi Kaplan gathered his family and guests for the Sabbath lunch. He made the blessings on the wine and bread. They ate and laughed and sang. When they were finished, they all dispersed to their homes or their rooms and went about their normal Sabbath routine for the rest of the day.

When the Sabbath was over, it quieted in the house. His family dispersed upstairs to either get ready to go out or just to change into less formal clothes. Rebecca went into the kitchen to prepare dinner and the Rabbi went to his study. He sat at his desk reading the Saturday newspapers and puffed softly on his pipe. Although not a regular smoker anymore, he allowed himself one bowl of tobacco every Saturday night. He found that he had been able to control the urge to smoke the rest of the week and he allowed himself this indulgence.

Rebecca loved the smell of the pipe and did not demand that he drop the habit even though she considered smoking to be disgusting in general. For all of his seeming easy demeanor, she knew that she was married to a very difficult man trying not to be difficult with the people around him. He had to have some way to vent the steam of his life and activities. So, he smoked on Saturday night.

Rebecca and two of their daughters set the table for dinner after the Sabbath. This meal was known as the Melava Malka. It was always a joyous occasion with singing, good food and conversation amongst the family and whatever friends came by.

Rabbi Kaplan and Rebecca had been blessed with three separate sets of fraternal twins. There was a boy and a girl in each set. As difficult as it had been to raise three sets of twins, the two of them had done it with the understanding that they had been given the greatest gifts. They loved the children and nurtured them as they continued to grow. The first sets of twins Mark and Sari were the most difficult and the babies had put a tremendous strain on their marriage. They were now 17. Daniel, who had answers for everyone, was clueless himself, about being a father. He had been an officer in the Navy when he was younger and was known for his quick and unemotional decisions in combat. Now he found himself fraught with fear and unable to handle a little baby. And there were two in his house. Rebecca watched in amazement at his inability to get anything right. He seemed to have no sense about what a child needed at any particular moment and always seemed lost in the clouds when one of the kids were crying. He didn't want to be like that and he hated himself for it being so. It took a very long time for Daniel to grow into fatherhood and because of that they waited almost six years before trying again to have children.

As the children grew up their distinctive personalities took shape. Mark was born first, but Sari had always been the boss. Mark had grown into a tall young man, well built with piercing brown eyes and a shy demeanor. Sari had discovered her beauty and was blossoming into womanhood. Nevertheless, she was a toughie and the boys knew it. She was shrewd and smart and no one walked over her. She easily dominated her brother by her quickness of thought and her frenetic spirit. Where he was easygoing and likeable, she was tough, sarcastic and demanding. She was nobody's fool and she made sure you knew it.

As luck would have it, the next time Rebecca got pregnant they again had a set of twins, David and Rachel. They were now 11 years old and each also had distinctive and individual personalities. This time Daniel thought he was ready. He dove right in and tried to help. But he still couldn't seem to get it right. But he was better at it. He still didn't like changing diapers and he still would drift into his own little world when one of the kids was tugging at him, but he loved the children with all of his heart and HE TRIED. Boy did he try!

David was roly-poly and into everything. The proverbial charmer, he would give his mother a mischievous look and scurry off to make more tumult. Rachel was sweet, quiet and the most naturally pretty of all the girls. She was also the most helpful of the girls. She was the Rabbi's favorite although he would deny that he had favorites. A denial that he would even tell to himself.

Five years later, when they tried again, another set of twins were born to them Ezra and Leah who had just turned six. By now, Rebecca had no expectations that Daniel was up to the job of being father to two new babies. But to her surprise, he took to the children like an old hand. He seemed focused and able to deal with the crying, the spitting up and the dirty diapers. He remained calm and controlled when the children fell or were sick. After a few months, Rebecca still couldn't believe that her husband had finally gotten it together. But lo and behold, he had!

Again, each of the children was a completely different person. Leah was born first and was strong from the beginning. Ezra was sickly for the first few months of his life. Although he was never in danger of dying, he was too sick to have his circumcision performed until he was almost ten weeks old. The boy was quiet and dark, somber in mood. In contrast, Leah was happy go lucky, with a skip in her feet and always singing a song and dancing around like a ballerina.

At eight o'clock, the doorbell rang and Rachel went to open it. Father Daniel greeted her and gave her a bottle of wine as a gift for the family. The Rabbi got up from the dining room table and shook the priest's hand. He thought to himself that the young man looked much better now than when they had met this morning. He seemed calmer and more in control. Rabbi Kaplan took the bottle of wine from Rachel and looked at it. He smiled and walked into the kitchen to show it to Rebecca. They both chuckled. It was undoubtedly a very fine and expensive wine, but it wasn't kosher, so they would never drink it. They put it on the floor of the cupboard for Daniel to give to the Italian family living next door.

After some polite greetings, the Rabbi invited Father Daniel to join with his family in the dining room. The family got up one by one, washed their hands and sat down to eat. The Rabbi made a blessing on the bread and everyone started to eat and talk. The Rabbi settled into his chair and ate a little food. As was their tradition, he sang some Jewish songs. When he sang, he closed his eyes. He had a beautiful voice and sang with tremendous heart and feeling. Then he blessed his family for the coming week.

As his family ate and discussed the happenings of the neighborhood and the news, Daniel Kaplan sat quietly and just listened. He encouraged Father Daniel to eat the pickled herring or better yet to try some of the lox. It was something the young man had never eaten before. The priest was pleasantly surprised that he liked it. He loved Rebecca's egg salad and tuna and ate heartily. The Rabbi smiled broadly. He was proud of his family and it showed. Slowly the children concluded their meals and sat quietly. Soon Rebecca brought in the dessert along with coffee and ice cream. Father Daniel could not believe how much food had been put out at one time, but he enjoyed it very much. As they all settled comfortably into their dessert, the girls asked the young priest about himself.

Rachel asked him how old he was. He told them,

"I am 25 years old".

Sari asked, "How long have you been a priest?"

"I have been a priest for 4 years."

She continued, " Was it hard, you know, becoming a priest"

"Seminary was difficult, but I did not find it hard. I wanted very badly to be a priest."

Ezra looked up from his dessert and asked, " Are you married?"

Rachel who was sitting right next to him, slapped him lightly on his arm and said, "Stupid, Priests don't get married."

The Rabbi flashed her a look,

"Rachel!"

"I'm sorry Abba (father)."

"Don't tell me. Tell Ezra"

"I'm sorry Ezra".

Father Daniel interjected,

"Actually, I am allowed to marry."

"You are? I thought priests couldn't marry.", Sari questioned him.

"Catholic priests can't marry. But I am not a Catholic priest."

"You're not? I don't understand what you are talking about."

She turned to her father and said,

"Abba, He's a priest, right?"

"Yes"

"And I thought priests couldn't have wives. I mean nuns don't have husbands, although they wear wedding bands because they're supposed to be married to . . . you know?"

"It can seem perplexing. But you know, we have a priest right here at our table. Why don't we let him explain it? Don't you think that's a good idea?

"Well" she turned towards Father Daniel and asked,

"You were saying that priests <u>could</u> get married?"

Father Daniel looked at the Rabbi and smiled for a second.

"Some priests can get married if they are not Roman Catholic"

"So, if you can marry, I can assume you are not Roman Catholic"

"Right"

"What are you?"

"Good question. I am an Episcopal priest,"

They looked at him quizzically.

"I am a priest in the Episcopal Church, The Church of England.

They were still confused.

"The Church of England broke away from the Roman Catholic Church centuries ago. Here in America, The Church of England is known as the Episcopal Church. In our Church, priests have always been allowed to marry."

There was silence for a moment while everyone at the table digested the information. Then all of a sudden, Ezra piped up again, breaking the silence.

"So! Are you married?"

Everyone laughed.

"Yes, Ezra, I am married."

They all looked at him. Then Leah said,

"And . . ", shaking her hands, for more information.

"And I have two little children."

"Boys or girls?"

"One each"

Ezra jumped in,

"I bet they're not twins".

Everyone laughed again. The Rabbi leaned over to the Priest,

"He's a little precocious, that one there, eh?"

They both laughed.

"Well, as a matter of fact, just like you are all twins, so are my children."

"You're kidding?" piped up David.

"No David, actually I'm not. My kids are really twins. Their names are John and Elizabeth. We call John, Jack. Elizabeth, we call Beth.

Rachel asked,

"Who was born first?"

"Elizabeth was born 6 minutes before Jack.

Sara looked up at the priest,

"What is your wife's name?"

"My wife?" He smiled, "Her name is Ruth Anne."

"Where are you from? You don't sound like you are from New York."

"I grew up all over the country. I was a military brat."

"A what?"

"A military brat. My father was in the military, so we moved all over the country, to wherever he was stationed."

Rabbi Kaplan interrupted for a second,

"Really, I was in the military when I was younger. What branch of the service was your father in?"

"The Navy"

Rabbi Kaplan smiled and shook his head.

"Me too."

He waited for a response from the young man, but got none.

"Are you surprised that a Rabbi like me was in the Navy?

Father Daniel shook his head no,

"Not really, were you a Chaplain?"

Rabbi Kaplan looked down into his coffee cup and shook his head yes.

Then the Rabbi gave his children a look. It was the look that he needed to be alone with his guest. The family said their goodbyes and drifted off, clearing the table, so that the men could talk in private. Soon Daniel heard the water running in the sink and knew that Rebecca was doing the dishes and it would be quiet.

He looked at the priest and said to him.

"Now young man, what can I help you with?"

Father Daniel took a deep breath, then he said,"

"I hope you will not feel upset by what I am about to ask, it is not meant as an insult or anything like that. It is just that I need to know that I am talking to the right Rabbi Kaplan."

The Rabbi looked strangely at him and made a circle with his hand through the air.

"I'm not sure I understand. There aren't too many Rabbi Kaplan's around that I know of here in Brooklyn"

"Well, maybe so, but could you please tell me a little about yourself, so that I may know if you are the right person."

"OK, What would you like to know specifically?"

"I am not sure, just tell me about yourself."

"Okay . . ." Daniel took a deep breath. Then he said quietly to the young priest," Listen, what's this all about?"

The priest turned red in the face. Rabbi Kaplan looked at him cautiously,

"If you were me wouldn't you be asking this yourself? I mean you are a perfect stranger? You can see my point, no? This is all very strange to me. I don't know what this is all about. I don't even know who you are? Just because you are dressed like a priest doesn't . . ."

The young priest seemed to get alarmed. Daniel could see it in his eyes. He put his hand out and patted the priest's hand. The priest calmed down and realized that the Rabbi was not accusing him of anything, he was only inquiring.

"Rabbi, I am not trying to put something over on you. I just have to make sure that I am conveying information to the right man. As for my authenticity as a priest, you can talk to my Bishop back in Virginia."

"I believe you" he looked the younger man in his eyes, "I do! Just what is it that you want?"

"I need to know who you are so that I can be sure that I am imparting some very important information to the right person."

"What information? Listen young man, tell me specifically what you want to know?"

"I'm not sure, I'll know it when I hear it."

The Rabbi frowned. The priest looked at him, almost pleadingly,

"Rabbi, can't you just tell me a bit about yourself, a history, so to speak, you know?

"You want me to tell you my biography?", Rabbi Kaplan chuckled.

"Well sort of". The priest smiled also, realizing how silly it sounded. Then the two men both laughed.

The Rabbi reached out and patted the younger man on the shoulder.

"But to what end? Why is this important?"

Father Daniel just looked at him. Rabbi Kaplan shrugged his shoulders.

"All right! All right! Whatever! I'll tell you my story. But I hope you have a little time."

Father Daniel smiled gently and nodded his head. The telephone rang in the kitchen. Rebecca answered it and could be heard talking in the background. Then she walked into the dining room and interrupted them.

"Daniel"

They both turned. She turned red and was flustered. When she recovered, she said,

"I mean my Daniel. Eh Danny, Mrs. Shugarten from the shul is on the phone."

"Becky, can you take a message for me, please?"

"Danny, she's at Maimonides (Hospital). Elliott was hit by a car and is in the emergency room. She wants to talk to you." She held the phone out into the dining room for him to reach.

He jumped up and grabbed the phone. He walked into the kitchen to talk.

"Hello. What happened?"

He listened patiently. As he listened he pulled a chair out from the kitchen table and sat down. He fiddled with the salt shaker as he listened to this distraught woman on the other end of the line. Finally, he interrupted her because it was obvious he could do nothing to calm her on the telephone. Finally he said to her.

"Miriam. Miriam. Don't worry. I'm on my way. I'm leaving right now. This minute. I'll be there soon. Don't worry, Miriam, I am going to get the car right now and drive over."

He looked at his wife. The longer he stayed on the phone, the longer it would take to get to the hospital. He handed the phone to

Rebecca and she spoke to Mrs. Shugarten for a few moments and then hung up the phone.

He looked at the younger man and said,

"Listen, I'm sorry, but I have to go"

Father Daniel nodded,

"I understand."

The Rabbi looked up at him and gave him a good look up and down. Then he sighed loudly to himself.

"Leave me a phone number where you are staying and I will call you when I come back. Maybe we can continue this tomorrow night?"

Again Father Daniel nodded. He reached into his jacket pocket for a card. He wrote down a phone number of his hotel on the back of the card and gave it to Rebecca. She looked at it for a moment and put it on the refrigerator door in the kitchen, so it wouldn't get lost.

The Rabbi put on his coat and hat. Then he went upstairs to get his keys and wallet. As he came running down the stairs, Rebecca stopped him.

"Daniel, You gave the car to Mark this evening. He left twenty minutes ago to go to Far Rockaway."

The Rabbi frowned and tapped his forehead remembering.

"All right, get a car service for me. Tell him to hurry."

"I'll take you", Father Daniel interrupted.

Rebecca and the Rabbi looked at him. He replied to them

"Where's the hospital. Is it far from here?"

"Not very. It's about 20 minutes from here. At this time of night, the traffic shouldn't be too bad."

"OK then, let's go!"

He looked at the priest and got him his coat. Together they went out into the night to the priest's car.

CHAPTER THREE

They drove off towards the hospital with the Rabbi directing Father Daniel where to go. They traveled down towards Borough Park, a section of Brooklyn that also has a large Jewish population. They turned up 60th Street, a main thoroughfare between Flatbush and Borough Park, riding until they got to Fort Hamilton Parkway, where the hospital was located. As they rode, they talked.

Rabbi Daniel looked at the young man and said,

"I guess this is as good a time as any to continue our conversation. You can start and whatever still needs to be discussed, we can finish tomorrow."

"OK", the young man nodded, "Tell me about yourself"

"Are you sure you don't want to tell me what you are looking for. I mean you can cut to the chase rather quickly that way."

The priest smiled, "I wish it was so simple, but I must be very careful. If I give the information to the wrong person, it will . . . well . . ." He looked at the Rabbi for a moment and took a deep breath.

"Please Rabbi Kaplan. Please indulge me. Just tell me about yourself. I know what I need to hear. Believe me I do. There is nothing dark or sinister here. I've simply got to know. . ." He grew silent as he peered out onto the street. The streetlights gave the road an eerie yellowish hue and he felt strangely out of his body."

"Please"

The Rabbi looked at him closely. He didn't know why, but he decided to indulge this young man. He also felt strangely out of his body and didn't know why. So he began to tell his story to the young priest sitting next to him.

"Well if you must know, I grew up here in Brooklyn. I come from a non-religious family, but they sent me to a Conservative Hebrew School, which met four days a week after school. Do you know the differences between the various groups of Jews?

Father Daniel answered," I understand the basics, I think. I know what you mean by Conservative Jews and how they differ from Reform and Orthodox. At least in theory, I think I do."

"Good" the Rabbi answered, "If at any time you don't understand something I say, please stop me. Anyway, I was raised as a non-observant Jew who participated in a Conservative synagogue. They had a Hebrew School that they called a Talmud Torah. The teachers that they hired were all Lubavitch Chasidim so even though we were not observant, we were taught all the things that orthodox boys were taught with the exception of the Talmud, the Oral Tradition. We learned to read the Torah and all the prayers, you know! When I was 14, we moved to Staten Island into a mostly Italian neighborhood. I went to high school there and then after graduating, I went to the State University at Buffalo, where I majored in partying and little else."

Father Daniel looked surprised at him. "Partying?"

The Rabbi shook his head yes. To the young priest looking at this older man with a long white beard, it seemed impossible to believe. Father Daniel laughed,

"No really!"

"You think I'm kidding?" Rabbi Kaplan asked him.

"No, It just doesn't seem to fit the image of the person sitting next to me right now." Then the young man sighed deeply, "But then again, I guess the world never seems to be the way we imagine it."

"I guess not Daniel". The Rabbi said. Then he continued,

"After three years of going nowhere fast, I came home and my parents told me that I would have to stay at home to go to school. Well that wasn't going to work, so I ran away from home and joined the Navy."

He smiled at the priest and then laughed gently.

"Perfect for a nice Jewish boy from New York. Everyone knew they hated Jews in the Navy, but what did I care, I was away from my parents."

He peered at the street sign,

"Make a right at the next light. That's Fort Hamilton Parkway. Anyway, the next thing I know, they ship me out to Great Lakes, Illinois near Chicago for boot camp. Because I had some college, they made me into a company clerk, which allowed me the freedom to walk around the base without a pass. They gave the clerks a white mailbag so that everyone knew who we were. So, I promptly caught a cold during one of the coldest winters in Chicago history. It rapidly developed into pneumonia. I could feel the fluid in my lungs. But I said nothing to anyone, although everyone knew I was pretty sick. But I didn't want to get recycled for medical reasons. That means I would have had to start all over again. So I muddled through. Finally, one night, I was walking past the dispensary and started coughing blood. This got my attention. I was scared. So, I walked into the clinic. The corpsman (Medical technician) on duty was some girl who started to yell at me for coming in without a pass after sick call. I was coughing so badly, that I couldn't even answer her. Finally, a Doctor stuck his head out of an office and told the corpsman to knock it off.

Then he walked down the hallway to the desk and said to her, "Can't you see that this sailor is sick. What are you yelling at him for." Then he took me into an examining room and after listening to my lungs, told me that I had pneumonia and that he is going to admit me to the hospital. I pleaded with him not to admit me, because they would recycle me and I was one week away from graduating. Somehow, I got him to agree to give me this enormous shot of penicillin and then he gave me a note, which gave me "sick in quarters" for two days. I made a deal with him that the day after I graduated, I would check myself into the hospital. I promptly did that right after I graduated from boot camp."

At that point, they pulled up to the hospital. The Rabbi directed him to the emergency room door and got ready to leave. He thanked the priest, jumped out of the car, and ran into the building. Father Daniel drove around the block looking for a parking spot. Three blocks away, he finally found one, parked the car and walked towards the hospital.

In the meantime, Rabbi Kaplan entered the emergency room and was greeted by Elliott Shugarten's uncle. He was ushered into a cubicle where the boy was attached to all sorts of machines. A ventilator was quietly humming in the background, breathing for him. He asked a nurse to send for the doctor who was treating Elliott. An intern soon joined him. They stood outside the cubicle while the intern quietly told him that the boy had been admitted with multiple lacerations and a collapsed lung. The child was thrown 30 feet and had landed on his head. They had successfully reinflated his lung. He had two broken legs and one broken arm. However, the worst was the damage that the boy's head had taken during the hit. The child had shown no neurological signs since he had been admitted. The doctor stated that the boy was brain dead. He had requested a "Do Not Resuscitate" letter from the family. But they had refused. Daniel shook his head in understanding. Then he thanked the doctor and ushered him away. He walked around to the boy and picked up his right hand. He felt a coldness in the boy's hand. His stomach tightened. The Rabbi felt that feeling of intense angst he always felt when there was nothing he could do to help the situation. He knew that it was in the Almighty's hands. He went out to the family. He gathered them around and let them cry on him. He spoke gently with the parents and tried to comfort them but he knew that it was grim. Elliott's parents knew that things were not good and that the likelihood for Elliott was not good. The Rabbi left them to rejoin the boy in his cubicle in the emergency room. He removed a small volume of Psalms from his inside jacket pocket, and began to recite various passages.

He prayed for a while, then took the boy's hands in his own and grasped them tightly. He rubbed the inside of the boy's palms with his own to warm them. He looked at the boy's eyes, which were half open. But there was no life in them.

The Rabbi leaned over the bed and gently talked to the boy as if he was aware of where he was. Daniel stayed with him throughout the night, talking to the boy about whatever came to his mind. He talked about baseball and hockey. He asked the boy about school and his friends and anything that could come to mind. He read to the boy from a small Bible. He smoothed the boy's cheeks and watched the steady rise and fall of his chest as the ventilator pumped air in. Periodically, he would go out of the cubicle to talk to the family, but he would quickly return so that the boy would not pass away by himself.

Mr. Shugarten, a short stocky man with a battered fedora came into the cubicle. He stared at his son from the foot of the bed. He looked at Rabbi Kaplan, sitting on a chair next to his son, holding the boy's hand and softly talking to him. He stood there at the foot of the bed for several minutes, saying nothing. He pushed his hat up off his forehead and scratched his nose. He did not cry, nor did he speak. Rabbi Kaplan looked up at him. He lifted up Elliott's hands as if to offer them to the father. The man blinked, but did not move. Then he turned around and walked out of the emergency room. Daniel felt very sad for him. The silence of death was too imposing for Mr. Shugarten. He could not say good-bye to his son.

More hours passed. The Rabbi still held Elliott's hand, still tried to warm them. He talked to the half open eyes but got no response at all. Finally he stood up and leaned over to Elliott's right ear and whispered into it,

"Elliott, nu? Are you planning on leaving us?"

Suddenly, the boy seemed to take a deep breath

The Rabbi leaned over the bed again. Once again he whispered into the boy's ear, but now he said.

"Please don't leave us Elliott, please don't." Daniel found his eyes welled over with tears. It caught him by surprise. He kissed the boy on the forehead, but he only response he saw was Elliott's chest rise and fall with the rhythm of the ventilator.

Earlier, Father Daniel had entered the emergency room and asked for Rabbi Kaplan. He was directed to the cubicle and had looked in quietly. He watched as Rabbi Kaplan spoke to the boy and held his hand. He saw the Rabbi gently pass a wet towel over the boy's lips. He then asked one of the nurses about the boy and was told that the situation was hopeless. The Priest went into the waiting area and sat down. He thumbed through some magazines for a while, but quickly got bored. Soon he was sleeping soundly. He awoke with a start and saw that three hours had passed. He went back into the emergency room and saw that the Rabbi was still holding the boy's hand, still talking gently to him. He saw family members go in and out of the emergency room and into the cubicle. But he never saw Rabbi Kaplan come out. He continued to wait. Finally he asked the nurse to tell the Rabbi that he was there in the waiting room. He also told her that she should not disturb him with that news until his vigil was completed. Then he went back to the waiting room, settled into a chair and went back to sleep.

He was awakened with a shake. He looked up at Daniel Kaplan's face.

"Well, what happened?"

The Rabbi looked sadly at him, he whispered, "He passed away a few minutes ago. The family is in with him right now. Why are you still here?"

"I had no other place to go and I still have unfinished business with you, so I waited. Do you mind?

"No. You can take me home."

"All right."

"We just have to wait for the family to leave. Then I must wrap the body and wait for the funeral parlor to send for the boy. I imagine they will have the funeral this afternoon."

"So soon?"

"We Jews bury immediately, unless there is some compelling reason to wait."

"Oh! I had heard that but I couldn't imagine it in practice. Live and learn."

They waited until an orderly called out the Rabbi's name. He got up quickly and walked into the cubicle. Father Daniel followed him and then watched as the Rabbi wrapped the boy in a sheet and tied knots on the head and feet. Then two orderlies moved Elliott's body to a gurney and began moving it to an elevator. Rabbi Kaplan followed with them. Father Daniel followed onto the elevator. The orderly pressed the button for the basement. When the doors opened, they maneuvered the gurney through a long passageway, passing the laundry and out into a yard between buildings of the hospital. They walked into this other building and down a passageway to a small room with a desk and a wall of doors that looked like small meat lockers. The second orderly opened one of the doors and slid out a stainless steel table. They lifted the boy's body and placed it on the table. Then they slid it into the locker and closed the door. The orderlies took the gurney and left the room. The Rabbi sat down at the desk and began reciting Psalms aloud. He said a few and then he looked up at the Priest and said,

"Do me a favor. Find the family and have them send the oldest boy to me right here."

So, Father Daniel went. First, he removed his Roman collar so that the family would not think that he was anything but a man in a black suit and black shirt. He found them all in the waiting room. Mrs. Shugarten was wailing inconsolably. Her husband sat on the edge of a chair. His head was turned down to the floor and he was holding his head by his ears. The Priest tapped him on the shoulder lightly and whispered to him what the Rabbi had told him to say. Mr. Shugarten shook his head in acknowledgement and snapped his finger at his oldest son.

"Follow this man to Rabbi Kaplan", he said to the boy. A teenager, this son, crying and pale followed him down the elevator, through the passageways until he reached the Morgue room where Daniel Kaplan was sitting. The Rabbi whispered gently to him and handed him the Psalms. The boy sat down and started reciting the passages. The Rabbi picked up the telephone on the desk, and dialed. He spoke animatedly to the person on the other end. Then he hung up. He looked around for a second, then went back to the boy, sat down and talked with him.

An hour passed before the funeral home gurney arrived. They gathered the body from its locker. Elliott's brother looked lost. The Rabbi led him out the passageways to the loading dock. They approached the hearse and he waited beside the gurney until it was placed inside the hearse. Then the Rabbi gathered up the family and sent them on their way. He followed the family out the door and once they had gotten into their cars, turned and returned to the emergency room.

He saw Father Daniel sitting on a chair. He looked at the priest wearily and said,

"Let's go."

The priest nodded his head and got up. They walked out together into the morning air. The sun had just risen recently and a slight chill could be felt. The wind blew trash and papers across the sidewalk in front of the hospital. As they passed the main entrance, a young couple was exiting with their newborn baby. The new parents stopped to pose for pictures in front of the hospital portico. Rabbi Kaplan stopped for a moment to watch them. The little baby was bundled in a blanket and was wearing a tiny blue stocking cap that had obviously been made by hand. The Rabbi was suddenly shaken. He thought to himself, "Before one is taken, G-d gives the world his replacement!" Then he sighed deeply, placed his hand on the priest's shoulder and gently guided him down the street.

CHAPTER FOUR

$\mathcal{S}$o, continuing the story. . . Where was I anyway?

"As I recall, you were telling me about how you had gotten pneumonia in boot camp and how you talked the doctor out of admitting you to the hospital."

"Oh yeah. Let's see now," he reflected for a moment. Yeah! After boot camp, I was assigned to Hospital Corps School on the other side of the base. I was made into the Class Adjutant and graduated with all these honors. The Navy shipped me out to the Marines at Camp Lejeune, North Carolina."

"Why the Marines?"

"The Marines didn't have medical personnel of their own. Navy Corpsmen were assigned to that function. We wore the Marine Corp uniform and were assigned to their units. If you were a good "Doc" to your unit, they would protect you and watch after you. I don't think I bought a drink, the entire time I was with the Marines. One day a sergeant came down to the field medical school I was training at and asked all the single corpsman to step forward. Then he informed us all that we had "volunteered" for Marine Reconnaissance.

"What did you do?"

"Believe it or not, I made it through the school despite everything. In truth I was too dumb to fail, which would have been the easy way to get out of Recon. I mean I was a poor swimmer and petrified of heights. Yet I learned to dive; parachute, and jump out of helicopters and fire all kinds of nasty weapons. I hated every moment of it. It was there that I became determined to become an officer. I thought that by becoming an officer, I wouldn't have to put up with all that nonsense."

"So what did you do?"

"I applied for Officer training and my Gunny sat on the paperwork so that I almost missed the deadline for getting accepted."

"Your Gunny?"

"Gunnery Sergeant, E-7. He was like a Chief Petty Officer in the Navy. Anyway, when I found out that Gunny had sat on my papers, I got really mad. I went to the Colonel who told me there was nothing he could do about it. Frankly, that was a line of B.S. but I was just a young Petty Officer and thought I had no recourse. However, I never knew how to take no for an answer. Not knowing quite what to do or for that matter any better, I found out the telephone number for the Navy's Education Command. And I called over there one day from a pay phone in the hospital. When I called it was late in the day. The person who picked up the phone listened to my story and heard the phone operator saying I needed to put more coins into the phone. The man I was talking to from Navy Education asked me where I was. I told him I was at a payphone. He asked me for the phone number and promised me he would call me right back. I gave him the number because I had run out of dimes. I hung up the phone and didn't know what to do. I waited for a moment. The phone didn't ring. I waited for what seemed like an eternity. Just as I was going to give up and walk away, the phone rang. I picked it up and sure enough it was the person I had been talking to. I explained again what was going on. He asked me why I was calling the Naval Education Command directly.

I told him, I felt helpless and I needed to know what exactly I needed to do so that the next time I applied, it would not get bogged down. He asked me if I had spoken to my Commanding Officer. I told him I had spoken to the Colonel and that he had told me that there was nothing he could do. The man got very angry when he heard that. He asked me the name of my Colonel and the name of my Gunny. He then asked me the name of the Commanding Officer of the Hospital. I told him what I knew. He then told me he would personally do whatever it took to get me ordered into the next class. I was delighted and gave him all of my personal information over the phone. I talked with him for over 40 minutes. He asked me all about myself, my hopes and aspirations. I mean he asked me really personal things. He spoke to me about the state of the world and what I thought I could do to improve the Navy. As the conversation neared its end I asked him for his name. I told him I wanted it in case I had to call back again. He told me his name was Riley and I needn't worry because I was going to Officer's School.

The next morning, I am called into the Colonel's office. A very angry Colonel wanted to know how I had the audacity to call Admiral James Riley, Chief of Naval Education and complain about him and my Gunny. I was dumbfounded. I tried to explain in between being berated by his screaming that I had just called to inquire how to do the process properly the next time I applied. That made the Colonel even more upset. I told him that I had spoken to some gentleman named Riley, but I thought he was some civilian. I never dreamed that he was the Admiral himself. Well the Colonel was besides himself because not only had Admiral Riley called the Colonel himself, he had called the C.O. of the hospital and the Commanding General of Camp Lejeune who had all called him to yell at him. Everyone was really pissed.

Anyway, Admiral Riley had immediately and personally cut orders for me to go to Officer Candidate School effective the next month. Well, that was great for me. But boy, was Gunny p.o.'d. He came down to my Battalion Aid station and threatened to make my life miserable until I left. I just looked at him without saying a word. While he was yelling at me, I walked over to the filing cabinet with all of the battalion's medical record. I searched through the files until I found his personal medical file. I pulled it out and started thumbing through it. When I found his shot record, I ripped it out of the file, wadded it up and popped it in my mouth. I chewed it up good and swallowed it down. When Gunny asked me what I thought I was doing, I told him that it seemed that his shot card had been "lost" and he would have to go through a full set of shots immediately. He glared at me and stomped out. "

"Well, did he ever get you?"

"Never bothered me until the day I left."

The young man sighed in his impatience. This was a great story but not quite what he wanted. The Rabbi was telling a lovely reminiscence but it wasn getting the priest nowhere. The story was just that, a story. He wanted to get straight to the facts that would verify the Rabbi's identity and he was listening to the old man's musings of day's gone bye. Finally, he interrupted.

"I don't want to seem rude, but I don't need the whole story."

The Rabbi looked at him incredulously. "Oh now, you don't need the whole story. Well what exactly do you need, young man?" he asked angrily

The young priest became embarrassed and stammered,

"That is not what I meant. I need to only hear a summary, where you were and when to make a confirmation.

The Rabbi looked quizzically at him.

"A summary? To confirm what?"

Then he looked on through the windshield and asked,

"When one of your parishioners comes to you with a problem, do you stop them and tell them to summarize?

"Sometimes, I suppose, but that's not what I mean, I just need to get some basic facts from you so that I know if I'm talking to the right person."

The Rabbi shook his head. He was weary from the night, but he had no idea what this young priest was driving at.

"Can I give you a piece of advice? And it doesn't matter if you are talking about Jews, Christians, or atheists. People coming to you with a problem have a story to tell. Often the story tells us more about the problem then the question they are asking us. Sometimes the story tells us what advice they are really seeking rather than what they think they are seeking from us. Often there are little telltale truths that can only be ascertained from how a story is told, what is left out and what the teller leaves in. If you don't listen carefully to the story, your advice can be worthless or worse, very damaging, because you did not understand the problem being posed to you. In this case, it is different, but the same. You asked me for a history. I do not know why you want it or who you are. You need it to satisfy yourself that you are talking to the right person. I, on the other hand know nothing. Yet you have asked me to tell you about myself and I am prepared to tell it as I have already begun to. Now you tell me that you only need "the Facts" to make a confirmation. I do not know what you want and what great secret you must protect. Frankly you seem rather confused yourself. Maybe if you tell me what you are seeking to find, I can help you. As it stands now, I am rather concerned for you, as you seem to be looking to clear a very big burden for someone. Tell me what you need, maybe I can help you."

Father Daniel shifted uneasily in his seat. He found a parking spot on the street and gently slid the car into the spot. He turned off the motor and turned to the older man. He took a very deep breath and looked deeply into his eyes. Through the older man's glasses, he could see clear hazel eyes, which had a tint of blue. The creases around his eyes were wrinkled, yet the eyes themselves seemed childlike. He knew that the Rabbi's rebuke was not done to hurt his feelings, but rather of genuine concern for him. He took a deep breath again and started to talk. But he stopped himself and pondered for a moment what he was going to do. Then he seemed to resolve it in himself and he said to the Rabbi,

"I know it may seem strange what I am asking of you, but please indulge me. You are right in saying that I am looking to clear a very big burden for someone. That is all I can tell you now. Believe me if there was some other way to do this, I would do it. As it is, I need to know your basic history now, not the details. If you are the right person for me to convey this information that I have, then there will be plenty of time for you to fill in the holes for me later. Again, please indulge a younger man, a younger man of G-d, to bring this situation to a conclusion."

He sighed breathlessly and looked closely again at the Rabbi's face. The Rabbi stroked his beard and looked at him, with deep concern and some foreboding. He closed his eyes and said nothing. He turned away from the young priest and shook his head.

"To the young, everything is such a drama! Why must it always be so? When I was younger, I made everything into a soap opera of Kafkaesque proportions and now that I am an old man, I can see what nonsense it was. Why can't you speak plainly to me? Why must this "situation" fall under such secrecy?"

He looked closely at the young man again. The priest looked straight out through his windshield and exhaled deeply.

"Ah, all right, when I was young, it was all so important. All right, young man of G-d. You should know that G-d is truth. In our way of life we call it Emes. The Master of the Universe is Emes – Truth. You should know it already. But all right, it is sometimes better to not be right about something. "

He looked directly at the young man and then put his hand on his shoulder and smiled broadly.

"So to continue. I went next to Officer Candidate School in Newport, Rhode Island and then was assigned to the Naval Air Station outside of Memphis. I was assigned there nominally, for in truth I was assigned to the University of Mississippi to complete my education before I was commissioned an officer. I was assigned to the Naval ROTC unit there and I stayed there for a year and a half until I graduated and was commissioned an Ensign in the Navy. I was assigned to the USS Tarawa, a big helicopter carrier for three months while they deployed and then back to San Diego, California for Surface Officer Training. I was pulled from that training before it started and assigned to the training that would make me a Special Warfare Officer. Then I was assigned to ”

The priest interrupted him.

"That's enough, thank you, I have the information I think I need.

"That's it", the Rabbi asked, "That solves the puzzle"

The priest just looked at him and quietly said, "Yes, that's all I need. You are the man I need to share my information with."

Rabbi Kaplan scratched his head, "Really?"

The priest answered back," Yes Really!

The Rabbi shook his head, "Well I'll be!"

The priest continued, "I would like to ask you something else."

The Rabbi shrugged his shoulder, now more confused then before.

"Sure, ask away!"

Father Daniel leaned down for a moment as if in prayer and then asked,

"What about when you were first in the Navy. What was your life like?"

"I'm not sure what you mean?"

"Did you go out?"

"Sure, I went out. What did you expect a young man in uniform to do, sit in the barracks?"

"No, I mean did you go out. . ?

The Rabbi interrupted,

"You mean with the ladies?" and laughed heartily.

Then he turned serious and said gently,

"I was not your "typical" sailor. I went to bars with the gang, but I didn't pick up women or go to the houses of ill repute, so to speak. I was very shy. If I went out with a girl, it was because I liked her and wanted to see if she could eventually be my wife."

The priest listened intently. Then he asked,

"Did you date anyone seriously?"

"Sure"

"How many?"

The Rabbi seemed amused,

"A few"

"Was there one who was particularly special?"

Rabbi Daniel turned to him with a very concerned look.

"There might have been. Young man, what is this about?"

"Do you recognize this name. . ? Karolyn German?"

The Rabbi took a deep breath. Then he turned white and pale. He said nothing and tried to hold his composure, although he was visibly shaking.

"Well?"

Still he said nothing, but tried to control his breathing with deep long breathes.

"I can see you know the name."

Rabbi Daniel thought he was going to die on the spot. His heart was racing out of control and all he wanted to do was escape from this car. But he made no move. Finally, he seemed to croaked out,

"You know her?"

The young priest nodded yes. The Rabbi regained a little composure.

"Is she still alive?"

The priest looked at the Rabbi quizzically, but nodded yes again.

He looked relieved to hear that.

"Is she one of your parishioners?"

"No"

"Then how do you know her?"

"I know her. Maybe you can tell me a little about her, from your point of view."

Rabbi Kaplan looked at him quizzically, "Why?" Then he shook his head and sort of smiled, "I know! For confirmation purposes", the Rabbi said slyly.

Father Daniel smiled and shook his head yes,

"Yes! For confirmation purposes."

The Rabbi looked directly in the young man's eyes. Then he squinted and his brow furrowed.

"Why do you really want to know, young man?"

"Because, she is my mother."

The Rabbi took a sudden deep breath. His head was spinning. The most unbelievable thing was happening to him. A lifetime ago of his anxieties had just been dropped at his feet. He had no way of dealing with the emotional overload he now felt.

"She is your mother?" stating it as if it was a statement and not a question.

"She is my mother!"

Still in disbelief,

"And you are her son?" again stating it as if it was not a question.

Father Daniel shook his head yes,

"I am her son! "

There was a long pause between the two. Then the priest continued,

"I need to know something"

The Rabbi looked up at him. Father Daniel looked at him with sympathetic eyes. Then he asked quietly,

"Rabbi, did you love my mother?"

"Did I love her? Why should it matter to you?

This was too much for the Rabbi to take. He pulled at the door handle and climbed out of the car. He stood looking at the car stamping his right foot into the ground again and again. He looked up into the sky and let out a cry of anguish. He turned to the right and walked a step and quickly turned about face and took another step. He twirled around and grabbed himself and stood there stamping at the ground like a rutting bull. He could not pull himself together. His face was taut. He was angry. He was in fear of the moment and the anguish of his youth had just invaded his carefully constructed world. He felt as if someone had stabbed him in the chest and the fiery pain was searing inside him and out. The priest, seeing the older man's reaction to all this jumped out of the car and stood at the driver's door looking at him across the top of the car. Father Daniel was afraid the Rabbi might hurt himself. But finally, the Rabbi settled down. He looked down at his shoes and then lifted his coat sleeve to his eyes to wipe away tears which had appeared in his eyes. Finally the Rabbi looked up at him.

"Did I love your mother?" he almost yelled," Did I love your mother?" he nearly screamed. "I loved her more than I loved myself."

Then he took a deep breath and composed himself again. He stood silently for a long time and then said quietly,

"Yes, I loved your mother."

The Priest nodded at him, "I know".

The Rabbi looked at him and said nothing. Then he shook his head in acknowledgement of what had just been said to him. He swallowed hard. Then he continued,

"She was my first true love. Not those fascinations young men feel are love. That "love" they feel until they are turned around by another pretty face. Yes, I loved her! And for the past twenty some odd, I guess it is nearly . . , no it is at least twenty-five years."

He looked up and out the side window for a moment,

"And for twenty-five years I have sought to bury that love. I built a totally new life. I found a wonderful wife and we have a wonderful family that you have yourself met. I have devoted myself to G-d and to the people around me and have buried the hurt that your mother caused me. Do you know what I am talking about? The Hurt! Do you?"

The priest softly nodded his head yes. Then he spoke quietly to the older man,

"I know about it. I do. So does Mom. Believe me when I tell you that she has carried it as a burden her entire life."

"Has she? Well good! At least I know that she was not without sorrow over our love. Is he your father?"

The priest was startled by the question,

"Ah, yes. Yes he was"

"He was?"

"He passed on about a year and half ago. Cancer."

"Was he decent man?"

"He was a good man in his own way"

"In his own way? What does that mean? Speak plainly to me. Did he treat her well?"

"He treated her as well as he could"

"What does that mean? As well as he could! Did he beat her?

"No, nothing like that, but he was a lot older than her, you know."

The Rabbi shook his head.

"I know. Any brothers or sisters?"

"No. Mom got sick after I was born and there were no others. I assumed it was because of her illness"

"What illness?" the Rabbi snapped.

"She had cervical cancer."

The Rabbi appeared shaken. The priest then added "But she apparently recovered fully"

"Oh", the Rabbi said, and he drifted off into his own thoughts.

The Rabbi stood quietly for a few moments. The wind picked up and he turned up the collar of his coat. He seemed in a trance. Then suddenly, he looked up at the young man.

"How is she now?"

"She is well. Still very active. She still plays racquetball several times a week. She works as a teacher in high school and is popular with her students."

"Good, I'm glad she is well. Good", he seemed to drift into his own little world again. The world of relived memories. Suddenly he shivered and reached for the car door. He looked up and said,

"It's cold, let's get back in the car."

He slid into the seat and the younger man followed. He looked up at Father Daniel and peered carefully at him. He sighed for a moment.

"Why did she send you to me?"

"She didn't, I came for myself. She doesn't know that I am here"

"She doesn't know?" Rabbi Kaplan seemed surprised, "Then why?"

"Why what?

"Why are you here?"

"It's a long story"

"You've come all this way to tell it, so tell it!"

The Priest took a deep breath and gazed out his side window,

"OK, . . . I will!"

The Rabbi settled into the back of the seat and looked forward through the windshield. He fished a pipe from his coat pocket and placed it in his mouth. The young priest began to explain.

"My father passed away on a Friday morning. He had been ill for a long time. He was a molder in the Navy and the metal and the smoke must have affected him over the years. Besides that, he was a heavy smoker to the end. I suppose it was inevitable that he would get lung cancer. At first, nothing changed much. He started chemotherapy and eventually had to have surgery to remove his left lung and part of his right lung. After that, he was essentially without strength to do anything besides sit in front of the TV and complain. Mom took care of him when he let her and he progressively worsened over about three years. Finally, he was hospitalized this last time when the cancer has spread to most of his body. I'm not sure if we were not more relieved than sorrowful that he passed on.

Mom seemed unaffected by his passing and did not even cry at the funeral. She was a perfect hostess greeting visitors to her home after the burial. She smiled at all the guests and comforted his side of the family. She took special care of my little family and me. We didn't want for anything because of her and that allowed us to be absorbed in our grief. Mom didn't lose her composure, not even once. I was sure that this was just delayed grief. However, in the next several months, she seemed to adjust very well without even the slightest hint of grief. One night she made dinner for my family and me. After the meal I finally got up the nerve to talk with her. Ruth Anne and I had discussed what was going on many times and we were both perplexed by her lack of grief. So, Ruth Anne took the children home and I sat down with Mom to talk with her. She must have known something was up, but I don't think she thought it involved her. I suspect she thought it had to do with some family problem with me and Ruth Anne or the kids.

Anyway, I asked her how she was doing, if she was holding up. She said to me that she was doing just fine.

Then she asked me if everything was all right. I mentioned that I thought it strange that she did not seem saddened by Dad's death and that I had not even seen her cry. I figured she would tell me that she cried in private. Instead she laughed. Then she told me that she had not cried at all over Dad's death nor would she. I was kind of shocked by that statement. It seemed so out of character for her to say something like that. She then explained that for many years, Charley, that was my father's name"

"I know", said the Rabbi.

"Anyway, She and Charley had lived apart under the same roof. She said that she had done her duty, as a good wife should. When he got sick, she took care of him, but the love and for that matter, the friendship had passed from their relationship a long time ago. I couldn't believe what she was saying to me. I told her that for as long as I could remember, the two of them always seemed to get along so well. I acted as if Mom was talking nonsense. But she wasn't talking nonsense. She said to me that sometimes people just get along. They rarely had anything to fight about. It was not that she didn't like him. She had always appreciated him. It was just that she didn't love him.

I asked her when she stopped loving him. Mom told me that in retrospect, she doubted that she had ever really loved him. That statement took me aback. I said to her that she had lived with this man for twenty-five years and it seemed a shame that she should go through life without having loved a man. She giggled for a moment, then she laughed again. Mom got up and went into the den. She rustled through some books in the bookshelf and pulled one out. She brought it back into the kitchen and sat down.

Mom opened the front cover and taped inside the cover was an envelope. It had yellowed with age. She opened it and inside were some photographs. Mom pulled them out, looked at the top one, and smiled broadly. She handed it to me and said that she had known love once as a young girl in the Navy."

The priest reached into his inside jacket pocket and pulled out a photograph. He handed it to the Rabbi. The Rabbi looked down at it and nodded his head slightly. He closed his eyes tightly and shuddered. Tears appeared on his cheeks and he wiped at his face with his hand. It was a picture of Karolyn and him taken in a restaurant sitting next to each other. It had been taken many years before in Chicago. The two faces were smiling broadly. They were both so young in the picture.

"How old were you then?" the priest asked the Rabbi.

"I would guess I was 23. Your mother was two years younger than me so she was probably 21"

"You were a nice looking couple"

The Rabbi shook his head yes and smiled. He stared at the picture for a long time.

"She went on to tell me that you were something else. And that's a quote directly from her mouth."

The Rabbi smiled weakly and shrugged his shoulders.

"She also told me that you were so driven to achieve, that she sometimes felt overwhelmed by you"

"I could see that", Rabbi Daniel said nodding his head yes gently.

"She also said that the separations from her while you were back in school made her very sad and she wondered if you would be there for her"

"I know I wasn't"

"You weren't?" the priest sounded surprised.

"Of course I wasn't. When you are young you can be remarkably unfeeling, all the time thinking you are the most sensitive. Growing older lets you look back and see things clearly and when that happens it allows you to regret."

"Do you regret not marrying my mother?"

The Rabbi stared out the window for a long time, and then he spoke up,

"I do! On some level, of course. First love is the freshest, the most intense. It is also the most senseless in many ways. When I look at my life now, I realize that I could never have married your mother. She was not my bashert. Bashert means my G-d given intended. Much like Rachel in the Bible. Jacob loved her the most intensely. But Leah was his woman for all time. It is she who is buried with him and it is she that was intended for him, even if he didn't understand it at the time. Later, he did understand it.

There is a part of me that will always love your mother, but Rebecca has been my wife for twenty years. They have been blessed years although they have not always been so happy. I am a difficult man, forgetful of others feelings sometimes because my head is often in the clouds. Rebecca herself is a difficult woman sometimes. She likes to argue with people and she takes stands that are often difficult for me. But as a mother I know no woman who can be called her equal. We have been blessed with three sets of twins. Each set has been a challenge and a great blessing and I could never have raised them myself. She has been there to make this family work and I love her dearly. Having children taught me that love is far more than the raging of hormones and childlike fantasies of romance. It is hard work and the feelings come and go and come again. This is life. Maybe it is not as exciting as my love for your mother once was, but it is much more real. And so, for that reason, I do not regret that my life has turned in this direction."

There was an awkward silence in the car for a moment. Each man seemed to gather together whatever inner reserve was inside of him. Each seemed to be shaping in their minds what further to say. Finally, the Rabbi asked quietly,

"You still haven't told me what you have come to me for?"

The priest bit his lip and thought for a moment.

"Let me continue the story for you, if that's OK."

The Rabbi shrugged

"Sure"

Father Daniel continued,

"I asked her why you had broken up? She said it was because she had married Dad. I asked what happened? She said she was seeing my father about two weeks and he asked her to marry him. They went down to Las Vegas and got married in one of those wedding chapels. I couldn't understand why she would do this if she were in love with you. She then told me that she knew in her heart of hearts, that you could never marry her because she was not Jewish. She said that she knew that no matter how much you loved her, even if you thought you believed otherwise, you couldn't do it. So when Dad asked her to marry him, she agreed to it and did.

I said to her, how could you do it so quickly? How could you be so calculating about it and give up on love? She told me that during the first week she had been seeing Dad, she had been waking up nauseous.

After three or four days of this she went to Sick Call where a Doctor informed her that she was pregnant. Not knowing what to do, when my father asked her to marry him she told him initially that she couldn't. When he asked her why, she admitted to him that she was pregnant. He told her he would marry her anyway and that he would raise the child as his own. I am that child. When I was born, she named me Daniel after you."

At first, Rabbi Daniel didn't get what Father Daniel was telling him. Slowly, this information filtered through his brain. When it finally registered within him, he looked over at the young priest incredulously. Suddenly, he felt his chest tighten up. The pipe dropped out of his hand and onto his lap, spilling lit tobacco onto his pants and the car's carpet. He gasped for air. He felt separated from his body, as if he was in a dream. He thought his heart would stop on the spot.

Suddenly, almost ferociously, he reached for the younger man's hand and turned it palm down. The priest tried to pull his hand back, but the older man was very strong. So the priest just let him hold on not knowing why the older man was looking at his hand. Daniel held the priest's hand up to the sunlight and looked carefully at the hand in front of him. He let the hand go and slumped in his seat. Rabbi Kaplan just sat in silence for a long moment. Then, he sat up straight, and picked up his pipe. He took a breath and then let out a loud sigh. He slumped back into his seat again, just shaking his head over and over. He reached for his eyes and rubbed them with his fingers. The priest watched all this curiously, not quite understanding what was going on. The young man looked down and saw the back of the Rabbi's hand. Then he understood. The Rabbi had vitiligo, a discoloration of the pigment of the skin. Father Daniel had the same condition on his hands. It was an inherited condition. He realized that with just one look, the Rabbi had confirmed for himself that the young man was in fact his son.

They looked at each other in silence. They looked for a very long time. They didn't speak, but they studied each other's features. The young man looked at his father closely for the very first time. He looked at his father's long lean hands and fingers, his long gray beard, the thin mouth and the eyes, which were filled with tears in front of him. Father Daniel looked at this man's innate elegance and saw the shattered look in his eyes.

"Are you all right?" the young priest whispered to his father.

"No, not really", the Rabbi replied, "Not really at all"

There was more silence in the car. Finally, the priest broke it by asking,

"Can you accept what I have just told you?"

The Rabbi nodded,

"It is not a question of whether I can accept, it is a fact and I do accept it. For me the question is why the Master of the Universe must test me again and why this time must the test be so impossible. Young man, can <u>you</u> accept that? I can accept that you are my son, as unbelievable as it may be to me now. Can you accept that I am <u>your</u> father and not the man who raised you all these years? And can we deal with all this, each of us, in some way together? If we can do that, well. . ."

The two men sat in silence for a very long time.

CHAPTER FIVE

e closed the door to the house quietly. He hung up his coat and hat in the front closet. Then Daniel walked into the dining room. Rebecca was sitting in his chair at the head of the table, drinking a cup of coffee and reading a magazine. She looked up at him as he settled into a chair alongside and looked at her carefully. A headband pulled her hair back and her robe was loose around her. She turned to him.

"Elliott? Nu?"

The Rabbi shook his head,

"He passed away, a little after five o'clock this morning. The damage was too great. He was brain dead when he arrived at the hospital."

"Do you know what time they will have the funeral?"

"They will call as soon as it is all arranged. Sometime this afternoon for sure."

They sat in silence for a moment. Then she leaned back in her chair and pursed her lips. She saw that his mind was wandering. She waited a moment and looked at him until she got his attention. Very softly, almost in whisper she said to him,

"So, were you able to solve the young priest's problem?"

"I'm afraid it is a very complicated problem. I am not sure I can solve it for him".

"How so?"

He shrugged his shoulders and gave her his familiar tortured look when he didn't want to talk about something. She took a sip from her coffee and looked at him.

"So, what's this big problem. Tell me, maybe I can help you solve it."

He shook his head sorrowfully,

"It's too complicated. In truth it is way too complicated for me. I really don't want to talk about it, if you don't mind". He took a breath.

She looked at him and said sarcastically, "Oh, please", almost spitting out the words.

He suddenly looked straight at her and said,

"For you, Rebecca dear, for you . . .it", he looked away towards the china closet, "It would be just impossible."

She looked at him quizzically. He made a face and gestured with his hands. He looked to the ceiling and said,

"Master of the Universe, this time you sent me a doozy"

"Oh, Daniel, stop the melodramatics. What's going on?"

He looked at Rebecca and got up from his chair and started to pace around the room.

"This one is beyond anything, anything I could ever have expected to encounter."

"How so?" ,

He didn't answer her. Instead, he paced around restlessly for a moment. Finally she said to him.

"Daniel, sit down."

"I can't! I'm overtired from being up all night and I have a bad headache. I don't know what to do. Do we have any aspirins down here?

He started to walk into the kitchen. Rebecca called out to him,

"Daniel, come back here for a moment. Sit down. I'll get you a coffee. Sit. I need to talk with you about something."

She got up and went into the kitchen. He sat down in his chair by the head of the table. He fingered the magazine lightly flipping through the pages but not really reading anything. Rebecca came back with a cup of coffee and two aspirins. She set them down in front of his chair.

"Good, you're sitting. Daniel, drink your coffee."

He sat down and looked into the coffee cup as if it was a mirror reflecting all of his anxieties back at him. She sat quietly for a moment watching him sip the coffee. She stirred for a moment as if she was going to say something, then shook her head and thought better of it. She watched him reach for the aspirins and put them in his mouth. He swallowed down some more coffee and took a deep breath. Finally in almost a whisper she said to him,

"He's your son, isn't he?"

He sprayed coffee out of his mouth and began to cough violently. When he recovered, he looked at her in amazement and yelled,

"What?"

She spoke again in an even softer voice.

"He's yours! Daniel, I know that he is your son."

"Who?"

"Who? The priest who! Whom else would I be speaking about?"

"And exactly how do you know that?"

"I know!"

"Oh my G-d, Rebecca!"

"Don't Oh my G-d me. He's yours Daniel. I know it!"

He stopped, took a deep breath and looked hard at her. She knew, somehow she knew. There was no point in trying to play it out. He was going to have to tell her eventually. And if she figured it out on her own, well, so be that too! He nodded to her, slowly but most assuredly, yes. Then he gently asked her,

"Really Becky, how do you know that he's my son?"

She reached into the pocket of her robe and pulled out a photograph. She slid it across the table to him. Daniel picked it up and looked at it. It was a picture taken of him years ago in his Navy diving suit. His hair was wet and slicked back. He was clean-shaven. In the picture, he was tall, tan and muscular. It didn't register with him what Rebecca was showing him.

"Look! He's the spitting image of you when you were in the Navy. When I got my first look at him in front of the house, I thought the Almighty had come to claim me. When he came to the house I studied him more closely. I thought I would lose my mind, because you could not recognize what was so obvious to me. I see you still don't realize the resemblance. Its eerie."

The Rabbi looked down at the floor. He didn't get it. All he got was just his confusion. He looked up at Rebecca, shrugged his shoulders in an act of desolation and asked,

"What are we going to do about this?"

She looked at him in shock for a moment. Then she put her hands on he waist and said angrily to him,

"I can't believe you Daniel Kaplan! We? What is this we? He's not my son. We? This is not a we. This is a you!", and pointed to his chest as she said it.

She was dismayed. She shook her head and said,

"We? Ugh! You say we?" She just glared at him. He looked down at the floor sheepishly.

"You say we? How do you dare say we? What a mess, Daniel Kaplan. This is some mess you have gotten us into. Me, the children. How could you have done this? We? Do you think I'm some sort of idiot?"

He stood up and started pacing the floor. He looked at her and answered,

"No Becky, I don't think you are an idiot. I'm just so confused."

"Well get unconfused. Get unconfused very fast Daniel. Do you hear me? Get unconfused!

Daniel looked at her in amazement. He was at a loss for words. Finally he caught his voice to speak,

"You ask me how could I have done this? Exactly, how was I to know a son I didn't know existed would show up on my doorstep? In my wildest imagination, who could have guessed this?"

She answered venomously,

"You should have known. You should have known that with your past, this could happen."

"That's absurd, Becky. You talk like I slept with women all over the place?

"Well how would I know you that you haven't?"

"You know because I've told you I didn't. And you know me."

"I don't know you! You are a mystery to me."

"How can you say that? Gee Beck, I can't believe you are doing this to me right now."

"To you?", she exploded, "What about me? What about the children? Come on Daniel, on some level, you must have known, your psychic in that way. You must have known. It was that lousy life you led before you met me. The Navy . . ."

Her voice trailed off.

He shook his head and just looked at her helplessly. She continued.

"You had no right to marry me. You knew! You had no right to subject me to this. . . This disaster. I should have known better. All my friends, my family said not to marry a Baal T'shuvah (a non-religious Jew who becomes religious). They all said you don't know what these people have done in their pasts. But no! I said to all of them. You were not that way then. And you had changed your life and were really trying to be an observant Jew. You didn't have all those horror stories, the girls all told about their Baal T'shuvah husbands and boyfriends. And now this! "

She started to cry. He went up to hold her but she pushed him away.

"Well, what are you going to do about this Daniel?"

"I don't know", he said with a tiredness that had completely overcome him.

"You don't know?" she screamed at him, "You don't know? Isn't it obvious to you? You have your whole life here. Your family. Your children. You are considered a pillar of this community. How could you even consider. . .?", she sputtered, "even consider having any further contact?"

He said nothing. He looked down for a moment then he looked up at her with pleading eyes. She looked into those eyes and she didn't like what she saw.

"You are considering it! How could you? How could you? After all of my sacrificing for you. You were nothing before you met me and you have the nerve to stand there and look me in the eye and tell me that you don't know what to do? It's obvious, isn't it? Isn't it Daniel?"

He just looked at her. He felt totally confused and totally alone.

"I guess its not so obvious. Well let me tell you something Daniel Kaplan. Rabbi Daniel Kaplan, you have to choose, him or us! You have a family here and we better count first, I tell you that here and now, Daniel Kaplan, we better count first."

She ran up the stairs, sobbing. Daniel just sat there in his chair stunned. What else could happen today to destroy his life any further? What else?

The next thing he knew, he was out of the house and driving his car away from the house. He drove down the street in a blind rage of hysteria. Daniel Kaplan's whole life had just blown the hell up. And he hadn't done anything. Yet now, all that he had ever worked for was gone. All his hopes, his accomplishments were now lost. That which he had tried to erase and thought that he had, they were now back with a vengeance. And they tore at him like a savage beast at work on its prey. But it was all done now and it could never be the same. And he knew now that it never would be.

So, he raced down Ocean Parkway, a huge avenue that dissected that part of Brooklyn, where he lived. His heart beat wildly; sweat was rising on his forehead. He swerved to avoid a car and drove onto the Prospect Expressway past the park and speeded onto the ramp of the Gowanus Expressway. There high above the buildings on the way to Manhattan, the traffic stopped him dead. Angrily, he beat on the steering wheel and then broke out crying in loud, long sobs.

The traffic inched ahead high on the bridging of the road. He could feel the whole road move from the wind and from the movement of the traffic. The smell of industrial soot and fumes from the cars made him feel sick. He closed his window and turned on the air conditioning. The traffic stopped again and he sat there frustrated and sad. Daniel had never felt so lost.

He looked out his windshield in a blind stare out at the cars ahead of him. A monarch butterfly alighted on the left wiper blade. It appeared to look at him. He took dim notice of it, hoping for a break in the traffic. He bounced his knee furiously, pent up with his complete frustration. Suddenly, the butterfly flew off. His eyes followed it as it climbed away, out of sight. He looked ahead at the traffic and sighed deeply over the lack of movement.

Then, it hit him. He shook his head and shoulders to awaken himself from the fog he was in.

"A Butterfly?", he asked himself. "What was a butterfly doing 100 feet in the air over the dirtiest, most polluted part of Brooklyn?"

Then a realization came over him. It settled over him like a calm warm wind and he could feel his heart slow down. His shaking stopped. It would all be okay! The butterfly! Of course! The butterfly was his angel. He took a deep breath. He was not alone. G-d was watching him! His faith, which had been so sorely tested today, well that would be what saved him.

He jumped from the sound of a horn blaring behind him. He stepped on the gas and got the car moving again. At the next exit, Hamilton Avenue, he turned off the road and doubled back. He was heading home.

He had his whole life to live and all the elements of that life were now taking shape. He didn't know what G-d had in store for him, but he wasn't going to run from the test now. And he knew that whatever it was to be, it would be.

CHAPTER SIX

ebecca Kaplan heard the engine start and listened as the car screeched out of the driveway. She hurriedly changed into her street clothes, put on a hat and left the house. She walked rapidly down to Ocean Parkway and turned left. From there she walked down the old bridal path past Kings Highway and Avenue R. She continued for three more houses and then turned and went into the fourth house. This house, a brick two story building with entrances on the side, served as a synagogue downstairs. Upstairs above the synagogue was the apartment of Rabbi Hillel Gerwitz, the renowned Rabbi and leader of much of the Orthodox Community around Kings Highway. Rebecca Kaplan was Rabbi Gerwitz' youngest child. She was the child of his advancing years and the apple of his eye. He had watched her proudly accept this Daniel Kaplan as her husband and had watched Daniel and Rebecca become leaders in the Jewish community themselves. Now she sat at his kitchen table in tears.

"Rebeccale (Little Rebecca), what is the problem? Sit down, have a tea. We'll talk", the old Rabbi said to his daughter after she had burst into the kitchen unannounced.

Her mother came into the room and gave her a kiss.

"So why are you here, baby?"

"Mami, I have a real problem"

"A real problem? Are you sick?"

Rebecca shook her head no.

"So what is it? Tell."

Rebecca recounted the story of the last night and morning activities to her parents. They sat in stony silence. They were horrified. Her mother became so agitated that she had to get up and leave the room. She went into her bedroom to lie down. Rabbi Gerwitz sat stunned. Finally, he leaned back in his chair, closed his eyes and took a deep breath. Then he reached out to hold his daughter's hand. He shook his head for a moment, then sat silent. He cleared his throat and coughed. Then he looked at Rebecca.

"Little One, he must never tell anyone about this, not even the ainecheles (grandchildren). No one is to know. Do you understand me?"

She shook her head,

"You go home right now. Tell Daniel to come see me as soon as he comes home".

"He has a funeral this afternoon."

"Then, when he gets back from the funeral. Tell him to come seem me immediately. I will set him straight, if he hasn't come to his senses all by himself. And Rebeccale, I'm sure, he will. You must realize that he is in shock. And if he has been up at the hospital all night, then he must be exhausted. He may not have even absorbed it into his head yet."

She looked at her father questioningly,

"You know, the ramifications of all this. It may not have sunk in yet. Really sunk in. But my daughter, this must be our secret. He can have no further contact. For the good of his family and this community."

"What if he decides to see this priest again? What do I do?"

"He won't!"

She looked at him doubtfully, He continued,

"But if you are concerned, I will say again to you that I will set him straight. He's a smart man and he is not rash. Have faith, Rebeccale; he will do the right thing. You will see, he will do the right thing."

"And if he doesn't?"

"You will demand that he give you a get (bill of divorcement) immediately and throw him out of the house."

Rebecca's eyes opened wide in disbelief at what she had just heard her father say. He looked at her and smiled softly.

"We pray and hope that he does the right thing, but we prepare for the worst and hope that we don't need those preparations. Now go home and send your husband to speak to me. I await him. Don't worry!"

CHAPTER SEVEN

Rabbi Gerwitz peered out of from behind the curtain on his front door and watched his daughter walk down the stoop and onto the street. He looked at his watch, it was not even eight o'clock in the morning and soon he would have a room full of men saying their morning prayers in shul downstairs. He shook his head. What a mess!

He felt deep sadness in his chest, not for his daughter, but for his son-in-law. He knew that in Daniel, there was found one of the most unique and genuine men of G-d. However, he also knew that what had just occurred could destroy everything for his son-in-law. Daniel Kaplan was the one man many in the Jewish community had hoped would become one of those great Rabbis, recognized by all in a generation as a leader in all things religious. A wise man, competent in law and compassionate in its enforcement, many people depended upon Daniel for guidance in their daily lives. He also hoped for Daniel, knowing that as the Elder in the community, he had grown older and was less able to carry on all of the active demands that arose. His own sons had shown little ability although all had great aspirations. Although Daniel had never indicated any desire, it had been Rabbi Gerwitz' intention to designate his son-in-law as his successor within the community.

"Feh," He shook his fist at the air, "Maybe, it's not all lost", he said out loud to no one in particular. He had to think about this. Maybe Daniel would see how impossible it would be for him to acknowledge this part of his past.

"Who knows?" he thought to himself.

He smiled broadly to himself remembering the first time he had met Daniel.

Five members of a nearby synagogue, Congregation Knesset Rambam, had visited him one Monday night. This congregation had at one time been one of the biggest in Brooklyn, but had since dwindled down to a few families. Their Rabbi had refused to retire or even give way to a younger man and the congregants felt it would be wrong to force his retirement. So, the shul had withered away slowly. Recent to their visit to Rabbi Gerwitz, Knesset Rambam's Rabbi had finally passed away. The Board of Directors had begun searching for a suitable replacement. It was their idea to bring in a new Rabbi who could draw younger families back to the shul. They had invested much time in interviewing a number of young men from the local Yeshivas and had found no suitable replacement. Most of these men were too bookish, stern, or argumentative. Few had any real speaking skills and the Board had become quickly disillusioned. One of the synagogue's members (who was not really Orthodox, although he prayed there and kept the Sabbath) had recently met with the Board and told of having gone to San Diego with his wife to visit their son who was in boot camp with the Marines out there. He told them of how on that Friday night, they had joined their son at the Jewish Chapel at the Main Naval Base at 32nd Street. The chaplain there was a young man who led a cheery service and who gave a beautiful and moving talk to the gathering. He spoke about how wonderful it was for them to be sharing the Sabbath. He talked of how special and how important it was for each of them to gather together, regardless of their backgrounds to pray and to sing and to be together. This congregant and his wife were very impressed. After the service, they joined the Rabbi and the sailors and Marines for a Sabbath dinner. They enjoyed it immensely. There was more singing and talk and lots of laughter. They learned from the Chaplain that he was one of only two Orthodox Rabbinical Chaplains in the Navy and that he had not always been religious, but had come to it from a deeply personal moving experience. The next morning they joined in again at the Chapel for Sabbath morning prayers and were again impressed with the young man's devotion to his sailors and Marines and to the guests. Again, he gave a beautiful and moving sermon and they were delighted with the whole experience.

So seeing that the Board of Directors were having such a difficult time finding a new Rabbi, he suggested to the Board that they contact this Navy Chaplain. They were skeptical at first, but feeling that they had nothing to lose by calling, they made contact with Lieutenant Commander Daniel Kaplan, Jewish Chaplain.

Chaplain Kaplan spoke with them at great length by telephone with the whole Board by conference call. Then he patiently spoke with each individual member, often at great length about his views and his experience. Each board member felt that Rabbi Kaplan had spoken to their particular needs. He seemed to them to be genuine and funny and very, very real. The Board met together and agreed to ask Chaplain Kaplan to come east to meet them and the congregation. Daniel accepted their invitation and a date was set.

The Board came to Rabbi Gerwitz for two reasons. They wanted his opinion about what they were doing. Second, they wanted Rabbi Gerwitz to have a talk with Daniel to assess his suitability and knowledge. Rabbi Gerwitz told them that he felt that it was probably unwise to seek a Rabbi from so far away. He also stated that military chaplains tended to be too liberal for a Brooklyn Shul. But the members of the Board were very clear that they had spoken with this young man and that they liked him very much.

Rabbi Gerwitz proposed that he could host the young Rabbi in his home for the weekend. Then he would give them an outside assessment of his abilities, his temperament and his suitability. It was arranged that during his stay, Rabbi Kaplan would spend the Sabbath eve with him, then go to Knesset Rambam, and give a talk on Sabbath Morning to the congregation. Additionally, Rabbi Kaplan would give another talk after Sabbath on Saturday night. He would stay with Rabbi Gerwitz until Monday, when he would return to San Diego. The Board of Directors agreed to the arrangement. Several weeks later, on an early Friday afternoon, a taxi pulled into Rabbi Gerwitz' driveway and a tall, elegant young man stepped out of the car wearing the dress uniform of a Naval Officer. His wife and daughter Rebecca gathered at the window and looked down at him in the driveway. He wore the gold stripes of a Lieutenant Commander with the Ten Commandment tablets placed above the stripes on each arm. He reached into the car, pulled a valise and a carry bag, and carried them to the door. The Rabbi sent Rebecca downstairs to answer the door and to escort the young officer up their apartment.

He came through the door to the apartment and warmly greeted the family. He shook the Rabbi's hand and nodded to his wife a greeting with a smile. Rabbi Gerwitz asked him about his trip.

"It was a long trip, but thank G-d, it was safe and I am here."

Mrs. Gerwitz asked,

"You must be very hungry, would you like something to eat?"

"Yes, thank you, a little something would be nice."

"What would you like?"

He laughed,

"What do you have?"

She laughed,

"Whatever, you want. I have a whole Shabbos worth of food. What would you like? I know… better, I'll serve you something and you'll eat."

He smiled,

"Agreed"

She and Rebecca went into the kitchen. A short time later Rebecca set a place on the dining room table and beckoned Rabbi Kaplan to wash and sit down. He went into the kitchen and washed his hands. He then sat down, took some bread, made a blessing on the bread and took a bite. He was famished. Soon Rebecca brought in a bowl of hot chicken soup with a matzo ball floating in it. He tasted it with relish.

"This is delicious! It has been some time since I've had a chicken soup like this."

The Rabbi's wife asked him,

"Your wife doesn't make for you"

"I am not married"

"You are not married? How old are you?"

"Thirty-five"

"Thirty-five and not married, how come?"

He looked at her sheepishly.

"I've been busy!"

"Busy with what? A man like you and a Rabbi no less, should be married. Hillel, maybe we know of some girls for him."

The old Rabbi groaned quietly and shot the younger man a look. The young man shrugged his shoulders and looked back at him with a wink. Rabbi Gerwitz smiled.

"Maybe I'll like this fellow", he thought to himself.

Soon Rebecca brought the rest of lunch to Daniel. It consisted of a piece of chicken and some kugels and salad. He ate it all and enjoyed every bit. He complimented the Rabbi and his wife for the meal. Mrs. Gerwitz said,

"Don't thank me, thank Rebecca, she cooked it all."

He turned to her and said,

"Well, thank you Rebecca. It was delicious and for someone like me who has to eat his own cooking all the time, it is nice to have a meal of this quality. Thank you!"

She turned red, then nodded to him, but didn't say anything. He finished up, said the Grace after the Meal and brought his things upstairs. He followed the Rabbi's wife, to a room that had been prepared for him. He had started to unpack when Rabbi Gerwitz came into the room.

"I hope that you find this room acceptable"

"Oh, it is just fine, thank you for having me"

"It is no problem. You must be very tired from your trip. Why don't you take a nap and relax until Shabbos? There are some towels for you to take a shower".

"Thanks"

He started to leave then turned around and stuck his head back into the room.

"Oh, another thing, we are having another guest for dinner tonight. A young man! We are trying to make a shidduch (match) for Rebeccale. Later, tell me what you think of him. He is a brilliant Talmudic student learning full time. I think you will find him most interesting."

"OK", Daniel looked at Rabbi Gerwitz puzzled; "I look forward to it"

"Have a good rest Rabbi Kaplan. You have a big day tomorrow. Sometime in next day or so, I would like to sit and talk with you about your life. A Jew in the Navy is most interesting", he smiled at Daniel.

Daniel smiled back at him and resumed unpacking his things.

CHAPTER EIGHT

To say that Hillel Gerwitz was intrigued by the young Rabbi staying beneath his roof would be giving too much credit to Daniel Kaplan. Rabbi Gerwitz had seen all types of young men come and go. He had married off three daughters, all to Rabbis, all steeped heavily in the culture of the Yeshiva. So to him, Daniel Kaplan was just another of these young men, albeit with a different uniform. He was intrigued with all of the ribbons over the young man's breast pocket and he was more than curious of the two gold badges he wore above and below his ribbons. He had personally counted six rows of ribbons. He knew that chaplains do not normally receive many ribbons in the military nor do they have chest full of badges, so there had to be an interesting story there. But aside from that, he expected Daniel to be quite ordinary as a religious man.

He listened to the chatter of the women in his kitchen. They were discussing their visitor and were very curious to find out about him. They were sure that he could not be that "Orthodox", so they were determined to show him what a real Shabbos was about. Rabbi Gerwitz chuckled to himself. This young man probably had more life experience than anyone they had previously met.

So this quiet Friday afternoon passed otherwise uneventfully, in the Gerwitz household. Around four o'clock, footsteps could be heard upstairs and then the sound of the shower being turned on. Soon, there was the sound of an electric razor and then shortly before five, Daniel Kaplan came downstairs dressed in a black suit with a white shirt and red tie. On top of his head he wore a large black wide-brimmed fedora. Everyone was sort of surprised to see him like that. He looked like he had just dropped out of the Yeshiva and not out of the Navy. He smiled and greeted everyone.

"How are you feeling Rabbi Kaplan? Rabbi Gerwitz asked.

"Good! Good, rested."

"We will go downstairs for Shabbos at 6:00"

"OK"

"Would you like a coffee, Rabbi?"

"Please, call me Daniel. I am not so formal"

Rabbi Gerwitz made a feigned surprised look.

"Well Daniel, if you hope to be Rabbi of a Shul, you'll become formal. It is sort of an occupational hazard. People expect their rabbis to be formal. And distant, at least a little. No one really likes his Rabbi to be too familiar. In this community, people expect you to make legal decisions, answers to the way they are to live their lives. So be formal Daniel with everyone, but your wife, when that time comes."

Daniel laughed gently and knowingly, but then he thought to himself that he really didn't know what that meant. He would not know until he was married. And he admitted to himself for the first time, that his consideration of a shul in Brooklyn was predicated on his hope of finding a wife.

Rabbi Gerwitz could see the wheels working in Daniel's head. He knew that he had guessed correctly about Daniel's motive in being in Brooklyn at this point in his life. Daniel was a decorated hero, who had chosen to become a chaplain. He was one of the few Orthodox Jewish Chaplains in the military and therefore could exert great influence. Yet, he was here, considering taking the mantle of leadership of a synagogue that was barely holding it's own in a community vibrant in Jewish life.

The rest of the afternoon passed quietly with Daniel reading and gathering his notes for his speeches the next day. At 6:00, he went downstairs to the shul and found himself a seat in a quiet corner. The men started to come in. They greeted him pleasantly, either with a nod or by coming up to him to shake his hand. He was a newcomer and a clean-shaven one in a shul full of beards. He settled into the rhythm of the prayers and was asked to lead the Sabbath evening service. He politely declined. He wanted to sink into that little place in his head that he needed for communicating with G-d. Soon Rabbi Gerwitz entered the shul. All the men stood up as he swept to the front pew. He shook hands with almost everyone. His entourage included two tall well-dressed young men who stood alongside him as if they were his bodyguards. After the service, Daniel waited a little while until the crowd began to thin and went back upstairs. He was greeted by Mrs. Gerwitz who bid him to wait for their guest and went into the kitchen.

Soon, he was joined by a tall, thin, almost ascetic looking young man. The man barely looked at him and said nothing to him. Daniel watched as he sat down in one of the big easy chairs and began to sway softly in his seat as if in meditation. Daniel, used to being more sociable, got out of his chair and walked over to the young man and introduced himself. He shook Daniel's hand weakly and without looking up, said that his name was Gershom Weiss. Rabbi Gershom Weiss! Daniel nodded and sat back down. The young man said nothing more and Daniel seeing that he was unfriendly, went back to his reading.

Rabbi Gerwitz came into the room dressed in his finest Sabbath coat and hat. The young man jumped up and stood stiffly, shaking the Rabbis hand. The Rabbi turned to him and said,

"Good Shabbos Gershom, Have you met Rabbi Kaplan?"

Gershom looked at Daniel in surprise. Then Daniel answered for him.

"We have already made our introductions"

"Good. Gershom, Rabbi Kaplan is a very interesting fellow. He is a chaplain in the Navy"

Again Gershom looked surprised.

"You are not Orthodox, I assume?"

Daniel smiled at him.

"Actually, I am", then he added, "There are a few Orthodox chaplains in the military"

Gershom seemed perplexed. Daniel looked at him for a moment and said to him,

"You seemed disturbed about what I said"

"No, No, I just had a question, but I don't quite know how to phrase it"

Daniel made a face,

"Just ask, I hear lots of strange questions all the time."

"Well this isn't really a strange question. I just wanted to know how you deal with the non-Orthodox Chaplains?"

Daniel was surprised by the question. He pondered a moment.

"The same way I deal with the Christian or Moslem Chaplains. I treat them as colleagues. I respect their opinions and experience. And I try to do the best for my Jewish sailors, most of whom are not Orthodox."

"Oh", said Gershom, shaking his head as he learned something new, "It must be difficult, for you to discuss religious matters with them? They are not really Rabbis, you know. They are taught some radical ideas in their seminaries."

"Sometimes it can be difficult, but not for that reason."

"I don't understand?"

"Neither did I at first. They chose to be Rabbis for the same reasons we chose to be Rabbis, for the most part. They felt a closeness to G-d. Their path was different than ours, that is all."

"I don't really understand?"

Rabbi Gerwitz interrupted them,

"Gentlemen, Kiddush"

They all gathered around the table. Some boys who were learning in the Yeshiva joined them for the meal. There must have been about 15 people around the table while Rabbi Gerwitz recited the Kiddush on the wine. They all then washed and sat down to eat. The men sat on one side of the table and the women on the other. Soon they were discussing many of the issues facing the Jewish community in Brooklyn and all the ramifications of this one's action or the other one's comment. The young men all attempted to show themselves off well by discussing and dissecting the difficult section of the Talmud each was currently learning. Then Rabbi Weiss spoke about that week's section in the Torah. He spoke in great detail and for a long time, bringing proof after proof. But Daniel was struck by the fact that he was repeating rote proofs, but not bringing his own original thought to his discussion. Daniel also noticed that Gershom never looked at Rebecca while he talked. And it was Rebecca, who ostensibly he was here to court. She in turn looked out across the table with a blank stare, her head resting on her hand. Daniel caught her eye and made a very subtle gesture with the crease of his mouth. She acknowledged his gesture with one of her own, indicating that she also found the whole dissertation boring and not very indicative of the man's depth of religious knowledge.

Between each course, the men would sing Sabbath songs and would talk some more. The women mostly gathered up plates or brought out more food. Daniel offered to help, but everyone looked at him as if he was from another planet. Finally, after the dessert was brought in, Rabbi Gerwitz said,

"It is a great pleasure to have two fine young Rabbis sitting with us tonight at our Shabbos table. Rabbi Weiss, whom you all know from the neighborhood and Rabbi Kaplan, who comes to us by way of San Diego, California and the Navy. As most of you know, Gershom learns full time at Mir Yeshiva from which he recently earned Semicha (Ordination) and teaches a beginners Gemara (a section of the Talmud) shiur (class) every day. Daniel, as this is our first time getting to know you, maybe you will tell us a little about yourself?"

Daniel nodded,

"I received Semicha from Yeshiva Menashe Frankfort, here in Brooklyn, four years ago."

Everyone looked shocked. Especially Rabbi Gerwitz, who was very surprised. He asked Daniel.

"You are a Menashe Frankforter?. I didn't know. I would have guessed that you came from Yeshiva University. Whom did you learn with?"

"My Rebbe (teacher/mentor) is Rabbi Avroham Aaron"

Rabbi Gerwitz was impressed.

"I know him well. He is a Gaon (A very holy man). A real wise man."

"Yes, He impressed me at my first meeting with him. I was planning to learn at Yeshiva University. A friend of mine asked me not to make a decision until I met Rabbi Aaron. However, he was away at summer camp and would not be back until the last week in August. This was in early July and I had to make a decision. So I accepted a place at Yeshiva. Anyway, my friend called me near the end of August and told me that the Rabbi was now home. I told him that I was already enrolled at Yeshiva. He asked me to call the Rabbi anyway and to talk with him. If nothing else, I would end up with some good advice. So I called him. When I spoke to him on the phone, he asked me to describe what I was trying to accomplish. Other than that he said nothing. At times I thought he was no longer on the other end of the phone. At the end of my conversation, he told me that I should meet him for morning prayers at Menashe Frankfort and after the service we would talk. The next day, I went to there and asked someone to point out the Rabbi. He was already in prayer, so I didn't disturb him. I put on my tallis and tefillin and began to pray. At the end of the service, I introduced myself. He then took me on a walk from the Yeshiva building down to Ocean Parkway, several blocks around, all the while talking to me about the Great Rabbi Hillel, and how people didn't have the right way of looking at the world. He told the story of the Gentile who asked Hillel to stand on one foot and tell him what Torah was all about. Hillel, of course, told him "Do not do to others, what you would not want done to you". He then explained to me the difference between that and the Gentile's Golden Rule of Do unto others . . . He talked of how people needed to put other people down to feel good about themselves. He emphasized that often times people's good deeds were motivated by a subtle need to put down those whom they were helping. He made me see how helping others must be free of the concept of payback, for it to be really effective. Then he talked to me about me. Who I was and why I had chosen to pursue this path. He talked to me about how the process of becoming a religious Jew from having been a non-religious Jew must be approached slowly. He talked to me about not giving up when the inevitable fall back would occur. And more important than anything else, he acknowledged to me that G-d could come to someone who was not religious. Then, he said something that struck me as one of those ultimate truths that I had been searching for. He said to me that we were all angels on earth. If we understood that and keyed into that, we could make the world a wonderful place. No man had ever spoken to me like that and I knew that I had to make this man my teacher. So I cancelled my registration at Y.U. and learned for four years with Rabbi Aaron. I worked full time as well in my own construction business. I would sneak out to go to class in the middle of the day and I would learn at night. I was very busy, but it was worth it."

Gershom seemed puzzled.

"You are a Baal T'shuvah (not originally religious)?"

"Yes"

"I hope your not offended by my asking, but why?"

"I am not offended. But why, what?"

"What? Well, I grew up frum (religious) and I can't imagine anyone wanting to give up all of the freedoms of the world. Why would anyone voluntarily take all of this on?"

Daniel leaned back in his chair and looked at the ceiling for a moment.

"Sometimes, what appears to be freedom is anything but. And what looks not to be freedom is the greatest freedom of them all. I don't know if that makes a lot of sense, but to me it does. And when I look back at the life that I had before this, I know that I was truly not free. I had no real direction, no sense of purpose."

Gershom pursued his line of questioning.

"But there had to be something, a moment that brought you to this?"

"Yes, there was one moment!"

They all waited. Daniel let some time pass before going on.

"I went to a place where G-d's presence was so clear to me, so loud, that I had to acknowledge it"

Rebecca interjected,

"Really", she seemed suddenly interested, "Where was it? I know, it must have been the Kotel (The Western Wall of the Second Temple in Jerusalem)?

Daniel smiled,

"No".

"Maybe you've been to the camps?"

Daniel looked at her quizzically,

"Camps? I never went to summer camp"

Rebecca laughed, then got very serious,

"No, I mean the camps in Europe, you know, the Shoah (Holocaust)".

"No, it was none of those places".

There was silence around the table. Daniel looked around the table uncomfortably,

"It was in Nagasaki, Japan"

Gershom asked,

"Nagasaki Japan?" He made a perplexed face," Nagasaki Japan? How could you feel G-d's presence there? I don't understand?"

Daniel spoke softly to him

"Do you know your history, Gershom?"

Gershom looked at him,

"Sure, I think?"

Rebecca asked,

"Isn't that where America dropped the Atomic Bomb"?

Daniel shook his head, acknowledging her,

"In part right. Nagasaki was the place where the second A-bomb was dropped. The first one was dropped over Hiroshima"

Gershom asked,

"Over?"

"Yes, over. They were air blasts. The bombs detonated in the air above the target. It essentially incinerated the immediate area."

Gershom said,

"But, I still don't understand. How could you feel G-d's presence in a place like that?"

Daniel looked Gershom squarely in the eye and asked, "Was G-d's presence felt in Betar (the site of a major massacre in Israel during the Bar Kochba War)?"

Gershom looked back at him perplexed. Daniel looked at the younger man and thought to himself, " Why do our young men have to be so foolish and closed minded?"

Then he asked the young man another question,

"Do you believe that there are places in this world that G-d's presence is acutely felt by people?"

"Yes, "

"Give me an example"

"Jerusalem certainly."

"Wasn't G-d's presence felt in the desert or on Sinai or even Egypt"?

"Well . . . yes"

"Were not some of the great centers of Torah learning in places outside of Israel?" Daniel asked Gershom pointedly.

"Yes"

"So why not Nagasaki, Japan?"

"Well . . . ", He became quiet and thoughtful. Then he said,

"But it happened to goyim (gentiles)"

"So? ", Daniel asked impatiently.

"You know Chinese, I mean Japanese, you know, Orientals."

Daniel made a face.

"So?"

Gershom seemed puzzled. Daniel looked at him carefully. Then he asked the young Rabbi quietly,

"Do you think that G-d only puts his presence amongst us Jews? "

He paused for an answer. None was forthcoming, so he continued,

"If you think about this logically, it makes no sense that G-d only brings his presence amongst us Jews? Do you believe that the Master of the Universe is so heartless that he would not bring his comfort to say . . . Orientals?

Gershom turned red.

"But they don't believe in G-d. They worship idols, you know Buddha" Daniel looked at him and continued,

"One, most Japanese believe in Shintoism. Which, as a point of fact, we would consider idol worship. But that doesn't mean that they are bad people, nor are they undeserving of G-d's comfort. People who suffer a great holocaust need G-d and he is there for them, regardless of where or who they are. Wouldn't you agree?"

The young Rabbi said nothing. Rabbi Gerwitz smiled softly beneath his great beard.

Daniel reached into his siddur (prayer book) and drew out a piece of paper.

"After I left Nagasaki and returned to the ship, I was very disturbed. I needed to deal with my raw emotions. I couldn't really explain how I was feeling to anyone, So, I started to write down what had moved me so deeply. I walked around Nagasaki and looked at my shipmates and I wondered if they felt what I was feeling. It seemed to me that they were not. Rather they were doing the tourist thing. But to me, well I felt such anxiety, such disruption inside. I felt like I was in a different place, like I had been enveloped by . . . something, someone. I felt separated from the world. I was so confused and I just didn't know why. The confusion continued for me. The more I thought about it, the more confused I became. But not in my head! I felt the confusion in my chest and in my stomach. I tried to analyze it. What I discovered was that for me G-d, the concept, was now G-d, the reality. He had reached out to me and my receiver became turned on, really on. And although I was flooded with these feelings, I didn't know how to process the anxiety, the tears and the love. I felt terribly afraid, but I also felt a great comfort because for the first time in my life, I knew."

Rebecca interrupted,

"You knew what?"

"I knew that G-d existed"

Gershom jumped in,

"But of course G-d exists. We all know that"

Daniel countered,

"But I didn't know that. And I suspect that most people really don't know it. They conceptualize, but deep in their heart, they do not know. For me, the heart joined with the mind and I knew as an adult what I had felt as a child. I felt together. G-d was real, substantive and close at hand. Just like I was as a little boy, G-d was my playmate, my confidante, my friend. And yet as an adult, all that frightened me. It still does! I would walk out on deck of my ship at night and contemplate how I could have that intensity of feeling not overpower me. I was so lost by the impact of my realization. I was the only Jew on my ship and had no one to talk to about it. I now understood that I would never look at life the same way again. I would sit on a bollard on deck and smoke my pipe. I would watch the sunset at sea. The beauty of the sunset stopped being just a beautiful act of nature to me but a reaffirmation of G-d's presence. But I had no place to go with all those feelings. Ultimately, I turned all of this raw emotion into a poem. May I read it to you?"

Everyone at the table looked at each other rather uneasily. Finally, Rabbi Gerwitz nodded yes. Daniel quietly read the poem.

NAGASAKI

I sat in the garden,
Flowers all in a row,
Where a bustling city stood,
Where the old men now go,

What remains of a church,
Are but bricks of her wall,
And the templates of happening,
Emblazon their fall,

If you listen you'll hear them,
Men, women and . . . child,
Hear their voices a calling you,
Call again and a while,

This garden's so peaceful,
Where hell knew her fury,
As for time immemorial
Let that be her jury,

When I was a young man,
I came to those gardens,
Naïve to my purpose,
So boldly, so hardened,

As I sat in those gardens,
At this place of no heroes,

G-d's presence 'still felt there,
Nagasaki – ground zero,

No person can cherish,
Until they've sat in that garden,
That once pilfered, polluted landscape,
Are we deserving of pardon,

A person can't reason,
Till they breathe for themselves,
That the quiet and peace now,
Are where . . . only screams dwelt,

I went as one person,
And left as another,
One cold January morning,
Life tumbled asunder,

The voices are calling,
Again and . . . again,
Their screams pass right through you,
Until you're insane,

You realize on earth,
N'ere to leave nor desist,
Where his presence is always,
These places exist,

For we all are his children,
And the destruction we wrought,
For whatever we're doing,
Did we gain what we sought?

There was silence in the room. Then Rabbi Gerwitz coughed uncomfortably and everyone seemed to wake up. They looked at each other around the table, then, they looked at Daniel. He shrugged, put the poem back in his prayer book and dug into his meal. They all followed suit and soon small talk overcame the table and the meal progressed in it's normal rhythm.

Soon, they said grace and drifted away from the table. Daniel stood up to leave the table, but Rabbi Gerwitz grabbed his wrist and beckoned him to sit back down.

"It must have been a powerful experience, for you to have written so emotionally?"

Daniel nodded.

Rabbi Gerwitz nodded back,

"You must tell me sometime, what it was like to have the Master of the Universe become your partner in life?"

Daniel looked at him perplexed,

"Rabbi Gerwitz?"

The great Rabbi raised his hand and looked directly into Daniel's eyes,

"You don't understand?"

"No"

"Sometimes a man spends his life in the search. He obeys all the commandments. He is stricter with himself than he is with anyone else, believing that through purity of thought and purity of action, G-d will truly become his partner. But he does not find. Then he meets another man. A man who maybe was not even looking. And that man finds what the other man has searched his lifetime for. Do you understand, Daniel?"

"I . . . am . . . not sure. I think . . ."

Rabbi Gerwitz raised his hand again,

"Rabbi Kaplan, the difference between us is that I chose him. The Almighty, however, chose you. I am jealous."

"But surely sir,"

The older man cut him off,

"No"

Daniel looked around the room. When he looked back at the Rabbi, he could see tears in the old man's eyes.

"Rabbi Gerwitz, you have spent your lifetime in pursuit of G-d's truth. You have been a judge, a teacher, a mentor to many and a friend to them as well. This whole community thrives because of you. Certainly, the Almighty chose you to be who you are and what you have become to all of these people?

The old man shook his head no.

"Please forgive me, Daniel, please forgive me for being so jealous".

"There is nothing to forgive. I just don't understand how you can feel this way?"

"It was something you said"

"What?"

"You said that you felt enveloped by something, someone"

"I know, I did"

"Tell me what it was like"

Daniel looked at him curiously. He shook his head and said,

"I don't understand what you want me to say"

Rabbi Gerwitz took a deep breath. He was old and suddenly felt very tired. His lifetime of work seemed inconsequential right now. He was talking to someone who might be able to explain to him what he had been seeking so strenuously for all of his 80 some odd years.

"Daniel, when this feeling came over you in Nagasaki, what did you feel?"

Daniel got up from his chair and paced a little. He put his hand on his chin and he closed his eyes. Then he leaned against the back of his chair grasping it with his hands and said,

"I felt a presence, like a haze. I could feel it against the skin of my face and my hands and then over all of my body."

Rabbi Gerwitz nodded.

"I looked around and the world had grown quiet. As I walked through this garden that the Japanese had set up at Ground Zero, I felt as if I could hear a million screams. . . of children. But the noise wasn't loud, nor was it frightening. I looked at the faces of the people around me, but I felt as if I was in a different place. I looked at the beautiful flowers growing, even in the bitter cold of winter. I felt detached and alone as I walked around the garden. Soon I came upon a stone monument that marked what was ostensibly Ground Zero. I took out my camera to take a picture of it, but my shutter jammed. I tried to advance the film, but had no luck. Finally, I just opened the back of the camera for a second and suddenly it worked again. Finally it was time to go and I left the garden with my shipmates and felt the envelope lift off of me as we climbed the long stairs out of the garden site. An interesting note, Rabbi, weeks later, when I developed the film, the print of the picture of the monument had a streak of orange and yellow light across it. Like a flame. It was eerie! Given the unsettled feelings, I already felt, it seemed to me that this was proof positive that G-d and I had made some incredible connection."

Daniel looked at Rabbi Gerwitz. The Rabbi's mouth was open and his head leaned heavily on the back of his chair. His eyes were drenched in tears and his hands shook slightly. Daniel became afraid and touched him on his hand.

Rabbi Gerwitz sprung forward in his chair and looked at the young man directly in his eyes. Then he said to Daniel,

"I am afraid of the Almighty, Daniel. I am afraid that in all of my years of intense study, of rigorous observance to his traditions and laws, that I have not learned anything about what makes G-d tick. I am jealous. Yes it is true, I am! I have stood by the Kotel many times, knowing that his presence was right there and still I felt nothing. I wept and people believed that I was weeping to G-d. But, I was weeping because I couldn't feel G-d. I give lectures every week to large audiences who tape my words and sell them in this community. People come up to me and say that my words inspire them, bring them close to G-d. I look at them in wonder. Why can I say over what I cannot even feel myself? My head has been in law books all of my life. Yet my internal spirit feels nothing. I talk about happiness and joy being a requirement of successful prayer. Yet now, after a lifetime, I feel nothing but intense sadness. Moses, our teacher, felt driven after almost a lifetime; certainly he was my age when he connected with G-d. So I can only hope that my time will come soon for me. Maybe then I can get to feel and experience being chosen by G-d as G-d has chosen you."

He looked up at Daniel and smiled. Then he said,

"And may you grow with the experience to be a leader of this generation."

Daniel sat dumbfounded. A great Rabbi had just admitted that he felt helpless regarding G-d. Daniel's own eyes filled with tears. He was an ordinary man who had felt G-d in his life and it was impossible for him to conceive that a man so devoted to Jewish life, as Rabbi Gerwitz would feel that he had been untouched by G-d. He didn't know what to say to the older man. He did not know how to comfort him. He sat down in his chair and looked at Rabbi Gerwitz as he wiped the tears from his eyes.

"Rabbi Gerwitz, I do not feel that G-d has chosen me for anything. I feel that he in heaven has opened a window a crack so I can slip a word in once in a while. But for you, Rabbi, he has opened not just a window, but a giant door. He has passed his light through you and that light has been felt by so many others. You may not feel that light pass through you, but its there nonetheless. You are a vessel of Torah and it fills all of these streets around you. You are who you are and you do what you do, because that is the way G-d wants it to be."

"But I don't feel it, Daniel. Not like you have felt it. All my life, I've wanted to feel it as this great miraculous force coursing around me and through me. Instead, I feel the aches and pains of an old man, dealing with people who are afraid to live their own lives and are dependent upon me to tell them how to.

I do not feel the "haze" pass over or through me. I read our Torah and I question in my heart what I read there. Does that surprise you Daniel?"

Daniel shook his head no. Then he sat down at the table. He reached across for a bottle of whisky. He opened it and poured a little in the old man's glass. Rabbi Gerwitz looked up at him. He nodded towards Daniel's glass. Daniel poured a little in his own one. The old sage smiled and lifted his glass. Daniel did the same and touched it to the Rabbi's glass.

"A L'Chaim to you"

"Amen", Daniel said smiling.

The Rabbi spoke again,

"Daniel, please do something for me"

"Sure, anything!"

"Give me a blessing from you"

Daniel was shocked,

"Rabbi, if anyone should be asking for a blessing it should be me asking it of you."

Rabbi Gerwitz dabbed at his eyes with a napkin. Then he smiled, knowingly, it seemed.

"Please bless me Daniel, Please"

"Rabbi, I've never blessed anyone before, I don't know how"

"Yes you do", he said quietly but firmly to Daniel

And so Daniel did. Rabbi Gerwitz took a deep breath and sighed mightily. Then he got up and wished Daniel a good night. This time Daniel took his hand and asked the Rabbi to sit down, Rabbi Gerwitz looked curiously, but Daniel nodded for him to sit.

He held the Rabbi's right hand in his two hands and he looked down at them as he said to the older man,

"May it be G-d's will, Rabbi Gerwitz that you should feel in your heart what G-d has given to your head. And may you realize that what is in your head has opened up so many hearts to G-d and Judaism. May your heart rest from your weariness because G-d has blessed you with the "haze" you want so much to feel. It is only that the tears of our eyes has washed the "haze" clear from our heart and purified us to live in this world."

Rabbi Gerwitz sat back in his chair. The tears streamed down both of the men's faces. Rabbi Gerwitz took his left hand and held both of Daniels hands with his own. Then taking a napkin to his eyes, he stood up, said "Good Shabbos" and slowly walked into his bedroom.

Book 2

DANIEL KAPLAN

CHAPTER NINE

He partied heartily throughout his first three years at Buffalo University. Then one morning he woke up and the gray cloud and haze that had been in his head cleared. Daniel Kaplan knew he had a real problem. After three years of college, he had no idea what to do with his life. His grades up to now were mediocre and he was unprepared to continue living the way he was. He knew that he had squandered the opportunity of going to college.

Scratching his chin as he got out of bed, he looked around his dorm room. He kept the room neat and clean, but only because he hated to sleep in an unmade bed. He grabbed a towel and sauntered off to the bathroom to take a long hot shower. Then Daniel went down to the dining hall and grabbed a cup of coffee. He lit a cigarette as he read through the campus newspaper. Seeing nothing there of interest, he looked around the room. Students were finishing up and moving on to their classes. Daniel should have been doing the same, but he had no interest. He lit another cigarette and sat back in his chair. Then he decided enough was enough.

Daniel got up and ordered a decent breakfast. When he finished, he returned to his dorm room and sized it up. He threw out all the beer in his little refrigerator. He collected the three bottles of scotch and two bottles of gin and deposited them on the common room table with a sign next to them that said "Take Me!". Then he turned his bedpost upside down and reached into his secret stash. He took out a half ounce of reefer. He put it in his pocket and walked back to the bathroom. He closed himself into a toilet booth and tossed all of the grass down the toilet. He watched it swirl around in the commode for a moment and then disappear. While he was at it he took the package of cigarettes out from his breast pocket and emptied it into the toilet as well. Then he went back to his room and threw out all the Playboy Magazines, the old newspapers, rolling papers, bongs, pipes and any paraphernalia, he might have acquired over the past three years. When his room was ready, he looked around and smiled.

Then he went down to his car and drove over to the Coast Guard recruiting office downtown. The recruiter was delighted to have him come in and readily arranged for him to enlist. When he went to take the physical, however, his eyesight was not good enough for entry. The recruiter told him not to worry, he could get Daniel a waiver and it would only take an extra week. Daniel's eyes were just outside the range, so the waiver would be automatic. However, Daniel believed that it was a sign of some kind that this was not the right thing for him.

So he returned to the dorm, watched television, listened to some music and smoked cigarettes. After lying around for two days in a state of depression, he got up and tried the Navy recruiter. This time, he was rapidly accepted. Vision was not an issue. His test scores were so high that they wanted to make him a nuclear trained technician. Daniel however, had decided that most of all he wanted to help people, so over the recruiters strenuous objections, he was enlisted as a hospital corpsman.

Daniel shipped out to boot camp at Great Lakes, Illinois during one of the coldest winters on record for the Chicago area. He was quickly assigned to be a company clerk, because he had college under his belt and he could type. He was also older than most of the recruits who were kids of 17 or 18. He quickly adapted to the training before succumbing to a bout of pneumonia, which he kept hidden until he couldn't breathe comfortably any more. Luckily, a kind doctor gave him strong antibiotics and he cleared up within two weeks and graduated with his company on time.

He was sent across the base after graduating to the Hospital Corps School Complex. Rather than sharing a barracks with 80 men, he was assigned a dormitory room with two other sailors and was not assigned to a class for three weeks, so he had time to relax and heal completely.

One day about a week before classes were to start, he was summoned to the school to be interviewed by the officer in charge of his class. He sat in a room with five or 6 men and four women. They filled out forms about themselves and spoke with the Class Officer. While they were waiting, Daniel looked across the room at some girls who were sitting there and checked them out. One girl stood out for him and he looked at her very carefully. He didn't know who she was, but he made himself a mental note. Based upon what he had seen, he was going to marry her. Now, Daniel had said that to himself many times before. Because of his shy nature, he rarely even asked the girl out. But this one would not be a passing fancy with momentary matrimonial dreams. He wanted to know this girl! He pointed her out to one of his buddies sitting next to him and told him that this was the girl he was going to marry. They all laughed together and kidded each other. They thought he was joking with them. He wasn't!

He was assigned as the class adjutant, the senior enlisted person in his class. It was like being the class president. He was responsible for making sure that everyone showed up and was ready. He acted as a liaison between the command structure and the students. Many a young sailor had Daniel to thank for saving them when they got into trouble. He had a way of cooling people down and bringing conflicts to a close quickly.

Needless to say he became rapidly acquainted with this young lady with whom he was so interested. She was assigned to help tutor anyone who might be falling behind. So she worked directly for him. But more important than that, she sat right behind him in class. And her name was Karolyn German.

It would take a number of weeks before he would get up the nerve to ask her out. But it was clear to everyone that these two were going to hook up together. You could see it in the way they looked at each other and the way he listened to her when she spoke to him. But he was very shy.

Finally one night, he was eating alone in the mess hall in the hospital. As he always felt uncomfortable eating alone, he was reading the latest issue of Time magazine. He had spread it in front of his cafeteria tray at the table. He was eating quietly and reading an article when she came over with her tray. Daniel didn't notice her at first. She stood there waiting for him to acknowledge her, but he was deeply engrossed in what he was reading.

"All you guys do the same thing. You sit by yourself reading magazines while you eat. Wouldn't it be better if you had someone to eat with?"

Daniel looked up at her and turned red. Finally, he put out his hand and waved it across the table and said,

"Please. . .join me"

"All right, I will", she giggled and sat herself down right next to him.

They talked for a while and finally he got up the nerve to ask her to go ice-skating with him that Saturday. She agreed and the date was made.

He picked her up at the women's barracks and went with her on the bus through North Chicago to where the ice skating rink was located. But they couldn't find it. Finally, when it became apparent that they would not find it soon, they decided to abandon the ice-skating and stopped at a diner to get warm. Over pie and coffee, they got to know each other. The owner of the diner kept refilling their cups. He was an Old Greek fellow who spoke with an accent and he must have thought he was helping them along, because they stayed there for over two hours. Finally, they caught a cab back to the base, cleaned up, ate dinner in the hospital mess hall and went out again to see a movie. After the movie, they went for coffee and then returned to the base. He walked her to the door of the women's barracks and as he approached the door with her, he put his arm around her waist and turned her around. She seemed unsure, but walked with him a short way. Finally, he turned to her and told her how nice the day had been for him and that he would like to do it again. She smiled at him and readily agreed to go out again. Then he kissed her lightly on the lips. She returned the kiss. They kissed again, this time more firmly and then they hugged each other for a long time. They walked back to the barracks holding hands. At the door, he gave her a final good night kiss. They said their good nights and she went up to her room.

Daniel watched her disappear up a stairs and then walked around for the next hour in the cold Illinois winter air. But he was warm. He walked over to the other side of the base and went into the bowling alley. Daniel wanted a drink so he went to the bar and ordered a beer. He was so wired up that the beer had almost no effect on him. So he ordered another one. Finally he turned in his shoes and took to bowling by himself. He ordered another beer and began by rolling a strike. Then he rolled another, and then the next ball was also a strike. He felt very loose. In Frame 4, he rolled another strike, then one in each of the next 5 frames. By now quite a crowd had gathered around his lane, but he hardly noticed. He tried to keep his emotions under control as he rolled the ball at the top of the 10th. A strike. The next ball was also a strike. The crowd was going wild. He stood at the line, walked down the lane and delivered . . . The ball looked perfect. It hit the pocket and there was a cracking sound. But one pin was left standing. The crowd groaned loudly. Daniel smiled to himself and easily disposed of the last pin for the spare.

As far as he was concerned, it had been a perfect day and a perfect night. Life could not get any better than that.

The next week was a whirlwind of getting to know Karolyn German. They ate all of their meals together. They took in movies every night at the base theater, where they sat in the balcony and explored each other by tentatively kissing. Then slowly and a little more tentatively, each other's body. His hand lingered on her knee and his arm would go over her shoulder and draw her near to kiss. But he was very careful at that early point in their relationship to remain respectful of the physical boundaries that existed with a woman one is just getting to know.

That Friday, after lunch, he disappeared into the hospital's flower shop and bought her a colorful bouquet in a glass vase. He told them to wrap it carefully for him and he wrote out a card, thanking her for the past week's company. He got to the classroom a little early and placed the vase on her desk. Then, he went about some administrative tasks in the reception office so that he would not be there when she saw the flowers for the very first time.

After the class was already seated, he walked in a few moments late, apologizing to the teacher for disturbing the class and he sunk into his seat.

He didn't turn around to Karolyn or even acknowledge her. The instructor, a nurse, started the anatomy lesson. Suddenly and quietly, he felt a pencil poke him between the shoulders. He ignored it, but soon another poke was felt by him. Still, he said nothing and didn't turn around. When the class ended and everyone went to take a break, she got up and gave him a light tap on the head. He turned to her and laughed. She laughed also.

"They're beautiful. I love them. Thanks"

He nodded gently.

"You didn't have to"

"I know! I wanted to"

She looked at him very closely. He shrugged sheepishly and turned red in the face.

"This is the first time anyone has bought me flowers"

He looked at her skeptically.

"No Daniel, Really"

"Well then, your previous boyfriends were fools."

She looked at him, smiled gently as he said.

"I am not the smartest guy in the world, but I know something special when I see it. Special persons need special gestures. So I wanted to give you flowers to show how special I feel about you, even though we know each other such a short time."

Later that night as they sat in the balcony of the base theater watching some incredibly lame movie, she reached across and kissed him deeply and held him tightly for a long time.

Book 3

KAROLYN GERMAN

CHAPTER TEN

Karolyn sat at her Grandmother Leah's kitchen table laughing and joking with her. They sat drinking coffee from tall mugs and shmoozed together. They truly enjoyed each other's company. They were more friends than relatives, and certainly acted nothing like grandmother and granddaughter.

Leah Deutsch was one tough old bird. Nothing escaped her even now as she approached her eightieth year of life. For all of those years, she made Batavia, New York her home, even when her talent and her drive would have taken her elsewhere.

As she sat reminiscing with Kary about the past few months, she could see that this granddaughter of hers had matured into a woman. And more than that she had matured into a woman in love. They talked about what love was like in the "old days". To Leah, it seemed light years away in attitude and practice. To Kary it seemed quaint and unsure. But the older woman knew that it was not so different. In fact, she reassured Kary that things were very much the same, if not in form then in practice. Leah saw that the love and romance of her early life was a pattern of behavior and that pattern was repeating itself with Karolyn.

Leah Deutsch was the third and last child of Benjamin and Marion Rosenblatt. The Rosenblatts had come from Russia at the turn of the century and settled initially on the Lower East Side of New York. They lived there about a year, but the crowded conditions and the lack of work convinced Benjamin to look upstate for work. Benjamin had been trained as a tailor in Europe and he hoped to find a place that would allow him to open a shop for himself. He traveled by train for a month scouting out locations with little success. When he arrived in Batavia, he was short on spirit and patience. But he found a small clothing shop whose owner was ill and together they made a partnership. Benjamin sent for his sewing machine and set up in the back of the shop. Business was reasonably good and after three months he sent for his family. By then the Rosenblatts had two young sons, Marc and Seth. Marion packed up the boys and settled into this town with a determination to make it a home for her family. Unfortunately, there were very few Jews living in the town and Marion felt more and more alone as time went by. Benjamin, easily adapted to the town, shedding his Jewishness with vigor and despite his accent, tried to come off as one of his gentile neighbors. Slowly but surely he slipped from the old ways and this became a source of friction between him and Marion.

After they had been in Batavia for a year or so, Marion gave birth to Leah.

Right away, it was apparent that this was a very special child. Unusually precocious, she quickly became her parent's favorite and easily overshadowed her two brothers.

Benjamin's partner passed away shortly after Leah was born and the partner's heirs offered Benjamin an opportunity to buy out the rest of the store. He accepted and arranged to pay it out over five years.

When the stock market failed and the Depression took hold, the store was forced to close and Benjamin was forced to open a tailor shop out of the house. Marion went to work cleaning houses for the rich families of Batavia as well as taking in wash.

They continued to struggle for a couple of years. Then things seemed to get a little better. Although they both still had to work, there was some consistent money coming in, even if it was very little. Their life seemed to be stabilizing when one afternoon, while the kids were in school, Benjamin and Marion went out shopping. They were out walking on the street on their way to the store. It was a drizzly day and suddenly a car skidded onto the sidewalk and mowed them both down. Benjamin was killed instantly and Marion went into a coma. She remained in that coma for a number of years until she passed away.

Their family from New York took the train up to bury Benjamin and to decide what to do with Marion and the kids. Marion was sent to a nursing home in Brooklyn. The boys were sent to live with uncles in New York. Marion's spinster sister Rose decided that she would stay in Batavia, live in her sister's house and raise Leah. All parties agreed and soon Aunt Rose was happily ensconced in her new home. Unfortunately, her ward was less than cooperative. In fact, she was downright headstrong, argumentative and moody. Being a lot brighter than her aunt, she was able to manipulate situations and this drove Rose crazy.

Now Leah was something else. As she grew through her teen years, she developed into a strikingly beautiful woman. She developed curves in all the right places and attracted the young men, like bees to honey.

By her seventeenth birthday, she was a force to be reckoned with. Sharp tongued and known for her quick retorts, she took on the demeanor of a "tough" girl, smoking, drinking and otherwise carousing. Much to her Aunt Rose's dismay, the parade of young men through the house and on the back porch seemed endless. Rose was afraid to look out her window for fear of what she would see. She tried to talk to the girl, but Leah breezily told her not to worry, she knew what she was doing.

Soon that pool of young men began to dry up. World War II approached and many of the young men were leaving Batavia for the Army, Navy or Marines.

One Saturday night a dance was held at the local high school gymnasium. Leah had just turned twenty and was working as a secretary for a local manufacturer. She still lived with Rose despite everything. For the dance that night, her date was a blind date made by her aunt. Rose had met this nice Jewish accountant on a recent trip to New York and she hoped that maybe a match could be made that would settle her niece down. It took a while to convince Leah, but finally Leah gave in and "Morty" took the train up from New York and took a room in the local boarding house. He came to introduce himself to Leah. Leah took one look at this skinny, timid man and she knew, "No way!" But she had agreed to meet with him, so she asked him to escort her to the dance. Whereas her reaction to him was disappointment, he was delighted in what he saw. She was the most beautiful woman he had ever seen and that made him even more timid and speechless.

Leah readied herself for the dance with the intention of showing off her assets. She wore a tight form fitting black dress and silver tipped black high heels. She pulled her hair back into a modified bun to which she attached a black bow. She wore a black crepe shawl on her shoulders. She looked terrific, like the fox she was and on the prowl.

She and Morty walked into the gym and all eyes turned towards her. She looked and felt great. There was a heady power in knowing that you could attract almost any man that night. She took Morty onto the dance floor, but he was hopeless as a dancer and she was soon dancing with anyone who could keep up with her. Out of the corner of her eye, she spied a young sailor in uniform, standing with one leg on a chair, drinking from a cup and listening intently to the group of boys and girls with him. She edged her partner closer. This sailor was very striking to her, almost familiar. But she didn't know who he was or why he seemed so familiar. She flitted around the room dancing ever closer towards this young man, maneuvering herself towards him. Her dance partner got annoyed and while spinning her towards the sailor, he let go. She spun right into him and they both fell onto the floor.

As they got up and composed themselves, the sailor got his first good look at her. He was thunderstruck. The rest of the room evaporated from around him and all that he could see and feel was this girl.

He didn't know what to do. Clearly, he wanted her, but he was shy and would otherwise be afraid to go up and talk to a girl who looked like this. He stood there, dumb and stupid. Finally the girl could see what was going on with him and smiled and said,

"I'm sorry to have knocked you down"

"Oh, that's Okay, I wasn't paying attention"

"I know", she said smiling, "By the way, I'm Leah Rosenblatt" extending her hand.

"Matthew Deutsch", he said taking her hand and shaking it gently.

"Matthew Deutsch? You're not the Matt Deutsch who grew up on Lake?"

"One and the same!"

She knew who he was now, she remembered going with her mother one day while her mother cleaned his house. The Deutsch's were among the elite of Batavia. She wasn't about to tell him that she had met him way back then.

Matthew Deutsch, heir apparent to the Deutsch Manufacturing Empire had run away to the Navy when he was 20. He did this much to the chagrin of his family and much to his own delight. Matthew's father had made a fortune in manufacturing containers for groceries, such as milk, meat, etc. Matthew, the logical successor, had no interest in the business and after two years at Cornell simply quit and joined the Navy.

His father used all of his influence to try and dissuade him. When that failed he tried to have local officials intervene so that the boy would be sent home. He went so far as to arrive one day at the Commanding Officer of the Boot Camp at Great Lakes, Illinois to convince the C.O. that they ought to discharge his son. The C.O. being a crafty fellow himself, called the boy in to confront his father. Matthew made it abundantly clear; that he wanted to stay in the Navy and that he didn't want to go home. That being that, the C.O. sent his father home and returned Matthew to his company. Matthew was soon sent to a ship stationed out of Norfolk, Virginia. As war was appearing rapidly on the horizon the pace of activities aboard ship to get ready accelerated. Matthew soon found all of this too confining for him. However, he managed to still do well and get the attention of his superiors on the ship.

When the ship went into the shipyard for upkeep, Matthew took some leave and went home. It was not a happy time for him there. His father made him feel like a failure for being in uniform and tried to make him feel guilty for not taking over the business. But he enjoyed the looks he received from the young women of Batavia when he walked the streets in uniform. When some of his old high school buddies suggested that he join them at this dance at the old high school, he really didn't want to go. Then he thought, "Why not?" For him this would be the most important "Why not?" of his life.

Because when Matthew met Leah, there was fire between them. He overcame his shyness and asked her to dance with him. He worried throughout that dance about what he would say to her when the song they were dancing to was over. When the music stopped, he just stood there, not quite sure of what to do. But Leah did not break away from him and when the music started up again, they continued to dance. They danced the rest of the night together. Even when the band played a fast number, Matthew and Leah danced a slow dance, up close against each other's bodies. He closed his eyes when they danced. He could feel her bosom against his chest and he breathed deeply of her fragrance. Her hair tickled his face, but he loved every moment of it. When the dance broke up, they looked around the room. His friends were gone as was Morty. They walked out into the summer night and sat on the front steps of the High School. They talked and talked until they saw the light of dawn peeking out below the clouds. They got up and Matthew asked her if she was hungry. She was. They drove into town and found a Diner. They shared pancakes and eggs and lots and lots of coffee.

During the remaining time of his leave, they were inseparable. Every night they went out. She listened intently when he spoke of the breech in his relationship with his parents. He listened to her when she complained about Rose and Batavia and life in general.

On his final night in town, he drove to pick her up for the night out. She was carrying a big shopping bag. She put it into the back seat of the car.

"What you got in the bag?"

"Oh, something special"

"For me?"

"Maybe!"

"Ah come on, tell me."

"No you'll see soon enough"

"Oh?"

"Yeah Oh. Now tonight, it is all up to me"

"Really?"

"Yes really. Tonight, you are my driver and I will tell you where we are going. You just follow my directions!"

"Yes sir! Eh ma'am. I am yours to command"

"Good and you best remember that later"

"What do you mean by that?"

She laughed and pointed in front of her,

"Just drive!"

They drove out into the countryside. She held his hand and he put his hand on her thigh. He kept looking at her, but she just looked ahead, with a slight smile on his lips. So he just tipped his white sailor cap forward, almost onto his eyes and smiled to himself. The girl was up to something. He would just let her have her fun.

They drove up by the reservoir and she directed him to a clearing off of the road. They got out and walked near to the water's edge. She put down her bag and pulled out a blanket and a pillow. Then she pulled out a smaller bag with sandwiches she had made and a bottle of wine. She handed him an edge of the blanket and they set up a picnic in view of the lake. The sky was clear and the stars shone brightly overhead.

They ate the food and drank the wine from paper cups. He held her tight upon his chest and they kissed. Soon she slowly began to untie his scarf and she lifted his shirt over his head. She looked at him in his tee shirt and smiled to herself. He tried to unbutton her dress but she coyly stopped him all the while, kissing him and holding him close to her. Finally she lifted his tee shirt off of his chest and nuzzled his neck and his chest. He loved what was happening but was confused as to exactly what to do. She lay on top of him, kissing him all over his chest. Soon she unbuttoned his trousers and slipped them off him and with no further to do, relieved him of his underwear. She ran her cheek across his whole body and he let out a sigh of enjoyment and contentment.

He tried again to take off her dress, but she stopped him again with a little laugh and continued to kiss him all over. She held him in her hands and brought him to his heights. He lay back near exhausted. She reached behind her back and undid her dress. She slipped it over her head and quickly undid her brassiere. He looked at her body and was just struck with awe to her beauty. She finished undressing and lay back down on top of him. She brought him inside her for the first of what would be several times that night.

The dawn sunlight woke them up. They quickly gathered themselves together and returned to town. He dropped her off at home. They kissed in the front seat of the car and his eyes grew teary at the thought of leaving her here in Batavia. He said nothing though.

As she exited the car, she closed the door and looked into the open window.

"What time is your train?"

"My train?"

"Yes, your train to Virginia"

"Oh, my train, yeah. It leaves at 2:02. My father got me a sleeper berth so at least I don't have to sleep on a bench. It's 14 hours to New York and then another 10 hours to Norfolk."

"Well, you have a good trip!" she said to him as tears started to flow from her face. "Have a good trip. . . and thanks for all of the good times and especially for last night. Can I write you on the ship?"

"Sure, I'd love that. Man, am I gonna miss you! Lady, you are one terrific gal. It wouldn't be fair of me to ask you not to see anyone else, but I'm not gonna see anyone else. And when my tour is up, I'm coming right back here to find you."

She smiled at him knowingly. He was a sailor and there would be another pretty face someplace in the world that would catch this man. She smiled at him again.

"Come back for me Matt. I'll be waiting for you."

Then she blew him a kiss and turned towards the house.

CHAPTER ELEVEN

His father's chauffeur dropped him off at the station. He stood alone on the platform except for a few business passengers who were going to New York. It had been a perfunctory parting with his parents, who reminded him again of their disappointment with him being in the Navy. His father offered to get him out again and reminded him that his legacy was with his families business and not as an adventurer around the world. Matthew couldn't wait to get out of there. So with some polite cheek kissing from his mother and a stiff handshake from his father, he left.

He found a bench and dragged his sea bag over to it. He set it up next to him on the bench and sat down. He had about three quarters of an hour to wait, so he settled in on the bench and snoozed with his head against his sea bag. He was awakened with a start. He looked up into the sun and his eyes could see the outline of a person. His eyes cleared and he saw her standing in front of him. She was wearing a gray dress and a white floppy brimmed hat. She looked radiant.

"You came to see me off?"

"No."

He looked at her quizzically.

"I came to go with you."

"Go with me where?

"Virginia"

He looked at her, but didn't understand.

"You're going to Virginia?"

"Yes, . . . with you!"

"With me?

"Yes. Don't you want me to come with you?"

He answered immediately, "Yes! That would be fantastic, but where are you going to stay?"

"With you silly."

"With me! I live on a ship."

"I know that. We'll find a place and we'll stay there"

He shook his head in disbelief.

"Well sailor, are you gonna take me along. . . or what?"

There was silence for a moment. Matthew was in shock.

"Well, do you want me or not"

"Absolutely, Yeah. . . of course. Of course, I want you to come with me. This seems so unreal. It's just sinking in to my head right now. Yes! Yes! Yes! I want you to come with me."

He picked her up by her waist and twirled her around. They kissed passionately, madly. Then he remembered,

"We have to get you a ticket. We'll get you a coach ticket and you can share the sleeper with me. Okay?"

She agreed. They spent the next twenty-four hours making love in the sleeper. When they got to Norfolk, They found themselves a motel room for the first night. The next day while he reported back to the ship, she looked for and found an efficiency apartment in Virginia Beach. They moved in together and she decorated it with bric-a-brac she found in shops by the beach. Curtains were made from tablecloths and tablecloths were made from sheets. She cooked him sumptuous dinners when he wasn't out at sea and they fell deeper and deeper in love. She was a steadying force behind him and everyone around him noticed the difference.

One day, the ship's chaplain came down to his bunk and left a note for him to come see him when he had a chance. Matt came up to the chaplain's stateroom and knocked on the door.

"Come on in" a voice called out. Mathew walked in to see Lt. Chastain, the chaplain lying on his bunk in his underwear. He got up and greeted Matt.

"Matthew, good of you to stop by", he said, shaking the boy's hand.

"Come sit down here", as he maneuvered a chair for Matt to sit down on.

Lt. Chastain sat back down on his bunk and looked up at Matt. Lt. Chastain was an older man, maybe 40 years old. He was well liked by the crew and a confidante of many. He looked at Matt closely. He liked the boy and he liked who the boy had become.

"Matthew, everyone around here is really proud of the efforts you have been making since you came back from leave. You have become noticed for your hard work and dedication. I suspect that it is in no little part because of that pretty little thing who stands on the pier every night to greet you."

Matt smiled broadly.

"She's really good for me and I am just crazy about her"

Chaplain Chastain looked up at Matt and frowned for a moment.

"That's the point Matthew, she's good for you, but are you really being good to her?"

"I don't understand, sir. I treat her very well.

The chaplain softened and smiled.

"I'm sure you treat her just fine son, just fine, but your not treating her well son, not well at all. You do know what I mean, Matt? Do you?"

"I'm afraid sir, I am a bit confused."

"Son, are you living with this woman?"

"Well . . . yes!"

"And you're not married to her, are you?"

Matthew turned bright red and sputtered, "Well no sir."

"Do you think by living with her you are being fair to this young lady, son?"

Matt thought for a moment, then he asked the Chaplain,

"In what way am I being unfair, sir?"

"Son, you don't think it's unfair for you to live in sin with this young lady?"

"It's what she wants."

"Is it? Don't you think she really would rather be your wife?"

"I don't know!"

"Why don't you know? Do you think that she is living with you without an expectation that you will marry her? Matt, if you were her and you loved someone, you might do what she is doing to try and preserve your relationship. But it's not fair to her. Some day, her reputation will be called into question and she will be embarrassed because she is living in sin with you. And what if she gets pregnant. What then son? These are important questions.

Matthew face dropped to the floor. The Chaplain saw that he had upset the young man. He spoke to Matt in a quiet way,

"Listen son, I may be a minister, but I am not a prude. I understand that young men and young women will be young men and young women. But you are a fine young man who has found a good woman. She is a woman who is good for you and to you. A woman who obviously loves you and cares for you and one who will build a life with you. Don't live in sin with her. Marry her or let her go. That's the only fair thing to do son. Marry her or let her go!"

Matthew sat kind of confused. He had not sought this situation out with Leah. She had taken it upon herself to travel down to Virginia and throw in with him. He really enjoyed having her around. She took very good care of him and he was extremely grateful. Not once had she ever brought up the subject of marriage to him. Not once. Sure the idea had crossed his mind a number of times, but since she never mentioned it, never even hinted about it, he had let the thoughts slide.

Chaplain Chastain woke Matthew out of his daze of thoughts.

"Matthew, do you love her?"

"Well. . . sure. . . I mean yes."

"Son! Are you or not? Or are you not sure?"

"No Chaplain, I am sure, I am crazy about her, just crazy in love with her."

"Well terrific, when can I schedule the ceremony?"

"What ceremony?"

"The wedding Matthew. The wedding!"

"Oh yeah. . . the wedding. Well I'll have to ask her"

Chaplain Chastain looked into his appointment book and pondered several entries. Then he looked up at Matt and said,

"Tell you what, I'll pencil you in for next Saturday. We'll do it aboard ship and have a fine little reception in the wardroom. So go on home and tell your sweetheart that you're going to make an honest woman of her. Oh, and another thing, son, go down to Schiffs, you know that jewelry store by the docks and pick her up a nice engagement ring. Tell them I'm your chaplain. He'll give you a good price. That'll make her feel really special and it will start you guys off right. So I'll see you both next Saturday at 1300 sharp. Dress Whites. "

Matthew stumbled out of the Chaplain's stateroom in a state of fog. He went up on deck to get some air and to think. It wasn't really a bad idea. She was practically his wife anyhow. So why not make her an "honest" woman. So when his workday was over, he caught a ride over to Schiffs and picked out an engagement ring. On a sailor's pay, he couldn't afford much, but he found a suitable ¼ carat ring which any young woman would be proud to have. He also bought two wedding bands. He was ready to make Leah Deutsch his wife. So he thought!

CHAPTER TWELVE

She had not been feeling right for about two days. She was somewhat dizzy and shaky. This morning, she threw up her breakfast. Her head was spinning and she felt awful. She stretched out on the bed and decided to close her eyes for an hour. When she woke up it was 2:00 P.M. She got up quickly and straightened the place up and started preparing dinner. When Matt came home, she mentioned that she had not felt well that morning. He was concerned and wanted to take care of her, but she told him that she was feeling fine now.

The next morning was more of the same. She threw up again and felt exhausted. By the end of the week, this scene had been repeated five times and she was frankly frightened. When she missed her period, she knew. Leah called one of the women with whom she had grown friendly in her building and told her of her suspicions. Her friend took her to a doctor who tested her for pregnancy. He told her he would have the results in a few days, but not to worry too much. Matt was getting concerned. He told her that she looked as if she had caught a bug. Leah agreed with him about that. Matt was so worried that he waited on her hand and foot for the weekend. She was very pleased that he had taken such good care of her. She had picked him right. Here was a kindred spirit, who appreciated her. The next Monday, he went off to the ship to get underway for a week. She kissed him goodbye at the pier and went home. The next day, she called the doctor, but he still had no results to report. Matt's ship pulled back in on Thursday, three days early and she still was feeling terrible. The next day, she told Matt that she could not meet him at the pier as usual because she was still feeling ill. Matt was very concerned, but she reassured him that it was just a bug. He was not convinced. He told her to call a doctor. She told him he was being silly and to go to his ship. Later that morning, the telephone rang. It was the Doctor's office.

"Mrs. Rosenblatt", he called her Mrs. because he assumed she was married. "Mrs. Rosenblatt, I have very good news for you. You are pregnant"

She was dismayed.

"When is the baby due, Doctor?"

"When is it due? Well let's see. Sometime in the winter, Mrs. Rosenblatt. We'll have to calculate it exactly later. You need to come in and see me so we can chart your progress."

She made an appointment for the next Monday and sat down in the kitchen to contemplate her fate. What a disaster! She broke out into tears. She cried for hours, flinging herself onto the bed and pounding at her pillows.

At around dinnertime she realized that Matt was not home yet. Leah was partially relieved at this. She didn't know how or even whether to tell him about her pregnancy. But she worried anyway, because he was usually always on time and when he wasn't, he always called. By 6:00 P.M. she still had not heard from him. Her heart started to beat wildly as she imagined all the worst scenarios. She told herself to calm down and sat in their easy chair while thumbing through a magazine. The minutes seemed like hours. Finally, she heard the key in the door and saw him walk in. She burst out into tears.

Matthew closed the door behind him and looked at Leah. Her eyes were swollen from crying and her hair was a mess. He was quite puzzled by what he saw.

"What's the matter, Honey? he asked

The girl continued to cry wordlessly as he came over to the sofa where she was sitting.

"What? What is it, Hon?"

She continued to cry. He put his arm around her and asked again softly,

What?"

Still he got no answer and she continued to cry, now pulling up her legs and hugging them tight. She put her eyes to her knees and shivered violently.

Being totally lost, Matt sat there and looked at her. Finally he reached around her and pulled her back to him. She resisted at first, but then let herself settle into his arms. As Leah calmed he asked her,

"Do you feel like telling me why you are crying?"

"I will", she whimpered, "but not right now"

"Uh huh, not right now! Okay, I can wait!"

He took in a deep breath and held her tight to him for a long time. Finally she fell asleep on his chest. Matt slipped out from under her and brought a blanket and a pillow out from their bedroom. He placed the pillow under her head and tucked the blanket in around her. Then he stepped outside the apartment and lit a cigarette. While he was smoking his mind raced to see if he could figure out what the problem was. Maybe someone in her family had died? Or she was homesick for Batavia? She had been sick on and off for about two weeks, so he figured that she was just tired out by having been ill.

He stepped back into the house and saw she was sleeping soundly. Dinner smelled good in the kitchen so he took a plate and helped himself. He sat down at the table and ate. Afterwards he read the local newspaper. Soon she stirred and awakened. She looked at him and then got up and sat down at the table.

"Would you like something to eat, sweetie?"

"Yeah, I'm very hungry. Don't get up. I'll take for myself."

She got up and prepared a plate and returned to the table. Matthew looked at her closely and said to her,

"Listen, I've got to talk to you about something very serious."

She shuddered slightly and tears started to well up in her eyes.

"No! No! Leah. No! It's not anything bad. Really! It's something good. At least I think it's good. I hope you do to. So calm down. . . and listen".

She stopped crying and looked over at him. She wiped her eyes with a tissue and blew her nose. When she was settled down, she said to Matt,

"Okay, what is it?" and nodded her head slowly.

"Well hon, it's like this." He reached into his pocket and pulled out a little box. He opened it and showed it to her. Her eyes opened widely and her jaw slackened open.

"Leah Rosenblatt", he said, getting down on one knee, "Will you marry me?"

"I can't marry you", she said and hurriedly got up from the table and ran into the bedroom. She flung herself on the bed and started crying hysterically once again.

Matthew just sat there. He was now terribly perplexed and very upset. A bomb had just dropped on his head and he had no idea of what to do. He sat there for a little while longer and headed for the door. He was halfway out the door when he got a better idea. He walked back into the apartment and went into the bedroom. He stood there with his hands clasped against his back, leaning on the door. Then he took a deep breath and got himself under control.

"I don't understand Leah. I don't understand what's happening here. You follow me down here. You live with me. We make love together all the time. So logically, I would think that eventually, we would get married. And now I've asked you and your response is "I can't marry you!" If you were going to say no I would think that your answer would've been "I won't marry you". But your answer to me is "I can't marry you". I don't understand Leah. What does that mean? I don't understand. What the hell is going on here?

Leah looked up at him. True, she had followed him to Virginia. True also that they lived together intimately. And she knew for herself, that she did want to marry him, but now. . . clearly there was no way! He came from a respectable family. Ultimately, she knew he would return to take over the family business. But he wasn't going to marry her. Why? Because she knew that he would not bring home a Jewish girl to be his wife, especially the daughter of their one-time cleaning lady. Furthermore, he would never marry her because she was pregnant. In her mind, that was unthinkable for him to do.

"Well? Leah come on! What's going on here? I love you and want you to be my wife. I don't get this. What's going on?"

She sighed deeply and turned towards him.

"Okay! . . Okay. It's like this Matthew. How can you marry me? What would your parents say to you marrying a Jewish girl?"

"I don't know! But what difference does it make? They're not marrying you, I am."

"Would it make a difference to you that I am the daughter of your old cleaning lady?"

"No! I've known <u>that</u> for a long time. I realized who you were soon after we met."

"Then why didn't you say anything?"

"I figured that since you didn't mention it, you must be embarrassed by it, so I didn't say anything about it either. And frankly, I could care less. So now you have no reason not to marry me. So let's go do it. Let's get married. The Chaplain . . ."

She interrupted him.

"Shhh! Matthew, please be quiet. Please! It's not that simple."

"Yes it is!"

She looked at him harshly for the first time since she knew him.

"Men, you are all so stupid".

He turned red in the face. She got up and walked up to him and looked him in the eye. He tried to look away from her, but he was suddenly very uncomfortable.

"Look at me Matthew. Look at me! This is very serious. Look at me! I'm pregnant Matthew. Pregnant."

"Pregnant?"

"That's right Matthew, pregnant."

She stepped back from him and turned away. He looked at her and took a deep breath.

"Pregnant", he said it as a statement, not a question.

"Pregnant . . ." Then he stuttered for a moment and said "How wonderful!"

She turned to him and gave him a quizzical look. He smiled at her, stood up tall and came to where she was sitting. He held her face and kissed her on her eyes.

"Yes wonderful! That's right Leah . . . It's wonderful. For me and for you."

He pushed her down onto the bed and kissed her hard and long. Then he picked her up, stood her on the floor, turned her around. Then he put his arms around her waist and twirled her around picking her off the floor.

"That's right Leah, we're going to be daddy and mommy and it's wonderful. Terrific. Fantastic. Outstanding. Wonderful. And we'll be the best mommy and daddy. We'll be the best, because we love each other so much and we'll love this child just as much. Please say you'll marry me Leah. Be in my life. Please!"

He kissed her deeply and held her close. She looked up at him. For a long time, she said nothing. Then she shrugged her shoulders and shook her head yes.

Matthew went crazy in delight. He jumped around the apartment like a tiger let loose from it's cage. In what seemed like one breath, he told her about Chaplain Chastain's conversation with him and the tentative plans for the wedding aboard ship.

Later, after they made love, they lay in bed talking. She asked him.

"Are you sure about this, Matthew?"

"Sweetie, I am as sure as anyone can be. I want you for my bride. And more importantly, I want you to be the mother of my children. You are so beautiful and lovely. Nothing else matters. So rest easy my love, I'll be there for you forever."

CHAPTER THIRTEEN

"Well that's just terrific! Just great! The boy runs off to the Navy and to top all things, this is what he does! Just great!" Milo Deutsch bellowed at his wife, Mathilda.

He was reading from the letter they had just received from their son Matthew. He held up the picture of the bride and groom and spat in disgust. He threw his cigar across the room and bellowed some more at his wife,

"You see what your son does? He doesn't give a damn about us. First he lives with this Jew girl, then he marries her! What is going on in your boy's mind, Mathilda? What?'"

"I don't recall having the boy by divine conception, Milo! He is also your son. As for the girl, Milo, get rid of her. The boy might be upset now, but he'll thank you later."

"You're right. You're right as usual, Tilde, You are absolutely right of course. How much could it take? The archbishop will annul it immediately. Not to worry Tilde. You are right. Let me talk to the young girl. I'm sure that she will see the error of her ways."

Milo calmed himself down. He reached into the liquor cabinet and poured himself a brandy. He sat down in one of his fine leather chairs to sip the liquor and to contemplate. Mathilda sat next to him in a leather chair of her own and seethed quietly. She was so mad at

Matt. Not only had he done everything possible to disappoint her, now he had brought discredit on the family by marrying a cleaning lady's daughter. The whole thing just made her sick. She laid her head back across her chair and looked up at the ceiling. What an utter disaster!

"Well Milo will figure it out and solve this problem", She thought to herself,

"He better or there would be hell to pay" Batavia's elite would never tolerate this.

"Well Milo, what are you going to do?" she asked her husband.

"I think it's obvious dear, what has to occur. The question is how much, Tilde, How much? But we will pay. What choice have we got? Then we're going to bring our son home from that Navy and I tell you Tilde, as G-d is my witness, I'll beat him to within inches of his life. Then I'm going to dress him in a suit and he <u>will</u> learn this business and become responsible. That is not a promise, Tilde, It is an oath!"

Mathilda twisted her jaw in disbelief. She looked hard at her husband. She was used to seeing him like this. Sitting in a chair, juiced up on liquor, pontificating on what he was going to do. Reality was such, that he really was a rather weak man. He was diffident to his children and unable to handle them. She sensed that deep inside, he was probably proud of his son for having done what his heart told him to do rather than rely on logic or the correct thing. Nonetheless, <u>she</u> was determined not to have this terrible blight hit her house and she would force Milo to do her bidding in getting rid of this girl. If she was lucky, no one would hear of the marriage in Batavia and Matthew would return unscathed by the incident.

The next morning Milo Deutsch went to his office as usual. At 10:00 A.M., he placed a call to his son's commanding officer asking him to have Matthew call home. He stated to the ship's captain that it was a family matter of grave consequences. Matthew was called immediately to the Captain's stateroom, where he was told that his father needed to speak to him immediately. The Captain offered his telephone and left Matthew alone in his cabin to talk with his father.

Matthew dialed his father's office and was put through to him.

"Matthew, it is good to talk to you. We received your letter on Saturday and honestly, your mother and I were a little shocked."

"And why would that be, Father", Matthew asked.

"Well son, we didn't even know you were serious about anyone and the next thing we know, you are married."

"So what, Dad? I found someone to love and that someone loves me back. What's wrong with that?"

"Well son, we are concerned. We hoped that you would have married someone from the right type of family. Someone who would be able to fit into your society. Someone who would be an asset to your career."

"And that is exactly whom I've married, Dad. She comes from a good family. She fits right in to my society and she is a good asset to my career".

Milo exploded,

"Career as what? Deckhand to a bunch of greasy sailors. I'm talking about when you are a captain of industry. What kind of impression will your little Jewish wife have on your associates then."

"Who gives a shit?, Matt screamed back on the phone, "I have no intention of being a captain of industry. Not now or anytime soon. And you best not say anything bad about my wife. I love her and she is good for me. Besides, she is soon going to be the mother of your first grandchild!"

Milo passed out with the phone still in his hand. He broke his nose when his face hit the sheet of glass that covered his desk. When his secretary walked in to tell him she was going to lunch, she saw the blood all over the desk and thought he was dead. She screamed!

CHAPTER FOURTEEN

"Well that's just fine, honey", Mathilda Deutsch said over the phone to her new daughter-in-law, "You and Matt can come here on his leave and stay as long as you like. Not to worry, Milo is a bit hotheaded, but I assure you everything's just all right."

Mathilda had a way of calming down the most hyper of people. She grew up the only daughter of a South Carolina tobacco plantation owner and her gentle southern accent had enchanted at first, a very ambitious boy from Batavia, New York named Milo Deutsch. That soothing voice had carried them through the toughest of times. When Milo became impossible with rage, she shielded the children and then calmed him back down. But she wasn't so easy herself. She had exacting standards and her house was always clean as a whistle and set up as if people would be dropping by to tour. Together they made one hard driving team and their children were made to feel foolish when they didn't live up to their parent's wishes and standards.

And it was with her famous southern charm that she was buttering up her new daughter-in-law. After all, she was carrying <u>her</u> grandchild. And well, that Jewish thing. Well, she planned to take care of that as soon as this girl hit her doorway. She'd have the priest down to the house and as quick as it takes, this girl would become a good catholic, just as she had done when Milo proposed to her.

She looked across the den to where her husband was drinking himself into oblivion, while grunting and phumphering.

"Milo", she said impatiently to him, "Milo, if you weren't always blowing up at the boy, maybe you would get your way. You see this as a huge catastrophe. But it isn't. Look, we impress this young lady of his into becoming a catholic, then we show her what life will be like, if Matthew was involved in the business. Use your assets Milo, charm the girl. Convince that it's in her best interest to have Matthew home. And believe me Matthew will be home."

"I see what you mean Tilde. That is a terrific idea. You know, I should have brought you into the business. You are so sharp."

"Oh Milo, don't make me laugh. The last thing you wanted was to have me so close to you during the day. You'd never be able to hit on those overly young secretaries you hire."

Milo turned red in the face,

"Now Tilde, you know that's not true. I've never said one untoward thing to any of the girls. And if you don't believe me, you can just ask anyone. I am a perfect gentleman."

"Uh huh", she looked back at him and shot back a wry smile.

CHAPTER FIFTEEN

Matthew had been out to sea for two weeks. Leah was very lonely, sitting in the house. She listened to the radio and sat out with the neighbors. But it didn't help. She missed her Matt. The baby growing inside her was now kicking up a storm. She could feel the baby moving around and at night she lay in bed and watched her stomach jump around. She talked out loud to the baby as if it could hear her and it comforted her to think that maybe the baby heard her and understood. In another two months, she would give birth. Matthew was so excited at the prospect of being a father. He embraced all of the potential problems with a "We can do it and we will!" attitude. He had been promoted to Petty Officer 3rd Class, so the extra money helped and the additional responsibility gave him much more confidence.

One evening as she was settling down to eat some dinner, there was a knock on the door. She opened it to find two Naval Officers standing before her. One of the men wore the four stripes of a Navy Captain. The other wore two stripes of a Lieutenant and the cross of a chaplain.

"Excuse us Mrs. Deutsch, I am Captain Sotherby and this is Chaplain Miles. Can we come in and speak to you?"

Leah became immediately frightened. She beckoned the men in.

"Can I get you gentlemen some coffee or something cold to drink?"

"No, thank you. We're all right. Please sit down Mrs. Deutsch"

Leah sat down at the table and crossed her arms on her shoulders. She hugged herself slightly, then took a deep breath and smiled weakly.

"What is this about Captain? Is Matt all right?"

Captain Sotherby looked at the Chaplain and frowned. He shook his head slightly and said to her.

"Look ma'am, there is no easy way to say this, so I am just going to say it."

Leah froze in terror at those words.

"Matthew was on deck trying to secure a hatch which had not been properly closed. This would not ordinarily be a problem except the ship was in the lee of a hurricane and the sea was washing onto the deck and flooding into this hatch. Matthew was swept overboard and his lifeline snapped."

Leah sat dumfounded. She took a deep breath and then she said to them,

"Where is he? Where is he?" She screamed.

"Ma'am, I'm sorry, Matthew drowned."

"Oh my G-d! Oh my G-d", she trembled, "Did you find his body?"

"Yes ma'am", the chaplain said to her. "He is being brought ashore by a merchant vessel which rendezvoused with his ship. They will arrive tomorrow."

The Chaplain opened up a file and passed a telegram to her. She picked it up and read it. She blinked back tears.

"His parents, I have to call his parents", she said tearfully.

"They are being told by Navy officials as we speak. Ma'am, are you going to be all right?

"No, I really don't think so. . . but. . .", she broke down sobbing. The Chaplain held her as she cried out in pain. Then she gathered herself up quickly.

"Gentlemen, thank you for coming. Where do I get Matthew tomorrow? I have to arrange for him to be shipped home."

"Young lady", the Captain said as he handed her a card," Come to my office tomorrow at 0900. The Navy will make all of the arrangements. Do you have any family who can help you?"

"Not here, but back in Batavia, my Aunt. . . Oh, I'll figure it out", she said bravely. "Good evening Gentlemen, I'll see you in the morning."

The men departed and Leah closed the door behind them and on the life she thought she had.

The next day, when she arrived at Captain Sotherby's office, she was surprised to see an older couple already sitting on his couch. She quickly realized that these people were her in-laws. Captain Sotherby greeted her warmly and not realizing that they had never before met, sat down behind his desk and began to sort through all the papers involved in this sailor's death.

Finally, Milo spoke up.

"Excuse me Captain, do you think we could have a few minutes alone. This is the first time we have met our daughter-in-law." The Captain excused himself. Milo and Mathilde stood up and approached Leah. Milo reached his hand out to her. "I am Milo Deutsch and this is my wife Mathilde. I believe you two have had some conversations on the telephone."

Mathilde embraced her new daughter-in-law and hugged her deeply.

"I tried calling you all last night, but there was no answer."

"We were already flying down here. We arrived late last night."

"Oh"

The Captain eventually returned and then proceeded with all the arrangements to release Matthew's body to his family. He wished them all well and released the family to claim the body that afternoon. Milo made arrangements for the body to be shipped by train to Batavia. Then they went to the hotel restaurant and had lunch together.

Milo said to her, "Leah, Tilde and I think that it would make good sense, if rather than you going down to the dock this afternoon, maybe you and Tilde can go back to your apartment and pack it up."

"Why would I do that?" she said to him.

Mathilde broke in at this point and gently said to her,

"Leah honey, certainly, you are not going to stay here?"

"I don't have any other place to go!"

"Yes you do. You have us. Come back and stay with us for a while."

"A while? How long is a while?"

"As long as you need, Leah. Certainly until the baby is born. And of course until you get yourself set up with the child. Really, you can stay as long as you want. I mean you are family now."

She looked at them and thought to herself," If I wasn't carrying their grandchild, they wouldn't know I exist," but she didn't say it, because she had nothing and nobody but the baby she carried inside of her. Besides, Leah was in such a state of shock by all that had happened that she was afraid of what the future would bring. At least like this, her immediate future would be taken care of. So she went along with everything Milo and Mathilde told her to do.

Later that day, Milo claimed Matthew's body from the ship. Meanwhile Mathilde hired a cab and accompanied Leah back to the apartment. They went to the local store and got some empty boxes and spent rest of the afternoon closing up the house. As she folded her son's clothing, Mathilde suddenly burst into tears and wracked sobbing. Leah held her until she calmed down. It was then that Leah thought to herself that this tall austere woman was actually a warm and loving mother. And that mother was genuinely grieving the loss of her son. It was a total contrast to how Matthew had described her. He had always referred to her as the "Ice Queen". Well the Ice Queen had melted in her son's tiny apartment on the beach in Virginia. When she had recovered, Leah made her some coffee and they talked for the rest of the afternoon, getting to know one another. Then they took a cab back to the hotel.

Milo arranged to ship all her things and she took one valise with some clothes and flew back to Batavia with them. She remembered the house well from her childhood and she commented to herself that it had hardly changed one bit. They set her up in Matthew's old room. She lay down on the bed and closed her eyes to take a nap. She thought that she could smell the faint wisp of Matthew, but realized that she had been dreaming. She arose several hours later and came downstairs. There she learned that they had made the funeral arrangements without her. But she was all right with this and sort of glad. As she stepped into the dining room she was greeted by a heavyset balding man, who, when he turned to her wore the collar of a priest.

"You must be Mrs. Deutsch, junior? I am Father O'Donnell. I am so sorry for you little lady, so sorry"

"Thank you, Father. I appreciate your concern. Are you the Deutsch's priest?"

"Well actually, no. I am an old friend. Milo and Mathilde go to the Monsignor's church. He is actually their priest. But I am making the arrangements for the funeral mass."

"The what?"

"The mass. You know the funeral mass."

Milo stepped into the room at that moment and whispered something into his ear. The priest looked up at him and said,

"So what! Matthew was a Catholic. She has to understand that. We have to give him a good Christian burial. Young lady, do you understand that we are burying your husband as a Catholic. It's what Matthew would have wanted."

She looked at the priest quizzically,

"Matthew probably could have cared less", she said to the startled priest and the now distressed Milo who retorted,

"Don't talk to the priest like that! He is a man of G-d."

"Now, now Milo. It's all right. She doesn't know. Young lady, do you have any objections to Matthew being buried a Catholic?"

She thought for a minute, then said,

"No. . . not really. He was a Catholic. I know that. He never went to church though."

"Maybe, he didn't want to hurt your feelings. I mean, you being Jewish and all", the priest said to her. Milo shook his head in agreement. She thought some more, "I suppose you're right. Well, it doesn't make any difference to me as long as you reserve the plot next to him for me. I'll pay for it. I mean I'll have to work out an arrangement to pay over time, but I want the plot next to him. Can you do that, Father?

Father O'Donnell looked kind of disturbed. He looked at Milo. Milo looked at him and shrugged his shoulders. Then he left the priest and Leah alone in the room. Father O'Donnell sat down on a dining room chair and put his forehead in his hand. Then he looked up at Leah and said,

"Young lady, I wish it was that simple. I really wish it were. But it's not. Not that simple at all. Come sit down here. Come sit down."

The priest sighed deeply.

"I'm afraid that young people often rush into things without knowing all the ramifications."

"Ramifications of what?"

"The ramifications of life, young lady, the ramifications of life", the priest said wearily.

"I don't understand"

"Well Leah. . , Oh, such a beautiful biblical name, tell me, when you married dear Matthew, who married you?"

"A chaplain from Matt's ship."

"Was he a priest?"

"I don't know. He wore a cross like you and that funny collar you guys wear."

"It's called a roman collar. But anyway, you don't know if he is a priest? Probably not. Most likely one of those southern Methodists or Baptists. No matter! Humm. It's like this young lady. Much as I'd like to get you the plot next to Matthew. I can't get it for you."

"Why not?"

"Because you are not Catholic"

"So what! He was my husband. What should it matter if I am not Catholic"

"But it does matter young lady. It does matter. You don't understand. You are a Jew. Matthew was baptized in the Holy Church. He was a Catholic."

"And now he's dead and I want the plot next to him. What is the big deal?"

"We can't bury you next to Matthew unless you become a Catholic.

"Well that's ridiculous. What about our kid? This kid is going to be a Catholic, right?"

The priest shook his head no,

"What do you mean? Matt was a Catholic. The father is Catholic, so the kid is Catholic!"

"No, you are the child's mother, you are a Jew. The child is a Jew."

"Well I'll raise the child as a Catholic. You know, I'll send the kid to St. Mary's."

"Leah, the only way that your child could be Catholic is if you had the baby baptized. But that baby's mother would still be Jewish. And you still couldn't be buried in a Catholic cemetery. Unless. . ."

"Unless what"

"Unless you accepted baptism and became a Catholic. Then we could get you the plot next to Matthew."

"Why does he have to buried in a Catholic cemetery?"

"Because he's Catholic."

"Well I'm his wife and I want to be buried next to him. This is all crazy. None of this ever mattered to Matthew. Why should it matter now?"

Milo walked into the room with Mathilde tagging behind.

"Because young people often act without thinking. I'm afraid that Matthew and you rushed into marriage without a clue as to who he was or what he would become. Now you must live with the consequences."

"And those consequences are?"

"Those consequences are that you are pregnant with our grandchild. Your husband, who was our son, is dead and you have neither the means to properly bury our son, nor the means to give birth and raise his child. For that you are dependent upon us. Since we are footing the bill, we will have the say. Matthew will be buried after a Mass of Christian Burial in St. Anthony's Catholic cemetery. If you want to be buried next to him, I suggest you convert. And if you want our help and let me remind you that we have considerable means to help you raise this child properly, then you best have this child baptized when the time is right."

With that, he turned on his heel and walked out of the room. Mathilde looked at her daughter-in-law and just shrugged. Then she followed him out of the room.

CHAPTER SIXTEEN

For years, Karolyn had listened to her Grandmother's story of love and the Navy. Every summer, Leah's house in Batavia became her escape for three weeks. Together, they would go shopping and eat in restaurants and just have fun. As Karolyn got older she found that she could tell Leah almost anything. But each of them had one secret that they held from the other.

Leah never told her granddaughter that she had been born a Jew. Each Sunday morning while they were together, Leah dressed up smartly and took Karolyn to church. There they prayed together and took communion together.

Years later, when Kary thought of her grandmother, she always saw her in her mind's eye with her Sunday best on, taking communion.

Kary for her own part, grew up rarely going to church. Her father hated it and her mother just didn't go, even on Christmas and Easter. Her two brothers grew up and also never went.

But Kary also had a secret. It was so terrible that she never told anyone. Not her mother, her brothers or even her grandmother to whom she could tell anything. From the time she was eight, her father had come into her room at night and molested her. It went on through her teen years. Finally, two years into college, she abruptly quit and joined the Navy. It was the first time in her life that the torment had stopped.

Then she met a young man, Daniel Kaplan. A young sailor who blushed when he looked at her. He was shy yet strangely gregarious, a loner with a way of commanding a room when he entered it.

She had sat down next to him one night in the hospital cafeteria and they had become inseparable over the next three weeks. One night after they were walking back from the other side of the base, he noticed that she had become very quiet.

"Kary, is everything alright?"

She didn't answer. He took her arm and turned her around. She looked at him and then looked down.

"Well?"

"You don't want to know."

"Don't want to know what?"

"Daniel, where are we going with this?"

Daniel seemed surprised. "I don't understand"

"Where are we going with this . . . this . . . are we just going out?"

Daniel smiled. He held both of her arms in his hands.

"No! I am crazy about you. I think that I am . . . no, I know that I am in love with you, Karolyn."

"Well you can't be"

"What?"

"You can't be, you hear me! You can't be. I am not who you think I am"

"You're not? Well, who are you then?"

"I'm me", She got frustrated with him, "Ugh, it's just that I have a secret."

"We all have secrets, Kary, so what?"

"No, if you knew this secret, you wouldn't want to have anything to do with me."

"How can you say that?"

"Because its true."

"You don't know me then. And I think I know you. You can tell me anything about you. It will make no difference, I love you."

"It will make a difference. You don't know! It'll make a difference, a big difference. You will not want me."

"That's ridiculous. What's the worst thing you can tell me?" He looked at her closely. He stared into her eyes and looked long and deeply. "Kary, I am going to tell you something. I have a secret too. So whatever your secret is, you can tell me or not, it will make no difference to me. I love you."

He looked at her again. "Kary," he said in almost a whisper, "If you tell me that you had been raped, it will make no difference to me. If you've been beaten up or molested, no difference. If you have a child, no difference. I really love you as you are honey. I was abused as a child, Kary. That's my secret."

He sighed and looked down for a moment. Then he looked up at her. "Sweetheart, tell me. It will not change how I feel about you one iota. Really, you can tell me, if you want to."

They sat down on a bench together. She looked at him very closely. Then in a moment she knew she would tell him. She didn't know if she could, but she knew she would.

So she began telling him and he listened. He held her hand and let her get the sadness out. While she was talking, he thought back to something he had once been told by his Grandfather. Daniel had asked his Grandfather why he had married his Grandmother.

His Grandfather grinned and then answered him,

"Someday Daniel, you will meet a woman who will mean so much to you that it will not matter what she looks like. You will be able to imagine the worst possible catastrophes with her and still you will want to be with her. Then you will know what love is."

As Daniel listened to Kary's voice, he heard his Grandfather's voice in the background and he understood for the first time that it was true. Daniel felt anger but not at Kary. He felt anger at what had been done and who had done it to her. He said very little to her while she talked other than to encourage her to continue her story. He squeezed her hand in support and brushed back her hair from her eyes. He took off her glasses and wiped them dry.

Finally, she took a deep breath. A great weight now sat on her chest. Would he really accept what she had just related to him? And if he could, would it really be possible for her to allow herself to love this man and be loved by him. She waited for a moment to see his reaction. All through the telling, he had not indicated anything other than to try and comfort her. Now, she wanted to know, needed to know, what he thought.

Daniel looked at her. He said nothing. He just looked at her. She looked at him, but was somewhat confused. He continued to just look at her. She looked down, but his hand caught her chin and lifted it up to look at him. He leaned towards her lips and gently kissed them. She returned the kiss. He hugged her tightly and she placed her head on his right shoulder. He held her for a long time. Neither of them said anything. Finally, she pushed gently back and looked at him.

"Well", she said to him.

He shook his head and pursed his lips tightly. He had been moved by her story and he didn't want to say the wrong thing. He wanted her to know that everything was all right and that if anything; he loved her even more now.

"Well", he said to her.

She looked at him. He looked down at the ground for a moment and then closed his eyes tightly,

"That is some story!"

He paused in thought for a moment. Then he said,

"But I want you to know two things, Kary. Two things! One – I love you with all of my heart. Second – I will never let anyone harm you like that again."

She looked at him silently. Then he said to her in a near whisper,

"Honey, despite what you may feel, you have done nothing wrong. You are the victim here. And I want you to know something else, I know what I am talking about. I got beaten up as a little boy. Why? I don't know. Certainly for reasons that I am still not sure about. I was a very good boy, but something led to those terrible beatings and I now know that it was not me, but his inability to control himself. I understand it logically, but not in my heart and it hurts. It hurts very badly. Kary, I understand. No, I think I understand that it hurts you for similar reasons. You may even feel that you were the cause of this abuse by your father. For a long time, I felt that my father was right in beating me. I had to be this awful person to have such a level of violence thrust upon me like that. I don't know if you feel that yourself, honey. I don't know. But if you do feel something like this, let me tell you that you were not the cause. A sickness was perpetrated against you. A sickness was perpetrated against me. As far as I am concerned, Kary German, all this tells me is that you are my beautiful love and I love you more now than before you told me this. As far as I am concerned, Kary, you will never have to tell me twice to stop. If ever I do anything that makes you uncomfortable, please let me know, so that I do stop. Wherever this relationship leads us, I want you to know that your body will never be violated by me. I believe that a woman has the right to say no and I mean it when I say that I will accept that unconditionally."

She looked at him. Then she stood up and pulled on his arm for him to get up as well. She pulled him close to her. Then they walked back to the barracks and he sent her to her room with a kiss.

Book 2

DANIEL KAPLAN

CHAPTER SEVENTEEN

The weeks that followed were weeks of pure joy for Daniel. Kary spent almost every available minute with him. They went to movies and bowled together in a mixed bowling league on base. She decided to get her hair permed. She hated her new style and frankly, so did he. But he loved her and it made for a very funny moment. He had the watch as the duty officer and was inspecting the woman's barracks when he came upon Kary sitting in the common room with her new hairstyle. He saw her and she saw him. She didn't want him to see the perm yet, but there he was, quite by accident. She looked up at him and gave him the raspberry with her mouth and stuck out her tongue. They both laughed and he went on his way.

One Friday night, as he was walking her back to the barracks, they made up to get up early the next day go into Chicago. Daniel returned to his barracks room after dropping her off. He got out of his clothes and looked around the room. Then he climbed into the top bunk. His roommate was already sleeping on the bottom bunk. Suddenly, he heard very loud and unusual snoring. He threw a towel down to wake up his roommate, but the man continued to snore. Finally, Daniel jumped down to shake the man and found an empty bottle of rum in the bed with him. He would not respond to the shaking and started to choke and turn blue. Daniel ran out of the room and pounded on the door of his neighbor and told him to notify the duty officer and get an ambulance. One of the guys ran downstairs; the other came into the room with Daniel. They pulled his roommate off of his bed and onto the floor. Daniel stretched his neck back to try and open the man's airway. His breathing stopped completely. Daniel and his neighbor performed mouth to mouth resuscitation on him until the ambulance arrived. The medics placed an airway into his roommate's mouth. Daniel went with him to the hospital where they pumped his stomach and stabilized him. It was 6 o'clock in the morning before Daniel returned to his room, cleaned the mess and climbed into bed hoping for a short nap. He lay down on his bunk and closed his eyes for a few minutes knowing he was going to meet Kary for breakfast in an hour. He woke up at noon. He jumped up, quickly dressed and ran over to the woman's barracks to call on Kary. The Duty Officer called upstairs and then told Daniel that Kary did not want to speak to him. When he started to protest, she asked him to please leave the barracks.

He walked over to the Hospital cafeteria to eat some lunch. As he sat down, he ran into Kary's roommate. He explained to her what had happened the night before and how he had just collapsed and fallen asleep. He asked her to explain it to Kary and please have her leave a message for him. She agreed to tell Kary. He finished his lunch and went back to the barracks. He didn't hear anything until around 3 o'clock. By then word of Daniel's actions had become well known within the barracks. Kary had initially doubted her roommate's story. However, it became evident that Daniel had been telling the truth. So she went to the men's barracks and had the duty officer call up to him. He came down and she was sitting in the lobby. She looked at him and apologized profusely.

The next week, she was sitting at dinner with him, when she suggested that they go into Chicago the next Saturday. They had done that several times for day trips to museums and both had enjoyed it immensely. They would take the train into Chicago and would go around to various sites. Daniel commented that he had seen in the paper that the Ice Capades were in town and maybe they would get tickets and go. But the show ended at 11:00 at night and Daniel was concerned about how late it would be to take a train back to Great Lakes.

Kary answered, "What difference would it make Daniel?"

"I don't understand"

"We'll stay over"

"Stay over where?"

"In Chicago, silly"

Daniel thought about that for a moment and couldn't believe that she meant what she was saying.

"All right. But where could we stay?"

Kary answered, " I've been looking at ads in the paper and they have a serviceman's special at the Omni. You know that used to be the old Playboy Hotel."

"What's the special?"

"$25.00 a night"

"Okay, so that will be $50.00 . . .", as he started figuring out the costs in his head.

"$50 dollars?", Kary asked him, "Where do you get $50 dollars from?"

"Well two rooms at $25.00. . ."

She reached out and held his wrist. She laughed for a moment,

"We won't need two rooms"

"We won't?"

"Believe me, we won't"

"Okay"

Daniel's head was floating. He was going to spend a night with Kary in Chicago and they were going to be together in one room. Now Daniel was not a virgin, but he always made sure that he was a gentleman with women and especially Kary, although lately, the balcony of the base movie theater was getting a little hotter for them than they would like. So it was a logical extension for them to go to Chicago together for an overnight. However, he was determined to show her a good time and to take her out for a romantic dinner and something after. He would take her to a show and then they could return to the Hotel. He was unsure about what she wanted, so he told her that he had no expectations from her and that they would only go as far as she was comfortable. She was fine with that and they had a good understanding of each other's intentions before they left.

That Saturday, they got on the train and went into Chicago. They checked into the Hotel and went up to their room. It was a typical hotel room but it had a little kitchenette area with a hot plate and refrigerator. It was on the 15th floor and had a grand view of Chicago's famous Loop. They looked at each other and hugged. They decided to go to the Natural History Museum and spent the afternoon browsing the many exhibits and enjoying each other's company.

They returned to the hotel at around 3:30 and made reservations at an Italian restaurant the desk clerk had recommended. They also bought tickets to the Ice Capades. The show started at 8:00 and they had a 6:00 reservation to eat. So they had a couple of hours to relax. They went back to the room and timidly began to kiss. Soon they were lying on the bed kissing and exploring each other, although they were still in their clothes. Kary removed his shirt and he removed hers. He felt at her bra and kissed her stomach and face. He reached behind her to unbuckle her brassiere and slowly released the snaps. As the bra slackened, Kary suddenly crossed her arms over the bra and she laid down flat on her stomach. The back of the bra was open and Daniel could see her back.

"Honey, is something wrong?"

She looked up at him, "I'm not ready yet"

"Okay, it's all right Kary. I understand. What would you like for me to do?"

"Well first, can you hook my bra back together again"?

"Sure"

She sat up holding the bra front with her arms and Daniel quickly put the bra hooks back together. Then he helped her into her shirt."

"Are you sure you are up to this? I can take you back to Great Lakes right now if you are uncomfortable?"

They sat at the edge of the bed.

"No, No, I'm okay, Daniel. I just wasn't prepared to go this far right now"

"Well, remember what I said. I don't want you to feel uneasy at all, so if you are. I'll take you back and it will be perfectly okay."

She got up and pulled back the curtain and looked out the window. She turned to him and said to him,

"Come here"

He walked over to her. She took him in her arms and gave him the most remarkable and long kiss. He looked at her, somewhat perplexed. She smiled and said to him,

"Daniel, I do want to be with you tonight. Right here in that bed. I promise you that when we come back here tonight that you don't have to worry about me taking off my bra for you. I want to be near you. So don't worry."

So they each took a shower and dressed for their evening out. They took a taxi to Ricardo's, a small but highly recommended Italian restaurant. They sat upstairs and had a delicious meal of lasagna and ravioli. They had a half decanter of wine. Ricardo's desserts were delicious. As they sat drinking their coffee, a photographer took their picture. A few minutes later, he brought it to the table and Daniel bought it for Kary.

After dinner they walked over to Chicago Stadium and watched the Ice Capades show. It was lovely and magical. As lovely and as magical as the night was turning out to be.

When the show was over, they returned to the hotel. Kary slipped into a nightgown and came out and kissed him. She removed his shirt and then his trousers. They slipped into the bed together. Daniel held her tight and massaged her back through the nightgown. Kary explored his body with her hands and reached between his legs to remove his shorts. She took him in her hands and kissed him on his chest and neck. He reached under her nightgown and slowly lifted it up over her. She let him remove it from her body and he explored her body. She let him remove her panties and touch her gently between her legs. The rest of the night, they got to know each other intimately although, they never came together. They fell deep asleep in each other's arms. In the morning, they cuddled some more and then finally, got up, and went to eat breakfast. They spent the rest of the day exploring Chicago and then went back to Great Lakes. The following week was torture for her, but for him he was very happy.

That next weekend, their class at Hospital Corps School had a graduation party at a local motel. Everyone got a little too drunk, especially Kary. She suggested to Daniel that maybe they should get a room together. He agreed. However, when he went to the office to register, he changed his mind. Kary had drunk considerably more than she was used to and he felt it was better for her to sleep it off in her barracks room. So over her mild protest, he told her that he was taking her back to base. They took a cab and he helped her unsteadily walk to the women's barracks. When he dropped her off, he asked the duty officer to please escort her to her room and make sure she was all right. He waited until the Duty Officer returned and told him that she had gone to bed.

The next morning, Kary didn't show up for breakfast. Her roommate said she was still sleeping. Around noontime, she came to the men's barracks and asked for him. The duty officer called upstairs and he came down. They walked towards the hospital to get some lunch. Suddenly, she turned to him and said most forcefully.

"Now I know what kind of man you are."

"I don't understand, Kary"

"Last night, you could have taken me to bed in that motel. And I would have gone with you. But you knew it would be wrong. So you took me back here. I love you for doing that, for caring about me so much that you wouldn't take advantage. Thanks for knowing me better than I knew myself."

CHAPTER EIGHTEEN

They had been at Camp Lejeune, North Carolina for almost a week. It was a dirty, dusty place with open bay barracks for 50-60 people. It was quite a difference from the clean orderly environment of the Hospital in Great Lakes. The place was very depressing and Daniel hated it. After a week of getting introduced to the Marine Corps way of doing things, both of them were tense, uptight and jumpy. Kary and Daniel decided to spend the weekend at a local motel. They were both sort of glum. After dinner, they decided to take a walk. They walked around Jacksonville, NC., the town surrounding the huge Marine Base. It was a three-movie theater town, two of which showed horror films. The town revolved around the Marine Base and pick up trucks. Everything about the place seemed backward and parochial to both Daniel and to Kary.

As they walked, Kary and Daniel talked about the change in their life and how precious his time with her had now become. She walked with him until they found a bench. Then they sat down. She looked at him and said,

"Daniel, I want to be with you tonight"

"You are with me tonight"

"No, I mean I want you inside of me tonight"

He looked at her carefully. She smiled at him,

"I want you to be the first man to have me, Daniel"

He felt very frightened all of a sudden. They got up and walked some more. They found a drug store and they went in. Daniel went to buy condoms but became so embarrassed that he could barely speak. The girl behind the counter gave him one of those knowing looks and he turned bright red. After, they walked out of the store; Kary took the paper bag from his hand. She sensed his uncertainty. They returned to the motel and undressed. They climbed into bed together and began to make love. Finally, he sat up in bed and looked at her.

"I know that this is going to sound crazy, but I am not ready"

"Not ready for what, Daniel?"

"I'm not a virgin, Kary"

"I know"

"But"

"Yes, Daniel"

"I just didn't think it would happen with you tonight"

"So?"

"Believe it or not, I'm not ready to go all the way with you yet"

"Your not? Why?"

"I don't know. I just wanted it to be different. Romantic and magical."

He looked around at the room. It seemed so seedy, although in fact it was clean and comfortable. But it was austere and he felt uncomfortable coming together with her in this particular place.

He shook his head again no. She looked at him closely, and then she smiled.

"It's all right, I understand"

"Do you?"

"Not really, but if your not ready, then I guess, I'm not either. Because, I want you to be my first."

He smiled weakly. He looked at her face and at her body lying in front of him. She was not what you would call a classic beauty. Other men might have found her quite plain. But to him lying in the dark next to her, she was extraordinarily beautiful. He loved her touch and he loved to touch her.

In point of fact she drove him wild not just sexually but emotionally.

"Daniel, I want you next weekend. Can you make yourself ready?"

He looked at her and nodded.

The next week, he found a lovely motel with beautiful rooms and a lovely restaurant. They checked in and put on bathing suits and went swimming in the pool. After they had spent the day sunning and swimming, they returned to their room and went out to eat dinner. A growing excitement, almost tension seemed to grow throughout the meal.

He brought her back to the room. He watched as she came out of the bathroom in her nightgown. He closed the bathroom door until just a crack of light was visible into the room. He moved towards her and gave her a little kiss on the cheek. She smiled and blushed. He touched her breast through her nightgown and traced his fingers around her collar. They embraced and kissed for a long time. Then she unbuttoned his shirt and loosened his belt. She drew off the clothing from his shoulder and pushed his trousers to his ankles. He held her as she helped him step out of them. Then she lowered his shorts and he stood before her naked. She hugged him and they kissed. He drew the nightgown over her head and kissed her breasts and cheek.

They climbed into the bed and cuddled for a very long time. Then she leaned back and opened the night table draw that was next to her. She drew out a little envelope and removed the condom inside. She gently felt for him and placed it upon him. They kissed and cuddled some more. Finally, he rolled on top of her and she opened her legs to receive him. He tried to be gentle and slow as he entered her, but she was tight and he knew that he was hurting her. He asked her if she was all right. She shook her head yes. Soon their rhythm increased and she accepted him more comfortably. Finally, he let go with a loud sigh. She drew him to her and he rested his head on her chest. She took his face and kissed him on the lips.

They came together four more times that weekend. For the rest of the time they were at Camp Lejeune together, they spent every possible weekend in that little motel, connecting deeply with each other.

CHAPTER NINETEEN

*D*uring the next two years, Daniel would receive orders to Officer Candidate School and would be ordered to the University of Mississippi to finish his education. Kary remained at Camp Lejeune, missing him terribly and trying to go through her days without him.

Daniel had signed up for training as a Naval Flight Officer. This would mean that he would be stationed at Pensacola, FL for at least two years. Kary was due for a duty station change and she put in for Pensacola. However her orders called for her to go to one of the first ships that had women. It was in the pre-commissioning phase so she was still ashore. The ship, the USS Nantucket was a repair ship. It was berthed in San Diego, CA

It was decided by Kary that she would travel to Mississippi to see him as she traveled west. She brought her parents along for company. They arrived on Halloween night.

Unbeknownst to Kary, Daniel had purchased an engagement ring for her from a local jeweler in Oxford during that summer. He had placed it in a bank vault, afraid that he might lose it or that it might get stolen. Oxford was the town surrounding the university and was and still is a quaint classic Southern town with a town square with the courthouse in the middle.

Daniel had bought the ring because; he was going to ask Kary to marry him. He had already told the Navy to switch him out of flight training and asked for orders to a ship in San Diego.

When she arrived, they all went to dinner in town. Her parents left her with him. He brought her to his room and they sat on his bed and talked. They kissed uncertainly as it had been a while since they had been together. Then he asked her to close her eyes for a moment. He went to his bureau and removed the ring from the top drawer. It was a simple setting with a quarter carat diamond. The diamond although barely more than a chip had a bluish hue and a sparkle that had made him want to buy it for her. He hoped that some day, he would be able to get her a larger stone, if she wanted that.

He got down on his knees and took her hands in his and said to her,

"Kary,"

He started to stutter from nervousness.

"Kary, would you please give me the honor. . . of . . . being my wife?"

She opened her eyes and looked down at him as he placed the ring halfway up her ring finger. She looked down at it and said nothing. Then she nodded yes and reached down and pushed the ring the rest of the way up her finger.

They kissed and hugged. They did not make love. Rather, they both took a walk around the campus, hand in hand. They talked about their future and their hopes and their dreams. They talked about their obvious differences in religion, but they agreed to learn each other's ways and respect them. Finally, as it had gotten very late, she returned to her car and left to return to her parents at their hotel. As he watched her drive into Oxford, his eyes glistened in happiness. He walked back into his dorm and there were people sitting in the lobby. They were all his friends and they all knew what he was going to be doing that night. As he walked in one them, a law student affectionately called Buddy yelled in his thick Mississippi drawl,

"Well Kaplan, is she going hitch up with a damn Yankee like you?"

Daniel laughed and then his eyes surveyed the room. He looked down for a moment at the floor and then looked up at his friends and gave them the thumbs up. Everyone rushed towards him hugging and patting him on the shoulders and back.

Buddy reached into a cooler that they had been hiding behind a couch and started handing out beers to everyone. Then he got everyone's attention and made a toast. He raised his beer can and said,

"To Daniel Kaplan. Before I met him, I never knew a Yankee that I liked. Nor had I had but a passing conversation with a Jew. And I hate New York", pointing his beer can towards Daniel, "So when this New York Jew Yankee came to live in this dorm, I would have been the first to say that I would have had nothing to do with him. But, he surprised me and I think us all by being, kindhearted, tough and funny as hell. And I've never seen anyone who scoffed down a pork roast faster than him. So to Daniel and to his new bride to be. By the way Kaplan, where is the girl?"

"She went back to her hotel to get some sleep"

Buddy shook his head knowingly. "Well to Daniel Kaplan and his now probably sleeping bride to be, may your love last a lifetime and your fortunes do the same. And now I think it's appropriate that we do the Ole Miss cheer"

And everyone including Daniel joined in, "Hoddy Toddy, Gosh Almighty, who in the hell are we, flim flam, bim bam, Ole Miss by damn. Hurrah!"

They all laughed and stayed up drinking some more until they could not keep their heads up any longer and started drifting back to their room to sleep.

In the morning, Kary's parents took him out for breakfast. Her mother was so excited. Her father was not a big talker, but he smiled as he listened to the other three talk. Kary just kept looking at the ring and smiling. Soon thereafter, they had to leave to continue on their way west. Daniel and Kary hugged each other tightly and kissed with an intensity that was beyond either of them. He watched in tears as her car drove away down the road to the highway.

After she had gotten established in San Diego, they decided that during his spring break, he would come to California and stay with her. It was a three-week break between quarters and he was very excited to see California and to start getting the wedding plans in order. The cheapest flight, he could book from Memphis flew into Los Angeles, so she met him there and drove him down to her newly rented apartment in Imperial Beach. Imperial Beach was south of San Diego and a beautiful beach town. She had an apartment on the first floor inside of a courtyard. It had a living room with a couch and chair, a bedroom and a small kitchen. The apartment complex had a small pool and was relatively quiet.

After he had settled in, she made him some coffee and they talked until about one in the morning. Then, she yawned deeply and looked at the clock . She took him by the hand and led him into the bedroom. As they went to bed, she told him that she had gone on birth control pills, because she wanted to really feel him inside of her.

"Can't they be dangerous, Kary. My mother had a hysterectomy because birth control pills made a tumor grow inside her."

"Daniel, they use much fewer hormones now. This pill is called lo-ovril. It is very safe."

"Okay, if you say so"

And they proceeded to make love. Both admitted that it was much nicer without a barrier and they made love often during his time with her in California.

Periodically during his visit, she would suggest to him that they should go up to Las Vegas. But Daniel, not being a gambler was not really interested. And he was enjoying being with her right there in their little apartment. So she let the thought pass and they didn't go during his visit..

On the last weekend he was there, he took her to a synagogue for the first time. They got up Saturday morning and drove over to a synagogue in Chula Vista. It was a Conservative Shul and they were very welcoming and friendly. He was called to the Torah and throughout the service he tried to explain to her what was going on. She watched him intensely sitting there next to her. She saw how much he enjoyed it and how much he wanted her to understand. But it was strange to her. It was conducted in a language with funny looking letters and a foreign tongue. But as she looked at Daniel she realized how deeply a part of it he really was. He seemed really moved and at the same time at peace in the synagogue. And it was a peace that she had never before seen in him.

On Tuesday, he flew back to Mississippi. The last two nights that Kary and Daniel were together, their passion ran fire red hot. They made love so many times that it hurt. She hung on him at the airport and he cried when he kissed her good-bye. But they knew that in three months, they would be together again. And this time it would be forever.

CHAPTER TWENTY

He arrived back in San Diego on a Friday night. He checked into the barracks and went across the street to the Officer's Club to eat. The place was full of Officers at Happy Hour. It was noisy and smoky and Daniel didn't know anyone. He decided not to eat there.

He left the club and reported in to his new command, the Surface Warfare Officer's School. He turned his papers into the watch officer and was told to come back on Monday morning at 7 o'clock for assignment. He asked if there were any decent places to eat in Coronado. He was told that there was a good Italian restaurant called Mama's, which was inexpensive and had generous portions. He walked back to his room in the barracks to change into civilian clothes. He diverted himself across the street back into the club hoping that it had quieted down. It had. He found a table and the waitress brought him a menu. He ordered a beer to start and perused the menu. He put it down because he knew that he really only wanted a steak. When the waitress came back he ordered another beer and a steak with mashed potatoes and fried onions. He left over the salad and sipped on his beer. The place was quiet and pleasant without the tumult of a crowd. He finished off his dinner with some apple pie and coffee. He paid the bill and walked out the front door and took a deep breath. He looked around and saw to his right an officer lying face down in the grass, obviously passed out drunk. He muttered to himself that at least the man could have enough self-respect to not drink in uniform. He bent down and turned the man onto his back. To his surprise, he saw three stars on each of his collars. He shook his head in wonderment. He tried to wake the Admiral up, but had no luck. Finally, he picked him up and put him over his shoulder in a fireman's carry and brought him across the street to the barracks office. The girl who was manning the front desk laughed when he walked in with the Admiral over his shoulder. Daniel didn't think it was so funny.

"Do you think you might have a room for the Admiral to sleep it off in."

"He already has a room here. He has a permanent room here. Admiral Riley is here regularly."

"Riley? Isn't he ComNavSurfPac"

"James Riley, the one and only", she replied.

She made a quizzical look at him and then she smiled at him. Then she handed him the Admiral's key. She was a good-looking brunette, but she couldn't have been more than 20 years old. He smiled back at her and carried the Admiral to his room and put him to bed. As he walked out of the room, he thought to himself that the name Riley sounded familiar. Then he remembered that it was Admiral James Riley who was once the Chief of Naval Education. This was the man who he had spoken to when his application to Officer Candidates School had been "lost". Daniel smiled, and thought of how once an unseen man had helped another. Now the helped man, now unseen, had returned the favor.

CHAPTER TWENTY-ONE

Monday morning arrived too early for Ensign Kaplan. He looked at his alarm clock and saw that it was 5:00 A.M. He groaned aloud and let his head fall back onto his pillow. Finally, he shifted his body out of bed and shuffled off to the shower. The hot water felt delicious on his neck and body. Soon, he awakened completely. He dried off and put on his uniform. He walked across the street to the Officer's Club for breakfast. He sat down at a table and motioned for the waitress. He ordered a coffee and borrowed the dining room's newspaper. The waitress brought coffee and he took a long deep swallow. Finally, he looked at the menu and ordered breakfast.

When he was done, he walked over to the building housing the Surface Warfare Officer's School. He reported to the watch officer and was given a packet of papers to fill out. He joined a number of young officers who were doing the same thing.

The Chief Petty Officer in charge of processing the officers told them they would be assigned to the next class being assembled. This class would convene the next Monday. In the meantime, he would be given temporary duty orders to the Naval Special Warfare Group across the street from the base. The purpose was for a naval intelligence orientation. He would go with any officers who arrived before the class convened. In the meantime, the officers were released from duty for the rest of the day.

Daniel headed back to the barracks to unpack. He spent the rest of the day trying to get oriented with Coronado. Finally, he got into his car and drove across the Coronado Bridge to the Naval Hospital in San Diego. He parked his car and walked up to the administrative offices asking where she worked in the hospital. He walked up to that office, but she wasn't there. He asked another corpswoman where she was. She told him that Karolyn was at a Doctor's appointment. He asked her to tell Kary that an old friend had stopped by to say hello. Then he went back to his car and drove away from the base. Finally, he pulled over to the side of the road and parked .

His mind wandered back six months. He was sitting on the bed in his dormitory in Mississippi. For four days, he had been trying to get Karolyn on the telephone. But she was not available. He had spoken to several girls who had answered the telephone in the hall of her barracks, but no one had seen her or knew anything about where she might be. Finally he called her ship and found out she had taken leave.

Then his mind wandered back four and half months ago. He had not heard from Kary in over a month and a half. He had just been commissioned and had been ordered to his first ship, The USS Tarawa. He had met the ship in Long Beach and traveled with the ship for a week until they returned to their homeport of San Diego. As soon as he arrived, he grabbed a ride with two officers from the ship who were heading back up to Long Beach. Two hours later, he had recovered his car from the pier and was racing back to San Diego to start looking for Kary. He called her ship to find out where they were berthed, but the clerk told him that she had been transferred off of the ship to the Naval Hospital in San Diego.

He drove straight to the Naval Hospital and inquired as to where Kary worked. He was dressed in his khaki uniform and was so nervous he was shaking. He went to the bathroom and when he went to wash his hands, the faucet erupted with a stream of water all over his pants. Using the electric hand dryer, he managed to dry his pants sufficiently, so as not to embarrass himself.

He started looking for the office where she worked and finally on the second floor, he found it. He walked into a long room with rows of desks lined two wide next to a wall of windows. He asked a lady corpsman at the front desk where he could find Kary. She looked at him perplexed. He realized that it was unusual for an officer to be asking to find an enlisted woman.

He walked up the aisle looking for Kary. His heart was beating so hard that he felt like he was going to explode. His head felt numb and he felt as shaky as he had ever felt. Then he saw her. She looked up and saw him. She turned red and then she smiled. She looked down for a second, then, she got up to great him. She escorted him onto the veranda of the hospital and sat down with him. She looked as beautiful as ever. Even more so. She had gotten a little heavier, but she carried it well. She looked so nice in her white uniform.

"I am glad you came", she said to him when they finally had settled onto one of the benches on the veranda.

"I've been trying to reach you for over a month, Kary. I've been worried sick. I've left . . . I don't know how many messages for you. What's up honey?"

"I know, I know", she said looking down at her hands. "I've gotten all of your messages".

"Then why didn't you call me? You know that I must have worried"

"I know", she said, "I just couldn't". She looked like she was going to cry, but she didn't. Then she suddenly sat back up straight, looked

Daniel in the eye and said, "Daniel, I have to tell you something and I am not sure how to tell you."

"Well, just tell me. There is nothing that you can't tell me."

"Daniel, I'm married!"

Daniel did not understand at first, the words didn't sink in for a few seconds. Then he felt a tightening in his chest and stomach as the impact of the words came through to him. He sat straight back with his head against the wall. He looked at her. He looked at her very carefully.

"Did you just say that you have gotten married?"

She shook her head yes. He leaned back against the wall with the full force of his body and closed his eyes tightly. Then he said to her,

"But we're engaged.", then he looked at her.

"No Daniel, not any more. I am married. I got married last week. His name is Charley. Charley Fiorentino."

He just sat there. He was shell-shocked at what he had just heard. He could not believe what he was hearing. He was sitting on a lovely veranda on a beautiful sunny summer day in San Diego with the woman he loved, the woman to whom he was engaged to marry and she had just told him that she had married some one else. Nothing could have prepared him for that shock. He took a deep breath trying to comprehend what was happening to him and finally he asked her,

"When did you meet him?"

"About three weeks ago"

"And you married him after knowing him two weeks?"

The question just hung there. He continued, "Do you love him?"

She shrugged, "I don't know, I guess."

He exploded, "I don't know, I guess? What kind of answer is that? What happened to us? We're engaged!. You ran off and married someone you know for only two weeks, knowing full well that you are engaged to another man. I don't understand", he said getting up and pacing in front of her, trying to keep calm in public, "I don't understand this at all, Kary, tell me that I'm dreaming."

"Your not dreaming Daniel! And I'm sorry. Right now, I feel like I am dreaming. I'm so sorry, I just couldn't bring myself to tell you. I should have."

She looked at him sadly, "But now you know."

Daniel tried to break through the fog that enveloped his head and his body.

"How old is he?"

"He's 42."

"You're 23!", Daniel exclaimed at her, "Twenty three, there is 19 years difference between you."

"I know"

"You know? What does he do for a living?"

"He's in the Navy. He's a Molder"

Daniel shook his head.

"Where did you meet him?"

"He was on the Nantucket. I was just transferred here three days ago, because married sailors can't serve on the same ship."

He looked down at the pavement in front of him. He ran his hand through his hair and then looked at his watch. It was almost 4:00 P.M. All he could think of was, "Today, I arrived in San Diego at 9:00 A.M. I made a 4 hour round trip to Long Beach to get my car so that I could go find her. Now, I arrive here and this! What a disaster! This is a colossal mess".

He had hoped to find out why she had disappeared and had thought that since he was permanently in San Diego, he could stabilize his life with her. Well, forget that Kaplan, your best-laid plans were down the toilet. Everything was now as complete a shambles as it could possibly be. It could not be a bigger disaster for him. He was so upset that he was actually shaking. He turned towards the wall and put the palm of his right hand out to support him as he looked at the ground. Finally he sat back down next to her. She looked down at the pavement.

"Why?", he said to her gently and almost in a whisper.

She just shook her head.

"Do you love him?"

"Oh, I don't know"

He paused to think for a moment, but couldn't get his thoughts organized.

"Did you ever love me?", he finally asked, not quite knowing where to go with all this.

"More than you can ever know"

"When did you stop?"

"Who says I've stopped?"

"Are you telling me that you still love me?"

She looked at him. There were tears in the corner of her eyes. She looked down again.

"Then Kary, I really don't understand"

"You can't"

"If it's a mistake Kary, then we can fix it. . .", He started to get up.

She reached up to him, "Daniel sit down!"

He looked at her for a second, then he sat back down.

"This is nothing that needs to be fixed, Daniel. I made my choice."

"But we were going to get married. We set a date."

"Daniel, you were never going to marry me!"

"You're wrong Kary"

"No I'm not Daniel. You know I'm not"

"You're wrong Kary. 100 percent wrong! Our deal was after I got my commission, we'd get married."

"And then what! There was always going to be something to be done that would come between us. With Charley, I'm it. Daniel, why couldn't you have just gone with me to Las Vegas and done it when you were here? There were plenty of times, you could have just gone up and said to me, Let's do it right now, let's get married and I would have. I didn't need a big wedding. I needed a husband. He didn't need to be an officer to have my respect and love. He needed to make a home for me. Charley stepped up and said, "let's do it" and I have. I am sorry that it hurts you, but".

She looked at him and saw that there were tears forming in the corner of his eyes.

"Daniel, I will always love you. You were my first love and first loves never die. But I'm married now and I have to give it a chance to work. Please let me do that."

He looked at her with tears filling his eyes and running down his cheek, "Okay Kary. I will." He got up with her to leave and she gave him a hug. He smelled her hair and held her tight. He kissed her forehead and whispered to her, "Have a happy life, Kary. I will always love you". Then he separated from her and walked back to his car. He was numb on the ride back to the Tarawa. He knew that a part of him had died that day. As he crossed the bridge into Coronado, he knew that he was forever changed.

The memory of that day was so powerful that even now he felt unsteady and was afraid to restart the car. He breathed deep to calm himself down. It took a long time. Then his eyes filled with tears and he wiped at his eyes with the back of his hand. He lowered the window of his car and took a deep breath of fresh air. He shook his head and told himself that he had to get over this. Only, he didn't know quite how. He felt totally lost. Finally, he shook himself out of his mood. Daniel put the car into gear and drove south to Imperial

Beach. He stopped by the apartment complex that he had visited Kary in four months earlier. He got out of the car and walked around. But he felt so empty that he just didn't know what to do. Finally, he drove back to Coronado and to the base, where he spent the rest of the day feeling sorry for himself.

CHAPTER TWENTY-TWO

The next morning, after he had eaten breakfast, he walked off the base and across the highway to the beach. He walked a short distance to a building with a fence and barbed wire around it. The sign on the door stated "Naval Special Warfare Group". He walked in and joined 6 other young officers waiting in the vestibule. They also were waiting for the Surface Warfare Officers (SWOS) class to convene and had been assigned temporary duty for this orientation.

The men were given entrance to a small lounge with a coffee machine and some vending machines. Some of the men bought coffee. Some of them milled around and smoked. Daniel chewed on his pipe and then bought a coffee from the machine. It was awful, but he drank it anyway to pass the time.

A Chief Petty Officer stuck his head in the door and told the officers to gather themselves up and follow him. They came together in a small briefing room. The room had a long dais like table, a movie screen and a table with a slide projector set up.

He introduced himself as Chief McIntyre and he was to be our instructor for this orientation on naval intelligence. He described further that the purpose was to familiarize the officers with intelligence systems and to help raise awareness so that they would not be the cause of an inadvertent security breech.

He dimmed the lights and the young men settled into their seats. The first slide was flashed onto the screen. The Chief said to the men,

"I want you to look carefully at this picture. Describe for me what you see. All right, the first officer on the left, describe what you see".

The first ensign stood up and looked at the screen for a short time. Finally he said, "I see a grassy meadow in what appears to be a valley of some kind."

The Chief asked,

"Do you see anything else?"

"No"

The Chief asked the next officer and got a similar response. Then he asked the next and the next and the next until all but Daniel had responded. All saw the same thing, a grassy meadow. Throughout this process Daniel felt an excitement rising inside him. He saw what was really there from the first moment the slide had been flashed onto the screen. He resisted the impulse to burst out with what so obvious to him. He was dumbfounded that his colleagues could not see what he clearly could discern. He knew that he was looking at a camouflage cover and he could clearly see the outline of an F-4 airplane beneath the camouflage blanket.

So when the Chief asked Daniel what he saw, he answered unequivocally. Chief McIntyre did not say anything at first. Then he said to Daniel,

"Sir, are you sure?"

"Yes Chief, I am certain."

"Show me!"

"Okay"

Daniel got up and walked to the screen. He lifted his hand and pointed to the edge of the camouflage cover. While he was standing there, the Chief flipped to the next slide, which showed an F-4, exposed, exactly where Daniel had said it was.

The Chief showed another slide and again no one could identify it but Daniel. Then he showed another slide, and then another. The results were still the same. In all, the Chief showed 20 slides and of the entire officer's group in the room, only Daniel was able to identify every picture.

At the end of the slide session, the Chief sent the men to the lounge for a break. The men all talked about the slides and asked Daniel how he deduced what was going on in each picture. Daniel shook his shoulders and told them that he didn't know how he knew, he just knew.

One of his fellow officers joked that he wished he had that gift.

Daniel got up and bought a cup of coffee from the machine. He fished out his pipe and lit it. He puffed gently and looked out the windows. He felt a hand on his shoulders and was directed to the door where Chief McIntyre was motioning to him.

"Mr. Kaplan, can I speak with you for a moment?"

"Sure Chief, is something wrong?"

"No, No, nothing's wrong. I'd just like you to follow me, the skipper would like to talk to you for a moment"

"Okay", Daniel shrugged and followed the Chief to the administrative offices. He was escorted into an office and told to sit down. Shortly thereafter, two senior officers joined him. They were Vice Admiral Ralph Press and his chief of staff, Captain Horace Impelizzeri. Daniel started to stand up but was motioned to stay seated. Admiral Press sat down behind the desk and Captain Impelizzeri sat in the chair alongside Daniel. Admiral Press looked at Daniel and smiled. Then he said to him,

"Young man, I'm told that you have some kind of talent there"

Daniel looked at the Admiral, then the Captain. He knew that from that moment, his life was about to change.

CHAPTER TWENTY-THREE

*O*ver the next few hours Daniel was barraged with pictures to analyze. Then he was tested on his knowledge of geography, history and world politics. So much information was being extracted from him that he started to make jokes to lighten the atmosphere.

Then he started to tell jokes in a mimicked Irish Brogue. Everyone laughed. Then he mimicked in a high English accent, then a cockney accent. Finally, he evolved into an Indian/Pakistani accent. They continued to laugh, but unbeknownst to him he had really gotten their attention. Soon the Captain was brought into the room and Daniel was told to do every accent he thought that he could do. He did a Russian, a Chinese, an Israeli, a Greek, an Italian, a German and a lot more. He had always had a gift for mimicry and now he was showing his talents. Everyone was laughing heartily at his jokes and writing down copious notes. Daniel thoroughly enjoyed this portion of the session.

This testing of Daniel went on for the rest of the day. He met with a psychologist and was administered a written test to test his mental state. He kept asking his testers when he was going back to the orientation, but they only smirked at him. He knew that he was being tested for a reason and his mind was going wild with what they might want with him.

Around 7:00 P.M. they finished with him and Chief McIntyre told him to come back in the morning. He told the Chief that he had to talk to SWOS to see if he could return. The Chief looked at him and said,

"Sir, I wouldn't worry about that. They've already been asked if we could keep you for the next few days. Your C.O. (Commanding Officer) already authorized your T.A.D. (Temporary Assigned Duty)."

"Really?", Daniel said, sort of surprised, "Chief, What's going on here with me?"

"Mr. Kaplan, what do you think?"

"I think you guys have some interest in me"

"I'd say you're probably right. But I don't know all the details."

"Well, I'll see you in the morning, I guess."

"Yes sir, See you in the morning."

The next day, he reported back and spent the morning going through more testing. First he was given an I.Q. test and then more psychological testing to assess his ability to think quickly and abstractly. By the end of the morning, Daniel's head was totally spinning. He was very, very tired and somewhat perplexed.

Daniel was told to get some lunch and come back afterwards. He walked over to the club, ate lunch, then stopped back at the barracks to pick up his mail and use the bathroom. He thumbed through the mail and saw nothing special. He flipped on the television and watched a few minutes of the noontime news. Finally, he shut down the tube and gathered himself up. He crossed the highway again and walked into the office. Chief McIntyre greeted him and escorted him down the hall to Admiral Press' office. He sat down in a chair and waited patiently.

Ralph Press was a pragmatic man. He had served in the Navy for over 30 years. However, for most of those years he was a CIA operative. As he grew tired of covert operations, he moved himself back into the Navy environment. He had trained many field operatives and had managed many of them during their covert operations. Press had always been struck with the poor quality of these field operatives and the incumbent problems they caused. Most of these operatives were either psychologically unstable or they had no real loyalty towards their mission, only loyalty to their advancements. Information leaks were common and the lack of realistic and timely information was constantly hurting operations and missions.

Throughout this all, Ralph continued to keep a look out for a particularly suitable type of young man or woman. They needed to fit the bill for unique and dangerous assignments. These persons needed to have the moxie and discipline to pull off the impossible and make it look ordinary and simple.

Admiral Press and Captain Impelizzeri came in. They waved Daniel to stay seated and sat themselves down. The Admiral looked at Daniel over his half moon reading glasses. He took a deep breath and made a tent with his fingers. He looked closely at the young Ensign sitting in front of him. Across the desk from him sat a man that he believed fit his bill. He tried to decide what his approach to this young man might be. An idea came into his head. He toyed with it for a moment then shook it off because he couldn't quite crystallize it in his brain.

The young man he had sitting in front of him had talents rarely seen. He was smart, confident, well spoken and what was truly important, he looked extraordinarily ordinary. He was a regular Joe who could mimic accents with ease. Daniel could remember little details that he had seen for only a second. These were powerful tools for someone. Especially, if that person was willing to participate in what Admiral Press and Captain Impelizzeri had in mind. They knew that a person like Daniel Kaplan came around so rarely that that person had to be cultivated very carefully, once they were identified.

Obviously, they could use their ranks and order him into covert operations. They could, but it would be counterproductive. For Daniel Kaplan to reach his full potential, they would have to convince him to join them voluntarily. Also they knew that if he accepted, rank would not matter any more, except for using it to perpetrate his mission. He would have to tell off many high-ranking persons and in some cases, disobey their orders outright.

Admiral Press had some advantages, however, in trying to convince Daniel to join them.

He had briefly eyed the intelligence report that had been hastily assembled about Ensign Kaplan. Something had caught his attention during his first perusal. He had made a few phone calls and had gotten some more information about it. Now, he shuffled the report across his desk and eyed it again. He picked up the summary, leaned back in his chair and appeared to be carefully studying the sheet. Captain Impelizzeri smiled weakly at Daniel, then at Admiral Press. The report detailed a man who had just had a devastating breakup with his fiancée. So Press knew that he was free to join them with no family encumbrances to interfere with operations he had in mind for Daniel.

He also saw that Daniel was Jewish. However, he came from a family that was not religious. In college, he had done the drug thing and stopped doing it by choice. He had pushed himself back to college, creating a very rigorous timetable for completion and he had succeeded with excellent grades and results. People who knew him described him as alternately very charming and very distant. He could hold an audience with a clever story or joke and he thought well on his feet when faced with a difficult situation. He never seemed to get disturbed or excited even when he was angry. Few people could ever remember him raising his voice.

The psychological profile presented a picture of him that was also very interesting. Driven, hyperactive and dynamic, he didn't trust anyone, but he never let anyone know that. He never discounted enemies, always assuming they might harm him if he let his guard down. However, he was not paranoid, only careful. He was very loyal to those he had a real affinity for and had only two known true friends. All of these tests confirmed to Admiral Press and Captain Impelizzeri what they all already suspected.

Daniel Kaplan had what they were looking for. Sitting in front of them was the Perfect Potential Intelligence Operative!! In other words – Spy Material.

CHAPTER TWENTY-FOUR

dmiral Press cleared his throat. He took off his glasses and looked at Captain Impelizzeri.

"Hank, what do you think?"

He looked back at Ralph Press and smiled.

"Ralph, I think Ensign Kaplan can be a home run for us."

Daniel looked at him quizzically, then at the Admiral,

"Excuse me sirs, but what are you talking about?"

Captain Impelizzeri looked him in the eyes and said,

"Young man, we are talking about you!"

"What about me?!", Daniel exclaimed.

Admiral Press interrupted.

"Daniel, tell me something. Did you always want to be a Surface Officer? "Well I, ugh"

"Daniel, let's be honest with each other. You didn't start out to be a Surface Officer. In fact, you don't want to be a Surface Officer at all. Am I right?"

Daniel just looked at him.

"Well Daniel? I can't blame you if you didn't. Personally, I always found ship duty boring and routine."

He shuffled through some papers on his desk. He found what he was looking for and held it up to read it.

"Dan, can I call you Dan?"

"I prefer Daniel but I'm not adamant about it."

"All right. Well Daniel, it says here that you originally requested assignment in aviation. Is that true?"

"Yes sir, I originally wanted to be a Naval Flight Officer."

"Why not a pilot."

"Without my contacts, I'm blind as a bat."

"So what made you change your mind?"

"Well sir, I was engaged to a young lady. Eh, ugh", he cleared his throat then continued,

"She was a corpswoman. I started dating her when I was enlisted. We fell in love and she asked for orders that allowed her to follow me to Camp Lejeune. When she was transferred to San Diego, I realized that I would have to be stationed in Pensacola for at least a year and a half and there was no way we could be married. So I changed my career path to surface warfare."

Admiral Press looked at him for a second and commented,

"And it did you a lot of good!"

Daniel looked at him quizzically,

"I beg your pardon?"

"You don't have to beg my pardon Ensign. I said it did you a whole lot of good. You did hear me Ensign? Didn't you? "

He leaned back in his chair and looked at Daniel for a moment. Then he leaned forward across his desk and said quietly,

"Listen, we know all about your relationship with Karolyn German"

"You do?"

"Yes and what we know what she did to you."

Daniel sat there in stunned silence. Admiral Press waited for the impact of his words to sink in before he continued,

"Let me tell you that my heart goes out to you, it must have been a terrible shock."

"Sir, if you don't mind . . ."

"Listen Danny boy, she did a really shitty thing to you. No matter how you cut it, it stinks. You may not like me saying that so bluntly to you, but I don't give a shit. She did you wrong son. And even if you don't think I know shit about what happened. . . well let me break some news to you, over the past two days, we've compiled a preliminary dossier on you that's already three inches thick and when we are done it will be a lot thicker. I know you've been trying to show a brave front to everyone, but get it son, whatever you think you could have done differently, she did you a big favor."

Daniel had turned all red in the face.

"Well sir, I made a lot of mistakes. . ."

Admiral Press roared at him from across the desk,

"Bullshit Ensign and don't bullshit yourself. She crapped all over you guy. Can't you see that? She could have called you, sent you a letter, a telegram, something. Instead, she ran off and married some old fool while she was still wearing your engagement ring. So don't fool yourself, your too smart for that. And don't blame yourself. It's a shitty thing to do and your too bright for that kind of thinking anyway. Son, you didn't deserve it, not one bit . . . the treatment you got from her.

Daniel exploded out of his chair and leaned across the desk and put his face right up to the Admiral's.

"Who the hell do you think you are saying that to me? What the hell do you know about what I am feeling or about the way we were? You have no right to talk to me this way. You think those stars make you so smart. Well let me tell you, Sir, you can take those stars and shove them right up your ass!"

Ralph Press stared right into Daniel's eyes. Daniel held that stare and made that unspoken challenge to Press to blink first. Finally, he looked away from Daniel and smiled. He shot a look at Captain Impelizzeri.

"Well Hank, what do you think now? I'm convinced. He's got the balls."

"Ralph, I think you may be right." he smiled back at Press, "He definitely has them. You can calm down Daniel. Let me explain what we have in mind for you."

Daniel sat back down but scowled. Impelizzeri continued.

"We believe, Ensign Kaplan, that you have a special talent."

"What do you mean by special talent?" Daniel barked back at him.

"Daniel, you made a very big impression on Chief McIntyre and he, ugh, doesn't impress easily. And you made a big impression upon me when I watched you analyze the reconnaissance photos. I was further impressed with the way you handled all of this testing. And most of all, you made us all laugh hysterically with your voices. That's a real talent and it made me sit up and take notice."

"All right, all right", Daniel said impatiently, "So sir, what does all this mean?"

Admiral Press leaned across his desk and spoke almost in a whisper.

"We think you may have a real talent for intelligence, Mr. Kaplan. But not just intelligence; special intelligence, covert intelligence. Call it what you will. And we'd like to invite you to join us at it."

"You mean here at Special Warfare Group?"

"Hell no son!, not here. Listen, this is just a base of operations for us."

"You mean. . .?"

"No. The Group really exists. We're just based out of here for convenience. You know, you have remarkable talents and we think you could be a tremendous asset to your government."

"Huh?, you've got to be kidding?"

Admiral Press looked Ensign Kaplan right in the eye. He leaned forward on the desk and pointed his finger right at Daniel.

"Do I look like I'm kidding? No son, we are not kidding! I am as serious as a heart attack. I don't think I've ever been so serious before."

Daniel turned deep red. He took a deep breath.

"But why are you asking me? You could just direct me to work for you?"

"Yes, I could". Then he leaned back in his chair and picked up a pencil. He started twirling it between his fingers. It fell out of his hands and embarrassed, he put it down on the desk. "Yes Daniel, I could order you, but what would be the point. A person like you couldn't be directed anyway. That's what we like about you. You work on your own. You trust only you. Listen, we are not looking for you to be one of our staff analysts. I don't believe that you are the type of person who could spend his days looking at photographs and writing reports. It's just not you. You are a doer. That's what we're looking for. A doer! So what we want for you is to be an operative."

Daniel thought to himself, "An operative? In what did he say? Covert Operations?" He took a deep breath and looked at the Admiral in amazement. Then he thought. "This is either some kind of a sick joke or the Admiral is out of his fucking mind?"

Daniel looked back at him incredulously. Then he looked at Impelizzeri, who appeared to be the more sober of the two of them. He asked the Captain,

"And you agree with his (pointing to the Admiral) assessment?"

"Absolutely"

"Really!" Daniel exclaimed. He looked down at his lap for a moment. His mind was racing and he needed to get some control over all of the myriad thoughts that were racing through him. Then he looked up and peered over to the Admiral and asked,

"Under whose authority are you making this offer?"

Ralph shot a surprised look at Hank Impelizzeri. The Captain leaned over to Daniel and said, "Mr. Kaplan, these uniforms are just for convenience. We are not U.S. Navy. Well, that's not really true. We are U.S. Navy, but only because it provides us with a perfect...," He laughed gently, "All right, imperfect cover." He shrugged and the Admiral nodded his head in agreement.

Daniel looked at him carefully. He looked at the eagles on Impelizzeri's collars and the three stars hanging on Press' shirt. He shook his head.

"If you are not really U.S. Navy, then who the hell are you?"

Admiral Press broke out into a broad smile. He leaned back in his chair and made a tent of his hands and placed them on his stomach. He looked up at the ceiling and chuckled. Then he stretched his arms up and put them behind his head.

"Daniel"

Daniel interrupted him,

"Sir, are you Naval intelligence?"

Ralph Press smiled and shook his head no.

"NIS (Naval Investigative Service)"

"No"

"Defense Intelligence?"

Press shook his head no again.

"Well gentlemen, what? Under whose authority do you make this offer?"

They both laughed for a second. Press looked at his Chief of Staff and said,

"You want to tell him or me?"

Impelizzeri pointed at the Admiral. He laughed again and leaned back in his chair.

"All right young man, you want to know who has given us the Authority to make this kind of offer?"

Daniel shook his head yes.

"I'm impressed with you, Daniel. No one has ever asked me at the very beginning under whose authority, I make this kind of offer. I guess they just assume that with three stars on my collar, I have the authority myself."

Daniel smiled, "Even I know that you must be acting under someone's authority. It would be inconceivable that you would go to all this trouble on your own."

"Really?" Press asked, "Why would you say that?"

"I'm an Ensign. And a very green one at that. You've invested a lot of time and effort in me over the past few days. Why would a three star Admiral be so intimately involved in trying to recruit me into something, when as I said before, you could just direct me to do your bidding. So it seems to me that I am asking you a fair question, sir. Under whose authority are you making this offer?

Admiral Press shook his head approvingly of what he had just been told by Daniel. He told Daniel that he had surmised correctly.

"To answer your question, Daniel. The Director of Central Intelligence"

Daniel didn't believe them

"You guys must be shitting me. In fact gentlemen," he said as he started to get up to leave, "I've listened to my share of bullshit in my life, but this takes the cake! CIA, what nonsense."

Everybody looked at each other. Daniel suddenly got embarrassed and started to apologize, but Admiral Press stopped him.

"Daniel, I'm afraid we're not shitting you. This is very real and we want you to work with us."

Daniel sat back down in his chair,

"With all due respect sir, I don't think so." And started to get back up.

"Sit on down, young man, we ain't done yet."

Daniel sat down again, "Son, tell me why you wouldn't do this?"

Daniel looked at him, shook his head and said,

"Admiral, tell me why I should?"

Ralph Press smiled weakly. The moment of truth had arrived. This was always the most difficult part of recruiting. Waving the flag rarely worked. But most people recruited were not asked to do covert operations, nor did any of their candidates seem to have such promise. They couldn't let Daniel Kaplan get away. And Ralph Press had decided that he wouldn't get away. What Ralph Press wanted, he usually got. And this was going to be no different, he assured himself.

Book 1

RABBI KAPLAN

CHAPTER TWENTY-FIVE

aniel climbed up the stairs to the Gerwitz residence with a weary sense of unease. He had barely walked in the door when Rebecca had sent him out again to see her father. He had told her that he would go later, but she insisted that he go immediately. So he drove over to the Gerwitz Shul and walked in.

Rather than go up immediately, he walked into the Sanctuary. He looked around at the fixtures, which were all too familiar to him. He leaned on the reading table and walked up to the ark and kissed the curtain in front of it. Then he sighed to himself and walked to the back of the building and up the stairs to the Gerwitz' apartment. He knocked on the door. Rabbi Gerwitz opened the door and let him in.

"Daniel, come in. Its good to see you." He clapped Daniel on his shoulder, "You're looking good. A little tired maybe, but good. Sit down, I have something very important to talk with you about. Sit!" He pulled a chair away from the table and beckoned Daniel to sit down in it.

Daniel sat down and turned towards the older man. Rabbi Gerwitz sat down across from him and hunched over the table as if he was going to tell a secret to Daniel. He folded his hand together and kept rubbing them together like he washing his hands. He cleared his throat. Then took off his glasses and put them on the table. Finally Daniel said to him,

"Dad, what's the problem? You're fidgeting like a little boy on his first day of school."

Rabbi Gerwitz laughed sheepishly. He put on his glasses and said to Daniel, "Rebeccale was here a little while ago."

"Becky was here. I didn't know that."

"I know. She was very upset."

"What did she tell you?"

"Everything"

Daniel looked down for a moment. Then he looked up at the older man and said quietly, "She could not have told you everything because she does not know the whole story."

"And what is the whole story?"

"Even I don't know the whole story"

"Rebecca said you were visited by a man yesterday, a priest. I think she said he was Episcopalian"

"Yes"

"She also said that this man, this priest is your son. Is that right Daniel?"

Daniel sighed out loud, "I am afraid that is so."

"Daniel, how can that be?"

"Obviously, Rebecca only told you part of the story that she knew."

"No, she told me about Karolyn German. I think that was the name she used for this young lady of your youth."

Daniel nodded yes. Rabbi Gerwitz continued, "Rebecca told me today what she has known for years, that you were engaged to this girl and she married someone else. Tell me Daniel, this girl wasn't Jewish?"

Daniel frowned for a moment. "No, she wasn't. She was Episcopalian."

"And you loved her?"

"Very much"

"And you would have married her?"

"I was engaged to her!"

"So what. Would you have married her?"

"She didn't think so. That's why she married someone else."

"Daniel, I'm not asking what she thought. I am asking you what you would have done?"

"At the time, I was sure I would have married her. Now after all these years, Rebecca and the kids, my life has changed so much, I wonder. I suppose the only one who could answer that is the Master of the Universe. I'll tell you a story. About five years after Rebecca and I were married, I was sitting in my office thinking about Karolyn. I remembered her birthday. Out of curiosity, I took out my Hebrew Calendar and checked her date of birth. It seems that she was born on the 9th off Av (the date of the destruction of the two Temples in Jerusalem, a day of mourning in the Jewish world). I found it so strange. I supposed that the Master of the Universe was telling me to finally put this to bed forever. And so I did. I concentrated on my wife and my family and my life as a Rabbi. And I forgot about Karolyn German. In time, I would just have some pleasant thoughts about her occasionally."

"And now what do you think?"

"I think I would have married her."

"You do?" Rabbi Gerwitz looked at him surprised, "Why do you say that?

"I can't say"

"Why not?

"Because I can't"

"Might I suppose it is because you are still in love with her after all these years?" Rabbi Gerwitz leaned back in his chair and played with his beard while Daniel pondered the question.

"No"

"Really! I would have guessed differently Daniel. I venture to say that you are still in love with her even now!"

Daniel looked up at him, "That's ridiculous, sir. Utterly ridiculous!"

"You think so?"

"I love your daughter like I have loved no other woman. I've built a life with her and have gone through good times and difficult times with her. We have a family together and she is my confidante and my best friend. That is why I say it is ridiculous."

"If that be the truth, Daniel, then I believe that it would be safe to say that you will not engage in any further contact with this young priest or his mother!"

Daniel almost choked when he heard those words come out of his father-in-laws mouth. It caught him very surprised.

"Well Daniel? Certainly you must agree that any additional contact cannot happen. Do you realize what a revelation like this would do to your standing in this community? For that matter, how could Rebecca, the woman you say you love like you have loved no other woman, show her face around here. How could she walk around this neighborhood after it was revealed that her husband had a child with a gentile woman over 20 years ago? And Daniel, what about your children? Do I need to go there? What about Sarila, she's almost a woman. How will you find her a match with the taint of this kind of scandal upon her."

Daniel sat in his chair, but said nothing. His eyes filled with tears, yet he still said nothing.

"Well? You sit there saying nothing. Certainly, you must have something to say? Answer me Daniel. You must cut off any further contact. That is obvious. It is obvious?"

Daniel looked down at the floor. He took off his glasses and wiped his eyes.

"Dad, twenty-four hours ago, I was just another Rabbi with a shul in Brooklyn. My life was simple and orderly. My biggest concern was helping people with their problems and writing my weekly sermon. A few hours ago, I learn that I have another son who was unknown to me for twenty-five years. And you say to me, cut off all contact, right here, right now!"

"That's right Daniel! You have too much to lose."

Daniel looked up at Rabbi Gerwitz. He stared into his eyes.

Daniel shook his head,

"I just don't know. I just don't know."

Rabbi Gerwitz spoke to him in a gentle but forceful way,

"Sure you do. You know what has to be done here, Daniel. These people are of no consequence to you and who you are in this community, your family."

Daniel looked up at the older Rabbi. Then in a near whisper, almost pleadingly he said,

"But he's my son. How. . .?"

Rabbi Gerwitz stood up from his chair with a fury that Daniel had never seen before. He turned almost purple before yelling out,

"No he's not! Daniel Kaplan, he is not your son. He is the result of a sordid affair that ended a quarter century ago. No! He is not your son. You are nothing like him and you have nothing in common with him. He is a Christian priest and you are an Orthodox Rabbi."

"But he _is_ my son. He is my flesh and blood."

Rabbi Gerwitz went near apoplectic, "He is not your son. He is the bastard child of an unwedded gentile."

Daniel exploded out of his chair, "Fuck you, old man!" not realizing that language he had not used in almost twenty years had escaped his lips. He stood eye to eye with the old Rabbi. The two glared at each other.

"I demand", the Rabbi Gerwitz yelled at him," that you give Rebecca a Get (Jewish Divorce) right now. Do you hear me? You give her a Get right now. I'll get a scribe up here immediately. You give her a Get . . . Now! You bastard! You give her a Get. I demand it of you."

Daniel started to move to the door, but the old man blocked his way.

"You are not walking out of here until you have prepared a Get."

"If Rebecca wants me to give her a Get, <u>she</u> can ask me. <u>You</u> can not demand me to give her one unless it is what Rebecca wants."

"Rebecca wants", the old man ranted at him, "Oh yes, and Rebecca wants!"

"Then", he said pushing the Rabbi away from the door, "She can ask me herself. I'll be home in ten minutes." Then he stepped through the door and went down the stairs and out into the driveway. Rabbi Gerwitz' assistant, Moishe Klosterman, a rumpled old Jew with a battered fedora, came running after him.

"Rabbi Kaplan, Rabbi Kaplan."

Daniel had walked out onto the sidewalk and was getting into his car when the assistant finally reached him.

"Rabbi Kaplan, is everything all right. I heard you yelling upstairs. What language Rabbi. I never expected to hear such language."

"Reb Moishe, I can't explain it to you now. I am sorry you heard me yell. But it is a difficult time for everyone. Please try to keep what you heard amongst us."

The assistant nodded and shrugged his shoulders. A burst of wind blew his hat from his head and he went chasing it down the street. For some arcane reason, Daniel thought it funny. He laughed for a moment and got into his car.

CHAPTER TWENTY SIX

Rebecca could not listen any longer. Her father was ranting on the phone about the bum she was married to, his filthy mouth and on and on and on. But when she heard him screaming at her to insist that Daniel give her a Get, she hung up the phone and took the receiver off the hook. She took a deep breath, walked into the dining room and brought out a bottle of brandy from her breakfront. She took out two shot glasses and put them on a tray with the bottle. She carried them over to the table, sat down and waited. She knew that it had been many years since Daniel had exploded and if he had told someone off as he had told off her father, than he must have been at the end of his rope. She wondered if he would come home immediately or whether he would wander off for a few hours to cool down. While she waited her mind went back to the first moments of their life together. She thought back to when Daniel was a Chaplain in the Navy.

She remembered looking down from the window as he pulled his bags from the car that first weekend when he came to Knesset Rambam to try out as their Rabbi. She really couldn't see his face as the visor of his hat shadowed his features. She had gone down to the door to let him in and she saw in her mind's eye that first smile. He had turned red and tried to overcome it. He dropped his hang up bag and fussed as he went to pick it up.

Later she remembered sitting at the dinner table watching him with feigned disinterest, but realizing that he couldn't stop looking at her. Her father had invited for the Shabbos meal that Gershom Weiss, who was more interested in her father than with her. She understood to herself that she needed to know more about this man from San Diego sitting across from her. And she needed to know before he returned to California on Monday.

When the Shabbos dinner was over, Rabbi Weiss left and Daniel surprised her by helping to clear the table with her. Her father chided him and told him to let the women finish their work, but he helped her finish the table and then joined her father. She looked out of the kitchen into the dining room. The two men appeared to be deep in conversation.

She could tell that he was very shy, but he looked her in the eye when he spoke to her and that was different from all the other men that she knew who for modesty sake looked through or away from her.

That night she awoke about two o'clock in the morning. She lay in bed and heard some noise in the kitchen. She got out of bed and looked in on her parents, but they were sleeping. She walked down the steps gingerly and saw Daniel sitting in his robe at the dining room table. He was sipping coffee from a cup and was reading quietly. She went back to her room and slipped back into bed, but soon curiosity got the better of her and she put on her robe and went downstairs.

"Couldn't sleep?', she said, startling him. He spilled coffee all over himself.

She laughed and then covered her mouth in embarrassment. He looked at her and laughed also. She came down to help him.

"Here, let me find you some napkins to clean this up."

"No. no, I'll do it. Just show me where they are."

"Its all right", she giggled, "I'll get them for you", and she helped him clean up the table. She then prepared him another coffee as well as one for herself. She sat down across from him and started to ask him about himself. She saw that soon his shyness had lifted and they talked began to talk. He found that she was a modern thinker although she lived in a rigidly Orthodox home. He talked to her about the Navy and his life. He felt comfortable confiding in her and he opened up about who he was. She let him talk and they were still sitting downstairs when the sun started to rise. They were still talking when her mother coming down to prepare breakfast interrupted them. It was then that they realized that they had not slept very much. But it didn't matter to either of them.

That morning, she walked over to Knesset Rambam and heard him speak to the congregation. She sat there amazed as he spoke powerfully and confidently. She saw that the congregation really liked what he had to say

And she was very proud of him. As he left the synagogue after services, she surprised him by being there. She told him that she had gone to listen to him and that he had been great. They walked to the Gerwitz Shul together talking and laughing.

After Shabbos lunch, he took a nap. When he woke up, he decided to take a walk. He said to everyone quite loudly that he was going to the old bridal path by Kings Highway. About a half hour later, as he sat on a bench, Rebecca surprised him. They spent the rest of the afternoon together talking and walking.

By the time he left to go back to San Diego, she had his address and office telephone number.

She called him almost every day and wrote him almost as often. To her amazement, he wrote her back just as often. Each letter was not very long, they were just these half page notes with stories about the men he worked with and other sundry stuff. He wrote almost every day. Some days she would receive mail from him in bunches. It was obvious that he would write a letter and forget to mail it immediately. So, he would mail them together.

That October, he got two letters of importance on the same day. The first letter was from Knesset Rambam. It offered him the position of Rabbi, when his active duty term was up in February. The second letter was from Rebecca. She said in the letter that she would be in Los Angeles during the Thanksgiving weekend for a convention. She hoped that he would be able to visit her then. She also wrote that if the answer was yes and he could see her in L.A then he was not to answer him in writing in his letter. She suspected that her father sometimes read her mail and he had already commented on the volume of mail from a certain Rabbi Kaplan. She told him to answer yes by saying that the coffee was better in L.A. or if he couldn't see her to answer that the tea was better in L.A. He laughed at that when he saw it, but when he answered her he told her the coffee was better. It really wasn't necessary however; because when she called him that day, he told her he couldn't wait to see her.

He answered Knesset Rambam that he would accept the position of Rabbi. He was delighted that he could come back to Brooklyn and lead a congregation there.

October soon became November and Rabbi Kaplan went about his duties as the Jewish Chaplain in the San Diego Naval District. He worked with homesick Marines in Boot Camp and with sailors and their families enduring the long separations. He continued his close contact with Rebecca Gerwitz in Brooklyn and looked forward to Thanksgiving weekend when he would drive up to Los Angeles to see her again. So it came as a total surprise when he walked into his office on the Monday morning before Thanksgiving and was told by the clerk that there was a young lady waiting for him in his office. As he stepped inside, he saw Rebecca sitting behind his desk, rearranging his things. She looked up when he entered the office and smiled.

"Doing a little housekeeping for me, eh?"

She winked at him, "Well its about time someone did."

"That's why I leave it like that. It gives my visitors what to do when they're alone in my office"

She laughed and came around from behind the desk. They looked at each other for a second. Then for the first time, they actually hugged. She held him tightly for a long time and he leaned his cheek onto the top of her head and smelled her hair. She stepped back after a time.

"Let me look at you", he said as she pretend curtseyed to him and spun herself around. She was dressed in a long denim skirt and a yellow T-shirt with flowers stitched upon the front. A small gold necklace hung from her neck. It had a pendant with her name written out on it in Hebrew. She was a contrast from when he had met her in Brooklyn. She had been more formally dressed and more formal in her manner. But here, in his office, she was relaxed and lighthearted and lovely. Her hair, both literally and figuratively were down for him and he liked what he saw, very much.

"What are you doing here?" he asked her. "I didn't expect to see you until Thursday."

"I came in early. I got in last night, supposedly to help with the convention. But instead, I rented a car yesterday. I got up early this morning and drove down here to surprise you. Now, I know you have to work, so don't worry, I'll go exploring around town until you are off work." Then she winked at him again and said, "Then you're mine!" and giggled her way out of his office as he shook his head and then followed her out to the parking lot. He helped her into her car and gave her directions of places to visit. He told her to return at 4:00 P.M.

She swept into his office at 4:00 with a breathlessness he had never seen in her before. She placed a basket on his desk and and with two more grocery bags full of Kosher food, she told him she wanted to picnic by the beach. He reminded her that soon the sun would be down.

"So what are our alternatives, Captain?"

"That's Commander to you. Actually you can throw a Lieutenant behind that Commander and you'll get the right idea."

She laughed, "Ridiculous", then with a sweeping bow she curtseyed to him, "So, Commander' she said stretching the word commander out, "Where's a young girl like me going to eat? Do you know of a decent establishment in which we can enjoy these victuals?"

Daniel could hardly keep a straight face. The two of them burst out laughing. He shrugged. Finally, she said to him. "Surely, you don't sleep in your office?

"What?

"Well, I assume you live somewhere around here?"

"As a matter of fact, young lady, I do!"

"Well, the food is getting cold and the wine is getting warm. I'll follow your car and let's get going."

He shrugged his shoulders again and helped her bring the food out to her car. She drove him to where he was parked and then followed his car out the gate and over the bridge to Coronado.

They pulled up to a small building and parked their cars. He helped her upstairs to his apartment. She walked in and looked around. It was small but cozy. He had a one bedroom with a terrace that looked out onto the street, but from which you could see the beach. It had a small kitchen and a small dinette area with a table littered with newspapers and mail. He had a small bureau on the living room in which had two pipe racks and a humidor. She walked into the kitchen and looked through the cabinets. On one side of the cabinet there was a little sign that said meat. The other side said milk. She saw that he had two services for four of inexpensive china and two separate services of four of silverware. As she emptied the food onto the table, she suddenly felt terribly sad for him. She opened the refrigerator to put the wine inside and what she saw was a typical bachelors cold keepings, three cans of beer, a package of salami and a half loaf of bread. Then she looked into his freezer. It was there that she was amazed. She saw that he had methodically stacked metal tins with food that had been frozen and dated. She would later learn that Daniel was a gourmet cook who prepared a week's worth of food on Sundays, and stored it in tins so that it could be easily defrosted and cooked.

She dispatched him to the bathroom to take a shower and get freshened up as she took over his kitchen. She found his Sabbath candles and sticks and set them in the middle of the table. She set the table and warmed the food. She looked through his music collection and found some quiet jazz records. She put one of them on for background. When he came out ten minutes later, he was dressed in casual tan pants and a golf shirt. His plain black skullcap had been replaced with a colorful crocheted one and he looked relaxed. She gestured for him to sit and they ate and talked and drank some wine. Finally with a flourish, Daniel asked her to dance. She looked at him with a pained expression. She had never danced one on one with a man before. She only danced with other women during celebrations. He assured her that it was easy and she soon found herself dancing cheek to cheek with him.

They both were enjoying themselves so much that they lost track of time. Daniel looked at his watch and realized that it was almost 10:00 P.M.

"Rebecca, it's very late."

"Daniel, it's okay."

"No its not. It is a two-hour drive to L.A. Come, I'll drive you back and grab the bus back in the morning. I'll say I'm on a field visit."

"It's not necessary. I'll stay in San Diego tonight"

"Rebecca, what about your family?"

"What about them?"

"Won't they be worried, if they call your hotel and you aren't there."

"Daniel, do you know how many conventions, I've gone to. My parents know that I travel around. It is not unusual for me to stay with a girlfriend or even in a motel on one of my side trips."

Daniel sat down on one of the kitchen chairs, "I don't know!"

"Daniel, what's not to know. I am an adult. I know how to handle myself."

"Okay, I guess" He got up and walked over to his magazine rack . He fumbled through it for a moment and finally pulled out the Yellow Pages. He started to thumb through them, when Rebecca asked him,

"What are you doing?"

"I'm looking for a motel for you. I'll pay, don't worry. I'll pick you up in the morning and. . ."

She slowly walked over to him and interrupted him by gently putting her hand on his shoulder. She moved her hand over until she had his chin between her fingers.

"Daniel", tilting his head up to look at her, "Close the Yellow Pages!"

"But"

"Close the Yellow Pages" as she bent down and kissed him lightly on his lips. He looked up at her and returned the kiss. She closed her eyes and kissed him again, this time more firmly. He felt her sit down upon his lap and reach around his neck, but his head was spinning and he wasn't sure quite what to do.

They kissed for a very long time, then she got up and led him to the couch, where they continued to kiss.

"Daniel", she said as she got up finally, "Do you have a T-shirt that I can borrow to sleep in?"

"Sure!" and he retreated to the bedroom and returned with one for her. He also had a pillow and a blanket in his hand.

"Rebecca, I prepared the bed for you. I'll set myself up here on the couch."

"No you won't, this is your house and I'm the one imposing. I'll sleep on the couch."

"No way! It's really not a problem, Becky. I sleep here a lot when I fall asleep reading. Its okay."

"Daniel, I insist. I'm putting you out of your normal routine."

"But . . ."

"No buts. Either I sleep on the couch or I drive back to L.A. right now."

She gave him a look like she meant business. He had no intention of letting her sleep on the couch, however, he wasn't about to let her drive north by herself at this hour. She looked at him and could see his mind working.

"I insist Daniel. I insist. The couch or L.A."

"All right, all right. Drive to L.A."

She smiled broadly as she went to set up her bed on the couch. She kissed him one more time and then shooed him into the bedroom and closed the door behind him.

"Good night!" and then she whispered "Sweet Daniel"

Daniel awoke foggily from his very deep sleep. The clock on the bed stand said 2:07. He looked up and saw Rebecca standing on the side of his bed with her back to him. He saw her lift the T-shirt over her head and drop it to the floor. She turned towards him, lifted the blanket and crawled in. She slid up next to him and slowly pushed up his T-shirt and helped him remove it. They started to kiss softly as she drew his shorts off. They held each other tightly as he ran his hand over her soft full body. He smoothed his hands over her breasts and gently touched between her legs. They learned each other's body but together knew that they would not venture past a point of no return. She rolled over and he brought himself up tight against her body and draped his arm over her and held her breasts in his hand.

"Daniel, I want to know something?"

"Yes?"

"Do you like my body?"

"Rebecca, I love the whole of you"

"But my body, do you like it?"

"You are the most beautiful, most sexy woman, Rebecca dear."

"Good. Daniel, I want you to know that the next time you can have my body is on our wedding night"

"I understand Becky", then he sighed. "I wouldn't have it any other way"

Then he drew her tighter to him, kissed her rounded shoulders and drifted to sleep.

She suddenly awakened realizing that she had been daydreaming. She wondered where Daniel was. She had the answer to that question rather quickly when she heard keys turning in the front door.

Daniel came in and lingered in the front vestibule for a few moments. She could see him putting his coat away and hanging his hat. She heard him sigh, but he didn't call out as was his custom to do.

He rustled through some papers in the front room. Then there was quiet. She smelled pipe tobacco burning and she knew that he was very stressed if he was smoking now. She waited patiently, but he still had not come into the dining room. Finally, she called out to him,

"Daniel!"

Still there was silence. She heard him sit down on a chair.

"Daniel, come in here please!"

Still there was silence. She thought she heard him move, but there was still silence. She got up and looked in the front room. He was sitting on the floor with his feet drawn up to his chin. He was just sitting silently.

"Daniel . . . Get up please" as she reached out to help him get up. He let her help him up and they walked into the dining room. Rebecca poured them both a drink.

"L'Chaim", she said as she took a sip. He just looked at the glass and let his hand surround it. But he did not pick it up to drink from it.

"Have a drink, Daniel, You need it"

He turned and looked at her. Then he shrugged, but he still didn't take a drink.

"I've been to your father"

"I know"

He nodded.

"Well?"

"Well what, Daniel?"

He just looked at her. She knew.

"No Daniel, I do not want a Get"

He nodded again. He picked up the drink and took a long swallow.

"What do I do, Becky?"

This time she was silent. She picked up her glass and took another sip. She reached out and took his hand. She held it up to her eyes and looked at the thin gold band on his ring finger. Always a maverick, he insisted on wearing a wedding band in a community in which it was rare for men to do so.

"The question Daniel, is not what you are going to do?"

He looked at her, "I don't understand!"

"Neither do I, Neither do I, but you are my husband"

"And?"

She looked at him wearily and shrugged, "You are my husband!"

CHAPTER TWENTY-SEVEN

The children were scurrying inside and outside of the kitchen getting their own breakfasts. They rushed along, trying to get ready to get out the door to meet their bus or their train so they could get to school on time. Finally above all the hubbub Rebecca gathered them all up around the dining room table.

"What's up Mom?" David quipped from the end of the table. Rebecca made a face at him and looked at all of her children. She shook her head and then said to them,

"I've called all your schools and told them you will be late today."

"Why Mom?"

"Your father and I have decided to call a family meeting"

"Why?" Rachel asked quietly

"Because there is something that we need to discuss with all of you"

"Mark asked his mother, "What's going on Mom? We've never had a family meeting before. Usually we just discuss things at dinner."

"I know honey, but this is different. Your father will be back from shul soon and will all talk about this then."

Sari said to Mark, "It must be something very serious. I hope that no one is ill." Mark nodded in agreement but said nothing.

An aura of dread descended upon the Kaplan home until Daniel came home from shul. He came in and sat at his place at the dining room table. Rebecca silently slid a cup of coffee and some Danish in front of him. He sipped at the coffee and ate a little of the cake. He looked awful. His eyes were red and his brow was deeply lined. His usual sunny disposition had been replaced with a glassy eyed look. He seemed almost indifferent to his children who were sitting there watching him and waiting.

Rebecca shooed everyone from the room. Daniel looked up and acknowledged what she had done with a quick look. He was thankful that she had done it because it gave him more time to think. Rebecca brought a cup of coffee for herself and sat down next to him.

"Danny, Are you okay?"

He pursed his lips and looked down.

"Dan, it will be alright. These children love you and so do I. Whatever happens remember that. Remember it Danny. We are with you."

He shook his head but said nothing. He stared into space. Rebecca watched him. She thought back to last night. He had stayed downstairs for a very long time. She had heard him come into the bedroom and start to undress. He had taken off his shirt and was sitting in his undershirt and pants at the edge of the bed. He sighed and then sat there for a very long time. She looked up at him and didn't know what to say. She knew it was still too fresh for him and he was still raw with the emotions of having discovered that he had fathered a child so long ago. She also knew that her own reaction had been a shock to him and well her father's conversation with him, ugh, that was an utter disaster. He was shell-shocked. The sadness she felt for him was overwhelming to her. But she couldn't reach out to him. She just couldn't.

Finally, he had taken off his pants and climbed into his bed. He leaned over and quietly kissed her as he always did and said to her, Good night sweetie, I love you." Then he had rolled over as if to sleep.

She had drifted off when she was awakened by his trembling and his tears next to her. He was sitting up rigidly with the blankets around his waist. His hands were covering his eyes and he was weeping quietly. She couldn't look, but then she did. His weeping ran right through her and she didn't know what to do. Was he weeping for his lost love? Or for her? Or for what? It seemed that there was no end to his tears. She lay in bed trying to close her eyes as tightly as possible. It seemed that if she could close her eyes tightly enough, she would not be able to hear his sobbing. Finally, he lay back down with his head on the pillow looking straight at the ceiling. She heard him whimper and saw him shake. She slid across the bed and put her head upon his chest. She could feel the salty tears that had wetted his shirt and could feel his heart beating so fast. He rubbed his hand through her hair and held her close to him.

And now, as she saw him sitting at the table, he would have to do something that was almost impossible for him.

She gathered all of the children in the living room. They sat on the comfortable couches and armchairs that had seen many guests and friends. Daniel pulled out one of the high backed dining room chairs and sat it in the middle of the room so that he could speak to them all.

They looked at him. Rebecca sat down in her armchair and waited with the children. Daniel sat in his white shirt and black pants alone in the middle of the room.

"I've gathered all of you together because I have to tell you some very important news."

Ezra asked, "What news Abba?"

Daniel smiled for a moment, then he continued, "Remember Saturday night we had a guest for dinner?"

They all nodded yes.

"He . . . eh"

"Yes, Abba", David looked up at his father.

"Well, ugh. Listen, the priest who visited us on Saturday, well he had a very interesting thing to tell me."

"What was that?" Mark asked.

"Well son, you see it's like this". He looked to Rebecca for support, but she looked at him with a look that told him that she was also at a loss for words. The children all looked at him. Finally, Sari said gently,

"Abba, just tell us. . . please!"

He looked at her, then at Leah who shook her head yes.

"What about the priest, Abba?"

"You see . . ." then he seemed to steel himself and he began to relate to them,

"My children, as you know, I was not always religious. Many years ago, before I met your mother, I knew a young woman."

"What was her name?" Rachel asked.

"Karolyn"

Sari sat up tall in her seat and interrupted him.

"Abba, . . . Abba?"

"Sari, It's alright, honey. Let me tell you."

Sari shook her head and listened intently along with the others.

"When I was 23 years old, I met a young woman named Karolyn. I met her when I was in the Navy. We fell in love and we decided to get married. So I gave her a ring and we got engaged. Then just before we were supposed to get married, she married someone else."

There was silence in the room for a moment. They all looked at each other in disbelief.

Leah ran up to her father's knee, "Do you mean, Abba, that you almost married someone other than mommy?," she asked him.

Daniel shook his head quietly, "I'm afraid so, sweetheart."

The children all looked at their mother. Rebecca shook her head in acknowledgement.

"It's true children! I've known about this woman since your father and I got together."

"There's something I don't understand", Sari said, as she got up and looked around the room

"And what is that?, Daniel asked her.

"What I don't understand, Abba, is . . . you were engaged, right?"

"Right"

"You loved her?"

"Yes"

"She loved you?"

"I thought so"

"And she married someone else?

Daniel frowned, "I'm afraid so"

"But why?", Sari asked incredulously.

"Well, for a very long time, little lady, I didn't really know"

"And you know now?"

"I think so"

"How?"

"Well it was something that the priest who visited us told me"

"Really!" Mark interrupted, "what did he tell you?"

Daniel took a very deep breath. He looked his oldest boy right in the eye and almost whispered,

"He told me . . .", then he stopped. Tears welled up in his eyes. He looked at Rebecca. She urged him on. He pursed his lips.

"What Abba, what?" cried his son.

Daniel gathered himself together. He stood up from his chair and put his hand on Leah's head. Then he sent her back to sit on the couch. He walked behind the chair and took it's back in his two hands. He bent over it for a moment and then pushed himself back up.

"It's like this my children. Father Daniel, who you met on Saturday night is your brother."

There was a hush in the room. No one except Rebecca and Daniel understood what that meant. Daniel looked at his children and saw their lost looks.

"What?", finally was the response.

Daniel answered right back, "He's your brother"

"How can that be?" Sari almost crying spoke out.

"It can be. . . because Daniel Fiorentino is my son!"

Sari got up, looked fiercely at her father and ran up the stairs. He started to follow her, but Rebecca stopped him and went upstairs herself.

Hours later, when the kids had returned from school, Daniel looked up from his desk in his office in the shul and saw his oldest daughter standing in front of him. She said nothing. He looked up at her. She was already a young woman and there were already many young men who had been proposed as possible husbands for her. Daniel was not so ready to let her marry. Now it probably wouldn't matter.

"Sari"

She stood there, ramrod straight with her books in her arms like a schoolgirl.

"Sarila"

Still nothing.

"You can sit down, if you'd like"

She looked at him stiffly and remained standing. She had an almost regal way of carrying herself. Even dressed in a school uniform with her hair tied back in a ponytail, she exuded the confidence of one much older. Much older!

"I just want you to know, Abba, that I hate you!"

Daniel sighed deeply. He threw down his pen and looked at his daughter. Their eyes met and they held each other's stare. Then she turned around and marched out the door.

CHAPTER TWENTY-EIGHT

Rebecca had been right to take the children away for the weekend. After two days of unbearable strain, she packed up the kids on Thursday morning and took them up to the mountains to the Fallsview Hotel. Daniel initially opposed it, but Rebecca prevailed upon him, explaining that she needed the breathing room and so did the children. Too much had occurred, too quickly for any of them to absorb and they needed as a family to put some distance between them. Reluctantly, Daniel agreed.

Rebecca had offered to set him up for the Sabbath with some friends, but Daniel declined. He would be all right alone. She wasn't so sure, but he reassured her. Nonetheless, she spoke to some friends to keep an eye on him, as she knew that he was very down right now. In fact, she knew that her separating him from his family right in his moment of crisis was devastating to him. But she needed the time away to heal and so did the kids.

Daniel came home to his house Thursday night and ate alone. He read the paper and then went upstairs to sleep. He fell into a very deep sleep. It was a sleep of exhaustion. He dreamed a very disturbing dream. When he awoke, he got up and sat at the edge of his bed. He opened the drawer of his night table and reached for a notebook that he kept there for recording ideas and dreams. Then he wrote down the following story:

PROLOGUE

I died at Dachau in 1943. Never mind that I was born in the 1950s, I know that I died there. Some people may think that I am crazy to believe this. Who knows? I might be! Nevertheless I believe. Now don't get me wrong I can't tell you who I was in that past life, only that I died there, in that gas chamber, unknown and unnamed, as were so many others. Sometimes a person sees things that they know didn't exist in their lifetime. Why they have been chosen to focus in on one of those events is a matter for G-d. For certainly, it is in his work alone that one is chosen to peer into those "special" things through the windows of the mind. They say that you only remember what you alone have experienced for yourself. I wonder!

THE TRAP

Now the room was large. Not overly large, but accommodating to the people gathered up inside of it. The walls were grimy black, soot layered and muddy- looking. There seemed to be a faint smell of cooking meat, which stirred the air. At least I think that was the smell, but I'm not sure. Could be my imagination.

The floor! I remember it most. Yes, the floor. It stood out from everything else in that room. Cement stained blackish brown, streaks emanating from little circles where liquid once pooled before being swept away. Yes, the floor . . .

To the side of the room a door stood large and metal. Next to its handle are two large locking devices, each about a third of the way from their respective corners. The door was closed.

The room grew suddenly quiet. Striding in swiftly was a tall man in an SS uniform. He had the arrogant confidence of a man who holds all within his sight in check, in control. I guessed that he was not older than perhaps 25 or 26, but already his face showed the lines of a man much older, of a man performing duties far beyond his years. His very presence cast a pall among all who were present. Even his own people were seemingly frightened by him. His blond hair was closely cropped under his pointed officer's cap and his jaw was distinctively square and jutting. A broad nose and full wide mouth finished his picture. He removed his black gloves slowly, one finger at a time and looked around the room. He wore his uniform as if he was born to it. He probably felt naked and uncomfortable clothed any other way. But it was in his eyes that bred real terror. Blue diamonds shone with a demonic luminescence that was transparent to his very soul. Those were the objects of his control, the cause of the fear he engendered. Through those eyes bred a terror so profound that it extended far past the inmates he interned and destroyed. It extended on through to his subordinates, his colleagues and even his superiors. It was the terror derived from a madness. And from just looking at him it was apparent that he was in fact, quite mad.

With nary a word spoken and with a dismissing wave of the hand, he signaled the guards around him to begin. They began to shout, to yell, prodding us with their sticks, ordering us out of our clothes. We were told to fold them neatly and place them on the floor in front of us. Each of us was given a dime size piece of soap and a dirty rag, which I presumed to be used as a towel. We were told that we would enter the shower room, shower and then be given clothing to wear while we were here. One of the guards instructed us to place the towels on the bench at the back of the room, which we did. We then waited while the large metal door was unlocked and opened. As it swung open, it appeared at first glance to be a large shower.

We were herded into the room prodded by the guard's sticks and their yelling. As I entered, I could see showerheads on the wall, all evenly spaced around the room. At least I assumed they were showerheads, although they looked different from any that I had ever seen. Must have been a new model. The walls appeared to be a dusky grayish white with a window towards the back. But it was out of reach and very small. Something didn't feel right, but here was nothing that I couldn't recognize as being wrong. I couldn't put my finger on it. I looked down at the floor, which was stained black brown, like a wood block stained with oil. Then I realized that...

There was no drain in the floor !!!

As soon as I realized this, I turned and bolted for the door, but the people moving in pushed me back. Yelling that it was a trap, others try to turn around but the guards pushed us in and slammed the door closed. I was swept back against my will. Every gain was soon lost, so I maneuvered to one of the walls.

EPILOGUE

So I was trapped, as were we all. I felt a familiar tightness in my chest, the rising tide of hysteria. The people around me were pushing, shoving, milling around and cursing. Sweat mingled freely and the stench of human tension mixed with the overpowering smell of the disinfectant used to previously clean this room. The smell was overpowering and it was difficult not to get sick. I held my breath so that the smell didn't affect me, but others were not so lucky. They were overcome and whatever little was still in their stomachs quickly departed adding to the already awesome aroma. Tired, I leaned against the wall, but quickly drew away from the cold on my shoulder. I looked up towards the window and saw a woman peering in. Suddenly, I was embarrassed by my nakedness and turned to face the wall. As it was, this allowed me to hold my position against the push of the crowd.

He now looked through the window, the bastard! I saw him standing there with a weak but distinct smile on his face. His eyes appeared to fire like rubies in the sunlight and the creases around his eyes seemed to trigger and shoot whatever was emanating in his head. The smile was really a smirk, no, really more of a sadistic satisfied look. It was the first emotion he had displayed to us. I wonder if that was the limit to his range of emotions. If it was, I felt strangely saddened for him.

I heard them sliding the bolts on the door into place. The sound of the steel left a resounding notice of the finality of the situation, of our fate. The room was now silent and tense. As the tumbler on the locks turned we all seemed to hold our breath. When the tumbler ceased to move, the room erupted into an outpouring of grief. There was no doubt now! A tumultuous purging of sanity manifested itself in waves of screaming, weeping, retching, pushing and shoving in the hope of individual survival. I tried to face the crowd and only with great effort was I able to turn around. But I was driven back into the cold wall, but now there was no pulling away. The cold on my back must also be endured and this filled me with dread. The crowd seemed to suddenly lurch and I slipped, but the crush of bodies kept me upright and I recovered my footing.

The screaming was now deafening. People choked for air. I was not sure whether this was real or imagined, but they coughed and gagged, some fainted and collapsed. Someone tried to climb over me, hoping to get above it all, looking for a handhold somewhere, anywhere. He fell onto a bunch of us, dragging us down to the floor, all of us yelling and cursing. It was truly bedlam here.

As if in response to all this a voice was now heard, a voice above all others, a voice that through it's tone began to quiet the crowd. His voice sang out, intoning the ancient declaration of faith,

"Shema Yisroel, Adonai Elohainu, Adonai Echod"

(Here O Israel, The Lord our G-d, the Lord is one).

He sang it out loud. I strained to see who it was, but cannot. Still I could hear him and that was enough.

"Shema Yisroel, Adonai Elohainu, Adonai Echod", again he sang out. And again, and again. With each verse, the din grew more quiet. Slowly, surely, sanity began to be

restored. With each recitation it got a bit quieter and more still. All you could hear now was his voice, chanting clearly. Others around me now started to murmur softly the same words, declaring their faith. We were all together now. Those who couldn't join in just listened, but we were all joined together in our hearts and our spirits. In the silence of this chamber, we merged together as one to ask forgiveness and to seek atonement. In our shame we were united, knowing death was imminent and knowing that despite all that has been done to us, we would die in dignity and thus preserve our humanity.

Standing next to me a little boy began to cry. I looked down to see large mournful eyes. It was obvious that these eyes had seen things at his tender age that men much older should never be forced to see. I patted his head, hoping to quiet him, to comfort him. Through his tears it was clear that he understood our fate and it was through him that we were meant to grieve. I reached down to draw him near. He put his arms around my leg and I felt his tears on my knee as he wiped his eyes on me. The child bowed his head on my dangling hand and I could feel his breath across my wrist. I began to measure the time of my life by the boy's breaths. Over and over the voice called us to attention. This makeshift congregation with our "rabbi", unseen by me, but I knew he was there.

Then he changed the prayer. He commenced to sing,

"Yisgodal, V'Yiskadash . . .", the opening words of the Mourner's Kaddish. I knew why he was doing this. Yes I knew. This was actually a song of life, for the living, not of death. It too is a declaration of faith and hope as ours

dwindled. As we emphatically answered "Amen" the feverish intensity within each of us reached a crescendo on the final "Amen" and we were all reduced to weeping.

After a moment he began the Shema again, reaching with his voice with an ever-increasing plea for forgiveness. It was like the end of Yom Kippur (Day of Atonement) with the gates of heaven closing to our prayer. I strained to see who was this man, but alas, he remained hidden from view and I knew that I would never see him. But I felt the comfort of his voice and knew that was felt by us all.

A light gray haze was now descending upon us. You could barely hear the hiss now. The people around me were beginning to choke hard and fall. The voice still was calling out to us, hearkening to those who could still listen. It was our strength. Through the garlicky pungent smell, I still could hear him even as the voice grew weaker and wearier with each chant. I looked down at the boy at my feet. Through his eyes, I saw acceptance. I looked away, my tears streaming down my cheek, wondering who was comforting whom. My hand rested upon his head, the soft burr of his shaven head under my fingers and felt the warmth of his cheek upon my leg. Soon that warmth would fade away and pass, as would we all.

THE END

Daniel put his pen down and closed the notebook. He got up and went downstairs. He felt deep despair in his stomach and he didn't know what to do. He went back upstairs and got into some clothes. He walked out of the house and down to Ocean Parkway. He sat on one of the benches on the old Bridal Path. He watched the cars passing by and listened to the Latin music from a radio being played by a couple that were making out on the bench about a half a block away. He felt awkward sitting there, so he got up and walked back home.

When he got inside, he poured himself a half a glass of scotch and sat down sipping it. He walked over to the dining room table and sat in his usual place at the head of the table. He picked up one of Rebecca's magazines and sat sipping and reading. When he finished the drink, he got up and brought the scotch bottle to the table. He poured another half glass and continued to sip as he read. He scratched his head as he began to get drowsy. He looked up at the opposite side of the table and he thought he saw something, maybe someone, sitting there. He rubbed his eyes, and when he looked up he saw what he thought was a person sitting there. He rubbed his eyes again and the person was gone. He shook his head and realized that he had been dozing off. So he went upstairs and went back to bed.

CHAPTER TWENTY-NINE

The Sabbath was sad for Daniel. He missed the kids. He missed Rebecca. He missed the noise and tumult. The house was just so quiet, that Friday night when he returned from synagogue. He had seemed distracted to his congregants and he was. Several of them had asked him if he was all right and he had told them that he was just out of sorts because the family was away. He received a number of invitations to eat dinner, but he declined, preferring to stay at home by himself.

He set the table and brought out a bottle of 12 year old scotch that he had put away for some worthy time. He wasn't sure if this was that time, but he felt like opening it anyway. He set out his dinner, made the blessings on his wine and bread and ate his meal quickly. He cleared the dishes and sat back down at the table with some books and a fresh glass with some ice.

He cracked open the bottle of scotch and poured at least four fingers worth. He took a large gulp and then put it down while he read at the table. Soon he felt more relaxed and sipped at his glass. Occasionally, he would pour some more scotch into the glass and continue to sip it down. Thus over a leisurely two hours or so, he had managed to consume about half the bottle. He knew he was drunk, but he was fine with it and he became engrossed in the novel he was reading.

"Eh, Daniel!"

Daniel looked up because he thought he heard someone call his name. He looked around and thought he was just imagining it or perhaps he had spoken his own name as he was want to do. He took another sip and went back to reading.

"Eh, Daniel!",

He looked up. Through the haze of his drunk, he saw a man sitting at his table. He was sitting to his right, two chairs away from him. The man was dressed in a white robe and had a long white beard. His hair was also white and long, pulled back and his forehead shined clearly. Daniel shook his head and closed his eyes. Then he reopened them, but the man was still sitting there.

"Daniel" , the man spoke clearly, "Your eyes are not deceiving you"

Daniel looked at him, staring. The man smiled, "Good Shabbos, Daniel"

Still Daniel said nothing. The man stood up and reached over the table to shake Daniel's hand. Daniel sat dumbfounded. The man waited, then looked at his hand and shrugged,

"O.K., If you don't want to shake my hand, it's O.K."

Daniel still said nothing. The man smiled again and looked across the table to the two seats on the left side of Daniel. They were now also filled with men in white robes, also with long white beards and with long white hair. Daniel looked to his left and saw them as well. The two men offered their hands to Daniel and he didn't respond. The first man said to the others,

"Not from the hand shakers, I guess."

Daniel suddenly responded and stood up as if he had just been awakened., "Not so! Please!"

The man directly to his left took his left hand in his and said,

"Its alright, we are here to be with you this Sabbath. A man should not be alone by himself on his day of rest."

They all sat down. Daniel still didn't know what to say. The third man had still said nothing. He looked out quietly and met Daniel's eyes with his own. Then he looked down at the table. It was silent for a moment, a pregnant moment. And just when it seemed that the first man was about to speak, this third man spoke without lifting his head.

"Daniel, Let me tell you who we are. But first . . . " He looked up at Daniel, then he stood up. He walked behind the second man and stood right next to end of the table. He took Daniel's hand in his right hand and the other man's hand in his left and began singing and dancing around the table. The first man joined in and for the next fifteen minutes these four men danced and sang out loud and made joyous Daniel's Sabbath. Then when he thought he could dance no more, Daniel sat down as did these other men. Daniel was smiling and was happy in his heart. He didn't feel drunk anymore. Rather he felt more alive, more in touch with his body and his mind than he had ever before.

"Who are you guys?", he asked in a bubbly fashion.

The first man sat back in his chair and smiled broadly,

"My son, my name is Abraham." He stood up and shook Daniels hand. The other two men did the same. He looked to his left,

"And you?" he said to the two of them. The one closest to him said,

"I am Moses, your Teacher."

The other man looked at him. "I am Elijah."

Daniel understood. He shook his head knowingly as if understanding had finally been given to him. Abraham spoke softly.

"You are crying in your heart, we had to come."

"But"

"We have known this day would come and now that it is here, even we do not have answers for you. We can only hold your hand and dance with you. We cannot make the pain go away."

He looked at them. "How do I make this work?"

Moses answered him, "The almighty has given you the tools and the insight. You have to make it work."

Then Abraham gave a mighty laugh. Daniel looked up,

"Don't you have anything to ask us? I'm sure you must. Let's face it, it is not everyday that you have a face to face with. . . you know . . . us!"

Everyone laughed including Daniel. Then he got serious for a moment and leaned his elbow down hard on the table and rested his head in his hands.

"Well actually, I've got a few. . . questions!, for all of you."

He looked to his left and realized that Moses and Elijah had vanished. He looked back quickly to his right, but Abraham was still there.

"The answer Daniel, to your questions", he paused, "And there is only one answer to all of your questions. What do you think that is?"

Daniel looked perplexed. "I don't understand what you are asking."

Abraham crossed his arms onto his elbows and sat quietly,

"Think about it!"

They sat quietly for a long time. Then Abraham spoke,

"Still don't get it, huh?"

"No, I'm afraid not. I don't"

"Think about it Daniel, Tomorrow is another day."

Daniel shuddered suddenly. Then he realized that Abraham was gone. He looked around the room. He was alone. He wasn't drunk anymore. He felt energized and very awake. He put on his coat and hat and took a walk around the neighborhood. He walked for hours on Ocean Parkway, all the way to Coney Island. He walked onto the boardwalk and then onto the sand of the beachfront. He stood there breathing in the soft sea breezes. He sat down on the cool sand and stretched out his legs. He sat contemplating. He watched the distant lights of ships steaming across the waters. He felt very complicated. Thoughts of his past rushed in and out of his mind. He blinked for a moment. He dozed and as he drifted off his mind went back to a different time and a different place. . .

Lieutenant Kaplan assumed the 4:00 – 8:00 A.M. bridge watch and accepted a cup of coffee from the boatswain mate of the watch. He looked out at the ocean. The Russian AGI they had been trailing for the last two weeks was drifting dead in the water. The Bristol was also dead in the water with her engines in standby to make adjustments when she drifted too close to the AGI.

"Another watch like this", Daniel thought to himself, "Drift around for hours. Then we chase the Russians at high speed for several hours, then drift around again. G-d, this is boring. Boo-ring!"

The sun was beginning to rise over the horizon and the sky was getting slowly brighter. Daniel sipped at his coffee and stared out the window. He lit his pipe and began puffing gently. The helmsman was telling a dirty joke and Daniel laughed with all the rest of the men. Daniel ran a tight watch, but his relaxed manner made him the most popular officer on the ship to stand watch with. This watch team had been together from the beginning of this deployment, four months earlier and it ran like a well-oiled machine.

These last two weeks of watches had been so boring that many of the men had a hard time staying awake in the middle of the night. Daniel figured it was a good time to teach any of the men who might want to learn, some ship handling techniques as well as navigation.

The men seemed to appreciate it and it made the time go by more quickly.

Daniel looked at his charts and the radar screen. He took another sip of coffee and looked out across at the AGI. He watched a sailor climb up to the gun mount. The mount was the equivalent of the .122mm mounts aboard Bristol. Daniel didn't pay much attention. During this period of chasing the Russian ship, this sailor had frequently been seen climbing onto the mount and working on it or just sitting getting some sun. So Daniel just watched and then turned away.

Suddenly, the bridge window by the Boatswain Mate of the Watch exploded into shards of flying glass. Blood flew everywhere. Daniel looked out and saw this Russian sailor raking the side of the Bristol with gunfire.

Daniel yelled,

"Everyone down. Left full rudder. All ahead 2/3. Senior Chief, Set General Quarters and call the Captain to the bridge . . . and help the Boatswain Mate".

The Boatswain Mate said to Daniel,

"I'm alright sir, just some cuts"

Daniel said to him,

"You sure?

"Yes . . . sir"

"Okay"

Daniel lifted his head up to where he could peer out of the bridge. He had pointed the ship right at the pilothouse of the Russian AGI and they were steaming right for it. The shooting continued and you could hear all kinds of screaming on the Russian vessel. The shooter stopped to reload and shot out all of the windows on the Bristol's bridge. Finally, Daniel reached the back bulkhead of the bridge and pulled the keys to the gun locker from its hanger. He opened the locker and pulled out a

30/30 rifle that was kept on the bridge as protection in case the ship was boarded. He dove out the door onto the bridge wing and stuck his head up long enough to place the rifle on the bridge wing itself. He sighted at the Russian gun mount and fired off a shot, but he had aimed poorly and it missed. The shooter sprayed the bridge wing and Daniel flattened himself to the deck and stayed down. Finally, he lifted himself up, positioned himself well and took careful aim at the shooter. He steadied his nerves and gently squeezed off a shot. The shooter sprawled back and dropped off of the gun mount. Daniel had gotten him right in the gut. Daniel ordered the ship engines slowed and then maneuvered the ship to a stop. The Bristol drifted to within a couple of hundred yards of the AGI. Daniel stood out on the bridge wing watching. He had become so nervous that his legs were shaking, so he placed the barrel of his rifle on the deck and leaned on the stock as if it were a crutch. There was all kind of noise on the Russian ship and the Bristol's Captain , having finally made some sense of the hubris on the bridge had taken over the deck from Daniel and was on the radio with the Russian captain. Things seemed to be calming down and then Daniel saw out of the corner of his eye a Russian officer hurrying down a ladder from their bridge to the gun mount area. This officer reached out for the shooter, and grabbed him by his hair lifting him to his knees. The man was thrashing around and spurting blood from his gut was washing all over the deck and bulkheads. Still holding his hair, this officer coolly drew a pistol from his pocket, put it against the side of his head and fired.

Daniel watching this screamed, "Noooooo!"

The shooter's head exploded all over the place. The ship's bulkhead was now crimson. The officer's uniform was completely red, yet he calmly stood on the deck and held what remained of the shooter's head by its hair. He looked across to Daniel, who was standing aghast at what he had just seen. Then the officer just shrugged his shoulders and nonchalantly tossed the remains of the man's head overboard.

Daniel immediately vomited all over himself. He stood there in shock. His Senior Chief walked over to him, put his hand on Daniel's shoulder and try to help him clean himself up.

"Are you all right, Mr. Kaplan?"

Daniel was incoherent, "Did you see that Senior Chief? Did you see what the fuck he did? Did you see that?"

The Senior Chief answered Daniel,

"Yes. . . sir. . ., I saw it. Yes"

Daniel looked at him,

"Why did he do that? The guy was disarmed. Why did he have to do that?", His voice growing louder and louder in dismay. What is wrong with those fucking morons? Are they nuts?"

The Senior Chief stood silently listening to Daniel rant. Finally he said to him, "Sir, what's the big deal. Your shot would probably have killed him anyway. You got him right in his stomach."

Daniel ferociously answered.

"But he wasn't dead. Not yet! If he was going to die so be it. But that fucking bastard, that son of a bitch, ahh." With that Daniel picked up the rifle and heaved it into the sea as if it were a javelin. Everyone just looked at him,

"Sir, why did you do that?"

Daniel glared at him. He put his hands up, shook his head and walked back into the pilothouse. Daniel turned away in disgust and went below, muttering, "He wasn't dead yet! He wasn't dead yet."

It got suddenly silent on the bridge. Everyone looked at each other in disbelief. They figured Lieutenant Kaplan had lost it completely. Finally, the Boatswain Mate yelled, "Hey what's everyone standing around for?" And everyone went back to turning the ship around and resuming its patrol. It had been one exciting morning.

Daniel learned some time later that the Captain had nominated him for a medal. He quietly asked that his name be withdrawn for the medal. Rather, he just wanted to know the name of the sailor he had shot. When he found out the sailors name, he wrote to the family apologizing for shooting their son. But he never heard back from anyone and wondered if either the Russians or the Americans had ever let the letter through.

He awakened with a start. He realized that he was very cold from the breeze off the ocean. He lifted himself from the sand and brushed himself off. He was very tired. He walked wearily back to Ocean Parkway. It was a long walk home and he could barely keep his eyes opened. Every two or three blocks, he would sit for a few minutes on one of the benches along the way. When he would get up again to walk his mind would wander. He seemed to be walking on automatic pilot.

He sat down around Avenue T. The cars passed by quickly and there were young people out and about. Daniel looked at his watch. It was after midnight already and Daniel knew that it would take at least another half hour to get home. His eyes started to drift closed as he sat, but he abrubtly caught himself and awakened. He watched the cars some more.

Soon his eyelids drooped down over his eyes and his brain returned him to . . .

"This is Blue Diver, I've just been blown off the stage."

"What!, Blue Diver, Blue Diver, say again."

"I'm off the stage, the current is sweeping me, and I'm hanging on my umbilical"

"Holy shit, how fast is that current." The Master Diver said to his Diving officer, Lt. Klieg.

Klieg yelled at one of the divers, "Quick, run up to the bow and pass a stick in the water. I need an accurate current speed."

The diver threw a stick in the water and measured how fast it took to go between two marks on the ship. He reported back to Lt. Klieg and the Master Diver,

"6 knots, sir."

"6 knots!. That can't be right. Do it again., Murphy go with him"

So it went, this time it was 7 knots. Everyone scratched their heads. When the stage went into the water with Lt. Kaplan and the young Korean diver the current was less than 1 knot. Now Kaplan was hanging on while Red Diver was hanging on for his life on a diving stage that was being thrown around at 125 feet below the surface. The crew worked slowly and carefully to winch the stage back onto the deck. But Daniel Kaplan was hanging onto his umbilical for dear life in the frigid waters just outside Pusan Harbor in Korea.

It was December. The USS Bristol had been summoned to help the Navy of the Republic of Korea (R.O.K.), the South Koreans. The situation? That August, a high-speed spy boat of the North Koreans had been hit and sunk by a fishing vessel going out to sea at night. The South Koreans felt that this boat was of such a unique design that they wanted to recover it. Except for two problems. They weren't exactly sure where the collision had taken place and where they thought it had taken place was too deep for their diving capacities to recover it. Hence, the Bristol's showing up in Pusan to assist in this endeavor.

The only problem was that Bristol's Captain, Jack First and the Koreans had different ideas as to what assist meant. To Captain First, assist meant that the Koreans were incapable of performing this operation and thus he would command the activities. To the Koreans, the Bristol was put at their disposal to conduct their operation, their way! So from the start the operation was a mess. Language difficulties, differences in sensibilities and culture guaranteed that this operation would be a disaster start to finish.

And for these reasons and a lot of bad luck, Daniel Kaplan hung by his umbilical in the treacherous waters off Pusan. He was approximately 100 feet below the surface and he was fighting just to keep himself attached..

"Blue Diver, Blue Diver"

"Aye"

"Blue Diver, whatever you do, do not remove your weights."

"No problem, its all I can do to hold onto the umbilical. Can't you guys start reeling me in?"

"That's a negative, blue diver. The currents too strong, if we reel you in we could break it. So just hang on."

"Great!"

So Daniel hung on. His arms grew tired and numb after a while. Since he was breathing a mix of oxygen and helium, he tired quickly. Realizing that he had to hold on, he managed to hold on with one hand long enough to twist a trailing line from the umbilical around his left hand to help stabilize him. Then slowly, he cinched up the umbilical until he had turned it so that he could get it between his legs. He locked his legs around it and then his arms. He laid his head on the hose part of the umbilical so that the strain on his arms was a lot less. Now he knew, he would not break free of the umbilical. He could only hope that the umbilical would not break free from the ship.

"Blue Diver, Blue Diver"

"Aye"

"How are you doing? There's a lot of movement on the umbilical. Are you all right?

"Aye, Master Diver, I just readjusted myself so that I could hold on better"

"Good, Blue Diver."

And so it went. For the next hour the dive team on the surface took turns talking to him. Lt. Klieg got his turn,

"Blue Diver, this is Klieg. How's it going."

"Joe, I got to take a piss in the worst way."

There was silence for a moment.

"Dan, if you piss in that suit, you got to clean it yourself"

"Fuck you, Joe."

They both laughed, as did everyone on the surface listening to the conversation. Throughout the hour, the current speed continued to rise. The Bristol rocked hard at her three point moorings and started to drag her anchors. They were going to lose him. The Master Diver spoke to the Captain about putting a small boat into the water to try and find Daniel in the water.

"Too dangerous Master Chief. Even if the were able to find him in this, they would never be able to haul him up from depths. We need the winch for that and it has to be done very slowly and carefully. Right now it's too dangerous to do as it is. Keep talking to him, but unless he seems to be in some crisis, leave him there. I'm not interested in recovering a corpse, or losing one for that matter."

The Master Diver shook his head. He disagreed. But the Captain was the Captain. Up in the officer's wardroom Rear Admiral Sung, the Korean commander, sat on the couch with one of his legs over the couch arm. He was waiting for Captain First to return to the wardroom.

"Well Captain, have we recovered your officer yet?

"Not yet"

"Why not?"

"The current is too fast"

"How much longer do you think it will take?"

"I don't know. We're waiting for the current to die down."

"Captain, you are dragging anchor and you will lose your mooring. Don't you think it might make sense to start your engines and reanchor?"

"Not while my diver's in the water"

"I realize Captain that you care about your officer, but the integrity of this operation depends upon you maintaining this anchorage. I order you to start your engines and reanchor this vessel safely."

"When Lt. Kaplan is safely onboard."

"No, now!"

"When the Lieutenant is back onboard this vessel"

"I believe that I am speaking plainly to you, Captain"

"And I believe that you can go fuck yourself, Admiral"

Admiral Sung looked at him.

"Is that how you talk to Flag Officers who are guests aboard your ship?"

"Admiral, let's understand each other. This is my ship. Lt. Kaplan is my crewmember. And until relieved by competent authority, I decide what goes on here. Get it, Sir."

Admiral Sung looked down at the deck, "We'll see".

Back at the diving site, Daniel was cracking jokes on the communications line and talking up a storm. All the guys on the Dive Station talked to him, telling him stories and jokes and then singing duets and triplets for him. Everyone felt the stress of having one of their own in trouble in the water. Divers are trained to be buddies under the water. Now, one was alone in the water.

As for Daniel, he was getting very sleepy. He knew that was not good. Hypothermia was setting in.

"Hey guys can you pump more hot water into my suit, I'm getting really sleepy."

Upon hearing that, the Master Diver called for the Captain. Daniel had been in the water almost two and a half hours. Time was now working against them. The current was still 5 ½ knots. They were going to have to risk winching him in. They told Daniel to hold on as tight as he could. The umbilical tugged hard against him but he gathered what was left of his strength and stayed with it. It took almost thirty minutes but soon Daniel saw the metal hull of the Bristol. Soon he was back on deck and being stripped of his dive suit. They took him right into the recompression chamber. There he sat with blankets around his head, drinking hot chicken soup.

After Daniel was finished with the recompression chamber and returned to the wardroom, the first person to stand up to shake his hand was Rear Admiral Sung. Daniel just decked him.

He was awakened by the sounds of screeching brakes and cars hitting each other across the street from him. He jumped in his own skin. He was chilled, even though it was a warm night. Daniel remembered what he had been dreaming about. He thought to himself that for years after the diving accident in Korea he had always felt cold. He would chill easily and suffered from wheezing. As time passed, however he had recovered his health, but now, suddenly, he felt that same kind of chill.

Then he got back up and walked back home.

CHAPTER THIRTY

e took off his hat and hung it on the peg by door. He drifted into the kitchen and looked at the refrigerator door. It was plastered with magnets and pictures from the kids. He sat down at the table and looked around. He took off his suit jacket and hung it over a chair and opened the refrigerator for a bottle of seltzer. He poured himself a glass and sat down again at the table.

He knew that he should probably go to sleep, but he felt very unsettled. He got up and went to his study. He stood at the door looking in, but he couldn't bring himself to go inside. He returned to the kitchen. He opened up the doors to all the cabinets, looking inside for what he did not know.

Soon he tired of that and picked up a small volume of Talmud and began to learn. He became engrossed in the reading, but soon his mind drifted off to his past. He thought of the implausibility of his life. It was such a life of contrasts and extremes. Sailor, Spy, Rabbi, . . . Father of six, no seven children. He grunted and tried to return to his learning. He bent over his volume of Talmud trying to stay awake enough to make sense of what he was reading. He closed the book and walked to the front of the house. He looked around the vestibule. It was all familiar to him, but now it didn't seem comfortable. He rubbed his arms. He was bored and half sleepy, but he didn't want to go to bed just yet. He opened the front door and stepped onto the front porch. He looked down the block but it was quiet and empty. Daniel sighed out loud. He stared at the folding chair on the porch for a moment, trying to decide whether to sit down or go back into the house. He sighed again and sat down. He rested his arms on the chair, but he felt uncomfortable. He knew that it was not the chair, he was uncomfortable in his own skin.

His life and his values were experiencing an explosive contact within his brain and he simply could not escape. Being alone on Shabbos only made it more difficult, actually more compelling. Moments in his life like this were almost stomach wrenching for him. He had tried to compartmentalize his life so that he could hide away in the boxes of his mind, those terrible things he remembered so well. They were when he felt helpless and afraid and he smothered those memories so that he could live. Since, he had met his son, all of those memories, those pains, erupted out of their little boxes in his head and reawakened his anguish. He closed his eyes and drifted off to sleep as he sat. His skin would not let him sleep long. He woke up with a start and realized that he needed to go to his bed. At least then if he fell asleep, he would be safe and warm.

CHAPTER THIRTY-ONE

*I*n synagogue the next morning, he seemed much better to his congregants. Daniel spoke with a fervor, he had not felt in years. His praying was powerful, internally and externally. But he walked home full of trepidation and fear.. He was very lonely and couldn't wait to speak to Rebecca on the phone when the Sabbath was over.

He prepared his lunch and sat down to eat. He ate slowly and listlessly. He finished his meal and put away his plate in the kitchen. He didn't feel like taking a nap. But the house was quiet and empty. So up the stairs he went to take in some afternoon sleep. Not feeling really sleepy, He took off his shoes and sat up in the bed fully clothed reading a book. Soon he drifted off with the book falling open on his lap. As his head sank deeply into the softness of his pillows, he began to recall those thoughts back in another place of one of those happenings. . .

"Man, is it hot!" came the complaint. Daniel took a deep drag from his cigarette. He held it in a moment, then blew out the smoke into his cupped hand so it would disperse without catching attention. He had been flat on his belly for over two hours, as was the rest of his patrol. In the tall grasses, the "Revolutionary Army" couldn't really see them, although they periodically sprayed the area with gunfire for good measure.

"Shut up, Josie", Daniel said in annoyance.

"Well it feels like we've been here forever, when are we going to move, Mr. Kaplan?" said the complainant, Petty Officer Joselyn to Daniel. Joselyn was the patrol's radioman.

Daniel and his patrol had been surprised as they walked out of the jungle into a clearing. They were to be picked up and extracted by Marine helicopter. When the firing began, the helicopter hovering over the landing zone took off and then tried to strafe the area with machine gun fire. Daniel, speaking to them on the radio, ordered them out of the area until the firing zone had cooled down.

Daniel then led his patrol crawling quietly through the grasses for the next 15 minutes until they were fairly sure that the insurgents had lost sight of them.

Still it was not safe and periodically, a grenade was lobbed in the general direction of where they had been ambushed, so they were careful not to move. They had hoped that the insurgents would get bored and leave, instead they had set up camp and were sunning themselves out in the open with a portable radio blaring away in the background. In answer to Petty Officer Joselyn's previous question, Daniel whispered,

"I think, Josie, when the boys over there get done with their beach party."

"Oh! Mr. Kaplan, can't you do something?"

"Shut the fuck up Josie! That's what I'm going to do. Tell you to shut the fuck up!"

Joselyn looked at him. Daniel smiled. They both laughed. They were getting really antsy. Under ordinary circumstances, Daniel would have ordered an attack at that point. The insurgents were exposed and many were napping. It would have been a perfect place and time to make a move at them and that would be their escape. Except that

Daniel Kaplan's little patrol did not technically exist and if they were caught, it would be a tremendous embarrassment to the United States government.

So they waited. It started to get a little darker as the afternoon sun ebbed in the sky. Daniel slowly disengaged himself from his backpack and beckoned to the radioman to slide over to him. He grabbed the handset and called in an air strike. Twenty minutes later 5 fighter planes came in and strafed the area. You could hear the insurgents screaming and running back into the woods for cover.

Then it was quiet. They waited quietly for some time. It was getting darker, but it was still light enough to see. Daniel picked up the radio again and ordered the chopper back in to extract them. The patrol gathered their things and moved towards the landing zone, very slowly.

"Stay down", Daniel called out to them in a whisper, "Stay below the grasses. Come on!"

They saw the chopper coming over the treetops. It skimmed down into the clearing and prepared to hover over the landing zone. Daniel beckoned his group to move slowly forward. The chopper was now three feet above the ground. Suddenly, a boom, and everything was on fire.

"What the fuck was that?" Daniel thought to himself as he threw himself down hard on the ground as fast as he could.

"Holy shit, they blew them up, Holy shit!", Lance Corporal Swifter, a tall kid out of Alabama, started screaming as everyone jumped away and through themselves flat, almost plastered tight to the ground as the debris from the chopper fell around them. Daniel looked up and suddenly was hit in the head by something. He looked over to his left. Down on the ground he saw fingers, then a hand, then an elbow and then the torn remains of where this arm had once been attached to its body. He reached up and touched his helmet. He looked at the red of blood on his own fingers. He rubbed his hand on top of his helmet. He

could feel goo on the palm of his hand and when he looked, he saw the red liquid dripping down the cracks of his hand and into the grasses below.

Daniel saw black smoke rising out from what remained of the chopper. It was totally destroyed. The headless, blackened torso of the pilot sat strapped into what remained of the cockpit. That cockpit now looked like a convertible car with the top down. Its tail lay crumpled and split apart. The rotors were all over the place and it was a miracle that no one on the ground had been hurt when they sheared off.

Daniel propped himself on his elbows in the grasses, just looking. He turned to his men and said,

"Let's get the fuck out of here. Now! Back away from here guys. Carefully! Move as quickly as you can and as quietly as you can. Those boys will be out looking for us any minute."

They retreated back into the grasses. Darkness was settling in. It would be hard for anyone to find them. The cover of darkness would work in their favor. When they reached a safe spot, they all rested.

Daniel whispered, "The smoking lamp is out. It's too dangerous guys. Just stay put and shut up. Starting now!"

The men all settled in. Daniel looked at his watch. And he waited. They could hear the insurgents out in the field looking for them, but they couldn't find them and soon gave up. The insurgents set up a field camp and lit a campfire. Then three of them went over to the chopper and started collecting things. One of them tore off the holster and gun from the dead pilot. The other two took the machine gun and carried it to where they were camped. They shot it into the air and laughed out loud. They examined the dead bodies and stripped jewelry and clothes from and whatever they could find. Daniel and his men watched quietly for some time. It was all they could do to not open fire on these animals. Then he gathered his men around him.

"Guys, this is where all this training gets used." He looked at his men. Joselyn and Swifter were just kids. Barely out of high school, they had been attached to Kaplan's detail over his strenuous objections.

"Too green to be any good to me", he had said to the Colonel and to Admiral Baxter who commanded this little advisory that the Americans were conducting down here in Central America. So of course, these guys were shoved down his throat. They had worked out, remarkably, and Daniel was now glad he had them. They had been patrolling these jungles for three months and had brought back tons of information without encountering any major obstacles. Now they were stuck in the biggest mess and quite by accident. He looked at Joe Polsky. Polsky was a Petty Officer 1st class and the best rubber boat handler Daniel had ever seen. Even better than himself and he was considered one of the best. He was a tall blonde haired man about 29 years old, who rarely spoke except to ask for a cigarette or a match. Fernando Baez was a short stocky Filipino who served as the patrol get-it man. You know, get this, and get that. He could rustle up almost anything and Daniel soon learned not to ask where the items Baez acquired came from. Ned Hasbro was the old man of the group. As dark a black man as Daniel had ever seen, he was built like the weightlifter he was, but fast like a gazelle running from a lion. He was the senior enlisted man in the patrol, a Chief Petty Officer. And he was absolutely lethal. Daniel trusted him instinctively. Unbeknownst to Daniel, Chief Hasbro trusted him and believed in his leadership, even if he thought Daniel was too young to be running such an operation. But Chief Hasbro had heard about Teheran and Daniel's "little task force". They had become legend amongst Special Force units. Hasbro knew that it had been Daniel's daring and creativity that had allowed the Americans to shut down all the power in the city. As tough as that was, what had impressed Chief Hasbro was how Daniel and his team had managed

to get out of Teheran in broad daylight. With the Iranians going crazy looking for the perpetrators of this act, Daniel had led his team to an escape into Afghanistan by traveling over seven hundred miles on foot. He had moved the "little task force" in some of the toughest terrain in the world at night for over three weeks until they could meet up with Afghan rebels who spirited them across the border in a scene right out of the O.K. Corral. So when Chief Hasbro finally met Daniel, he found it hard to believe that this slender, bookish, almost kidlike person was the man he had heard so much about. But they got on well together from the start and at some point, the Chief had nicknamed him DK, which was Daniel's initials, but was also short for "Doc" because Daniel had been a hospital corpsman in his enlisted days.

Daniel looked at these men. These were men with whom he had spent three solid months doing some of the most dangerous surveillance and even more dangerous search and destroy missions.

"Well, Chief", he whispered to Hasbro, "Is it worth it?"

"I don't rightly know there, sir"

"What do you think?"

Hasbro let out a low whistle and shook his head, "I think we might be better off sitting tight for the moment. What do you think?"

"Shit if I know!"

Hasbro chuckled quietly, "We're supposed to get in and get out. We're in, but man. . . How the hell do we get out? We can shoot it up with them. They're a sucker target. But we can't get a chopper in here till morning. It's too dangerous. If we start firing, they'll send in the bulls. DK, you know what we got to do!"

"Ugh huh, put some distance between us and them"

"You got it there, sir. Let's get out and set up another LZ somewhere else, someplace safer and quieter so that we can be extracted"

So they began a long slow retreat from the area in the hope of putting considerable distance between them and the insurgents. It was dark and slow and arduous. The men moved steadily without a break for about three hours. Then Daniel sat them down to gather some strength. It was chilly out now and when you looked up at the sky, you could see the whole universe. Then they got up and continued to walk. As day started to break, Daniel called in new coordinates for a new helicopter to get them out of there.

Soon they hear the thumping sound of the helicopter in the distance. They set up a landing zone and watched for enemy fire. As the helicopter came into view, Daniel suddenly became violently ill. He threw up for what seemed like several minutes and broke out into a cold sweat. As the chopper approached the landing zone, he seemed to calm down a little bit. Soon everyone was safely aboard and they were flying out. Daniel sat in his seat, leaned back on the bulkhead and closed his eyes. In his mind he could see the dead pilot. He could see the charred body. He could see it had no head anymore. He saw the torn arm and felt the pain of those who had been killed to fulfill his order. What had he done wrong? Dead men were on his conscience. And he felt as if there were no place to go.

As they traveled back to base camp the other men in his group sat with their feet out the open door of the plane and were chattering away. Hasbro sat opposite from Daniel. He reached into the pocket of his jacket and pulled out a pack of smokes. He shook the pack up and pointed the protruding cigarettes at Daniel. Daniel reached for one with shaky fingers. He put the smoke to his lips and Hasbro reached over and lit it for him with his lighter. Hasbro had the most remarkable lighter. It was an oversized Zippo with a big fat naked lady engraved on one side and on the other side the word "MOM" was engraved. Daniel had always been curious about the seeming abstraction of this, but he never asked. Now as he sat in the chopper, he looked across at Hasbro,

"Hey Chief, let me see your lighter for a second."

Hasbro handed it to him. Daniel looked at it carefully turning it on both sides. Then he handed it back to Chief Hasbro.

"DK, what you want to know?"

Daniel shrugged.

"I ain't gonna tell you! Its personal."

Daniel shook his head in understanding. Then he put his head back against the seat and closed his eyes.

"DK, there was nothing you could do"

Daniel looked up at him. "I fucked up Chief. We were in such a rush to get out of there. I didn't cover the LZ properly."

"Bullshit, sir. That pilot could have aborted, man. The LZ was cold. The bugs were back in the woods. They got lucky. We couldn't have stopped that if we were blazing away at them with our 16s. DK, we were too far away to make a difference."

"They came in on my say so, Chief. My say so! And I had to leave them there. Leave them there!", he said harshly. "I had to leave them there while the bugs stripped their bodies, Chief. Leave them fucking there."

The Chief became quiet. Nothing in this business disturbed him more than having to leave the dead behind. It was not his way, but his mission often demanded it. And he had done it before.

"DK, is this your first time?"

"First time what?" he asked angrily.

"First time you had to leave someone behind?"

Daniel grew very quiet. His eyes filled with water as he looked down.

"I have never had a man die under my command. . . until today."

Chief Hasbro looked at him thoughtfully.

"Then you ain't a virgin no more, sir."

The chopper made a steep turn down into a field airport, which served as the base for the advisory group. Hasbro's words filled Daniel's head,

"Then you ain't a virgin no more!"

Suddenly, he felt himself being shaken awake. He opened his eyes and looked around the room. But he saw nothing. He looked at the clock on his night table. It said three o'clock. He mumbled to himself and got out of bed and went downstairs.

He took a glass of soda and sat down at the dining room table to read some of the Jewish newspapers that Rebecca collected for him every week..

Soon he caught something in the corner of his eye's view. He looked up and saw another man sitting to his right, two seats away. The man was wearing a white robe like the men he had seen last night, but this man's hair was curly dark and so was his beard. Daniel quickly looked to his left.

"Its just me, Daniel, No one else."

Daniel looked at him. Then he slowly put his glass down.

"Daniel, have you figured out the answer?"

"What answer?"

"The answer that my father was helping you to find"

Daniel looked around at himself and felt vaguely uncomfortable.

"You are not drunk now. And I am here. Feel my hands."

Daniel got up and reached over the table to shake the man's hand. The man grasped his hand with both of his own.

"I feel real. Don't I?"

"Yes"

"Its because I am real"

Daniel turned red in the face.

"Daniel, a man's spirit is just as real as his body. Well maybe a better way to say it is that it's just as tangible as his body. So I can be here, really here with you, just as my father and Moses and Elijah were with you last night. Not like a dream, not like a drunken stupor, but real, tangible".

"Then. . ."

"If they had come to your table when you were sober, it would have killed you. When that time came last night, when you were no longer drunk and you were able to dance with them, then they were tangible and their help could be real. And their help was to prepare you to talk with me."

"What about?"

"You"

"What about me?"

Daniel shuddered for a moment. Then in front of him stood the man dressed in a long black coat with trousers and a big rabbinical hat like Daniels.

"Let's take a walk", he said and moved right for the front door.

"Hey, wait a minute, who are you?"

"Who am I?", he laughed, "My father was here last night, you know, Abraham. Does that give you a clue?"

"I guess!", Daniel laughed also.

"Come on then", the man put his arm around Daniel's shoulders and led him out onto the street.

CHAPTER THIRTY-TWO

*I*saac led Daniel through the neighborhood as if he had been living here for many years. They walked down wide Avenue P and walked up East 7th Street towards Avenue O. As they walked up the street talking, Isaac abruptly stopped in front of a house. The address on the door said 1652. The house was the left side of a semi-attached brick house. The stairs leading up to the door were concrete painted red and there were ledges alongside the stairs with cast concrete pots filled with petunias and marigolds. Isaac seemed particularly interested in the back and walked up the driveway to peer into the backyard. He pointed out to Daniel the ten-foot high brick lattice wall and smiled when some kittens came out of the garage next door. He bent down and picked one up, scratching its ears and tickling its stomach. Then he deposited the kitten into Daniel's jacket pocket.

"What did you do that for?"

"She needs a home . . . and a friend"

"How can I carry it, its Shabbos"

"First of all, don't call her an it. She's a she. Second, no one will know you're carrying it, except us. And third, she needs you and more important, you need her. "

Daniel peered into his pocket. She was cute. All orange with white across her nose. She had fallen right to sleep in his pocket nuzzling against the inside of his coat. He could feel her against his hip.

"Take her home, Daniel. It will be good for both of you."

"But what about . . . ?"

"Rebecca and the kids. They'll be alright with it too, you'll see!"

Daniel shrugged his shoulders. He was talking to a spirit, who had just deposited a kitten upon him. He knew nothing about cats. But. . .

"You shouldn't worry so much Daniel. Life is really not that hard.'

Daniel shook his head again.

"I'm not so sure about that"

"Why would you say that? Do you think that finding out about a son you never knew about is somehow bad?"

"Well?"

"Surely, you must be kidding. This is your son we're talking about. How can that be bad? This is such a tremendous miracle for you! You should be overjoyed that the Almighty has given you the chance to get to know him."

Daniel shook his head. "You wouldn't understand"

"What makes you think I can't understand. I may be a retired shepherd", then he chuckled, "How about that. Retired shepherd", he laughed again.

Daniel just stood there looking at Isaac.

"I don't get what's so funny?"

"Exactly!", roared Isaac, "Listen Daniel, let me tell you a story." Then he thought for a moment, "No, better yet. You can ask me any question about myself. Any question and I'll tell you about it. Anything, but just one question." He looked at Daniel intently, "Ask?"

They walked for a while and then turned onto Ocean Parkway, They sat down on one of the benches.

"The sacrifice"

"You want to know about my father's sacrifice of me?"

Daniel looked intently at him, "Yes".

"And what do you want to know about it?"

"I don't know, everything."

"Everything is a very general thing. Do you want to know how I felt or what I was thinking?"

Daniel seemed perplexed. "I don't know. From the time I was a little boy I was curious about the story of your sacrifice. Now as an adult, looking at you, with an opportunity to ask the actual source, I find that I don't know what I want to know. So I want to know everything."

Isaac chuckled,

"Daniel, if you don't know what to ask, how can you ever discover the truth. Even the <u>source</u> tells you something from their perspective. And even that perspective is skewed. So think Daniel, I was there and I cannot answer your question."

Daniel thought about it for a moment. Then he asked,

"But why? You were actually there. You experienced it, felt the emotions, and understood what was happening."

"What makes you think I understood anything?

"Well, I was taught that you when you figured out that you were the sacrifice, you walked boldly with your father at your side. And then you insisted that your Father tighten the bonds so that you would not move and possibly invalidate the sacrifice. Is that what really happened? Is it all true?"

Isaac looked at him sadly,

"Do you believe that the Torah is the truth, Daniel?"

"Of course I do."

"So why are you asking this question of me?"

"I don't know. I guess hearing it from you verifies it for me"

"But you just said you believe the Torah is true. What difference would it make if I verify the events or not?"

Daniel pondered that for a long time. Then he looked at Isaac and said,

"I guess then maybe I have some doubts"

He hung his head in shame and started to cry. Isaac put his hand on Daniel's shoulder.

"Believing the Torah is true is only part of the process of accepting G-d's will in our lives. Even the Torah has to be questioned for it is such a deep statement of the truth that often what appears in text is just the surface of an underlying truth. Certainly you understand that, Daniel? Because the Torah of Laws is also a Torah of Heart. Scripture is the truth, but it is only an escalator to the deeper floors of understanding. So whatever I would tell you to verify the Torah would have no meaning.

Daniel looked up at him perplexed,

"Why is that?"

"Because I am only a man. Even in spirit, I am still only a man. The events I experienced are colored by my experience. I cannot verify what G-d as the writer of the truth has said took place.

Daniel seemed confused. Objectively it all made sense, but Isaac was sitting in front of him and suddenly he wanted to know all the details of what was in Isaac's mind during the sacrifice. He looked into Isaac's eyes,

"But weren't you terrified?

Isaac smiled broadly.

"Of course I was terrified."

"You were?

Isaac looked at him a moment.

"Sure, wouldn't you have been? Would you have liked the Torah to record that I was weak in the knees. Or that my mouth was all dry and I couldn't swallow. Would it have added anything to the purpose of the story if G-d had wrote" And Isaac was afraid?""

Daniel looked at him for a moment. He didn't say anything. Then he closed his eyes as if to imagine in his mind how it must have been for Isaac.

"Well I was all of that. And yes I walked boldly with my father at my side. And do you want to know why?"

Daniel shook his head yes.

"Because, I asked the right question, Daniel, the right question. I didn't know if I was going to be a sacrifice right to the last moment. But if that was what had to be, then it had to be. I didn't ask G-d why he had chosen this test for me and especially for my father. I asked how can I fulfill G-d's purpose, even though to my mortal mind, the purpose was inconceivable. But if it was required that I lay down on an alter to become a sacrifice, then G-d must have a greater good that was to come out of that. And if that was so, then I might as well do it right. So I made sure my father tied me down tight enough. Then, I made the world I was living in at that moment, right. I lived my life to the absolute fullest from the moment I realized G-d's plan until my father drew the knife over me. I made sure that during that time, I became right with myself and by doing that I became right with my world. I could die now, because whatever unfinished business, I had with my world, Daniel, I made it right as I ascended the hill. I'm not talking about being right with the whole world. I'm talking about being right with my world. Who I was and whom I wanted to be remembered as. Daniel, are you right with the world that you are living in now?

"No, there are terrible things going on in the world."

"That's not what I mean. Your world! Is your world right? You don't know why the Almighty has shown you a son at this time of your life, in this place. But you feel sorry for yourself. You see it as a problem, rather than embracing it as a miracle. Don't you?"

"I. . . don't really know."

"Yes you do! When G-d chose to test my father by sacrificing me, I asked the right question. That question was why is G-d giving me this miracle. It would seem that he was punishing me or acting without reason. But the question was not about me and it <u>was</u> about me. Would I recognize the miracle and be right with my world or would I not recognize it and die treifah (unkosher)? Lets face it Daniel, you feel terrible living in your world. There is so much undone. So much unsaid. So much unknown and so much you don't want to know. You have your life and it's comfortable. Any little disturbance causes you worry because it makes you feel unbalanced. Well, when you live your life on the head of a pin, it is easy to become unbalanced. When you make that pinhead grow and expand and absorb it into who you are and where you must be, then and only then, will those little disturbances be what they are. Little! Do you understand?"

Daniel understood the abstract nature of the thought but not its implications. Isaac looked into his eyes and saw the fear within them.

"Daniel, no one needs to be told what is the right thing to do. Inside, we know. Deep inside. Down within your heart, its very clear. But its frightening, because we put on the clothes of what we are expected to wear to be what we are expected to be. We do that rather than being who we are and what our core really stands for. My father told you last night. . . What?"

Daniel shifted uneasily in his seat., "I'm not quite. . ."

"My father said to you that the answer to your questions is. . .", he paused, "and he left you thinking. The answer to your questions,

Daniel, is you! You have a heart and a soul and a conscience. You know what is the right thing to do, each and every time. You know! YOU KNOW! What do you do about your son and how will it impact your life? You know what has to be done. Look at what's important here. These big black hats we are wearing are only symbols, Daniel. They represent us to be something that we are not. They are as artificial as most of the people wearing them. They wear them because everyone does. But it has no meaning in reality. It's just a hat! It is not important what the rest of the world thinks of you. It is important what you think of you. It's what is your conscience. And your conscience is pure, Daniel. Pure. It tells you what is really right. Not what is legally right, rather, what is really right in the universe, your universe. Because G-d gives each of us that tool. We ignore it at our peril. We act confused because we're afraid. But of what are we afraid? The Master of our Universe knows everything , he sees it all. He gently guides us, but he leaves us free choice. If we use our influence to pervert it then this big black hat is just a big black hat and you are playing a part in a play you call your life. It is your conscience that counts. It teaches you to ask the right question. The right question is always more important than the right answer, Daniel. And I'll tell you a secret. If you don't think you know or are afraid of what your conscience dictates you to do, then ask your wife. She knows and will lead you in the right direction. If you must be lead, Daniel Kaplan, let her lead you. If you can lead yourself, walk up that hill, tighten the ropes around you and let G-d decide whether you are to be a sacrifice or not. But whatever you do and however you do it, walk up that hill. And walk up it boldly. Even if you are terrified, do not look back. The future is always ahead of you. And you alone can control it by taking the truth you know and living it. But it can only happen if you ask the right question".

Daniel closed his eyes to think for a moment. When he opened them again, Isaac was gone. Daniel took a deep breath and leaned back on the bench. The kitten stirred within his pocket. He took her out and scratched her head. She crawled up his shirt and he laughed as he pried her off and returned her to his lap. Then together, they sat and watched the cars whiz by on the Parkway. And they sat for a very long time.

CHAPTER THIRTY-THREE

He sat in his little corner in front of the shul. He was wearing his talis and his tephillin were wrapped around his arm and around his head. The morning service was over and the men were drifting back to their homes to eat their Sunday breakfasts with their family. Soon it was quiet. Daniel sat alone looking around at the sanctuary. But he felt no sanctuary. He only felt tumult and anxiety.

He was very tired. His bones ached and his teeth clenched down upon each other, grinding noisily until his jaw hurt. He had slept little over the past three days. All he could fathom logically from the whole weekend is that somehow; he had acquired a little cat. He wondered if Rebecca would think he had lost his mind when she saw the little fur ball. Anyway, he was just exhausted.

Daniel leaned back into the pew and rested his head back. He glanced at the carvings on the Ark that held the Torah scrolls. His eyes traveled to the menorah and then he began to recall. . .

He stepped off of the plane at Washington's National Airport and moved quickly to pick up his luggage. It had been a long two days flying and he was exhausted from the lack of good sleep and the terrible food on the plane. He wearily picked his luggage off of the carrel and walked out of the airport and hailed a cab. He sat back in the taxi and pulled out his orders and checked them again. Then he directed the driver to take him to the Pentagon.

He paid the taxi upon arrival there and walked into the security area. He handed his military I.D. to security and showed his orders to the Sergeant in charge. His papers were checked against a list and he was told he would have to wait for an escort. The Sergeant picked up a telephone and spoke to someone on the other end, reading off Daniel's name and rank. Then he handed the papers back to Daniel and turned back to his duties. Daniel stepped back from the counter and waited. After a few minutes, he felt a tap on his shoulder. He turned around and saw a Marine Gunnery Sergeant standing before him.

"Lieutenant Kaplan?"

"Yes Gunny?"

"Sir, I'm Gunny James, I am your escort."

"Good, where am I going?"

"Well sir, first, I will take you to a hotel where you can freshen up."

"That's good. Maybe we could find a place where I could get some chow on the way?"

"Well sir, the hotel is very close by, so I'll drop you off and you can check in. Then I will be back at 1500 (3:00 P.M.) to pick you up and drive you to your meeting."

"You mean, I'm not meeting at the Pentagon?"

"No sir."

"Then where is it?"

"It's at the State Department sir. I can't tell you anything else because, I don't know. But if I can make a suggestion sir, you have time to get your Service Dress Blues dry-cleaned. I would do so. You're meeting some very important people. So get yourself up right, if you know what I mean."

"I thank you Gunny for that information. I'll make sure I do that."

"Good sir, let's go."

Daniel climbed into the car and thought to himself that everything was so deliciously secretive. He smiled to himself and remembered when Chief Radioman Rayburne had come down to his stateroom five days ago with a top-secret message. The message directed the Captain to sail into Guam and await further orders. Attached to this message was a blind message for Daniel's eyes only. That message directed him to fly to Washington immediately and report to the Pentagon Security Officer. An additional radio message was also shown to Daniel. This reported the death of his brother and authorized emergency leave upon arrival at the nearest port of call. Except that Daniel had no brothers. This was his cover. So when they arrived in Guam, Daniel was the first person off the ship, with his flight bag and emergency leave orders to New York. When he got to Hawaii, and got off the plane to make his connection, he walked to an agent and changed his flight plans from an arrival in New York to a flight to Washington. He waited two hours and then flew off into the night on the rest of his very long odyssey.

After Gunny James left him off, he checked into the hotel and went up to his room. He unpacked and called the valet to pick up his uniform for cleaning. Then he sat on the edge of the bed, lit a cigarette and turned on the T.V. Daniel peeled off his clothes and watched. He idly picked up his shoes and grabbed for his shine kit and began shining them. This was a kind of therapy for Daniel, a kind of mindless activity, which relaxed him. He finished his cigarette and stepped into a hot shower and washed away the days of travel. He got dressed into some casual clothes and walked out of the hotel and looked around. As he walked down the streets of Georgetown, he found that he liked the atmosphere. On one corner, spying a small restaurant, he looked inside. It was still early, around 8:30 A.M. and he was very hungry. People were inside having breakfast. He looked around for a newsstand, bought a paper and then walked inside and ordered a large breakfast of pancakes, eggs and Virginia ham. Finishing off with some coffee, he fished into his shirt pocket for some cigarettes, but thought better of it. He saw some cigars in the counter by the cash register. Daniel got up and bought two, one for now and one for later. He sat back down, got a refill of coffee from the waitress and lit up. He perused the paper and just relaxed for some time. The girl who ran the place smiled at him, but seemed in no rush to have him move on, so he stayed. Finally, he got up, paid his bill and went back to the hotel. He asked for a wake up call at 1:00 P.M., pulled the drapes and climbed into bed.

When he awakened it was not quite 1:00. He took a quick shower and called the valet to see if his uniform was ready. They told him that they would send it up at once. After his uniform was delivered back to him, he busied himself with getting ready. When 3:00 arrived, he was already down in the lobby waiting when Gunny James arrived. They walked to the gray government car and he got in. Gunny James drove away through the streets of Washington. Daniel looked out the window at the familiar sights and wondered what awaited him.

Finally, they pulled up to the State Department. A young woman wearing a bright red suit opened the door to his car. She greeted him and shook his hand.

"Lt. Kaplan, I am Anne Sothern, Deputy National Security Advisor."

Daniel smiled and accepted her hand.

"Daniel Kaplan, ma'am, nice to meet you."

She put her hand on Daniel's back and steered him into the building. She led him through the building until they arrived at a conference room. She asked him if he would like some coffee. He declined and she sat down with him to wait for all the parties to assemble. Daniel looked at his watch. It was five minutes to four. He waited. Ms. Sothern signaled him to get up and follow her. She escorted him into a large office and directed him to a chair in front of the desk. He looked at the other men sitting there and recognized the Director of Central Intelligence. There was another man in a business suit that he didn't recognize and an Israeli Major that he did recognize. The man was Major Avraham Baruch and rumor had it that he had either directly run or had planned every significant Mossad operation during the past five years. He was legendary. But to look at him would be deceiving. He was short, stocky, barrel chested with close cropped short hair and an impish grin. He looked like a little elf. But make no mistake about it, he was deadly.

Daniel did not know the fellow sitting behind the desk, but he was busy talking on the telephone and had not yet acknowledged him. Daniel waited, nervously biting the inside of his lip and trying not to fidget. The smell of dry cleaning fluid from his uniform was annoying him particularly, but Daniel realized it was his heightened awareness brought on by anxiety.

Finally, the phone call was finished and the man behind the desk walked around and greeted Daniel.

"Daniel Kaplan, I am John Breckenridge, Assistant Secretary of State for Middle Eastern Affairs"

He presented his hand and Daniel shook it and smiled weakly.

"These other gentlemen are Joseph Walker, Assistant Secretary of the Navy for Intelligence"

Daniel shook his hand.

"Douglas Steuben, Director of Central Intelligence. I don't know if you have been formally introduced before, but he's your boss, you know".

Daniel laughed and shook the Director's hand and they all laughed.

"And finally, Avraham Baruch, Israel's answer to James Bond. Proving again that you can look like a bull and still get the girl".

Everyone laughed at the Secretary's joke, but Daniel thought it was quite lame. After all, Baruch's exploits were incredible and the Secretary appeared to be one of those self-righteous government hacks. Nonetheless, Baruch did not seem disturbed by the comment, so Daniel let it rest.

Finally, they all settled down and got down to business. They handed Daniel a folder and he opened it and looked inside. It was a dossier on an individual. He perused it awhile and then looked up. The Secretary began to explain.

"Dan, we brought you here because we have a difficult problem and we feel that you might be able to solve it for us."

Daniel felt around inside his jacket for his pipe. He found it and put it between his teeth.

"Okay!", Daniel said cautiously. "What's the problem?"

"Well as you can see from the papers in front of you, our problem is a man named Peter Kopolowitz. Let me give you an overview and then you can read the dossier and address any particulars that you might have."

Daniel nodded okay. The Secretary continued.

"The man works as an intelligence analyst for the Navy. He is 42 years old, married with no children. He has a Bachelors degree in Romance Languages from Harvard and has worked for the Navy for almost five years here in Washington. We were informed by Israeli intelligence about six weeks ago, that this man was attempting to deliver classified material to their embassy."

Daniel looked at the Secretary with a quizzical eye. He lit his pipe and took a puff.

"Why?"

The Secretary looked perplexed.

"Why what?"

"Why would he be delivering classified material to the Israeli's?"

"We don't know!"

"You don't know?" Daniel asked as if he didn't believe the Secretary.

"No, we don't know", he repeated.

Daniel sat upright in his chair. He pulled the pipe from his mouth and pointed it at the Secretary.

"Get real Mr. Secretary. How is that possible you don't know? You must know. Why would this man be doing this?"

He turned to Major Baruch and raised his eyebrows.

"Was he spying for you?

Major Baruch looked at him carefully and said quietly,

"No, he is not one of our operatives, assuming of course, that we have operatives engaged in intelligence gathering against our ally, the United States."

"Right", Daniel said sarcastically, "You wouldn't think to do that. Listen Major, cut the crap. I've stopped counting how many times you guys have tried to turn me, so don't tell me you don't do it. I've filled out reams of Contact with Potential Foreign Agents forms due to you guys. Believe it or not, not every Jew in the military is a potential secret agent for Israel.

Baruch laughed. He looked Daniel in the eye and said jokingly,

"Well, we can certainly try, can't we?

Daniel smiled at him.

"He's spying for you against the U.S.?"

Baruch smiled and shook his head no.

"No, he is not an agent for us. What he is, sir, is a big pain in the ass!"

Daniel raised an eyebrow.

"A what?"

Major Baruch was more direct with Daniel.

"*You heard me right the first time, this idiot is a major pain in the tuches. We have had to waste countless hours trying to convince this shmuck that the information he insists on giving us is information that we already have. We share vital intelligence on a regular basis. This Kopolowitz insists to us that he has information that the U.S. is deliberately keeping from us. At first, we took him seriously until we evaluated it. After it became clear, that most of this was information we already had, we politely asked him not to come around any more. But not only does he continue to come around, he makes a big stink and drives our security people crazy disturbing our operations. So we indulge him, we take his files and send him on his way.*"

Daniel looked at the Secretary and said,

"*Why don't you just arrest him?*"

The Director spoke up.

"*We have a vested interest in not having a public exposure of the fact that our allies might conduct intelligence operations against us. If we arrested Kopolowitz, we would have to explain our relationship, intelligence wise with the Israelis. Worse still, there are those who would exploit the fact that Israel conducts intelligence operations within the U.S. The President would be sorely damaged politically by this disclosure.*

"*So, what do you want from me?*

"*You sir*", *the Secretary stated in a matter of fact way,* "*Are going to get this fellow under control and make this situation go away!*"

"*I am?*" *Daniel said quizzically,* "*And exactly how am I going to do that? Tell me,*" *he said sarcastically,* "*What do you have in mind?*"

The Secretary smiled at Daniel,

"*You . . . are going to tell us!*"

"*Tell you what?*"

The Director of Central Intelligence spoke up for the first time in his deep rolling voice,

"You are going to convince this fellow to stop and desist"

"You've got to be kidding!". Then he looked around at the men in the room." I guess, you're not." Daniel shook his head, "And if he doesn't?"

"Do whatever it takes to make him cease and desist"

"And "whatever" means?"

"Any means necessary"

"Do you mea. . . "

The Director interrupted him.

"Young man, any means necessary, as long as it doesn't embarrass the President"

"Why do you need me? Wouldn't it be easier to just make him disappear?"

"We've thought of that", Major Baruch said.

"Well if you've thought of it, why haven't you done it?"

"We have our reasons"

"And those might be?

At that point, Breckenridge interrupted,

"Gentlemen, this isn't getting us anywhere. Look Dan, we have our reasons for bringing you here. It's your mission to get this guy under control."

"But you just told me to use whatever means necessary. Well gentlemen, my means and method are to make this fellow disappear. And like immediately.

Does that suit you fellows?"

Secretary Breckenridge looked extremely unhappy,

"I'd say not"

"You'd say not. So that means, I can't use any means necessary, right?

"Well . . . right"

"Uh huh" Daniel nodded knowingly to all of these men. "In other words, you guys have no fucking ideas, and you've brought me in to baby sit this fellow and keep the lid on all this. Right?"

There was silence from everyone. Daniel sat back and drew deeply on his pipe. He had no idea how to approach this. Clearly neither did anyone else. He was thrown to the wolves and if it failed, the blame would rest only on him.

"So Gentlemen, what have you dreamed up so far? What's your plan?

The Assistant Secretary of the Navy spoke up.

"Daniel, you will be assigned as head of the intelligence desk that Kopolowitz works for. Over the next month, you are to befriend him and get his confidence. You are to play the part of an active duty officer who is an active Zionist and whom is struggling with the knowledge that certain intelligence effecting Israel is being kept from them. We will feed you with false intelligence information so that you can build yourself up in his eyes. But you are to remain the loyal American despite everything. You will make a big deal about doing your duty and swearing allegiance to our flag and so forth. We hope that in seeing you as a mentor and as a torn individual with a strong sense of duty, you will turn him away from what he is doing"

Daniel took a deep breath, then he looked incredulously around the room at the men assembled.

"Gentlemen, with all due respect, and I do mean with all due respect, but this is the most asinine thing, I've ever heard! Either you guys are the most naïve bunch or I'm missing something. Since, I know that you are not naïve, I must be missing something. Because, I cannot believe, for even one instant, that any of you believe that this would or could work. Am I wrong? I mean, I'm the kid here. Gentlemen, make this guy disappear!. Geez, the mafia does it, you mean to say that either the CIA or Mossad can't just make this fellow disappear?

The two Americans looked at each other. They knew he was right. But to let Daniel in on the missing pieces was equally dangerous. Furthermore, the Israelis had been threatening to kill this man for a month and only because of diplomatic intervention was Kopolowitz still alive. Lt. Kaplan had put their back to the wall. As far as Baruch was concerned, Kopolowitz could take a bullet and that would be the end of it. But Kopolowitz was married to the daughter of one of the wealthiest and most influential men in the country. He was a personal friend of the President and a major contributor. His influence had gotten Kopolowitz his job with the Navy in the first place. This whole problem had the potential to explode in different directions, no matter what they did. And there were things about Kopolowitz that the Americans believed even the Israelis didn't know.

Joe Walker spoke up again,

"Well, Daniel, we know how you feel, nonetheless, this is what we want done. Can you do it?"

"I guess I can, Mr. Secretary, but I'm not sure why?"

"Don't worry about why. Over the next few days we will brief you in depth. If you have any ideas, please speak up. Study the dossier closely. You'll start next Monday. Report tomorrow to me in khaki's and will start the briefing process for you. Oh, and another thing . . ."

He tossed Daniel a small box. Daniel opened it up and saw the gold oak leaves of a Lieutenant Commander. He looked up at the Secretary questioningly.

"That's right Commander, starting immediately"

"But I just became a Lieutenant six months ago"

"Well consider yourself very early zone. Congratulations. Now make this work. We need this problem to go away quietly."

CHAPTER THIRTY-FOUR

What Daniel never knew was that the meeting had continued on after he had left. What had happened was this:

Brenckenridge, Steuben, Walker and Baruch looked at each other with vaguely bemused looks.

"That young man must think we are crazy", Breckenridge said to his assembled guests.

"Why would you think that?" Walker countered.

Director Steuben stood up and took off his jacket. He hung it on the back on the Louis IV style chair in which he had been sitting. He rolled up his sleeves and surveyed the room with his eyes. He looked blankly at Undersecretary Walker and disgustingly at Major Baruch.

"I don't like what you are doing here!", he stated emphatically,

"It stinks and it's stupid. The kid is right, arrest or get rid of this creep. This plan of yours is no plan at all. We are supposed to be part of the intelligence brain trust of this nation but clearly. . ."

His voiced trailed off. Walker jumped up and said harshly to him.

'Well what would you have us do? Tell him everything?

"Yes, he is an operative. He knows how to keep a secret and he definitely has a need to know."

Breckenridge disagreed,

"I'm not sure that's true"

"What are you not sure is true?"

"I'm not sure he has a need to know. I think this is way above him."

"I think", the director countered, "that you are an idiot"

"Now Doug, there's no reason to get nasty."

"No reason? You're going to hang this young man out to dry. He's my agent!. You have no plan. How are you going to stop this man without there being publicity. Well?"

Breckenridge quietly said,

"We'll leave it to Kaplan to get him under control."

"And if he doesn't, or isn't able to? Then what? Ahh, you guys are remarkable. The blind leading the blind. I don't like this at all! I do not like the way you are planning to handle my operative."

Walker said, "I beg to differ with you Mr. Director, but Daniel Kaplan is not your operative, he is Navy and thus mine!"

"You also are an idiot, He's wearing that uniform for convenience. He's CIA, remember that. He's mine, not yours. Mine, got that! I'll pull him out of that uniform and send him to Langley so fast your heads will spin. Mine!, he's my man and you can't have him unless you do this my way. Frankly, I think he has more brains then the rest of you combined."

Then smiling at Major Baruch, and making a sweeping bow before him,

"Except you Major, I wouldn't think of calling the old master an idiot. So what do you think of this fiasco in the making? You can't be buying into something so ludicrous."

Baruch smiled broadly and looked the Director in the eye. He reached into his pocket for a cigarette, crossed his legs and hiked up his leggings. He took out a lighter and lit the smoke. He drew deeply and looked at the Director a moment and then turned and faced Secretary Breckenridge.

"American cigarettes, they are much better than Israeli. I stock up every time I come over here" He took a breath and then looked at the ceiling. He took another deep puff and slowly blew the smoke out up towards the ceiling.

"Your right Doug, I don't buy into this as an operation, I do buy into this as a concept piece, however. Kopolowitz is dangerous to both you and us. Us being the Israelis, but more important to the Prime Minister. Clearly, no one knows how dangerous he is. He can be an overzealous patriot for us or a total crank. Whatever he is, however, does not matter to us. We do not want to deal with him. Why? Because he is unstable. The problem with him being unstable is that he is a risk to embarrass us during these difficult times. For you there is a similar risk, that of embarrassment. Additionally, you do not want the world to know to what extent you allow friendly foreign agents to gather information here. We do not have this problem. I suspect that most people would believe that we operate our agents here in the U.S. I'd further suspect that most people assume that we are working together on many intelligence fronts and share information. So, we do not have the same public relations problems with this that you do. We just don't want to deal with him because he is weird. You, however, must measure what the bigger risk is. Should you let him operate in a dummy mode and we at the Israeli embassy act as the conduit for planted inconsequential material or shall you try to stop him, either in the manner described today or in some other fashion. Lt. Kaplan asked the exact right question. Why don't you just take him out of circulation or arrest him. But that is your question and not mine. We are prepared to eliminate him as a problem, but we must control the situation so that it does not appear that we are conducting covert assassinations on American soil."

Walker chimed in. "Baruch, that's a lovely speech. But it says to me that you are telling us, solve the problem for ourselves".

"Well, yes and no. We want you to make this man go away. But you know more about Kopolowitz than I do. You know what kind of man he is. You have to weigh the risks."

"So, what do you suggest?" Breckenridge asked.

"Tell Kaplan the whole story. Lay it all out for him. Then together with him devise a strategy, which takes your basic premise of what you want Kaplan to do and make it operational. If you want Kaplan to convince him to cease and desist, you have to give him the tools. Because Kaplan's too smart and he will suspect your motives. Lay it all out on the line for him. Make him a part of the process and he may find a way to get Kopolowitz under control. You have until next Monday. Get him in here and start getting him ready."

They all looked at each other and shook their heads in agreement. They got up and filed to the door. Director Steuben gently steered Major Baruch to a small vestibule.

"This whole thing doesn't have a prayer. Am I right", he asked the Major.

"Not a chance, but maybe it could work out in some other way which protects you guys politically."

"I agree. I want to minimize my exposure here. We're already under the gun for funny business overseas. I'd hate to have this blow up on my front step."

"Well, Director, if it does, you have a brand new Lieutenant Commander, you can blame it all on"

"That's true. That's true!"

They both chuckled. Then they shook hands and went their separate ways.

CHAPTER THIRTY-FIVE

*D*aniel's dreaming continued.

It seemed to Daniel that he had been cast into an impossible position. It was clear to him, well nothing was clear to him at all. In fact, he was so confused by the events at the State Department that he didn't know what to think. Who was Peter Kopolowitz? What was he doing that had caught everyone's attention. Furthermore, what was the Israeli's involvement. These four guys had cooked up a scheme, but were leaving the follow through to an unknown. Why?

It was obvious that these gentlemen were to remain blind operators. Daniel wondered why there had to be such deception. Arrest this fellow, if he is a danger to National Security. Why such a convoluted plan? And why no real plan, just a hazy idea of what they wanted and orders to make this problem go away quietly?

His mind traveled back to the Israeli again. Major Baruch was known for his meticulous detail in planning operations. Yet it seemed, at least on the surface that he was a part of this surreal endeavor.

He went back to his hotel in very agitated state. He thought that maybe over the next few days, they would come up with a real plan of action for him to carry out.

Daniel Kaplan reported the next day to the Pentagon to be briefed. There were also functional meetings to create a strategy to solve the

Kopolowitz mess. Daniel knew that he was being placed into the position of pawn for some very high flung chess players and he didn't like it one bit. He had watched while four of the administration's most powerful men had hemmed and hawed their way through his meeting with them. He was convinced that nobody really had a clue and that they were looking for some distancing room. And he was that distancing room.

Daniel realized that he had to solve this problem himself. The results would be either little or no recognition if he were successful. And if he failed, massive blame and disrepute.

He sat in a booth in a coffee shop near the White House and pondered this fate. He was between a rock and a hard place and no amount of rationalizing this would change that. He laughed when he thought of his promotion to Lieutenant Commander. He knew that it served as a bribe of sorts to convince him to take this untenable situation.

So he decide that he had to chew this one up and figure out how he to get through this. He decided to do something unusual for him. He would do a personal code of conduct for conducting this operation. He would not compromise himself from its principles in any way. Then whatever developed, he could be guided by these principles and even if it turned out badly, he would know that he had done the right thing. So often, intelligence operations skewed the line between right and wrong and Daniel knew that he had to be prepared for it. Not to say, he would not engage in unorthodox methods to accomplish something. But in this case, it was clear to Daniel, it was different. Here, he had to have guiding principles that were absolute.

He reached into his bag and pulled out a legal pad. He knew that to even do what he was about to do was a violation of all the principles of intelligence. Nevertheless, he felt this was so important that he would develop his own modus operandi to guide him through this minefield.

*Across the top of the page, in large block letters he printed out
AMERICAN. He underlined it to emphasize its importance to his state
of mind. Underneath that he wrote in block print: JEWISH in capitals.
Under that he wrote in script: Supporter of Israel and underlined that.
Then he took a deep breath and looked at the paper carefully. He
thought to himself,*

*"Okay, I am going to protect my country. I will protect this country,
even if I do it despite itself. Let's look at this clearly. These jokers up in
the upper echelons are not trying to solve an intelligence problem. They
are trying to solve a potential public relations problem. But what if
Kopolowitz really got his hands onto something? What if he gave it over
to Israel? And what if what he gave over to Israel was damaging to the
United States. I am an American. I love Israel and support them. But
I have reported it each time the Israelis have made contact with me."*

*He thought to himself about Kopolowitz. He was clear that he
didn't agree with Kopolowitz' motives. Now how do we neutralize the
potential danger. Let's find out as much as we can about Kopolowitz.
The easiest way is from the horse's own mouth.*

*Over the next few days, he received numerous briefings and was
shown to his section. The section was told that LCDR Kaplan would
be taking over on Monday.*

*When Monday arrived, he moved into the section leader's office
and began a series of personal meetings with all his new staff. Most
seemed earnest and confident. Then he met Peter Kopolowitz in his
office for the first time.*

*Kopolowitz sat down in front of him and peered over the desk as
Daniel was finishing on the telephone. What he saw intrigued him. He
realized that his section leader was Jewish when he saw a small prayer
book lying on the desk with a Chumash (Hebrew Bible) lying open on
the corner nearest to Daniel's chair.*

Daniel finished with his call and stood up and reached across the desk to shake Kopolowitz" hand.

"Daniel Kaplan"

"Peter Kopolowitz"

"Nice to meet you Mr. Kopolowitz"

"Oh please, call me by my first name. We're kind of informal around here"

Daniel smiled,

"Good, you can call me by my first name in the office also. In the office my first name is Commander. And I will assume your first name in the office is Mister?"

Kopolowitz shook his head, smiling weakly and thinking to himself that his new boss was just another Pentagon hack. But he was curious. He was clearly making no bones to anyone about his religion. The military world had always discriminated against the Jews. Sometimes subtly, sometimes openly. Yet this man was boldly showing the world who he was.

"Where are you from, Mr. Kopolowitz?"

"Originally, I am from Ohio, although I grew up in New England."

"Where did you go to school?"

"I went to Harvard. I got a degree in Romance Languages from there"

"So, how did you end up working for the Navy"

"My father-in-law called in a favor"

Daniel shook his head knowingly. Then Kopolowitz asked him a question,

"Commander, do you find it hard being Jewish in the Navy?"

Daniel looked at him for a moment.

"Not particularly"

"Really, I would have thought . . . "

Daniel quickly interrupted him,

"Thought what?"

"Well sir, the Navy does not have the best reputation in how they treat Jews."

"Has anyone here discriminated against you because you are Jewish, Mr. Kopolowitz?"

"Well . . . Not overtly."

"But subtly?"

Kopolowitz nodded yes.

"Well welcome to the world Mr. Kopolowitz. The world has little appreciation for our people, even though we are probably responsible for more technological growth than any other people. But our reality is that we are hated, for who we are, not what we are. Sure, I feel discriminated against. But that's not going to get in my way to protect my country."

Kopolowitz nodded,

"Tell me something, Commander"

"Yes"

"What do you think about Israel?"

"I don't know what you mean"

"I mean are you Pro-Israel"

"Of course, I am a Jew"

"But you are a Naval Officer"

"So?"

"If you had to make a choice between America and Israel, who would you choose?"

"The question is out of context. I am an American. My first duty is to my country"

"I see. Well sir, if you don't having anything else for me, I would like to return to my desk."

"Certainly", he stood up and shook Kopolowitz' hand again. "It was nice to meet you"

"Same here, sir. Maybe some evening, you and your wife and me and mine can get together for dinner or drinks. I'd be curious to hear your views of the Israeli-Arab conflict. I imagine that it would be most interesting to see it from a line officer's perspective."

"I would love to except that my wife has not been found yet."

"Oh, I'm sorry, how long has she been missing?"

Daniel smiled, "She's not missing, she just hasn't been found yet"

CHAPTER THIRTY-SIX

Over the next few weeks, Daniel made it his business to become friendlier with Peter Kopolowitz. He went out with him for lunch or stopped to shmooze with him at his cubicle. The section found Daniel easy to work for and things seemed to have a flow of their own. Kopolowitz opened up to Daniel about his frustration at seeing information vital to Israel was not being shared with them.

As he became friendlier with him, he was invited to his home for dinner. There he met Jean Kopolowitz, a tiny woman who was a power package of energy. She was as rabidly pro-Israel as Peter and Daniel wondered how much she knew of his activities. He continued to come to their home for dinner or barbeques and the like. He became a somewhat frequent guest and a sounding board for Peter and Jean to rant to about how the Israelis were getting screwed by the American Intelligence community. Jean was very combative, asking openly, why Daniel as a Jewish Officer didn't say or do more.

He remembered that one morning, he had received a telephone call from Avraham Baruch.

"Daniel, how is it going over there?"

"So far, so good, Major."

"Not so formal Daniel, besides I'm now a Lieutenant Colonel. You know, for convenience."

"Well Mazel-Tov Colonel"

"Thanks, but seriously Daniel, how is our little project proceeding?"

"I think we're right on schedule. Why do you ask?"

"We got a visit yesterday"

"From him?"

"No"

"I don't understand Avraham"

"Maybe we should meet?"

"I guess that would be all right. Where would you like to meet, here or by you?"

"Neither. Listen Daniel, Get on the Metro and take it to Falls Church. When you come down the stairs to the street, look for a red taxi with the name Max's Cars written on it."

Daniel listened intently and quietly started to write all of what he was hearing onto a scrap of paper.

"When you get into the cab, say to the driver that you want to go to the best steakhouse in town. He will answer you that there are no good steakhouses in town. Then you say to him "Take me to McDonalds" . Okay Daniel, you got all that?"

"Avraham, this sounds like something out of a bad novel."

"Good, it's supposed to sound like that. Daniel, be in Falls Church by 5 o'clock"

"Okay"

Daniel hung up the phone. He laughed to himself as he filled out a contact form. Then he picked up the phone and called Director Steuben.

At 5 o'clock Daniel climbed down the stairs from the Metro Station in Falls Church, Virginia and looked around for a red taxi. Daniel had changed out of his uniform and was dressed in casual pants and a light jacket over his polo shirt.

Soon a red taxi pulled along side him and he reached for the door and climbed in.

He looked at the driver and said,

"Take me to the best steakhouse in town"

The driver laughed out loud,

"There are no good steakhouses in town"

Daniel looked at him for a moment. He was a little unsure about all of this but he said anyway,

"Then take me to McDonalds"

The driver looked back at him and reached his hand through the glass separating them to shake his hand,

"Colonel Baruch sends his regards"

"Where are we going?"

"Not to far. Why don't you sit back and relax. I'll get you there in one piece"

Daniel thought to himself, "They always say that!"

He leaned back on the cushion and the driver drove for almost an hour west until they reached a large horse farm. They drove through the gate and up to a very large and grand house.

The driver stopped the car and got out to open the door for Daniel. Daniel got out and looked at the house and walked to the door and rang the bell. The door opened to reveal a beautiful dark slim woman wearing a floor length shift dress.

"Please come in, Commander", she said with a hint of an Israeli accent. She reached out and took his hand and escorted into the house. It was a huge mansion with an imposing foyer and she led him back through the house to a large glass enclosed sunroom. Seated on a chair, drinking a tall Bloody Mary was Avraham Baruch. Next to him was a tall, elegant man who spoke English as if he had grown up in the states. Daniel recognized him as the Israeli Ambassador to the United

States, Reuven Ashenazi. As Daniel walked into the room, both men rose and shook his hand. Daniel felt sort of out of place, but they bid him to sit down in one of the comfortable wicker chairs and asked him if he would like a drink. He pointed to Colonel Baruch's glass and said,

"One of the same"

Soon the woman who had originally greeted him returned with a glass for him. He took a sip. It was a deliciously made drink. He stopped for a second and put the drink down on a side table. He made a face.

"What's the matter, Commander? Do you think we spiked your drink?", Colonel Baruch said laughingly.

Daniel chuckled lightly,

"Well, I must admit the thought crossed my mind, but why would you do it to me anyway?"

"Exactly", Ashenazi agreed, also chuckling, "What would be the point?"

They all laughed, Finally Daniel looked at these men and asked why he had been brought here.

Baruch giggled, "Well certainly not to enlist you"

They all laughed again. But finally Ashenazi tapped Baruch on his elbow and motioned him to start.

"Not yet, Reuven, we are waiting for one more."

So they continued to drink and make small talk until a large white haired gentleman joined them. He was introduced to Daniel, but Daniel did not need an introduction. Daniel knew the Prime Minister of Israel when he saw him.

They all sat down and Baruch started laying out the problem to Daniel.

"We have been visited in the Israeli embassy by a Chinese gentleman who had been enlisted as a conduit to pass on "vital information" to them. We looked at the documents he brought. Then we asked him how *he had gotten the information. He told us that an American gentleman had come to the embassy and offered to provide the Chinese with some information if they would act as his conduit with the Israelis to transfer these documents and others like it periodically."*

He handed Daniel a file to look at. Daniel opened it and saw some of the "intelligence" which he had fabricated for Kopolowitz.

"Did he give the Chinese anything?"

Ashenazi interrupted, "We have to assume so"

Daniel shook his head. Kopolowitz must be out of his mind. Who knows what information is being sent to whom. Daniel would have to assume that other countries besides China had been contacted. He looked at the Prime Minister,

"Sir, why are you here?"

"Commander, I am here because I just happen to be in Washington for a fundraiser. However, you must of course understand that this is now a matter of grave new importance to both your country and ours. Our relationship with China is our own. Your relationship is more adversarial. Regardless, you don't know what this man is giving them in exchange for him "helping us"."

"Which begs the question, sir, why am I here and not Director Steuben?"

"He knows why you are here."

"Again, I'm confused, why are you talking to me?"

"Because you no longer have the luxury of time to get him under control. Who knows what secrets he's giving out to whom in his misguided desire to help us poor Israelis."

"I don't understand. We've put in place a mechanism to feed this moron fake intelligence to give to you guys. Now this fake intelligence is being conduited by another country because of what?"

"Because, the embassy personnel here in Washington have been told to not let him in."

Daniel looked at the Ambassador incredulously,

"So let him in. Make him feel welcome. Take his papers and burn them for all I care. We are going to an awful lot of trouble here guys. Why don't we just arrest him?"

The Prime Minister looked up at Daniel.

"Commander, you are an intelligent man. You know that often times political considerations drive the way things are handled. I disagree with your President in this regard. As far as I'm concerned, I would just as soon have him eliminated, but you people are not going to allow it to happen. Kopolowitz made a scene at our embassy only last week. And now this. Obviously, you have to take this man out. But time has run out. Young man, either arrest him or eliminate him in some way. But get rid of him and do it immediately. I know you will want to talk with Director Steuben about this. Feel free to use this telephone. It is a secure phone and the Director is expecting your call."

Daniel got up and placed the call. The Director told him to relieve Kopolowitz immediately of all assignments and have him escorted out of the Pentagon first thing in the morning. He told Daniel to tell Kopolowitz that he would be arrested if there were any other incidents.

Daniel hung up the phone and looked around the room. The Israelis had been pretty patient up until now. As he looked at the Prime Minister's face, he knew that they had run out of patience.

They invited Daniel to stay for dinner, but he declined and asked for a ride back to the hotel he had been staying at during this assignment. He shook all of their hands and left the house shaking his head.

CHAPTER THIRTY-SEVEN

Daniel arrived in his office at 5:30 A.M. He prepared a cup of coffee and then made a phone call to the Pentagon Security Chief. Daniel hoped that he would be able to get Peter out of there without a scene. He wanted as little tumult as possible because if the Press Corps at the Pentagon got wind of this, everything was screwed.

At 8:00, Daniel looked through the window of his office to see if Kopolowitz had arrived yet. He didn't see him in his cubicle yet. The rest of his section began shuffling in and going to work. An hour passed, still Peter was not at his desk. Daniel asked his secretary if he had called in sick. She told him no one had heard from him.

At 9 o'clock, Daniel called the Kopolowitz home. He left a message on the answering machine and waited. By 10, Daniel had already spoken with Director Steubing and expressed his concern.

Around 10:45, he received a call from Avraham Baruch. Baruch was very upset.

"Daniel, that putz tried to get into the embassy again today. We turned him away. He is pacing like a lunatic in front of the building and my security people are getting very upset."

"Well Colonel, what do you want me to do?"

"Do something, because if he's not gone in the next half hour, we are going to shoot him dead. You hear me Daniel? Dead in the street. And who knows what he has with him."

"Avraham, that's crazy! Don't shoot him. What will that accomplish?"

"Listen Daniel, you better come down and get him or we are going to kill him."

"Okay, but Avraham, promise you won't do anything until I get there. Promise me Avraham."

"I don't know"

"Promise me! If I can't get him out of there, he's on his own. But you better promise to do nothing until I get there. Maybe, if we're lucky, he'll get bored and leave"

"We can only hope Daniel, Get over here fast."

Daniel grabbed his jacket and flew down the Pentagon corridors. He hit the door running and caught a cab.

"Take me to the Israeli Embassy and there is an extra ten in it for you if you get there as fast as humanly possible."

The driver burned rubber and soon Daniel could see with his own eyes the scene Kopolowitz was making in front of the Embassy. He was screaming at the guards and they were screaming at him. Daniel threw the fare at the driver and bolted out of the car. He ran up to Peter and put his hand on his shoulder and turned him around.

"It's over Peter", he said quietly, "It is over!"

Peter looked at Daniel in his Khaki Naval uniform and saw a man shaking his head yes at him and repeating,

"It's over Peter. We've known about you for months. We've tried to keep it quiet out of respect for your family, but it's over! Let's go quietly and not make a scene."

He started to gently move Peter away from the embassy front, but he pulled away,

"How dare you? This is Israel we're talking about. You are a Jew, Daniel. How could you?"

"Yes I am a Jew, but I'm also an American. And what you have been doing is wrong. Fundamentally wrong."

"Fundamentally wrong?", he screamed at Daniel, "They are withholding information that is vital to the Israelis. How can that be wrong? How?"

Daniel sighed deeply,

"Listen, you don't know what the Israelis do and don't know. Do you think you are the only one to decide what to share with them."

"If need be, Yeah!"

"And what if they don't want what you determine they need so badly?"

He looked at Daniel for a moment. His face drooped.

"Peter, it was the Israelis who told us about you in the first place. We tried to keep a lid on it. But Peter, the Chinese, how could you?"

Peter's eyes lit up, "You know about the Chinese?"

Daniel nodded yes.

"Well, I will do whatever is necessary to get vital information to the Israelis"

Daniel just looked at him sadly, "Please Peter, let's move on. You've made enough of a scene here" and he tried to get Peter to walk away from the Embassy with him. But he resisted Daniel. Then suddenly he punched Daniel in the stomach as hard as he could. It caught Daniel by surprise and knocked the wind out of him. He stood there retching on the street until he could get his composure. Then, really pissed off, he walked over to the nearest pay phone and dialed the F.B.I.

"Hello, this is LCDR Daniel Kaplan and I must speak to the highest ranking officer present. I am reporting a National Security Breach."

He was quickly shifted to the station head and explained the basic elements of the problem. Those elements being that Kopolowitz was making a scene in front of the Israeli Embassy and the Israeli's were poised to shoot him dead in the street. He also mentioned that the Navy was investigating Kopolowitz for espionage.

In what seemed like seconds, cars came flying out of nowhere and Agents carrying rifles and shotguns flew out of the cars. Quickly they arrested Peter and took him away. Daniel watched all of this from a distance and when things had quieted down and the people watching had dispersed, Daniel started to leave. But then he decided to take the rest of the morning off. He returned to his Hotel and settled in front of the T.V. with a cigarette. He tried to relax, knowing that he would be going back to the office in a few hours to start debriefing the operation.

Then he heard a knock on his door. He got up to answer it.

"Who's there?"

"This is Charles Stevenson from the F.B.I."

Daniel opened the door and looked at a man who was displaying his badge to him. His partner stood by quietly. The man said,

"Are you LCDR Daniel Kaplan?"

Daniel nodded yes and smiled,

"Hang loose a moment, gentlemen, I'll go get my coat"

CHAPTER THIRTY-EIGHT

Rebecca had made the phone call, unbeknownst to Daniel while she and the children were away at the Hotel. It was Sunday morning and she was packed up, ready to leave after lunch. The children were running around the Hotel enjoying their last few hours. The room was quiet. She drew the curtains closed and turned on a table lamp. She kicked off her shoes and looked through her pocketbook for a slip of paper upon which she had written the telephone number of Daniel Fiorentino in Virginia. She had gotten the number from directory assistance and throughout the weekend she was very anxious about having it in her bag.

She took out the paper and dialed the number. As it rang, she stretched out on the bed and propped a pillow behind her back. The phone rang three times and then a woman picked up the phone.

"Hello!"

"Hello, I'm looking for the Fiorentino residence"

A light southern accent crossed over wires to Rebecca's ear,

"Well, you've reached the right place. How can I help you?"

"I'm looking to speak to Ruth Anne Fiorentino"

The voice on the other end laughed gently,

"Well you got her. The one and only. At least, I think that I'm the one and only", Then she giggled happily.

Rebecca smiled.

"Ruth Anne, my name is Rebecca Kaplan. Do you know who I am?"

She heard the phone drop on the other end. It was quickly recovered and Ruth Ann returned to the phone. She seemed out of breath. Rebecca asked her,

"Are you all right, Mrs. Fiorentino?"

"Oh yeah, I'm fine. And please call me Ruth Anne"

Ruth Anne had sat down at her kitchen table and was shaking. Damn, Daniel wasn't home from church yet. She did not know what to say to this woman on the other end.

"Ruth Anne, I know that this must be very difficult for you. I am Daniel Kaplan's wife. My Daniel does not know that I am calling you. And I am calling to speak only to you."

Ruth Anne took a deep breath on the other end of the phone. Her knees were shaking.

"I am calling because this has been a great shock to my husband, as you can imagine. I expect that it has been a great shock to your husband."

"Yes, it has been a very traumatic thing for my Daniel as well. Thank you for saying that."

"Ruth Anne, we could all ignore this and pretend that it hasn't happened and I am certain life will go on much the same for both you and me. But my husband, I know him and I know his heart. He not only learned that he had a son, but that he had two grandchildren. I know, even if he doesn't say it, he wants and more importantly, he needs to see them and be a grandfather to them. So I would like to ask you to come visit us here in New York next weekend. I can't believe that I am saying this, but, please I want you to come, really!"

"I don't know, I'll have to ask Daniel."

"Please Ruth Anne, don't ask him. Tell him. Bring the children and let our families begin to heal. Please say yes."

Ruth Anne was in tears with the phone in her hand. She was sobbing loudly and Rebecca got very concerned. Finally Ruth Anne returned to the phone and whispered,

"Yes, we'll come"

"Good, let me give you my home phone number so that we can be in touch and make all of the arrangements together. Thank you. You don't know how important this will be to all of us!"

"It's okay Rebecca, I think I do. And it will be G-d's will that it shall be a wonderful reunion. Good bye"

"Good bye"

Rebecca hung up the phone. She thought to herself that the first hurdle was now overcome. There were many other hurdles to jump over the next week, but she was sure that they would successfully jump them together.

CHAPTER THIRTY-NINE

The family had been home for two days now, but nothing was the same. The children avoided their father, in part because of the revelation. In part because he was so depressed that he seemed dazed and confused. Rebecca tried to draw him out, but with little luck. She thought that his depression was based upon being in overwhelm. She did not know that he was grappling with the conversation he had with Isaac over the weekend. He could not even explain to her what had occurred. She would have thought he had gone daft. Frankly, he wasn't sure if he had not.

Finally, after dinner on Tuesday, she cleared the dishes and sent everyone upstairs. Daniel sat at the kitchen table drinking a coffee. She sat down next to him.

"Daniel, there is something I must tell you."

He looked at her,

"And what is that?"

"I've made a decision. And its final! Nothing you can say will change it. So don't try to convince me otherwise because it will not work. Do you understand?"

His stomach turned in knots and his face grew flush. He shifted uneasily in his seat and didn't know whether to look at her or off into the distance.

"Daniel, have you heard what I just said?"

He nodded yes.

"Well good"

He took a deep breath as if to steel himself against the worst possible circumstance. In his mind, he was convinced that she was about to ask him for a divorce. If she did, he knew that he would just die. Die right there!

"Becky, and what have you decided?"

"Daniel, don't hate me for doing this"

He started to shake. He knew what was coming.

"Daniel, while I was away, I called Ruth Anne Fiorentino"

"Called her, what? On the telephone?"

"Yes"

"Why? I don't understand Becky. Why would you have called her?"

"She was very nice Daniel. And she knew all about us"

"So?"

"They are coming here to visit with us this weekend"

"What?"

"All of them, Daniel, Ruth Anne and the twins"

"And when are they coming?"

"Friday, they are going to spend Shabbos and Sunday with us"

"With us, where will they stay?"

"Here in the house"

Daniel looked at her in amazement. He couldn't believe what he was hearing.

"But Rebecca, why did you do this?"

She reached out and took his hand in hers. She looked down at the table and shook her head.

"You are this young man's father, whether I like it or not. And this son of yours has children of his own. They are your grandchildren and just like our children they are twins and are a boy and a girl. If ever the Almighty has sent you a sign that this is the way it is supposed to be, then this sign seems to me at least, to be very clear."

He looked at her with tears forming slowly from his eyes. She continued,

"Daniel, I know that our life is about to change dramatically. Clearly, you cannot continue to be the Rabbi of Knesset Rambam. They would be mortified by the knowledge of all this. We will move upstate to the country and you can find a shul, maybe a Modern Orthodox or even a Conservative shul to serve or you may have to take a job. Who knows?"

He shook his head in acknowledgement. Rebecca looked at his eyes and said to him,

"Your path in life has had many dog legs. This is another one. But I will be there to live it with you. Why? Because I believe in you, I don't know why? But I do! I believe in your innate gentle kindness and in your faith in G-d. And more than that I love you!"

He stood up and drew her to him and held her in his arms with all of his might. He looked in her eyes and saw that she was crying too.

CHAPTER FORTY

The Torah was being put back into its Ark and the Sabbath service was now at the point where the Rabbi gave his sermon. Rabbi Kaplan stood up and walked over to the lectern. He looked out over the congregation in front of him. He looked up into the balcony where the women's section was. Rebecca was sitting there as she always had. He looked up at her and she nodded to him yes, as if to say it would be all right.

He took a deep breath and waited for everyone to get settled. Then he put on his glasses and opened his notes.

"The Torah speaks repeatedly about how ordinary people came to live extraordinary lives. It talks about Abraham. He was our first convert. It talks about Ruth, a convert who is the mother of the Davidic line and precursor to the Messiah. It talks about those who strayed and returned to the fold. Moses, our teacher, King David, King Solomon, etc. What the Torah does not do, except on rare occasions and at least on the surface, is talk about these peoples lives before their conversions or their return to the fold. It does that because, the lessons Torah is trying to teach us is about the virtues that were found by being true to Torah.

When tragedy strikes us, we turn to G-d and say, Why me? We rail against the perceived inequities of the world and G-d's participation in it. We expect, like a child, to be taken care of by the Almighty as if he was a parent taking care of our every want and desire. And we assume that when those wants and desires are not met that G-d has either forgotten us, or that he is not who we thought he was or even worse that he doesn't exist. We try to find the pathway that will bring us closer to him. Some insist it requires in-depth study of the law itself. Others throughout the ages have argued that it requires dancing and joy and song. Others have studied the mystic ways, looking to bring themselves close. And some go through the motions of whatever path they choose, because they need to be a part of the group. These people rarely find G-d in their hearts or in their thoughts, but have perfected the look and the sounds of someone who has found G-d within him.

The Torah rarely tells us of whether or how a person's past life can intrude upon their life now that they are in G-d's fold. Rather it treats that past life as if it did not exist or was of little consequence. Again the reason for this is simple. Torah is showing us the results of finding G-d.

But it is the process of finding G-d that concerns me today. And it is the reality that for some of us the past sometimes does intrude into the life we have chosen. And that sometimes, this occurs when it is least expected and certainly least wanted.

I spoke to a number of gentlemen over the last few weeks, because just such a thing has happened to me. I was angry and perplexed that G-d would force upon me such a terrible trial. I had become secure in the knowledge that I was doing everything proper and that my reputation in the community carried tremendous weight. So what has befallen me, in my own mind, put that into jeopardy. I feared that a lifetime of good works would dissolve in an instant. I remembered the old Navy adage that states: One awe damn, and that's not really the word, but one awe damn can kill all of your attaboys. It means that whatever good you have built up over time could be destroyed by one mistake.

These gentlemen helped me to examine the situation, not as a man who has a reputation within the community to uphold, rather as a man of G-d and to look at why G-d was doing what he was doing to me at this moment in time.

One gentleman in particular taught me a tremendous lesson from a struggle that he had. To paraphrase him: When looking at why, you must seek to ask the right question, rather than seeking out the right answer. Those who seek the answers often don't know what to ask. But if you seek to ask the right question, then surely the right answer is within yourself and can be clearly seen as the product of the Almighty.

And so my friends, my loyal friends. I have been your spiritual leader for over 20 years. When you hired me, you knew that I was not always religious. You came to rely on me because, I hope I was sensitive to your problems and your lives.

But as I said to you, I was not always religious. When I was a young sailor, I fell in love with a lovely lady named Karolyn. She was not Jewish. I fell in love with her just the same. We knew each other three years. We became engaged to be married. In fact, for a short period, I lived with her. When I went back to school to get my commission, she was transferred to California. I visited her there during a school break for three weeks. We were intimate. Then I returned to school and got my degree. However, just before I was to graduate, I lost contact with her. I was frantic. As soon as I was commissioned, I met my ship in Long Beach and went to sea with the ship for a week. When we pulled into San Diego, I went looking for her. I found her stationed at the Naval Hospital. It was then that she told me that three weeks before, she had met a man and after a two-week courtship, she had married him, even though she was still engaged to me.

As you can imagine, I was heartbroken and it took me a very long time, many years actually to recover. But I built a wonderful life as a Rabbi with a beautiful and lovely wife, Rebbetzin Kaplan. My life has been one of remarkable miracles.

Two weeks ago, I was visited by a young man. To make a long story short, he was this woman Karolyn's son. He is an Episcopal priest with a family of his own. But what I was to learn much to my horror was that he was not the son of the man Karolyn married instead of me, rather he is my son. A son I had never known about."

There was a hushed silence throughout the room. People looked up into the gallery at Rebecca, but she remained steadfast.

"You see that sometimes your past life can intrude. Why G-d has chosen this moment to reveal this to me. I must face it and face it openly. I acknowledge this man to be my son and I am proud of who he has become. However, it is clear to me that given the circumstances, I cannot remain the spiritual leader of this shul.

I have loved being your Rabbi for all these years and pray that you will look kindly upon me and my family. I wish you all the best. This test is also a miracle. And I will learn to live with and within it."

He sat back down. Nobody moved. Not a word was spoken by anyone. Daniel took off his prayer shawl and folded it and put it away. He got up and walked down the aisle of the shul and out the back door. Rebecca got up as well and joined him outside.

CHAPTER FORTY-ONE

She smiled at him and hooked her arm around his. They walked home from the shul. As they approached the house, they stopped and looked at it for a long time.

When they stepped inside, they were greeted by a house full of people. Ruth Anne and Father Daniel were sitting at the dining room table. They got up.

The two men shook hands and then Daniel kissed his son's cheek. They had been together for almost twenty-four hours. Despite the cultural differences, both families seemed to meld into one. The children all fell in love with each other and Daniel looked upon his grandson and granddaughter with a pleasure that he had never known.

The two men had spoken together late into the night. They found out so much about each other. Rebecca and Ruth Anne couldn't stop commenting about their similar mannerisms and reactions to things. The men talked about how G-d had affected and effected their lives. Finally, Rebecca came downstairs and sent them to bed.

Father Daniel asked his father,

"How did it go?"

"I don't really know, they seemed so shell shocked"

"I'm sorry for you father"

Daniel sighed deeply,

"Daniel, you can call me Dad if you want?"

The younger man thought for a moment, then he said,

"All right, Abba"

They all laughed. Then Rabbi Daniel placed his hands upon his son's head for the first time and blessed him formally. He kissed his son on the forehead and whispered that this was the most incredible miracle. Both men started to cry. All of the children and grandchildren gathered around the two men and hugged them. Rebecca took Ruth Anne by the hand and hugged her as well, saying,

"It is good! It is good!"

All this was interrupted by a knock on the door. Everyone looked but no one moved. A knock was heard again. Finally, Rebecca went to open the door. Standing on the porch were at least twenty members of his congregation. Another thirty were on the steps and pathway and milling on the sidewalk in front of the gate.

"Well what do we have here?", Rebecca exclaimed to the crowd.

One of the men yelled, "We want to see the Rabbi"

"Well I'm afraid that he is. . . "

"Please, we want to see him"

Rebecca walked back into the house and said to Daniel,

"They want to talk to you"

Daniel shook his head and walked out onto the porch. Everyone started to speak at once. Finally, Daniel quieted everyone.

"My friends, I am here. I will answer any questions you might have"

One of the congregants, Joe Rubin was the President of the Shul. He spoke up in front of everyone.

"Rabbi, as you can imagine, we were horrified by your story this morning. It is a real surprise and we are shocked, just shocked."

Daniel nodded in understanding.

"We are shocked that you didn't ask us our advice. We are shocked that you would consider leaving us for an indiscretion that happened before you became religious. And mostly we are shocked that you would assume that we would no longer want you as our spiritual leader."

Daniel looked at them. He was surprised by what had just been said. But as he looked out onto the crowd, he could see kindness, where he had assumed that he would be ruined.

"There may be people in this shul who are offended by what you have said. And they may choose to leave this congregation. Well if that be the case, be gone with them. We do not accept your resignation, Daniel. We do not accept it. You have led us for a generation and G-d willing may you lead us for many more. Well Rabbi, are you in?"

Daniel looked at these people. His eyes started to fill with water. He had known most of these people a very long time. Now they were saying to him that he was still who they loved and respected. Still who they wished to come to for comfort and judgment. Still the man they wanted to lead them.

He shook Joe Rubin's hand and nodded yes. Then the crowd milled around him and brought him near to them. Rebecca, standing in the doorway, started to cry. And Daniel the priest looked out through the porch at the miracle happening before his eyes.

Book 4

KAROLYN AND FATHER DANIEL

CHAPTER FORTY-TWO

She returned the ball against the wall with one of her killer shots. The ball simply hit the base of the wall and rolled back away, making it impossible for her opponent to return it. Even at 49 years of age, Kary German-Fiorentino could still outplay most of the men at the racquetball courts. She played almost every day. Today's opponent was one of her favorites. Tall, handsome, lean and muscular, he was just 26 years old. She looked at him with an approving eye. Then she ran him ragged and sweaty across the court for almost an hour. Kary laughed inwardly as she decisively beat him in each of the three games that they played. She bent down and picked up a can of balls and placed the one they were playing with back inside. She put her racquet into its case and draped a towel over her shoulders. The young man came over and smiled at her. He shrugged foolishly. She hooked her arm across his back and gave him a kiss on the cheek. He turned red. She giggled at his embarrassment.

"You think it's funny, don't you?" The young man said to her.

"Actually, I do" She replied and continued to giggle. "What are you afraid of? People might talk?"

"Well actually, they might!"

"Too bad! If a mother can't kiss her son in public, then its too bad for all of them"

"But Mom, that son is their parish priest!"

"So what?" She looked at him with a grin.

He shook his head. As she got older, it seemed as if she had gotten younger. Certainly, she had gotten bolder. Since she had become a widow, she seemed relaxed and laughed a whole lot more. To her son, Father Daniel Fiorentino, the young parish priest of St. Michael's Episcopal Church in Tidewater, Virginia, she seemed genuinely happy for the first time in many years. She actually looked better now than he had ever seen her. And for him it was sort of a relief. And for Daniel Fiorentino, these past several months had forever changed his relationship with his mother. The world he had known, one of orderly ways and organized living, had become completely topsy-turvy.

He looked at her again, this time more closely. He had to admit, she was in shape. And she was taking good care of herself. Even her colleagues at the high school had remarked that she seemed to be a changed woman. Many of Daniel's parishioners had started pulling him aside, asking him if maybe his mother might be interested in an evening out. But she had resisted their efforts and their inquiries, stating that she was having too much fun to be tied down to anyone.

Daniel understood that. She was finally free. Free from the burden of Charley's illness and free of the burden of guilt she had long felt over a lost love named Daniel Kaplan. And her son knew that she felt free of this guilt from Daniel Kaplan because he had orchestrated a meeting between father and son. It was that meeting that had revealed to Daniel Kaplan something that Kary had hidden from him for 25 years. What she had hidden was the knowledge that she had a child and that the man she had married, Charles Fiorentino, was not the child's father at all. The real father was Daniel Kaplan.

And for Daniel Fiorentino, he now understood that this man who was really his father had a history with his mother. He was a man his mother had once almost married. A man she had been engaged to but did not marry. All this Daniel Fiorentino had only learned about within the last six months.

This man Daniel Kaplan was an interesting fellow. Like his son he was also a man of G-d. On the surface this shouldn't really have been a problem for the young Priest. But his father was no ordinary man of G-d. He was a revered leader of his Jewish community.

He looked at his mother and laughed with her. They went down to the locker rooms, showered and changed. Then they went over to a local diner for some coffee and dessert. They sat down at a booth by the window. Both ordered coffee. Daniel ordered some apple pie. Kary just wanted her coffee.

"Daniel, how is your father doing?", she asked him after they had been served.

"I spoke to him yesterday on the phone. He seems fine. Rebecca spoke to me afterwards and said that he had been working very hard, but that he was good."

"I'm glad. Danny". She smiled softly, then she asked him,

"What is she like?"

"Who?"

"His wife, Rebecca?"

Daniel laughed and shook his head, " I like her actually, very much. But that's one tough customer. She runs that house like it was an army. My father walks around in this fog, it seems. At least he did the three times we've visited them. He is really . . . how would I describe it? His head is in the clouds all the time. Yeah, that's it. He seems perpetually surprised at the life he is leading. But he's great! He's easy to talk to. Not judgmental at all. He loves Ruth Anne and the kids. I mean he really does love the kids. He dotes on Jack and Beth and they adore him."

"Does he talk religion with them?"

"Nope", he shook his head, trying to swallow a piece of pie as he spoke, "He talks all kinds of sports to Jack, especially baseball. I've seen him rummage through an old box and pull out some baseball gloves. . . I mean he must have five or six of them."

She looked at him cynically.

"Really, I'm serious, he's a real fan. We've gone out in his backyard and thrown a baseball around with him. But he also takes special time with Beth. They sit together and have these deep talks. I've seen them disappear for several hours. She says they sit on these benches on Ocean Parkway, which is a main drag in Brooklyn and they talk away. What about, Ruth Anne and I have no idea. But she has connected to him very strongly. He takes time to read to them and he tells them these wonderful stories, sometimes from the Bible, sometimes he tells them about growing up in Brooklyn. And believe it or not, he is a puppeteer"

"A what?"

"A puppeteer!"

She gave him this perplexed look.

"He has these hand puppets and he makes them seem so real. Even Ruth Anne says it. He becomes the puppet characters so completely that the children sit there entranced. And he interacts with each child. They are crazy about their Grandfather, Thank G-d"

She smiled, "I'm happy for you Danny. For you, Ruth Anne and the kids." She paused for a moment. Then she shook her head lightly.

"And for him also. I'm really glad for him. Tell me, does he ever discuss me with you or the kids?"

"He asks about you always, but I've never heard him discuss you other than to discuss with me what happened when you were seeing each other. Even then, he seems to say little. I push him for details sometimes and he answers my questions, but you can see that he is very reserved when he talks about you."

"I think I can understand that", she said.

Then she frowned for a moment and looked out the window. She drifted off into some recess of her mind and Daniel could see that she was disturbed by what she was thinking.

"Mom, are you upset that we have spent so much time in Brooklyn these past few months?"

"Oh no" She shook her head and looked at her son.

"Well, maybe you should come with us for a visit? I'm sure that you would have no problems with Rebecca"

Kary laughed out loud. Daniel made a surprised face.

"Of course you would say that! You're a man. And you are his son, not her husband's lost love" She was quiet for a moment. Then she started to ask a question, but stopped. He noticed that she was uncomfortable about something,

"Mom, is there something wrong?"

"Oh no! Not really. Tell me something. Does he ever discuss religion with you?"

"Of course, he does. We talk about G-d all the time"

"No, not G-d. That's not what I mean. Does he ever discuss your faith with you? How you came to the decision to become a Priest?"

He looked at her carefully, but she continued, looking most uncomfortable while asking,

"Does he ever question your belief in Jesus?"

"You know, he has always discussed G-d in this macro way. But he acknowledges my belief in Jesus, even if he doesn't believe himself."

"Tell me Daniel, do you believe in Jesus?"

Daniel looked at her like she was crazy.

"Of course I do, I'm a priest!"

"I know that", she snapped at him," That's not what I am asking you?"

He seemed confused,

"Well, what exactly are you asking me?"

"I don't really know. I guess, I want to try to understand how you believe in Jesus within your heart?"

Daniel was very confused,

"What's this all about, Mom?"

"Oh . . . I don't know. I was just wondering", She paused for a second,

"If you became a priest because you felt the pull of G-d or the pull of Jesus?"

Daniel pondered the question for a long time. He took a sip of his coffee and a bite of his apple pie and thought. His mother looked at him the whole time, trying to decipher what was going on in his head.

"Mom, I don't rightly know! I've never thought of it before. To me, it is all rolled together as one."

"You realize that to your father, it is not. To him, G-d is a very solo experience."

"A what? I don't understand"

"When your father and I were dating, we would discuss the differences in our religions. It was easy for me to discuss it with him, even though we were of different faiths. You know why?"

"No", Daniel said, shaking his head.

"Because, I could conceptualize G-d, but the story of Jesus seemed to me to be unreal. Even though, I still go to church, I'm not really sure I believe in Jesus. Yes the man, I believe in, it's just that whole son of G-d business. I always have had trouble with it, even as a little girl.

"I can explain it too you if you'd like?"

"You don't need to explain it to me Danny. Its all gobbledegook to me anyway."

"What?"

"Its gobbledegook. Nonsense, you know?"

Daniel got very upset,

"No I don't know Mother! To me this gobbledegook as you call it, is my life."

"Oh Daniel, its not your life!"

"I beg to differ with you" he said in the most annoyed way.

She sighed in exasperation, "Oh, its not that. Listen to me my son, Mr. Priest. When your father and I were together . . ."

"Courting, he likes to say"

"Thank you for interrupting. Anyway when your father and I were courting" She looked up at him, "We talked about faith, our beliefs, etc. Daniel used to say that when G-d split the Red Sea, three million people were there to witness it."

"Actually 600,000"

"No that was 600,000 men. And men of fighting age. Actually there were about three million people at Mt. Sinai, if you include all the old people, women and children"

"Gee Mom, I didn't think you knew so much about the Bible"

"Why, because I never go to church?"

"Actually, yes!"

"There's a lot you don't know about me"

"As I've learned", he said to her with a slight grin.

"Touche! My point is, however, even if the whole story of the crossing of the Red Sea sounds ludicrous on it's face", She paused, "Even if it sounds outlandish to believe that the sea actually split, there is eyewitness verification. And not just one or two persons verifying, but millions."

"Okay"

"Then Daniel would point out to me that Christian Scripture does not do that".

"Does not do what?"

"Doesn't verify!"

"Sure we do, just look at the Gospels"

"Exactly my point! We know of the events of Jesus' returning from the dead but not from eyewitnesses. Rather it is the testimony of men who came much later. No?"

Daniel looked at his mother with wonder.

"So"

"I've always been disturbed by that contrast. Haven't you?"

She looked up for a moment and then started playing with her spoon, spinning it around on the table. Daniel looked at her perplexed. She continued her speaking as if reading his thoughts and answering them,

"When you told me that you wanted to become a priest, I had to make some choices."

"What choices?"

"Well one, to have exactly this conversation with you."

"And?"

"Whether to tell you about your real father while Charley still lived"

"And?"

"And what?"

"Well obviously you didn't tell me while Charley was alive, so why discuss it now?"

She made a face. She was sort of sorry she had brought it up at this point. But there was no point avoiding it now. It was out on the table anyway.

"I chose not to discuss it with you because I didn't want to dissuade you from something that your heart seemed so taken with. But I couldn't figure out why? Where had this affinity come from. Certainly not from Charley, he avoided Church like the plague and I always felt that I was going through the motions. But I never mentioned it but, I've always wondered what attracted you. G-d or Jesus?"

He shrugged. "And now seeing that your actual father ended up in the same place, I wonder?"

She stared out the window for a second and started to pick at his pie with her fork. She sipped her coffee and looked at him kind of sheepishly. Daniel looked at her with wide eyes and a growing discomfort.

"Whew, who'd have thought?" he said to himself, shaking his head, "Honestly Mom, I don't know." He sighed deeply for a moment, "Actually. . . ." he paused, "Interesting!" He looked down for a moment then looked up at her, " You know, I have never questioned the difference, never really considered it as different. Certainly in seminary, no one ever debated the issue". He pondered the question while taking a bite of pie. As he drew the fork out of his mouth he said to her, "Its good food for thought for me. Its something . . .I guess I will have to discuss with my father."

He paused for a moment in thought, and then he shook his head,

"I don't really know! Gee Mom, what's this all about?"

"Daniel has never tried to lead you into any kind of discussion about Jesus?"

"No. Never!"

"Interesting"

"You seem surprised?"

"I am!"

"Why?"

"I don't know", she looked down, still playing with her spoon. Daniel reached across the table, grabbed her hand and stopped her. The spoon rolled down off the table onto the booth cushion on which she was sitting. She quickly recovered it.

"What, did you think he was going to do? Try and convert me?" Daniel asked laughingly. She didn't laugh however. Rather Kary looked her son right in the eyes. She moved the coffee cup away from in front of her and put both of her elbows on the table holding up her head.

"Daniel, I want to see him!"

Daniel was startled. He took a drink from his water glass and looked very carefully at his mother.

"You heard me right! I want to see him, Daniel"

He took a deep breath and replied, "Mom, I don't think that's a very good idea, not a good idea at all!" He shook his head resolutely.

"I have to see him. A few moments ago, you invited me. You said I'd get along fine with Rebecca."

"I know Mom, but really!" He shook his head definitively, "Out of the question! Its just craziness, Mom.

"Why?"

"Why??? I can't believe you are asking that question." He looked at his mother sharply. "I can't believe you would even consider asking me this question?"

"He'd want to see me, Daniel"

"No he wouldn't. What the hell has gotten into you Mom?

She took a sip from her water. "Remember what you asked me a moment ago?"

"No"

"Yes you do!. You asked me if I thought that your father would try to convert you? I never answered that question."

"So what? What has that got to do with you wanting to see him?"

"It only matters if you let me answer the damn question!" She said testily to him.

He looked at her perplexed. "So answer it already!"

She continued, " The answer is that he wouldn't have to!"

"He wouldn't have to what?" Daniel said.

"He wouldn't have to convert you!" She repeated more directly.

Daniel looked at her closely. She looked down at the table and picked up a packet of sugar in front of her. She held it up to the light and examined it for a moment. Then she looked out the window at the bright sunny street. Daniel saw that she was drifting into her own head again. He reached out and touched his mother's arm again,

"He wouldn't have to convert me?" He was very confused.

"No"

Daniel leaned back against the booth and looked at his mother very carefully.

"What are you talking about?"

Kary sighed deeply and looked her son in the eye,

"He wouldn't have to convert you because you are already a Jew!"

He slid his back upwards against the booth, and then he dropped back down to the cushion he was sitting on. She could see his Adam's Apple moving furiously and his eyes grew strict and angry,

"That's preposterous, Mother. What would ever get you to say something so absurd?"

She sighed deeply. Then she looked down onto her seat for her pocketbook. She pulled it onto the table and unzipped it. She rustled around inside for a few moment and then withdrew a small bottle of pills. She opened the bottle, removed one and took it with some water. She returned the bottle to her bag and returned the bag to her seat. She looked at Daniel, gently with sad knowing eyes.

"Times like these, I wish that I still smoked. I could use a cigarette about now."

He looked at her quizzically. He never remembered her smoking. Charley always was smoking, but not Mom. He was very confused.

"Mom, you don't smoke."

"I know, not any more. There was a time when I first met Charley that I started to smoke. It would relax me. I've stolen occasional smokes over the years to calm me down"

"Mom, what was that you just took?"

"A tranquilizer. Just something to help me cope when I get anxious"

"Anxious about what?"

"Oh, just things"

"Like what?"

She took a deep breath and seemed to suddenly relax and refocus. It was as if the tranquilizer had taken effect.

"Danny, I'm all right. Really I am"

"Mom, you're not all right. Something is bothering you. You've asked me the strangest questions and then you tell me I am a Jew. I know my father is a Jew, but you are not a Jew and religion passes through the mother, at least according to my father's beliefs. It all seems very clear to me"

"No it isn't!" she said angrily. Then she calmed down and smiled, "You see my Daniel. Everything is not black and white. To you life is black and white, but by now you should have figured out that life, our life, Father Daniel, is anything but clear. It is a gray world son and very complicated. But trust me when I say to you that you are a Jew".

"And how do you arrive at that incredible conclusion Mother?"

"Because . . . my son . . . I am a Jew!"

He looked at her incredulously,

"That's not true Mother. You were baptized in the Church"

"I know but. . ."

"But what?", he said fiercely at her.

Kary sighed deeply again. The waitress came to their table and refilled their cups. She stirred some sugar into the cup and placed the spoon on her napkin. She looked up at her son and shook her head.

"I need for you to absorb the fact that your mother is Jewish and therefore so are you."

"But I'm baptized as well. I am not Jewish at all. I am an Episcopal priest"

"Be that what it may, you are the son of a mother who is Jewish"

"Mom, you're talking nonsense. Are you going to tell me that Grandma is Jewish?"

"Yes"

"I don't think she would consider herself a Jew"

"Probably not, but she is nonetheless"

"How?"

"Your great grandmother, Leah Deutsch was born a Jew and acknowledged herself as such, even if she wasn't religious about it."

"You're talking about Grandma Leah. Why that's not true! She went to church every Sunday. She took communion. I've seen her. I've actually handed her the wafer."

"I know, but what you don't know was that she followed a boy named Matthew Deutsch to Virginia and married him."

"I know all about how he ran away to the Navy and was killed in the war. Great Grandma told me the story herself."

"Well what she didn't tell you was that she was Jewish. What you also don't know is that Grandma Leah became pregnant with your grandmother before Matthew was killed. She had nothing and nobody but the baby she was carrying. So she returned to Batavia with her in-laws. They took care of her and helped her raise my mother. But they gave that support conditional upon Leah converting to Catholicism.”

“Why?”

“Because they were mean, selfish people”

“Okay, knowing Great Grandmother. . . I mean, She was tough. I just don’t see her converting unless she wanted too.”

“She wanted to be buried next to Matthew”

He shook his head in understanding, then he asked,

“But he died so long ago”

“Well she is buried next to him. She never remarried and she turned her life over to the church. I suspect it was because she felt no other place to go with her emotions and it allowed her to remain close to Matthew’s memory all those years. We are Episcopalians because that is what my father was raised to be. My mother being a “Catholic” easily adopted his faith because it really is Catholicism in another form. Charley was Catholic, but couldn’t care less.”

“So what has this got to do with being Jewish. Everyone’s been baptized. We’re all Christian. What’s the big deal?”

“For us, it is not a big deal. For your father it is”

“How so?”

“I always let your father believe that the reason I pushed him away and married Charley was because I knew that he would never marry me because of my religion.”

“And?”

“Well you see, son, I knew by that time that it made no difference. From your father’s point of view and as I have learned from asking several Orthodox Rabbis, I am Jewish. The fact that I was baptized as a child means very little in the big scheme of things. Jews don’t believe that you can convert out. Even if you convert in and change your mind afterward, they still consider you a Jew.

Hence, you are my son. I am a Jew and so are you!"

Daniel looked into his mother's eyes. He sat quietly for a long time.

"Mother, why are you telling me this now?"

She breathed in deeply and looked around the diner.

"Daniel, I have always lived as a Christian and could accept that there is a G-d. But as I told you before, I always, even as a child, questioned the whole concept of Jesus and the Trinity. When I was dating Daniel, I thought to myself how easy it would be for me to just become Jewish. After we got engaged and he was still in school in Mississippi, I went to see a Rabbi in San Diego about converting. I was going to surprise Daniel by starting conversion classes. The Rabbi I met with asked me all these questions about my family history. I didn't understand why he was asking all of these things of me. Finally, he took a deep breath. You know, I can see the whole conversation in my mind right now as I tell this to you"

"Well?" Daniel said impatiently.

"Well" she leaned in towards him and spoke very quietly, "He said to me that no conversion was necessary. I told him I didn't understand. He smiled at me and said to me, "Child, you are already one of us. You are already a Jew." I was floored by what he said. He must have thought I looked stricken, but he explained the law to me. According to Jewish Law religion passed through the mother. So I had always been a Jew and didn't have to do anything to marry Daniel as a Jew"

"So why didn't you tell him? I'm sure it would have made him very happy"

"It probably would have. In retrospect, I think I was in a bit of shock. Suddenly, how I had defined myself had changed. But also Daniel was so all over the place. And then when I realized I was pregnant . . . and well . . . "

"Life", answered her son.

She smiled weakly, "Yeah, life!"

"Mom, I'm still confused. Why are you telling me all this now?"

"Well strangely enough it goes back to my original question to you"

"That being?"

"Is you service to G-d based upon G-d himself or Jesus?"

Daniel again pondered the question,

"And what difference would it make anyway?"

Karolyn bit the bottom of her lip for a moment, then she rubbed her cheek with her hand. She looked up at her son. He was kind and sweet and loving. He was devoted to his parish and to his family. She saw him entirely different now than she had ever envisioned him.

"Because I think that if your service to G-d is based upon Jesus, then you have found your place in the world and should remain a priest"

"Who's considering not being a priest?"

"Let me continue, please. Daniel. If your service to G-d is based upon G-d, then I believe that you are in the wrong place. And that place. . . I can't believe, I'm actually saying this", she shook her head in wonderment, "is in the world of your father"

Daniel looked at her flabbergasted,

"Surely, you don't mean. . .?"

She shook her head yes.

"Well I'll be!" He paused, "I'll be!"

"Arrange for your father to meet me again. This is also a secret I never told him. It is a secret that I have held from him for twenty-five years. I need to tell your father that I knew that I was Jewish when we were together."

"That would just kill him! Meeting him is out of the question. If you want him to know, I can tell him for you. Kind of break it gently to him, you know"

"Daniel", she said in a quiet plea, "just arrange for me to meet him. I need to tell him and I need to ask his forgiveness after all these years. Please son, make it happen."

CHAPTER FORTY-THREE

*D*aniel Fiorentino sat back in the tall black office chair that had been a gift to him from Ruth Anne when he had gotten appointed to the Parish of Tidewater. It was soft leather on five wheels and a person could easily fall asleep in it. He had done so himself many times. As he surveyed the papers on his desk, he couldn't help but fidget. He had no intention of trying to wade through it all today.

He had returned from the coffee shop with his mother to her house. He walked around and went upstairs to his old room. He looked around. It was basically unchanged from the time he was a child. He looked at the large wooden cross hanging over his bed. He reached over the headboard and took it down. He held the brown wood in his hand and turned it over. Burned into the back was his name. He had made the cross himself when he was 9 years old, using his father's tools. He had sanded and finished it with extreme care. His father had been angry at him for using the tools without his permission, but remarked about its beauty and simplicity even if he didn't like religious articles. But his Mother had told him how much she liked the cross and hung it up over his bed.

He gently hung it back up above his bed and sat down on its edge. He looked around. The sunlight streamed through the Venetian blinds and reflected on the floor. The colors of the rainbow could be clearly seen at its edges.

"Black and White", he thought to himself. It's how he had viewed the world from the time that he was a little boy. Black and White! And life pretty much was that way for him for a very long time. Right was right. Wrong was wrong.

Then his whole world had changed. His father was not his father at all. His mother had loved another man and he was his real father. And amazingly enough to himself, he had come to accept all that.

"I can live with a father who is Jewish", he said to himself. "I can live with it because it is so. I <u>can</u> love him even if our worlds are so different. But now . . .Our worlds are not different. I think! Oh' I don't know!" He shook his head in self-doubt.

"Are you okay?"

He looked up and saw his mother standing in the doorway.

"You looked like you were deep in thought."

"I was"

"I know", she said with a little smile, "I was talking to you one moment and the next thing I know, I'm talking to myself."

"Its all right Mother, I just came up here to think"

"Has it helped?"

"Helped? Ugh . . . yes. Actually no"

"Well as the cause of your problem can I do anything to help? Although I know you probably have heard more than enough from me today", she laughed gently.

"No, it's not like that". He stood up and hugged her. "I just feel so out of my body"

"Kind of like I must have felt when the Rabbi told me that I was a Jew?"

He looked at her. Closely.

"What did it feel like Mom? And what did you do?"

She sat down on his bed. He joined her. She held his hands. She looked at them, very closely. Kary looked at her son. When she looked at him she saw two things. Her son and the remembrance in living flesh of the man of her youth. It made her shudder inside.

"I'll tell you what it was like. Although I was luckier than you in a way"

"Why?"

"Grandma Leah"

He shook his head in understanding.

"I walked out of the Rabbi's office and got into my car. As I drove back to the ship I started to shake."

"Why?", he asked a little confused.

She pursed her lips for a moment and then looked around the room. Daniel looked at her and whispered to his mother,

"Why?"

"At first I thought that it was because my whole identity as a person was changed. I am not Episcopalian, I'm a Jew. But something gnawed in me that told me that wasn't true. I couldn't figure it out. Anyway, I settled down and drove on. Later that day, I called my grandmother."

"Leah?"

"Yes. I told her about the meeting with the Rabbi"

"And how did she react?"

"She was silent on the other end of the phone"

"Silent?"

"Yes, absolutely silent"

"I don't understand?"

"Daniel, she was dumbstruck"

"But certainly, she must have known this all along?"

"Daniel, people make their own realities sometimes"

"I don't understand"

"Grandma asked me if I was going to marry Daniel?"

"Why did she ask that?"

"That's what I wanted to know as well. I told her well of course, this cinched it, we were meant to be together."

She took a breath. Daniel made a face,

"And?"

"Grandma said to me something I have never forgotten", Kary said dramatically.

"What was that?"

"She said to me that whatever I did and whomever I married she would love me just the same"

"And?" Daniel was getting impatient.

"I told her that I knew that. That's why I was calling her"

"What did she say to that?"

"She told me something else"

"What?"

"She told me that the most important thing for me to consider was not whether he was the same faith as me but whether he'd be home every night."

"WHAT?" Daniel exclaimed, "That makes no sense. I don't understand. You were telling your grandmother that you were coming full circle back to her roots and she told you that?"

"Yep", Kary said shaking her head, "But I understood what she was talking about. At least I thought I did. And so I took her advice."

He looked at his mother for a moment. He saw that her face was suddenly dark and sad. He smiled at her. She shook her head yes, knowingly. Then she looked at her son closely and softly said,

"And Daniel, she was wrong!"

Book 5

CONCLUSION

CHAPTER FORTY-FOUR

The telephone rang in the room. Rebecca looked at Daniel then at the phone. He walked over and picked it up. He spoke quietly into the receiver, shook his head and then put the phone down. The moment had arrived. He was not ready.

"That was Daniel", he said without looking at Rebecca.

"So, she's here!" Rebecca said quietly with no sense of emotion.

"I shouldn't do this. This is wrong! I chose my way of life and it is with you."

"Daniel, my Daniel, we've been all through this. I want you to meet with her. In many ways, I need you to. But more important, you need to. For if you don't, you'll never know and if you don't know, you will always have doubts, about me, about your choices in life, even about our children."

"No!" he almost screamed, "There can never be any doubts about the way I feel about our children. I love them with everything that I have. Just like I love you".

She looked at him carefully. It would be so easy to say to him that it was all right, don't meet with Karolyn. She would win by default. And she didn't want to win by default. She had devoted her entire being to this man and she didn't want to share him with anyone, especially, his memories. She had too much riding on it, but she was prepared to lose. For once, she had no back-up plan. There could be none.

"You need to know, even if you are unwilling to admit it to me, I know that you need to know. I've wrestled with this as much as anybody and it is so clear to me that you must know. So like the old song, I am letting you fly free, if you come back, you are mine, if you fly away, then you were never really mine. And I can live with it. I may hate the idea of it, but I can live with it."

He sighed and his eyes filled with tears.

She continued,

"More important than any of this, you must see if what drove you to G-d was anguish or feeling. I pray for you that it was feeling, true feeling. Because I know if it is that, then you are mine. If it was anguish, then you are hers and you cannot continue to be a man of G-d, because that was never really your path. So you see my sweetheart, it is very important that you go downstairs and meet with her. So go!"

"Come with me", he whispered as he gathered her into his arms and hugged her tightly.

She let him hold on for a long time. Then she separated herself from him and said,

"I'll come down with you, but I will not go with you to her. That you must do on your own. Do you understand?"

He shook his head yes and reached onto the night table for a tissue to dry his eyes. He looked closely at the women he had shared his life with. He knew that he had been unfair to her in what he had carried in his head for so long. He had tried to bury it and had been successful for long stretches. Then something, a bit of music, a smell of something cooking, something, would trigger it back and he would think of Karolyn again. Even when he was engrossed in his rabbinical duties, she would intrude into his brain and into his memories. And he had often wondered what had become of her, but he had done nothing to find out.

And now, because of the efforts of the son that he did not even know existed, he was going to have the opportunity to have the answers to the questions that had eluded and confused him for so long. But he was afraid. He did not want it that the beautiful life he had so painstakingly built with Rebecca should be based upon lies. Well not lies exactly, but half –truths of the heart. But he wasn't sure of anything anymore. The strapping young man who was his son was still a stranger to him. How was he to bring the two diverse histories of his life together and make them work? Could they ever really work? Or would he have to again surrender his heart and his soul?"

Rebecca saw what he was thinking and said nothing. Finally she reached out and took his hand.

"Come, let's go"

He nodded briefly and accepted her hand. Together they left the room and walked to the elevator banks. They rode down in silence, each in their own head.

Finally, the elevator reached the lobby and the doors opened. They walked out together and then she let go. She shooed him away in the direction of the lobby to where she had seen his son Daniel sitting. She could see the back of a woman, but not the face.

She turned around and went back into the elevator, then she stepped back out and sort of hid behind some potted plants.

He walked stiffly towards the lobby and then saw his son sitting there. He was about to turn around and run, when young Daniel saw him and rose. He looked impressive with his black suit and starched Roman collar. How strange Daniel felt as he looked at him. He was also dressed in a black suit, with an ordinary tie and his rabbi's wide brimmed hat.

Karolyn turned around in her seat and looked at him. She saw a tall older man with a long white beard wearing the garb of a respected Rabbi. She did not recognize him. She looked up to her son and said,

"Danny, is that him?"

"Yes mother, that's him"

"I don't recognize him!"

"Wait till he's a little bit closer. You will."

She continued to look and as he approached she looked at his eyes and gasped. It was him! She would recognize those piercing hazel eyes anywhere. She thought to herself,

"Is this the man I loved so passionately, so many years ago?"

She followed him with her eyes some more and answered the question in her head aloud.

"I guess it is him", she whispered to herself.

"What did you say Mother?"

"Oh nothing, it is him Daniel, I do recognize him."

Daniel continued to walk through the lobby towards their grouping of soft chairs and sofa. Young Daniel stood up and greeted him. The two men shook hands and then young Daniel gently guided his father to the place where his mother was sitting. She rose from her couch and turned towards the two of them.

"Hello Daniel", she said quietly and reached for his hand.

He was momentarily dumbfounded. He looked at her carefully. She had barely changed. She still had the smooth cheeks and the big eyes that he had first noticed so long ago. Only now, those eyes showed the telltale signs of aging with little crow's nests at the outside corners. She was still fit. Her hair was still in a short cut, but now had highlights of gray. She looked as if she had grown older gracefully, but had not grown old.

"Hello Kary", he chokingly whispered. He accepted her outstretched hand and took it in his own. He looked in her eyes for a long time and said nothing. Suddenly, she pulled him towards her and kissed him on his cheek. He turned all red in the face.

She laughed for a moment. They sat down together on the couch. She to his right, he to her left. Young Daniel settled into the easy chair directly opposite them. There was silence. Both looked up independently at their son. He made a confused look at both of them. The tension was very strong. You could almost cut it with a knife.

Neither Daniel nor Kary looked at each other. Nor did they say anything. Daniel was getting very anxious. His breathing became very hard and labored. Karolyn asked him,

"Are you all right?"

He took a deep breath, then another. He looked straight out over the lobby.

"Did I not deserve to know that I had a son?"

She sighed. He continued,

"Well?" he waited. She said nothing.

"Why? Why didn't you tell me? Was our relationship of such little value that you would hide **this** kind of information from me. Did I hurt you so badly that you would deny a father the right to see his own child grow up? To keep the very fact of his existence a secret for so long?"

Young Daniel sat upright in his chair and moved to intercede.

"No son!", he exclaimed, "This is between your mother and I!"

He looked at his mother, asking with his eyes if she agreed. She nodded in agreement and said quietly,

"Yes, it is between your father and I. Do not be upset. Your father is asking a fair question. I am sure that he has lots of questions. Most of those questions have remained unanswered for a very long time. He has every right to be angry and every right to know." She looked straight at her son and said," I asked him to come down here and I intend to settle my account with him. So Danny, you can go and leave us alone right now. It will be all right."

Their son shrugged his shoulders and looked at both of them separately. He grimaced but got up and said, "O.K., I will see you both later." He walked away looking back at both of them as he continued to the back of the lobby. But curiosity got the better of him. He spotted a low wall with a long flowerpot filled with petunias. He ducked behind it so that the petunias were hiding his face. He looked to the left and to his surprise, he saw Rebecca standing there doing the same thing. They looked at each other for a moment and laughed. Then unsaid, they watched together the unfolding events.

CHAPTER FORTY-FIVE

She turned toward him. He looked straight ahead and said nothing. She looked at him. He continued to stare out. She looked at him closely. Beneath the white beard, the profile was still the same. His eyes were still greenish-blue and his lashes still uncommonly long for a man. She had loved those beautiful eyelashes when she first met him. She was still intrigued by them, even today. Those lashes had become speckled with gray lashes, but they were still long and beautiful and stood out against his weathered face.

"Look at me, Daniel. Look at me . . . please. I've asked you to come here to make amends."

He continued to look straight ahead, but finally he spoke,

"Tell me something. Had that young man of yours not pursued this, would you ever have told me? Would I ever have known of his existence?"

"You are asking me an unfair question."

"An unfair question? You say that this is an unfair question? What could be more unfair than what you put me through all these years? Not to know that I have a son, not to see that boy grow up, to share moments in his life? So don't you talk to me about unfairness. I've been on the short end of that stick with you for a very long time."

She sighed loudly and looked away from him. They sat silently for a long time, both looking straight ahead and refusing to acknowledge the other. She seemed to want to say something, then she would back away and remain silent. He just glared out into space. Finally, she got up the courage to speak,

"I'm sorry Daniel. I am sorry for having been a foolish young girl and for being so afraid. I'm sorry for having remained afraid all these years. Most of all, I am sorry for having denied to you the opportunity to know your son up until now. I know that you would have been a very good father to him. I am sorry for your missed time with him and I am especially sorry for having hurt you so long ago and not explaining it to you more clearly. I would like to tell you that eventually I would have found you and told all this to you, but it is probably not true. Oh yes, I would have liked to, but time has a way of numbing the wounds and making memories remote and I cannot say that I would have been more brave and found you. I do know this, Daniel Kaplan. Since my husband passed away, I set into motion the process that brings us together today. I did not have to tell Daniel about our love. I could have made up some story about getting along with my life. But no, I told my son the deepest secret that I had and freed him to decide for himself whether to seek you out. That he did. While you would probably attribute it to G-d's work, but frankly, I don't know anything about that. I'll tell you that I did not discourage his search for you and I secretly hoped he would find you so that eventually an opportunity to ask for your forgiveness and to make amends would come my way."

She stared out into space for a moment and was silent. Then she took hold of his arm and turned towards him. He did not look at her, neither did he remove her hand from his arm. She talked into his ear,

"I beg your forgiveness, Daniel. With all of my heart, I beg that. I pray that you are not really angry with me and that you can overcome my hurting of you and forgive me."

She stopped. She stopped because she could not control the torrent of tears from her eyes. He stared forward and did not acknowledge what he had just heard. She sobbed quietly, still holding his arm. Finally, he took a deep breath. He turned to her and looked at her through the tears. Tears running down her cheek. He reached out tentatively and wiped them away from her cheek with the back of his hand. He looked at her, just sitting there and his speechlessness was relentless. He simply did not know what to say.

He reached into his inside jacket pocket and drew out a packet of Kleenex and gave her a tissue. Kary wiped at her eyes, but was still crying silently. Still he said nothing. She got control of herself and said to him,

"I'll understand Daniel, if you cannot forgive me. I will understand. I know that I hurt you very badly years ago. Our son says that it was a powerful hurt. A far deeper hurt than I thought or could have imagined. I guess it was because you were out of sight. And I'm sorry for having never known the extent of the pain that I caused you then. I'm sorry Daniel, truly I am. And I know that the recent truths for you have been too heavy to hold. So I will understand if you send me away without your forgiveness and without letting me try to explain."

He looked down at the back of his hand. Her tears were still wet upon them. He remembered back to another time when he had wiped away her tears. He looked at her. It was if they were transported back in time and she was 20 again. He shuddered. For a moment, he had recaptured his youth and the memory was pure and true. He shuddered again. He looked down at the floor.

"It is very hard for me, this meeting you again like this", he said in a voice barely louder than a whisper., "It is very hard for me to wipe away 25 years of hurt with the words "I forgive you!" Well Kary, . . . I forgive you." Then he sighed wearily and looked at her closely. Daniel peered into her eyes and shook himself, "Yes", he said, looking down at the carpet in front of him, "Yes Kary, I do forgive you, but what does that really mean? I wish I could know. I have probably always forgiven you. In all the years of pain, I never once blamed you for what happened. Rather, I always blamed myself for being too weird or quirky or whatever. I have been told by others who know about this, that I was the one who was wronged. On some level, I came to accept that. It made it easier to move on with my life. . ."

He stopped for a moment to clear his throat. But he didn't say anything. He took the end of his beard in his hands and started fiddling with it, almost unconsciously as if in deep thought. Kary started to say something but before the words could come out, he raised a finger to stop her and she let him continue.

Daniel spoke again, this time much more passionately, "I forgive you Kary, but what does it mean? To me and what should it mean to you? Well, I don't know? The pain was so powerful in the beginning that I wanted to take my life. Thankfully, G-d does not permit that and even then, I understood that I could not do it. Despite my pain! Whoever said that time is the great cure all is both right and wrong. Time deadens the pain but does not make it go away. Each succeeding year, the pain is deadened a little more. First to the point of toleration, then to the point of forgetting. So that you can move on and rebuild your life. For me that has meant meeting a wonderful woman who became my friend and my wife and to whom together G-d has blessed with children, all twins. And each set a boy and girl. What a miracle! I have been blessed that G-d allowed me to get close to him and serve him".

He paused for a moment to gather his emotions together,

"And he let me forget. That might have been his greatest gift of all. Sometimes there would be reminders and the pain would come back like an ugly raw wound, but between G-d and Rebecca, the pain was allowed to subside and my life continued to prosper and grow. "

He raised his head, but did not look at her.

"It is very hard for me to wipe away the years of hurt. But the intensity of that pain passed from me a long time ago. Meeting our son brought it all back. This pain, agh, I thought was too much too handle, too hard for me to endure again. I wanted to run away from my world and I tried to. I drove away as fast as I could until I found myself on a highway in Brooklyn high above the industrial area. The traffic had stopped moving and I was trapped in the car with my own frustrations. It was maddening and I beat on the steering wheel. Finally, I looked up and saw a butterfly on my windshield. I asked myself what would a butterfly be doing in this place. Certainly a butterfly alighting on my car in such a place was rather unlikely. Yet, this beautiful mammoth butterfly was sitting on my windshield wiper and looking at me. I was so distracted that I barely noticed it. But then it flew off and I realized that it was an angel. And I knew that I could survive even this test of my life. G-d was sending me a guardian angel to help me through. So Karolyn, I forgive you. Why? Because I do! Our son, Daniel has filled in a lot of the pieces for me on the objective front. The rest is history and the history is history!"

He looked at her and gave her a soft short smile. He shrugged his shoulders. He had carried a terrible burden for so long, yet he decided in an instant to give it up. He didn't know what it really meant to either him, Karolyn or to Rebecca.

There was silence from her. He saw a frown grow on her face.

"Terrific Daniel, it's a terrific story, very lovely actually. It probably plays well in your synagogue. You know what it means to me Daniel?. What it means to me is that you think that it is all about you. After all these years, you are still off in your own little dream world."

He looked at her in amazement. But he let her continue without interruption.

"You see butterflies on your car and they are angels telling you that G-d will help you. Does that make sense? You are still trying to live your fantasies with no concept of their effect on the people around you. You still live in the hope that it will all end happily ever after. Well, it doesn't. And no amount of wishing it will make it so. I know I hurt you Daniel, but you hurt me too. You said you loved me. You said that you wanted to marry me. You even gave me a ring and I am sure that you really loved me. But you were such a child, a man-child, who danced to his dreams, who wanted it all on his own terms. I was pregnant and you were on the other side of the continent. Your head was in the clouds. I knew that you wanted me to convert, but aside from taking me to temple once, you never tried to explain why it was so important to you that I convert. After I married Charlie, I kept track of you. I knew that I had hurt you. After Daniel was born, I thought that I might even tell you, but I heard that you had taken some very dangerous assignments. Yes, I knew about Daniel Kaplan, CIA. And I knew about you returning to the Navy as a Chaplain. Did you think that I would not keep track of the father of my only child. I also kept track of when you got married and to whom. I learned of the birth of your twins and then I stopped keeping up. I felt that now you had children of your own and that my keeping Daniel from you no longer meant that I was denying you fatherhood. For once, I felt that I could have my son free from the guilt because you had ones of your own. But even that was not to be. How often I would wonder where you were and how you were? But I never again attempted to look for you. You know why?"

He looked up at her. She peered into his eyes and could see a mist of defeat in them. Kary continued,

"Because I couldn't afford to make a life with a dreamer. I needed someone grounded and in the real world. I am glad Daniel that you have found someone who allows you to still dream. I am so glad for you. Really, I am! It was the dreamer I fell in love with. It was that dreamer who fired my imagination who got me to believe in myself. I cleaved to that dreamer, but he didn't cleave to me. At least I didn't think that you did. Now I'm not so sure. Something tells me now, after all of these years that it was probably a misread by me. But at the time, I believed that it was a dreamer, I could not afford to live with. I couldn't be a part of your dreams, because my reality was so hard. I saw in you that you would achieve great things, because dreamers are the only ones who do. But, I couldn't stomach the roller coaster that it would have meant. When Charlie died, I thought about finding you again, to look for myself, but I didn't. But I told your son, because this wasn't about me anymore and he had the right to know. In all the years, I lived with Charlie, I never loved him. I made a home for him and he was a good father to our son. I lived year to year with the ingrown frustration of having chased a cloud named Daniel Kaplan. And it was with sadness to watch that cloud keep disappearing just as it was within my grasp. So I chose not to chase clouds or dreams or love. I knew that you would never go away and pursue your heart's dreams unless I forced you too".

She stopped to take a breath. She dabbed at her eyes with her finger and looked away from Daniel for a moment. She closed her eyes and continued,

"I once talked with my grandmother about you. Her name was Leah. She talked to me about how difficult it would be to convert and how I would never feel welcome. She knew because she was born a Jew. You once told me that Jewishness was passed from one generation to the other on the mother's side. Daniel, she was my mother's mother. I know you know what that means."

Daniel nodded his head gently. He thought for a while to himself. Suddenly he grew very weary. He put his hand to his head and looked up at the ceiling.

"Then we could have married?"

He just looked at her. She nodded yes.

"Yes we could have, but we didn't and our love was not enough to overcome that regardless. Our religion didn't matter. You were not ready to marry me or anyone else. You didn't know who you were and you were chasing dreams that were not even your own. I had a son in my womb and I could not risk it. Do you understand that, Daniel?

He shook his head in disbelief. He nodded yes to her because she was right and her words were true. He sat quietly looking down at the floor, his eyes filling with tears.

"You know that our son, the Episcopal priest is a Jew?" Daniel asked Karolyn.

"Yes I know. I have always known that, but I couldn't stop him because that is who he is. And because I needed to hold onto this secret at all costs. That is my failing."

"Does he know about your grandmother being a Jew?"

"Yes, He knows."

"He knows? How long has he known? Daniel has never said anything to me about it."

"I know" she said to him.

"You know?" Daniel asked totally surprised.

"Yes! I know that he has never spoken to you about it, because I didn't want you to hear it from him. I wanted you to hear it from me. That's why I asked our son to set up this meeting."

Daniel sighed wearily. He looked at Kary and shook his head as if to say, "What more can happen?"

She saw it in his eyes and she gently said to him,

"Even Daniel did not know this until last week."

"Was he alright with it?"

She shrugged her shoulders, "Who knows? It was quite a shock to him, I can be sure. But I doubt he would ever tell me just what he feels. It's not just you who I have hurt in this. Our son has also had a few too many shocks from all of this."

They stopped and looked at each other. They smiled at each other. They knew that whatever had been, was. G-d had not meant for them to be together. He accepted that for the first time in his life. G-d had meant for him to be with Rebecca because <u>she</u> was his soul mate, not Karolyn. Even now, as he realized that religion was never an impediment, he knew that it was not the love he was supposed to share his life with. They shared a son and therefore she would always be a part of his life. But he was no longer angry. The absence of anger after all these years allowed him to walk away from her. He knew that whom he really yearned for was upstairs, in their hotel room, probably crying her eyes out. He got up.

"Kary, I must go now. My wife will be worried. We will continue this talk at another time, someplace else."

"I know Daniel, I know. It was good seeing you after all this time. Stay well."

They hugged and held each other tightly. She kissed him on his cheek, brushing lightly against his beard. They smiled and separated. From behind the plant boxes Rebecca and her stepson saw him rise.

They got up quickly and ran into the nearest open elevator. Daniel walked through the lobby to the elevators. He waited patiently for the next car to arrive. Suddenly, he changed his mind and turned around. He walked through the lobby and out of the building into the sunlight.

CHAPTER FORTY-SIX

He walked down the street for a block or so. Then he turned into a park that was alongside the river. He bought a soda from a vendor's cart and found a quiet bench under a tree looking out onto the water.

It was hot, so he took off his coat and folded it up neatly. He placed it on the bench next to him. He took off his hat and placed it on top of his coat. Then he rolled his sleeves up over his elbows, just like when he was a young man in the Navy. He opened his tie and unbuttoned the top button of his shirt.

In front of him, he watched some children go bye. One boy rode a bicycle. These children reminded him of his own children and suddenly he was carried back to memories of sitting on the old bridle path on Ocean Parkway in Brooklyn, watching his children running and playing. He would sit with Rebecca for hours and they would marvel about the growth of the children and their capacity to be funny and deliciously inventive. He started to hum lightly to himself. He always did that, now it was almost unconscious. He popped open the can of soda and took a long slow guzzle. The cold and the bubbles hurt going down his throat and he coughed. But it tasted good and he enjoyed it. He took a deep breath and tried to separate himself from what had just happened. He chided himself for not going directly to see Rebecca, knowing she would be upset, but he needed the time to gather himself together before he saw her.

A cool breeze dried the perspiration from his brow and he started to relax. He took another sip of soda and sat back contented. Suddenly, he burped out loud. It made him laugh. For the first time in a very long time, he started to feel the great weight on his head and shoulders lifting. He drew a deep breath and closed his eyes. He saw swirls of many colors and then a big red spot in front of his eyes. Soon that changed to yellow, then brown, then blue. It was then that he realized he was crying. Not weeping, just crying softly. Daniel reached into his pocket and pulled out a small packet of tissues. He cleaned his face of the tears and breathed more easily. He felt much more in control. He drew a deep breath and patted his chest. The scenery was very calming. He whistled at the birds and watched the sailboats float lazily by.

When he finally felt relaxed and in control, Daniel picked himself up, gathered his coat over his arm and his hat in his hand and walked slowly back to the hotel. Approaching the door, Daniel turned around and looked back at the park. He sighed, but this time with relief. He stood there for a long time and then proceeded through the revolving door.

CHAPTER FORTY-SEVEN

ebecca heard the key in the door and was startled. She had expected him some time ago, but he had not returned. She suspected that he needed to clear his head, but as the time dragged on, she became worried. Her mind was going in circles of confusion and angst and although she was worried, she was also relieved that she didn't have to deal with it so quickly. But now he was here.

She splashed some water on her face, toweled off and stepped from the bathroom. She turned to the right and saw him closing the door behind him. He looked at her and she at him. They stood silent for some time. Slowly, his coat slipped from his arm onto the floor, then he let go of his hat and it fell to the floor too. He stood there looking at her. Looking at her through the mist forming in his eyes. He stood there, silent and dumb, unable to move or explain himself. He stood there, knowing that he had hurt her and wishing that he hadn't. He stood there, knowing he loved her more than anyone in the world and in fear that she would not let him remain in her life.

She stood there, with her head slightly cocked, pursing her lips together to get control of her emotions. She stood there, silent and dumb, unable to tell him that it was all right and that he could come to her. And that she wished that he would. She stood there, hopelessly hurt by the situation and hopeful that it was now over forever. Then maybe she could have him completely.

He seemed to move forward towards her and she held out her arms to him. He almost ran the few feet to her and held her with all of his might, all that was dear to him. He cried upon her shoulder and she upon his chest. He wept violently and moaned his anguish to her. She held the back of his head and ran her hand through his hair to comfort him. He kissed her, deeply and with feeling that she had never known him to have. She returned his kiss and he kissed her again and again and again. He looked at her and kissed her on her cheeks very lightly. He touched her face with the back of his hand and kissed her forehead and then her eyelids. She breathed deeply when he ran his lips down the back of her neck and when he turned her around and held her back close to him.

He swayed her towards him and held her very tightly. He kissed her again and again. His arms were tight against her belly and he lightly ran kisses down the nape of her neck. He unbuttoned the front of her dress with the hesitancy of a young boy with his first girl. She let him. Then he slipped the dress off of her shoulders and kissed them. He let the dress slip from her body as he turned her around and held her tightly. He rubbed her back and hugged her again. Then they kissed for a very long time until they both seemed to run out of breath.

He led her to the bed. She sat down on its edge and reached for his jacket and took it off. Soon her fingers were opening his shirt and then his pants. He sat on the edge next to her and they started to kiss and hold each other. He removed her brassiere and underwear and looked at her as she lay on top of the blanket. She was magnificent to look at, even after all these years and six children. But now, he saw her differently. He saw just how magnificent she was, he saw a beauty that he had never seen in her before. They made love the rest of the afternoon. When he joined with her this time, it was like he was starting anew, like a virgin again. They knew each other's bodies, but now they discovered each other's bodies and souls. Their joining climaxed with such joy between them that they both couldn't believe that they had lived through so much and for so long without reaching this level. They were transformed into the upper reaches of heaven.

The afternoon stretched into the evening, then the evening into the night. Daniel and Rebecca made love again and again, rediscovering each other anew each time. Late into the night, Rebecca awakened and got up. She put on her robe and pulled back the curtains and looked out onto the street below. She looked at the bed. He was lying there, sleeping soundly, his lips moving quietly as he always talked in his sleep.

He was her husband. She knew that. And she was his wife. And she knew that he knew that. But today, tonight, she was a bride and her Daniel her groom. For the first time in her life, she knew that he really belonged to her, that he was the one who was meant for her and she was the one meant for him. The miracle of their family was real. The miracle of his love was real. And this wonderful difficult man was hers for eternity.

She heard him stir and turned to the bed. She saw him looking at her, quietly. Then he reached out to beckon her to join him. She climbed in next to him with her back to his front and felt him reach over to her belly and pull her towards him. He kissed her neck softly and told her he loved her. Then she heard the soft sound of his breathing as he drifted back to sleep.

THE END

9 781963 050349